RETURN TO BAYEUX

RETURN

— TO —

BAYEUX

A Novel

CILINDA STROUD

Cilinda Stroud

Published by CMS Creations LLC
Email; cstroudauthor@gmail.com

Printed in the United States of America
First Printing 2024
First Edition 2024

Cover design by Richard Ljoenes
Interior design by Danna Mathias Steele

10 9 8 7 6 5 4 3 2 1

Paperback ISBN: 979-8-9868040-0-2
eBook ISBN: 979-8-9868040-1-9

This book is dedicated to Ted, Stephanie, Charles, Alex, Gabriel, Mark and Erin.

RETURN TO BAYEUX

CHAPTER 1

A Soldier Returns

1918
Bayeux, France

Thankfully, the villagers were oblivious to the hollow-eyed soldier who intensely watched them, as they flocked toward the massive stone church. The December wind was cold and blustery, causing the townspeople to burrow their heads deep into the collars of their coats, and cast their eyes downward to shield them from the icy snowflakes, averting their gazes away from the disturbing presence watching from the shadows.

The rhythmic clanging jolted him with memories that shrouded this place, and his life before the war. It had been four years since he left with his brother, but only one of them had returned. It was painful to remember the last time he had been in this town square, basking in the joyful send-off celebration, as the brothers eagerly left with other local boys to fight the Germans. He had worn his new uniform so proudly, as beautiful Sophie tearfully clung to him, kissing him goodbye. He had not seen or heard from his beloved Sophie since that fateful day. The mystery of it still fogged his memories, and he was no longer certain if he had really loved her, nor if she had loved him. Henri breathed deeply, trying to calm the torment sweeping through him, threatening to make him walk away from this place, walk away from the memories.

With the calculated eye of an experienced sniper, he took in the town of Bayeux. The ancient, cobbled streets were as he remembered them. The mosaic of intricately crafted gray stone buildings that bordered the main street radiated a mysterious aura of resilience and history. But there was a visible sense of tiredness, too. The small stone shops and restaurants that charmingly bordered the main street looked neglected and were devoid of any greenery in celebration of the Christmas season. The war years had obviously been hard on the town. Looming over the tired little French village was the magnificent Bayeux Cathedral. The towering Roman and Gothic architecture seemed very much out of place amidst the humble local businesses. Dating back to the time of William the Conqueror, the Roman Catholic Church had been the center of life in Bayeux for centuries. Surprisingly, most of the stories and history surrounding this impressive bastion of religion were unknown to the average citizen of the town. They simply knew this imposing structure as their church. It was the life center of all events in the village. If the walls of the Bayeux Cathedral could talk, the stories would be mostly of christenings, weddings, and funerals. But intermixed with the routine rituals of life, there would be damning stories, too.

Henri had powerful memories of this church. It had been an important part of his childhood. As the church bells rang out and summoned the local parishioners to Sunday mass, Henri was drawn, almost trance-like, to the ancient structure.

As he prepared to step into the town square, he was suddenly aware of his appearance, and he began to brush the dirt and dust from his tattered uniform, while also trying to smooth his dirty hair. He had not shaved since he had begun the long walk back to Bayeux from the battlefield in northern France, and his dirty facial hair gave him a disheveled, haunted look. Cautiously, reluctantly, he hid his sniper rifle under a scraggly bush at the edge of the town square. The lethal artifact had been a part of him, keeping him safe throughout the war. When his unit was disbanded, after the armistice, he walked away with it, his only companion on the long journey home.

With a wariness that had become integral to his survival, Henri stepped into the main street. He tried to blend inconspicuously into the crowd of people who were making their way to the entrance of the church, but his presence was anything but inconspicuous. The soiled, tattered French uniform and his haunting, battle-worn appearance made people instinctively step away from him. He was barely recognizable even to these people whom he had known all his life. The change in Henri was dramatic and more than a little frightening. In his youth, he had been a friendly, charismatic boy. The hollow-eyed, weary looking soldier who walked among his fellow parishioners appeared to be a disturbing shadow of his former self.

Father Bernard was standing at the entrance greeting his people and welcoming them into the church. The priest had stood with these parishioners through all the grief of the war, and it had aged him. Perceptive as always, Father Bernard immediately noticed the gaunt, troubled-looking soldier making his way toward the church. His heart lurched with concern, as he watched the parishioners suddenly grow quiet and wary, as Henri walked among them. The priest had been anxiously waiting for the return of this soldier since the war had ended over a month ago. Awkwardly, Henri stopped in front of the priest, his troubled gaze silently communicating volumes, as their eyes met. The priest smiled slightly, trying hard not to let his concern cloud the moment, as he quietly welcomed him home. Henri nodded numbly, as he silently acknowledged the priests welcome, before making his way to a seat in the back of the crowded church.

Father Bernard had welcomed several of the local returning soldiers in the last weeks since the war ended. The town's surviving warriors had come trickling back to their community, to their families. A number of these returning soldiers were obviously injured, but many had a troubled, vacant look that communicated much more than the spoken word. Over one-third of the town's young men had been killed in the war, and these few survivors were looked upon with reverence, as hope slowly ebbed back into the town of Bayeux. There was a growing sense of excitement and anticipation as these war-weary soldiers returned to the place of their birth and families. It was the Christmas season, and the year of 1918 seemed unusually blessed. So much had been endured and lost by the people of Bayeux, that there was an almost unrealistic expectation that these few surviving warriors could somehow heal the gaping emotional wounds that affected the entire community.

As the priest looked from the back of the church at his people, his community, he could not help but feel pleased. The beautiful morning light shone hopefully through the colorful stained glass, illuminating the scene in the crowded church. Tightly packed in the ancient wooden pews, the parishioners seemed to bask in their togetherness. There was an expectant air, as spicy incense infused the ancient church with the fragrant aroma of spirituality and hope.

Sister Marguerite stepped forward to direct the restless group of children in faded choir robes. The children were excited, as they knew this was a special mass. The town was celebrating the return of their soldiers, and it was also the Christmas season. The children had been deeply impacted by the war. Several had lost family members, and the toll on the youngest members of the community could be seen in their serious faces. But children are instinctively natural survivors. At times when it was known that enormous battles raged across northern France, it was the children hopefully singing their hymns that inspired the congregation to keep the faith. As the pretty, middle-aged nun nodded to the children and signaled to the organist, Henri suddenly looked up and took notice of this woman. She was a talented children's choir director, and it was apparent in her orchestration of the clear, harmonious voices singing the hymns of the season. There was hardly a dry eye in the church, as the music filled the soaring space, and somehow brought the community's pent-up joy and emotion bubbling to the surface. The returning soldiers were particularly moved by the coalescence of togetherness, music, and incense into the religious celebration.

At the completion of the opening hymn, Sister Marguerite turned and overlooked the congregation from her elevated perch. She discreetly scanned the crowded church, searching for him. Her heart fluttered as she spotted a dirty, disheveled soldier in the back pew. He looked thinner and hauntingly older, but she was sure that it was him. Marguerite struggled to maintain her composure, suddenly feeling faint. With deliberation, she turned her back to the congregation and fought to control the surge of feelings that threatened to overtake her. Stoically, she took a deep breath and focused her attention on the choir.

The priest noticed the stricken look on the nun's face, and he knew that she had spotted Henri. He secretly worried that Sister Marguerite's reunification with this beloved young man would prove to be painful. Father Bernard knew this family well. If he were being completely honest with himself, he would admit that he loved them. He knew their secrets and had been with them through painful times. When Marguerite's sister, brother-in-law, and nephew had been killed in the war, it was Father Bernard who had tenderly cared for the nun, and patiently coached her back from despair.

Father Bernard proudly looked out over the crowded church from his elevated pulpit. Having arrived in Bayeux, newly ordained, twenty-three years ago, it was in this little Normandy village where he found his true calling. Oddly, it was the community that anchored him in their faith and gave the young priest a sense of belonging that had been completely absent in his youth. Several times, Father Bernard had struggled with the church hierarchy as they sought to reassign him to another parish. Through luck and circumstance, he had somehow managed to stay in Bayeux. The villagers loved and respected him. He had been with them through many a storm, and they accepted him as one of their own.

He did not look like a typical priest. Even under the cover of the long black robe, he appeared muscular. His face was chiseled with dark, expressive eyes. The handsome face was oddly an anomaly for a man of the cloth. In addition to his uncommon, good looks, there was something innately alert and perceptive about him. He had proven himself to be compassionate, but also practical. His humanity had been his guiding principle as he provided leadership in a sometimes inflexible, judgmental religion. Father Bernard had done things that would never have been sanctioned by the church leaders, but he was mostly at peace with himself.

Father Bernard sensed the emotion within the confines of his crowded church and kept his sermon simple and brief. The message was succinct, but powerful. It was time to heal, and time to celebrate the return of the town's soldiers. These battle-weary men would need the support and gratitude of the townsfolk to rebuild their lives. The losses within the community were obvious as you looked at the families that were missing their young men. Father Bernard urged his congregation to remember, but not let bitterness reign. Hate and bitterness would waste the freedom that these young men had fought so hard to preserve. A life well-lived must encompass love and hope.

As the last hymn was being sung in an eerily harmonious manner, Henri visually scanned the crowded cathedral, looking for Sophie. His mind was a jumble of confusion as he thought of her, desperately searching, hoping to somehow find her. But he knew that this young woman who still haunted his memories would not be there. The circumstances and tragic decisions of the last few years could not be so easily undone. Henri stood quietly with his head hanging, as the parishioners filed eagerly out of the church in anticipation of celebratory feasts.

Sister Marguerite slipped away as the choir was dispersing and moved to the back of the church. She stood in the shadow of the massive stone arch as the church emptied. Quietly, intensely, she stared at him. Marguerite loved this young man with her whole heart. Sensing her presence, Henri looked up and met her concerned gaze. The flicker of recognition in his troubled eyes was unmistakable. A small nod communicated much to Sister Marguerite. When they were finally alone, the nun approached Henri slowly, taking in his vastly different appearance, almost afraid of what she might discover about him. She reached out to him like he might be a terrified animal, and finally their tear-filled eyes met. He stepped forward and collapsed into her open arms, both sobbing convulsively. Thankful for the privacy of the empty church, they held each other for the longest time. This woman that Henri had known as his aunt was remarkably similar in appearance and mannerisms to his deceased mother. She had always been present throughout his young life, but her unfaltering love and devotion to him during the last year of the war had almost certainly kept him alive, as he struggled to find a reason to go on. Her regular letters and packages had been a steady stream of love and connection that kept him afloat as he floundered in a sea of despair.

Marguerite looked up with reverence and sincere gratitude as she prayed out loud, "Thank you God for bringing him safely back to me."

Henri instinctively recoiled in anger. Visibly shaking, he shouted in the tenor of a wounded animal, "No! Do not give thanks to this God!"

Marguerite was stunned and a little frightened by the outburst. She struggled to compose herself and respond to Henri in a reassuring manner. The nun reached out to comfort the distraught young man, but he pulled back. In a near whisper, Marguerite said, "God is still with you. He has not abandoned you."

His voice escalating, Henri responded in an almost feral shout, "You have not seen what I have seen!"

Marguerite could hardly breathe as she took in the wreck of the young man before her. Gaunt, with a wild-eyed look, Henri was almost unrecognizable. But it was his obvious mental torment that she found most disturbing.

Sister Marguerite innately understood the lapse in faith. Henri had fought for four long years and had endured the loss of many friends, but most poignantly he had lost his mother, father, and brother. He was questioning his faith in a God that would allow such suffering. Sensing the fragility in this young man, she quietly embraced him.

Hearing the outburst, Father Bernard hurried back into the cavernous main seating area of the cathedral to find the gut-wrenching scene. He could sense the pain and turmoil as he quickly took in the drama. Hiding in the shadows, holding his breath, he listened. Finally, with a heavy heart, he slipped away to his office so that they might once again have the freedom of privacy.

In a state of agitation, Henri uttered, "I need to get to the farm." But Sister Marguerite knew that he was not emotionally prepared for what he was likely to encounter. With a forced calmness that she did not feel, she said, "You'll be there soon enough."

"No, I need to go now."

She sighed as she said, "Well, you will be back on the farm before you know it. But it looks to me like you're in need of a bath, and a haircut, and a shave. And something tells me that you've probably picked up a few unwelcome travelers....in the form of lice."

Henri smiled weakly as he said, "Oh, yes, I've definitely been carrying some unwanted travelers."

Marguerite slipped her arm around Henri, gently guiding him to a nearby building where she occupied a single room. The room was simply furnished, but it had all the essentials for a comfortable existence. A small cast iron stove was emitting wonderful heat throughout the relatively small efficiency apartment. Marguerite added wood and proceeded to stoke the fire, as she prepared to heat water for Henri's bath. There was a bathing tub in the corner and a pile of clean clothing on a nearby chair. It was obvious that much thought and preparation had gone into the anticipation of Henri's return.

Unfolding a privacy screen around the bathing tub, she instructed the man-child to remove his clothes. He was embarrassed and began to protest, but Marguerite was undeterred. Reluctantly, he handed her individual pieces of his military clothing. One by one, the nun fed the lice-infested articles of clothing into the wood burning stove. She handed a bar of strong lye soap and a brush over the top of the screen. As Henri sank his tired, dirty body into the warm water, a sense of calm started to settle into him. But the calm was quickly disrupted by Marguerite's instructions to scrub hard. When Henri was done,

Marguerite handed a blanket over the screen. As he huddled in the corner wrapped in the blanket, she emptied the shockingly dirty water. Refilling the tub with clean, cold water, she added heated water to make the temperature tolerable. Again, Henri submerged himself and scrubbed until Marguerite finally agreed that he might indeed be free of pestilence.

Henri emerged from behind the screen wearing an odd assemblage of coarsely woven, warm clothing. Although the boots were worn, they had no holes and fit quite nicely. The luxury and pure comfort of clean, warm clothing brought tears to his eyes. He was embarrassed by his blatant expression of emotion, but Marguerite pretended not to notice. She was indeed proud of her ingenuity in putting together such practical, warm clothing for her returning soldier. Marguerite had scavenged through the clothing donations that had been made to the church to assemble the outfit. She had even managed to find a coat and gloves.

Clean and clothed, Henri was instructed to sit in a chair by the stove. No longer protesting, he sat quietly as Marguerite combed and cut his hair. There was an ease settling between them, a trust returning. Next, she gently, gingerly shaved him, and the transformation was quite remarkable. Although thinner and harboring an older, wearier look, he was ruggedly handsome, and he was her Henri. Marguerite studied him with the knowing eye of someone who knew deep secrets. Henri had the unmistakable eyes of his father. Light green with flecks of brown, they were his most arresting facial feature. The thick brown hair with blonde highlights was another reminder of his paternity. Henri's fine facial features were chiseled and aristocratic, but his body was lithe and muscled, and it told of his sturdy Norman lineage. He truly was a beautiful young man.

CHAPTER 2

The Telling of a Dark Tale

1918
Bayeux, France

As Henri sat by the warmth of the wood stove, Marguerite poured him a glass of his father's home distilled Calvados. Smiling in memory of the man, he sipped, savoring the spicy brew, as a warmth crept through him, slowly relaxing him. He had a need to tell the tale of the war years, and it came tumbling out, unfiltered, and painfully truthful. Marguerite listened, not wanting to impede the flow of words that seemed to need to be let out. The story was more than she wanted to hear, but she knew he had to tell the tale. It was like a purulent wound that needed to be lanced; only then could the healing commence. Initially, Henri spoke mostly in a dull, matter-of-fact manner, but when he began to tell the story of his brother's wounding, Henri began to cry, his words muffled through his tears. Marguerite listened, spellbound, and horrified by the events, and all that Henri had experienced.

Marguerite offered him a piece of her homemade apple pie. He ate ravenously, talking between bites, consuming three pieces of pie before feeling somewhat satiated. The taste and texture of the pie was exquisite. Marguerite started to prepare a dinner of roasted chicken with potatoes and parsnips, all the while listening. She was comforted by the familiarity of his voice, but she was saddened and troubled by his revelations.

Henri first spoke of his older brother, Louis. The pain was so raw that even Marguerite was initially taken aback. She understood the closeness of their bond, but she had no idea what they had endured together, over the last few years of trench warfare. Henri shook his head in disbelief, as he recalled the memory of their initial eagerness to join the war effort. In retrospect, their innocence was almost childlike. Only one year apart in age, the brothers had proudly donned their uniforms and basked in the town's celebratory send-off. Henri's military fervor had an additional motivation. He wanted to prove his manliness and patriotism to his girlfriend, Sophie, and to her father. But he now knew the truth. Sophie's father had never intended to condone their relationship and had welcomed Henri's departure to hopefully end the love affair. The allure of adventure, and the romantic excitement of war quickly fell away, as his letters to Sophie went unanswered. Devastated, Henri threw himself into survival mode, trying unsuccessfully to forget her.

Henri and Louis ended up in the same battalion, which was a comfort to their parents. But the horrific nature of trench warfare abruptly dispelled any romantic illusions that the brothers had about the glory of battle. The two brothers found themselves utterly unprepared for the shocking carnage. Reeling under the reality of constant danger, they were predictably traumatized, and floundering to find hope amid the chaos of war.

Pulling together, they leaned heavily on each other to survive. Early on, they made a joint pledge that they would live to see the end of the war. As a part of their survival plan, they agreed to never volunteer for high-risk missions. They also honed their already considerable rifle skills, both achieving the designation of sniper. Skilled sharpshooters were viewed as extremely valuable to a brigade, and not likely to be ordered to charge across open fields into withering enemy machine gun fire. And so, the brothers had a strategy to survive the terror of trench warfare.

Their letters home to their parents were lighthearted and reassuring, and entirely deceptive. They agreed that they could not share the horrific details of their daily lives, not with the parents who had so lovingly raised and nurtured the two boys. At night, huddled together for warmth and emotional comfort, they spoke of their lives before the war. These intimate nighttime conversations became the thin thread that kept them sane and gave them hope.

But the war ground on, and as the carnage became more widespread, it had a profound effect on them. The loss of close friends and neighbors was eating away at their resolve to survive, and this was particularly true of Louis. For once in their young lives, it was the younger brother, Henri, who was constantly watching over Louis and encouraging him to stay sharp and minimize his exposure. It was becoming increasingly apparent as the war continued that Louis was becoming mentally unstable and starting to act recklessly. Henri could clearly see the change in his brother's behavior and in his emotional affect. During a lull in battle, Henri crept away to make an impassioned plea to his commanding officer. He literally begged his commander to send Louis home on medical leave so that he might recover from the mental ravages of combat fatigue. But the Battle of the Somme was in full swing, and the commander had no patience for the desperate appeal.

Upon his return from the failed encounter with the commander, Henri discovered that his brother was missing. Panicked, Henri stumbled through the disgustingly muddy and bloody trenches asking all whom he encountered as to the whereabouts of his brother. Finally, a battle-worn private reluctantly told Henri that his brother had volunteered to serve as messenger between the forward troop placements and the main command. Henri cried out and collapsed in despair. Ignorance was one of the few reprieves from the reality of trench warfare, and the poor, hapless soldier deeply regretted having shared this acutely worrisome information with Henri. The battle raged until finally it was completely dark.

Henri crawled out into the desolate land between the lines of battle. He desperately called out Louis' name, as he searched for his brother among the wounded and dead. Finally, he heard a familiar, weak cough, a residual from the mustard gas, and he recognized a distinct, yet hoarse voice calling out his name. It was unmistakably his brother's voice. Henri belly-crawled through the slimy, blood-soaked mud. The coldness of the night, and the rank smell of human carnage, vividly assaulted him like a nightmare. Intermittent flares being sent up by the warring armies illuminated the macabre scene. Bodies of the dead and dying were scattered everywhere. Numb and shaking, he finally made it to his brother.

Louis lay sprawled in a very unnatural position, his face looking up at the flare-lit night sky. Even in the eerie light of the floating flare, Louis looked ghostly white, his midsection dark with congealed blood. Tenderly, Henri kissed his brother. Louis smiled and weakly reached up to caress Henri's face. The love and comfort radiating from this contact between brothers calmed them both, and communicated a bond known by very few. In the dark of the night, Henri tried to determine the extent of his brother's injuries. No doubt it was a serious wounding, and Henri worried that moving him would result in his death. But he also knew that the darkness of night was dissipating, and he had a limited amount of night cover to get his brother back to the Allied lines. Slowly and methodically, he dragged Louis across the macabre landscape between the warring armies. Just before dawn, he lowered his brother back into the French trenches. Louis was barely conscious, but he was acutely aware of Henri's love for him.

Henri rode in the ambulance that transported his wounded brother to the makeshift field hospital. The carnage and suffering scattered chaotically around the tents of the triage area was hell-like. Only one mile behind the raging battle, the concussive sound of exploding artillery added a surreal quality to the life and death scene. The gray-haired combat surgeon who greeted their ambulance left little doubt as to the gravity of the situation. Calmly and pragmatically, he examined Louis and gave a sigh of resignation. He turned to face Henri and explained that Louis was gut shot and had lost a lot of blood. No doubt there was extensive damage to his bowels and internal organs. The bleeding had stabilized, but he did not think that Louis would survive surgery. Somehow, Henri knew this to be true even before the weathered old physician spoke the words.

At this point in Henri's recounting of his brother's grievous wounds, he softly began to cry. Marguerite reached across the simple wooden table and steadily held his trembling hands. No words were spoken between them, but the acknowledgment of the unresolved grief and loss was palpable. It took quite a while for Henri to resume the cathartic, sad tale of his brother's wounding. Finally, as though uncertain that he could really recount the emotionally ravaging events of the last year, he began to speak in a halting, almost whispering tone.

Communication of war casualties to families was generally sporadic and unreliable, especially in the chaos of the major battles of the war. Henri knew this and took it upon himself to contact his family. A telegraph was sent from Central Battle Command to the town of Bayeux to relay an urgent message to the LeBlanc farm, notifying them that their son, Louis, had been gravely wounded during the Battle of the Somme. Adele LeBlanc had lived in dreaded fear of this moment, as the battles raged across northern France. With war casualties mounting, there was barely a family in the region who had not suffered a loss. The sense of foreboding that fell over Adele as the messenger walked through the arched gate made her weak in the knees. She knew what he had come to say before a word was spoken. Her husband, Gabriel, saw the messenger approaching the farmhouse as he left the barn, and he shuddered, barely able to breathe. He listened in numbed silence to the news about their older son. Within the hour, Gabriel and his wife Adele had packed a light cart with blankets, bread, cheese, and ham. Gabriel had carefully chosen his sturdiest horses to assure that the distance could be covered in the shortest amount of time.

Bad news travels fast in small communities, and so it was with the news of Louis' wounding. As Adele and Gabriel were hurriedly packing for their journey to be with their injured son, Leo arrived. He embraced Gabriel and assured him that he would care for his livestock while the family traveled to be with their son. A life-long friend and fellow farmer, Leo understood loss. He had lost his only son in the war a year earlier, and Gabriel had been his constant support through the ordeal that followed. There was no argument from Leo about the futility of traveling over 190 miles to the battle site. Leo understood the need of the family to be with their dying son.

It was well after midnight when Henri reached the most painful part of the cathartic saga, the part of the story that Marguerite could barely allow herself to listen to, the events so brutal, and the losses still so real. As he told of Adele and Gabriel's arrival at the field hospital, Marguerite could no longer hold back her tears. She envisioned the final goodbye and tried to block out the thought of the instantaneous death of her sister, brother-in-law, and mortally wounded nephew, as they tried to escape a German artillery assault. This time, it was Henri who reached across the table and tried to comfort Marguerite. She cried openly, letting the pain out, as she thought about the death of her sister. Adele had always been her rock, her counsel, her unwavering support, and the lifelong friend who knew everything about her. The loss, even two years later, still stunned her.

Deep into the night, Henri finally talked himself out. It was like a candle that had burned brightly, then flickered, finally extinguishing itself. Marguerite led him to her humble bed and tucked him in like a child. He did not resist, as she pulled the quilt close around him, tenderly kissing his head. Surprisingly, he quickly settled into a deep, deep sleep.

Placing a quilt on the floor beside him, she laid down, but she could not sleep, her mind retracing her life, her choices. As the first light of dawn started to illuminate the little apartment, Marguerite came to the decision that she had to make a change in her life. She had to fully commit herself to this young man whom she loved so completely, to help Henri rebuild his life.

CHAPTER 3

The Dying Speak Only the Truth

1916
Field Hospital at the Battle of the Somme, Northern France

While Gabriel and Adele were beginning their journey to be with their wounded son, the brothers were huddled together in a dark corner of the old stone church that had been converted into a field hospital. Most, but not all, of the stained glass had been blown out in the previous days' battle, allowing the cold air to stream in, contributing to the discomfort of the wounded within. The old wooden pews had been removed and replaced with cots which were filled with all manner of wounded soldiers, some moaning, some crying out in pain, and others eerily quiet, near death.

Henri was exhausted, his mind fogged by grief and fear, as he watched over Louis, diaphoretic and pale, slipping in and out of consciousness.

The old surgeon had been watching the two brothers, and he walked over and handed Henri a coarsely woven, heavy blanket. He said with a voice of authority, "You need to get some sleep, son."

Henri seemed almost incoherent with grief, as he shook his head and said, "No. I want to stay awake and watch over him."

"You will not be doing yourself, or him, any good if you're exhausted. Get some rest. I'll watch over Louis."

Henri trusted the old man. There was something about him that reminded him of his father. Reluctantly, he nodded and said, "You'll let me know if he needs anything."

"I will. Now get some sleep."

No longer fighting his exhaustion, Henri placed the blanket beside Louis' cot, and laid down, collapsing into a restless sleep. Hours later, Henri was awakened by the sound of Louis moaning, as Dr. Lamont examined his abdominal wound. The old doctor's face radiated concern as he peeled back the dressing and saw the thick, purulent drainage, becoming assaulted by the smell of infection.

He sighed as he said to a barely conscious Louis, "The bleeding appears to have stopped, but you do have some infection in the wound, which is not too surprising, given the internal damage. How's your pain?"

Louis was emerging from his drugged state, and he tried to sound cogent as he said, "Not too bad."

"I can give you more pain medicine to keep you comfortable."

Louis suddenly became agitated, as he answered, "No. I need to talk to Henri. I must tell him."

Dr. Lamont looked puzzled, but he understood that Louis wanted to stay awake, needed to stay awake, to talk with his brother. He reassured Louis, "Ahh, you want to stay awake to talk with your brother? Of course, we can hold off on the pain medicine. You just let me know when you want more medication. Is there anything else I can do for you? Any questions I can answer?"

Louis sounded suddenly more alert as he answered, "No, Doc. I think I got the picture."

Dr. Lamont looked at Henri as he said, "Okay, boys, I'll leave you two alone so you can talk."

Henri had an odd feeling, a sense that he was about to be told something troubling, something that he did not want to hear. Louis reached out to grab his brother's hand, his movement drunken, shaky.

Henri captured his brother's clammy hand in his own, looked at him with concern, and said, "Calm down. I'm right here. I'm not leaving."

There were tears in his eyes, and he seemed upset, not the usual restlessness associated with pain. "I'm sorry. I didn't want to hurt you."

"Louis, what are you talking about? Try and relax. It's the drugs making you feel this way."

Speaking haltingly, through waves of pain, Louis said, "No, it's not the drugs. I have something to tell you."

Suddenly, Henri stopped, took a deep breath, and braced himself. "Okay, I'm listening."

Louis understood that he was dying, and it created an urgency, a need for truth between the brothers. He bluntly said, in his weakened voice, the combination of the medication and the pain making his speech halting and hoarse, "Sophie…was pregnant…when we left… for the war."

Henri gasped, a look of disbelief on his face, as he dropped Louis' hand, and looked stunned.

"I don't understand."

Louis, openly crying, confessed, "I learned about the pregnancy… from Bernadette…in a letter."

Henri's anger was rising, and they were once again just brothers. There was nothing held back, no sympathy for Louis' mortal wounds – just raw, unfiltered anger. "What? You knew this and didn't tell me?! You listened to me night after night, wondering and crying about Sophie not writing to me, and you didn't think I should know she was pregnant with my child?!"

Louis' words were stumbling, drunken, as he explained, "I was wrong…so wrong."

"Why would you do this to me?"

Again, the words tumbled out, hesitantly, as he struggled to speak. "Well…I told myself…I did it to protect…you. I knew that you… would want to marry…her. I couldn't stand the thought…of you…

being with her...and her deplorable father. He hated...you...and I thought...he would ruin...your life."

The words were sinking in, and Henri was suddenly quiet. From across the room, Dr. Lamont was watching, taking in the scene, concerned for his patient. He started to walk toward the brothers, but then stopped, deciding to let them finish their conversation.

Henri seemed to accept the words, as he asked, "Why didn't Sophie write? Why didn't she tell me?"

"I don't know. Bernadette wrote...that her father...sent Sophie... away to a convent...to have...the baby."

"Where is Sophie now? Where's the baby?"

Louis was getting weaker, his speech even more halting, and barely audible. "The last letter...a long time...ago...Bernadette wrote...that Sophie's father...promised to put her up...in a fancy...Paris apartment...if she left...the baby in...the orphanage."

Henri looked crushed and horrified. He instinctively knew that his dying brother was telling the truth. The revelation was shattering, in a way that made him call into question his very perception of his love for Sophie. It could not have been real, and that hurt. Deep in his thoughts, Henri came to the realization that Sophie had ultimately made the decision to not tell him about the pregnancy. She had chosen a convenient, pampered life over him and their child. It was a gut punch, a brutal reality, at a moment when life and family seemed so tenuous.

Henri took a deep breath, as he struggled to not let anger be his last message to his brother whom he loved so completely. He took Louis' hand, and with complete sincerity, he said, "Louis, listen to me. I'm glad that you told me the truth. I forgive you. I do, and I love you, brother."

Grimacing with pain, Louis smiled weakly, relieved that the truth had been shared with this brother he loved more than life itself. Henri looked to Dr. Lamont, and he motioned him over.

The old surgeon could see that Louis was writhing in pain, and he offered, "You look like you could use more pain medication?"

Louis nodded, as he said weakly, "Please."

Surprisingly, over the next few days, Louis seemed to almost stabilize, with longer periods of lucidity. The brothers talked, laughed, and cried. They did not waste a second of their remaining time together, it was so precious. They talked about everything, from their childhood together, to their parents, as well as Aunt Marguerite, and Sophie. There was unfiltered honesty between them, along with acceptance of all that had happened, and an emerging peace between the two. By the third day in the crowded field hospital, it was apparent that Louis was deteriorating rapidly. During his lucid moments, he was increasingly obsessed with Henri's future, openly worried that he would not recover from all the losses of the war. It seemed like such a selfless, loving act, and it was not lost on Henri. He knew that Louis loved him, and that he wanted the best for his younger brother.

Louis struggled to speak. His voice was trembling and barely audible. "Promise me...promise me...that you'll live...a good life... you'll be happy...find a good woman...someone who...deserves you. Promise."

Henri teared up, the thought of the future incomprehensible as he watched his brother dying. He wanted to reassure him, put him at ease. "Louis, I'll try."

"No! Promise me!"

Henri sighed as he looked at his brother, and tried to sound convincing, "I promise."

Louis seemed to settle, to find comfort in his words. "Sophie... had a...little girl. You have...a little...girl. Find her. You'll be...an amazing...father."

Henri didn't know what to say, he was so numbed by the spectacle before him, but strangely he felt a comfort in the knowledge that he had a child. It was a lot to take in, to truly comprehend, and he was heartened that Louis thought he would be a good father. It was a thought that stayed with him, somehow guiding him toward a future he could barely imagine.

Surprisingly, Louis made it through the night. As the light of dawn filtered into the old stone church, it was apparent that the end was near. Henri hovered, anxious and panicked over his brother. He had known that his brother would die, but suddenly the finality of it hit him in a wave. As he took in the sight of Louis, his skin ashen, his breathing shallow, Henri laid his head on the cot and started to cry.

Louis opened his eyes, and somehow laid his hand on Henri's head, as he suddenly mustered the strength to say, "Don't cry. I will be with you always."

"Louis, I can't imagine life without you."

"You'll be fine. You're stronger…than me."

Henri shook his head. "I don't feel strong. Louis, don't leave me."

Louis had an amazing sense of clarity, as he said, "Remember your promise…you'll find happiness, and a good woman…someone who deserves you. Find your…little girl."

Henri tried to pull himself together, to stop crying, as he said, "I promise."

Louis seemed more at peace, just hearing the words. Then he said, his voice barely a whisper, "I just want to see them again…one more time. I know they're coming."

Henri reassured his brother, "Yes, hang on Louis. I sent a message four days ago. They should be here today. Please, Louis, hang on."

"Tell them I love them…and that they were incredible parents."

"Louis, you need to tell them yourself."

The sounds of the escalating battle crept closer, as Louis slipped into unconsciousness.

CHAPTER 4

Final Farewell

1916
Field Hospital at the Battle of the
Somme, Northern France

Gabriel knew horses, and he paced the animals to cover the distance to the Somme as quickly as possible. The horses were as sturdy as the couple driving them, steadfast and diligent. Resting intermittently for short intervals, the determined family was traveling over forty-five miles a day. The animals seemed to sense the urgency, and they kept going, despite obvious fatigue. Four days later, they were approaching the Somme battlefield. Gabriel struggled to calm the edgy horses and urge them on, as the sounds of the ongoing battle grew steadily louder, and more concussive, the closer they came. Ambulance crews and the military traffic that they had encountered directed them to a stone church, sitting high on a hill, that had been converted into a field hospital. There was no guarantee that they would find their son there, but it seemed a likely place.

As Gabriel urged his exhausted horses toward the old stone church, he was aghast at the scene before him. Briefly, Adele and Gabriel stopped. They gave each other a look of disbelief and dread, as they visibly steadied themselves, moving forward purposely through the hell-like landscape in search of their son. Obviously, the open meadow had been the site of a great battle. Scattered throughout the cratered rolling hills were the remnants of shattered carts, and the bodies of dead horses. The stench was nauseating. As though oblivious to the carnage around them, a steady stream of wagons, and motorized ambulances were coming and going from the field hospital. Surrounding the stone church, were clusters of wounded and dying men scattered haphazardly around the normally bucolic place. Moans and cries of pain could be heard when there was a lull in the concussive sounds of artillery, and it created a sense of misery that hung heavily over the place. Despite the obvious gravity of the situation, there seemed to be a certain order and calmness among the staff attending to the wounded. An old man in a dirty, blood-covered apron seemed to be directing the operation. He moved from one wounded soldier to the next, methodically assessing wounds and making decisions as to their treatment. The dead were quickly cleared away behind the old church, and the wounded were separated by the acuity of their injuries. The old man spoke directly to each injured soldier, and he seemed to have the ability to reassure them all, despite their injuries.

By this time, the little horse drawn wagon was approaching the triage area. The middle-aged couple looked tired and determined. Doctor Lamont knew who they were, before they even introduced themselves. He had been expecting them. Walking directly toward Gabriel and Adele, he greeted them. The formality and warmth of his greeting was oddly out of place in the chaotic scene, but he seemed like mercy itself. It was a surprising revelation to experience such kindness and humanity in what seemed to be nothing less than a hell-hole of brutality and suffering.

Doctor Lamont stepped forward and said, "You must be Louis' parents."

Gabriel nodded and said, "Yes, we're here to be with our son. I'm Gabriel LeBlanc and this is my wife, Adele."

The doctor extended his hand in greeting, but then retracted it, as he became aware of the blood dripping from his fingers. Despite the chaos surrounding him, Dr. Lamont seemed to have the ability to block it all out and focus on the obviously distressed couple before him. He introduced himself, "I'm Dr. Lamont, chief surgeon. I've been overseeing Louis' care."

Adele, obviously anxious, impatiently asked, "How is he?"

"He has a very serious gunshot wound to the abdomen, which has caused a lot of damage to his internal organs. Unfortunately, infection has set in, and he is not going to survive. I'm so sorry to tell you this," he answered honestly.

Adele gasped and struggled to remain upright. Gabriel steadied her by putting his arm around her.

He nodded that he understood what the surgeon had explained, and then asked, "Is he conscious?"

Dr. Lamont answered, "Well, he's drifting in and out of consciousness. Your other son, Henri, has been with him since he arrived here. They seem to have quite a bond between them. It's been remarkable to observe them over the last few days. Obviously, they have had much to say to each other. I do believe that Louis has just been hanging on, so that he might see you both one more time. He's a lovely young man."

Gabriel was choked with emotion as he asked, "Can we see him?"

Dr. Lamont nodded and said, "Of course you may. Both of your sons will be relieved to see you." He pointed to the entrance of the church and said, "You will find your sons in the back of the church. I must get back to my duties here."

With those final words, he turned and redirected his attention to a young soldier who was obviously panicked and crying out in pain. His reassuring words could be heard as the couple walked toward the church entrance.

Adele and Gabriel hesitantly walked into the shadowy church. Most of the stained-glass windows had been blown out, creating wide swaths of natural light that cut through the darkness. Everywhere, there were wounded soldiers lying on cots. The scope of human suffering was almost beyond comprehension. Although Adele had been mentally preparing herself for what she might encounter, she felt faint and could barely walk between the cots that were filled with wounded soldiers. Looking earnestly, Adele and Gabriel finally spotted their sons huddled together in the back of the church. Louis was a ghastly shade of pale gray. His eyes fluttered, and his breathing had a disturbingly rapid and shallow quality. Even at a distance, he looked like he was dying. Instinctively, the parents rushed, scrambling around wounded soldiers, toward their sons. Henri saw them, and he felt an enormous rush of relief and gratitude. The little family fell together, and for one fleeting moment, the grim reality fell away, allowing them to feel only the love between them. Despite an effort to stay strong for the boys, both parents sobbed openly. Adele could not stop touching her boys. It was as though she needed to feel their physical presence for as long as humanly possible. Barely conscious, Louis smiled and held both of his parents' hands, sending them a message of appreciation and love.

His weak voice could barely be heard as he said, "I knew you would come."

Initially, Adele and Gabriel were so bereft with grief that they could not speak.

Breathing shallowly, Louis stated, "I have been incredibly lucky… to have been born into such a loving family."

Gabriel tearfully responded, "No, we were the lucky ones…to have been given a son like you."

Adele nodded in agreement as she said, "You do know…that we could not love you more. You have been such a gift to us."

Although clearly uncomfortable, Louis smiled, and sighed with gratitude, his last wish granted. He was at peace in the presence of these people, his family. They instinctively knew and understood that Louis was ready to give up the struggle for survival, and they reluctantly understood, their faith in God ever present.

As the death scene unfolded, there was a flurry of frantic activity, as the field hospital was preparing to evacuate in the face of an enemy breakthrough. The Battle of the Somme had been a series of murderous campaigns that had been fought back and forth, over the same war-torn ground. The medical staff was in the process of pragmatically deciding which patients could be moved in the emergent escape. Louis was dying, and it was decided that he was to be left behind.

Gabriel was enraged when he heard this, and vowed, "My son will not be taken captive by any damned Germans!"

The aged surgeon was focused, pragmatically directing the evacuation, his voice calm and authoritative. He understood the family's angst, but he was undeterred in his decision, and calmly proclaimed, "Your son is dying. I must focus my attention on evacuating the wounded, those who have a chance of surviving their injuries. I'm so sorry."

Gabriel's rage was frightening to behold. He stepped forward to confront the gray-haired surgeon, his anger and grief overwhelming him, making him irrational, and threatening. Quickly, Henri stepped between the two men, gently pulling his father away from the doctor.

Henri understood the unfolding battle, and urgently warned his parents, "You have to leave now, before the cart and horses are commandeered for the evacuation!"

Without hesitation, Gabriel used his considerable strength to gently scoop up his barely conscious son. Like he was a small child, the father tenderly carried his mortally wounded son between the cots, to the humble cart outside of the ancient church door. Adele hurriedly followed, equally determined. Without speaking, she climbed into the back of the wagon, quickly making a bed of blankets for Louis to lay on. Cradling her dying son's head in her lap, Adele had the look of a fiercely protective mother.

Their anxious goodbyes to Henri were cut short by the authoritative command of the old surgeon. "You need to get moving! There is no time to waste! The Germans have broken through our lines, and they will be here in minutes!"

Overcome with grief, Henri looked upon his brother for what he knew would be the last time. Louis stirred as he lay in the back of the wagon.

With one last strained effort, Louis looked at Henri and weakly whispered, "I love you, brother."

Although Henri could not hear the words spoken over the din of the escalating battle, he knew what Louis had communicated.

Without hesitation, Henri looked tenderly into his brother's eyes and loudly proclaimed, "I love you, too."

Adele and Gabriel were shaken to the core by the finality and tenderness of the exchange between their sons. Unable to speak, they both sobbed softly, nodding their own goodbyes to Henri, their eyes communicating so much. No words were needed. Gabriel hurriedly urged the frightened horses forward, as Henri turned away from his family, his eyes filled with tears.

He moved toward the approaching battle, his sniper rifle in hand, suddenly mentally engaged in the life and death struggle before him. Henri did not look back to his escaping family. He could not look back. It was too final, too overwhelming. Instead, he focused on the killing of Germans, the foes who had mortally wounded his brother. The reckoning would be fierce, his grief and anger so strong. He knew that he could not leave this fight, did not want to leave this fight. With purpose and skill, he headed into battle.

Artillery rounds were starting to fall around the congested line of ambulances that were making their escape from the advancing Germans. Gabriel fought to maintain control of his terrified horses, as the sounds and explosions of the erupting battle moved closer. The sturdy farm animals could not be steadied; the environment was so foreign, so frightening. The team of horses started to gallop wildly, uncontrollably, away from the slowly moving caravan of evacuees. The jostling cart was careening haphazardly across the cratered field when a round of artillery hit it squarely. The impact of the exploding shell shredded the occupants of the little cart. Their deaths were blessedly instantaneous, and thankfully not witnessed by Henri.

CHAPTER 5

Highly Effective Killer

1916-1918
Battlefields of Northern France

The battle convulsed back and forth over the contested ground for three long days. Finally, there was an exhausted lull, as the soldiers on both sides seemed to literally fight themselves out. Although the losses were almost incomprehensible, the armies were in approximately the same position as when the battle started. The barren land between the warring enemies was littered with dead horses, and the remains of mutilated soldiers. The smell of decay was inescapable.

Henri had collapsed against the muddy wall of the trench when the messenger approached him. He was dazed from lack of sleep, and the prolonged back and forth of the murderous battle. The young orderly handed Henri a handwritten note that was smeared in blood. Hesitantly, he opened the folded paper and read the simple message. It was only four words, but somehow it communicated so much more.

> *Please come see me.*
> *Dr. Lamont*

A sense of foreboding overcame Henri, as he climbed out of the trench and slowly trudged toward the field hospital. Despite the back and forth of the battle, the French had reclaimed the contested ground surrounding the old stone church, which was once again a busy field hospital. The futility of the lives lost for such a small gain seemed unreal to Henri. He recognized the stooped figure of Dr. Lamont from a distance. The old surgeon was hunched over a gravely wounded soldier, assessing his wounds. He appeared calm and completely in control as he made his determinations. Henri quietly approached the doctor, waiting for him to finish his assessment. Finally, Dr. Lamont looked up and nodded to Henri. The old man and the young soldier stepped away from the triage area.

Turning toward Henri, he took a deep breath as he said, "I'm so sorry to tell you this, but I have some very bad news for you."

Henri felt numb as he looked at the old doctor.

Dr. Lamont gently placed his hand on Henri's shoulder as he revealed, "Your family was killed in the retreat."

Stunned, Henri struggled to stay upright. With a sense of dazed disbelief, Henri asked, "My family? My…my whole family was killed?"

The surgeon responded in his most reassuring voice, "Yes, an artillery shell hit their wagon as they were leaving the hospital. There was no suffering. They died instantly. I'm sorry."

Henri fell to his knees, as a faintness overcame him, his grief visceral as he retched and vomited. Dr. Lamont knelt beside him and held Henri as he sobbed. After several minutes, Henri seemed to somewhat regain his composure. Slowly, he pulled himself to his feet and picked up his rifle.

He looked through tear-filled eyes as he said, "I appreciate you telling me in person."

The battle surgeon, who had delivered his fair share of bad news through the war, emanated compassion as he responded, "I have been impressed with you and your brother. Obviously, you two were very close. And I could tell your parents were lovely people from the few moments I spent with them. I'm so sorry for your losses."

Unable to speak, Henri nodded in response.

Dr. Lamont took on a paternal tone as he said, "Son, listen to me. You need to survive this war…for the sake of your family. They would want you to go on. It's going to be tough to get through the next few months, but you need to find a way. This war will end, so stay safe. I'm putting you on medical leave for the next two weeks. You need to get away from the front lines and take care of yourself. Get your head straight so you can survive this war. Do you hear me?"

Henri shook his head in resistance as he said, "That's not necessary."

"It's absolutely necessary and it's an order, soldier." Appealing to his sense of duty, Dr. Lamont went on to say, "You're an extremely valuable sniper, and we can't afford to lose you to battle fatigue. Do you understand?"

His military training instinctively kicked in as he responded, "Yes, sir. I understand."

The doctor then said, "I've already notified your commander that you will be on medical leave for the next two weeks. So, go take care of yourself." Abruptly, he turned and focused his attention on a wounded soldier who was nearby in the triage area.

Henri spent the next two weeks in a tented enclave two miles behind the battlefront. In many ways, it was a great relief to be away from the imminent threat of enemy attack, but it was anything but comforting. The occupants of the little tent community were mostly wounded, convalescing soldiers, but there were victims of battle fatigue too, and their bizarre behaviors startled him. He was both mesmerized and horrified by the population of mentally broken soldiers. One traumatized young man would intermittently scream out in horror when he heard even the most remote sounds of battle. It was unnerving, and it made Henri aware of his own mental fragility. He was determined not to fall into the abyss of madness.

His mind swirled with sadness and disbelief as he tried to process the loss of his family, along with the realization that he had a child. It was a truly confusing time. Henri pulled back into himself, unwilling to interact with other soldiers. He wanted to be completely and utterly alone. Surprisingly, he was able to sleep at night, and this did wonders for his state of mind. He was still sad, but his mental fog was clearing.

Henri was relieved when the two weeks had passed. The time away from the front had provided him an opportunity to grieve away from the danger, and it had allowed him to rest and sleep, which seemed to give him much more clarity of thought. He acknowledged his sadness, his losses, but in some strange way he wanted to return to his life as a sniper. It had been his life for over two years, and he felt a sense of belonging with his comrades, and with the routine of war. Initially, it was uncomfortable, as his fellow combatants struggled to offer their condolences, silently wondering about his mental stability. Henri quickly distanced himself from their awkward expressions, clearly sending the message that he did not want to talk about his family. Instead, he quickly and effectively got back to the business of killing Germans.

A numbness set in, one that methodically pulled him through the battles, through the very personal killing. In the months ahead, he became a highly effective sniper, revered among his fellow combatants. Calculating, and supremely aware, he used his excellent rifle skills to kill an astonishing number of Germans. He didn't seethe with hate. The truth was, he barely felt anything. He just wanted the war to end, and he knew that it would be a fight to a draw.

Henri's cool, methodical approach to battle was strangely calming, and it inspired confidence among the inexperienced replacement soldiers. For that reason, the floundering soldiers gravitated to Henri. The youngest, most inexperienced soldiers were alarmingly childlike in their reactions to the chaos and terror of battle. It was not uncommon to find them huddled in the bottom of the trench, sobbing uncontrollably. Emotionally spent, Henri had little tolerance for these rookie soldiers. But slowly, over time, he began to offer insight and strangely distant and pragmatic instruction to the fledgling soldiers. They listened attentively, desperately wanting to survive. At only nineteen years old, Henri was perceived as a rarity, a battle-hardened survivor.

One of these young replacement soldiers seemed particularly drawn to Henri, attentively taking in his instruction, and quickly proving himself as a highly effective sniper. The boy, Theo, was only seventeen, but he looked much younger. Scrawny and unimpressive, he had a look of fragility about him. Although reluctant to get close to any of the young combatants, Henri did start to take this young soldier under his protective wing. He guided him through sniper training, and calmly called out encouragement and direction through the chaos of battle. Theo saw something in Henri, buried deep beneath the numb, methodical killing. There was a glimmer of compassion, and a willingness to help the vulnerable, inexperienced young soldiers. Theo admired him, and in turn protected him, as he recognized Henri's internal struggle. Slowly, the two began to reveal small bits of information about themselves. The conversations were mostly at night, and were short, cryptic revelations. There was more unsaid, than said. Yet there was a mutual understanding between the two young men. They both had experienced tremendous loss and were trying to find their way out of the darkness.

It was often said that there are no atheists in foxholes, but Henri wasn't convinced. He was experiencing his own crisis of faith. Raised in religion, he felt anger, guilt, and doubt as he questioned the benevolence of a God who could allow such devastation. He had been brought up to believe that faith would sustain you through the darkest times. But his faith was clearly wavering.

Theo was similarly raised in religion. In the quiet of the night, the young, childlike soldier reluctantly confessed his own faltering faith to Henri, and his disbelief that God could allow such carnage.

Theo shook his head in the shadowy darkness, wondering out loud, "My mother is a very religious woman, and she raised me to be a strong Christian. But, to tell the truth, it's hard for me to have faith in a God that would allow all this killing."

Henri listened, completely understanding. He said, "I feel the same way. I used to pray, but I can't anymore. If there is a God, I don't think he's listening."

Theo thoughtfully said, "You know, maybe when this war is over, and we can see some good in the world, our faith will return."

Henri marveled at this young soldier who seemed to be a deep thinker, and surprisingly devoid of bitterness. He was wise beyond his years, an old man in a young, rather unimpressive body. In the macabre backdrop of trench warfare, these conversations about God and religion were such an oddity, such a contradiction to all that was happening around them. Two highly effective killers of men were debating and lamenting God. But these deep conversations about religion seemed to be the thread of sanity that anchored them emotionally through the final months of the war. They trusted each other, and that was the beginning of a deep friendship, and the reemergence of their humanity.

With the entry of the United States into the war, and the cautious renewal of faith in their command, the French troops, along with their Allies, fought doggedly to the end. The losses were horrific. France had paid an enormous cost in lives lost and soldiers wounded, but finally, in November of 1918, the war was at an end. The news of the armistice spread quickly through the trenches, followed by a wave of jubilation, and then exhaustion, as the troops tried to recover from the long ordeal. The French military command quickly moved forward with plans to disband their troops and get them home for Christmas.

Henri and Theo stood restlessly in line, waiting to turn in their weapons. One could sense their reluctance to part ways, to head back to their pre-war lives. They both seemed adrift in the crowd of young soldiers. Suddenly confronted with their inevitable parting, there was an undeniable yearning for more time together, more opportunity to know each other away from the war. They were not blood brothers, but they had gone through hell and back together, and they had formed a close, brother-like bond.

As the time of their departure grew near, Henri turned to Theo and asked, "So what is your plan, now that this war is over?"

Theo responded wistfully, "Guess I'll head back to Cherbourg and check on my mother. I haven't received any letters from her in a couple months, but the mail is unreliable. She's all I got left."

Henri nodded as he said, "I don't have much family left either."

"I suppose you're going back to your family's farm near Bayeux?"

Sighing deeply, Henri responded, "Yes, I'm going back to our family farm, but it's going to be hard. It's been two years since my family was killed, and the farm has been deserted for all that time."

Theo asked, "Did your folks have animals?"

Henri brightened as he said, "Oh, yes, they have raised Normandy cattle for five generations. My father was so proud of his herd. I'm not sure what happened to the livestock after he died."

"Sounds like a pretty nice farm."

Henri went on to say, "It's a beautiful little farm. It's not anything fancy, but there's a nice stone farmhouse and a pretty good size stone barn for the animals. The house sits up on a hill, overlooking a large apple orchard. It's a peaceful place, been in my family for over one hundred and twenty years."

Theo smiled at his friend as he said, "Yeah…you're a farmer. I can see that in you. I bet you'll have that place whipped in shape in no time."

Henri shook his head and said, "No, it won't be that easy. There are so many memories in that place. It's going to be hard to go back. I worked that farm with my father and brother. I can hardly stand the thought of them not being there."

Theo reassured him, "You're the strongest person I've ever known. I'm betting that you will build a nice life for yourself."

Henri appreciated the sentiment and responded, "Thanks for the vote of confidence. And Theo, if you ever want to give farming a try, look me up."

"I appreciate the offer, but I need to go back to Cherbourg and take care of my mother. She hasn't been well for quite a while. I'm all she has."

Henri nodded as he said, "I understand completely."

The progression of the long line of soldiers who were waiting to turn in their weapons had stalled. Henri looked at Theo and said, "I have never had much patience for lines, or military protocol for that matter. You know, I think I've earned the right to keep this rifle. It's gotten me through a lot."

Theo chuckled. "I'm feeling the same way."

Henri stepped out of line and turned toward Theo as he said, "Let's get out of here. We've both got a long journey ahead of us, and we may as well get started. We can at least walk part of the way together. I don't want to get all sappy, but I'm going to miss you."

Theo beamed as he responded, "I'm going to miss you, too."

Quietly, the young soldiers slipped away from the long line, and walked over the muddy, battle-scarred hill, with only their rifles in hand.

CHAPTER 6

Regret

1918
Bayeux, France

It was almost dawn when Henri finally stopped talking. The narrative of the last few years had become steadily more pragmatic as the night, and the story, wore on. Marguerite had listened attentively, inwardly wincing, as Henri unfolded his tale. Guiltily, she had listened in silence, as Henri told of the discovery that he had a child. She knew more about this child than she felt safe to divulge. It was a thorny tale that was painful for her to even contemplate telling. Frankly, Marguerite was worried about Henri's emotional stability. The thought of introducing more strands to an already convoluted story made her shudder.

He seemed a shell of the vibrant, confident young man who had left for war. Henri's state of mind, as well as his outlook on life, were mirrored in his appearance. Physically, he looked tired, much older, and more worn than his twenty-one years, and there was an edginess that told of his inner turmoil. As Marguerite watched over Henri, finally sleeping, after his tale left him exhausted and spent, she was troubled and riddled with guilt over decisions that she had made regarding him.

Not able to sleep, her mind racing and conflicted with the thoughts of someone about to make a major change in her life, she watched as the light of dawn eased through the small apartment window, and she quietly slipped out of the door. Marguerite loved this time of day. There was something calming and ethereal about the dawn. She always did her best thinking and had her best conversations with God at dawn.

Marguerite used her strength to open the massive wooden door leading into the cathedral. The heavy, forbidding looking entry door made it seem an unlikely haven. Reverently, she walked towards the raised altar. The early morning light coming through the stained glass gave a heavenly ambiance to the beautiful cathedral, and it had a calming effect on Marguerite. Trance-like, she knelt on the altar steps and began her conversation with God. Marguerite had found solace in this place, on this altar, after the deaths of Adele, Gabriel, and Louis. Initially, her grief had assaulted her like a tsunami, washing over her, drowning her. But she was better now, not completely healed, but able to appreciate life. The busy routines of her life as a nun had given her structure and purpose, and had helped her cope with the losses, but the decisions of her past still weighed heavily on her. Of course, they had always been there, submerged in the busy routines of her life as a nun. Though, as she thought back over her life, she had to acknowledge that there had been a steady drip, drip, drip of regret, and lost opportunity. In her most honest moments of reflection, it was undeniable.

Marguerite had convinced herself that she had made the right decision for Henri when she gave him up to her sister. The ease with which Adele loved and incorporated Henri into her family gave Marguerite comfort and was a cause for jealousy. The older sister had been a natural mother, loving and effusively happy in her role. As Marguerite observed the little farm family from afar, she could not help but feel the loss. She too, felt that she had the capacity to be a loving mother. But as time went on, she sadly had to admit that she would never know that happiness.

Gabriel and Adele had a loving marriage, and that was mirrored in the care of Louis and Henri. Unable to have any more children, the couple had welcomed the addition of Henri to their family. Adele and Gabriel wanted to support Marguerite in her time of crisis, so the plan to raise Henri as their own was an easy solution. They loved Henri from the start. He was their child in every sense that mattered. The couple were in total agreement, Marguerite should have the opportunity to spend time with Henri, and be a valued part of his life, but she was to be known to Henri, and everyone else, as his loving aunt. Initially, Marguerite had felt that this was enough.

As time went on, Marguerite came to resent her limited role in Henri's life. Adele and Gabriel were strict parents and had the expectation that the boys learn to work on the farm at an early age. When Marguerite voiced her disapproval to her sister and brother-in-law, it was not well-received. Gabriel was polite, but forceful. It was not her role to offer advice. Adele and Gabriel were the parents. Marguerite was devastated, but quietly hid her feelings, purposely trying to live with her decisions.

Adele and Gabriel were well regarded in the community. Henri knew acceptance and respect growing up in the LeBlanc family, and for this Marguerite was thankful. In her most benevolent moments, Marguerite told herself that she had made the right decision in giving Henri up to her sister but doubt and regret inevitably crept back to the surface.

For over two hours she was on her knees, praying and trying to make sense of the thoughts racing through her tormented mind. The nun had experienced spiritual crisis before, and had always successfully sought solace in this place, on these altar steps. But this inner battle was shaking her concept of herself, and her role in religious life, to the core.

Father Bernard walked into the cathedral and was startled to see Marguerite kneeling on the altar steps, intensely in conversation with God. He knew the gravity of Marguerite's conflict. He knew her well. There were no secrets between them. Father Bernard had cared for Marguerite when she fell into despair after the deaths of Adele, Gabriel, and Louis. He had seen her when she was most fragile, and he feared that this crisis would send her spiraling back to madness.

Silently taking in the scene before him, Father Bernard fought the urge to rush forward and intervene, but he realized that he had no right to interject his influence into her decision. The trust between them had been crafted through pain and turmoil over the past twenty-two years. Both had been dedicated to God's work, but they both had also known sin.

Marguerite, hearing someone enter the church, turned, and caught Father Bernard's imploring gaze. Much was communicated, as they steadfastly looked into each other's eyes. No longer able to resist, Father Bernard slowly moved forward and fully embraced Marguerite. They fell into each other, guiltily soaking up the consolation of physical contact. The embrace was both comforting and strangely intimate. They both felt it and were unnerved by its intensity. Both had known and distantly acknowledged their draw to each other, but their vow of celibacy had prevailed through all the years they had worked together. In many ways, the relationship had developed more fully because of the lack of physical intimacy. Carefully, away from the prying eyes of their fellow nuns, priests, and the congregation, the two had managed to share the pain and joy of their lives. They knew each other completely.

It was Marguerite who spoke first. "I have to do this."

His sorrow was visceral, as he said, "No, you're being impulsive. Your work here is not done."

"I will not abandon him again."

"You have always been with him. He was raised in your sister's loving family and has enjoyed your constant love and support throughout his upbringing. He draws his identity from this family. The brother that he lost in this terrible war was a true brother. The adoptive parents who raised him, never thought of him, or loved him differently than Louis. Telling him now will only confuse and anger him."

"He is my son!"

"He is your son, but he has endured tremendous loss and he needs time to heal."

"He deserves to know the truth!"

"Yes, he does. But now is not the time."

The pain and anguish gushed out, as Marguerite loudly confronted the priest. "I was young and scared and stupid! I have been haunted by my decision to give up my child, even to my sister's loving care."

"Henri has known a loving and stable home life. The decision was made with his well-being in mind. Marguerite, you're torturing yourself."

"I did not have the courage to face those who would condemn me."

"Those who judge us rarely have our best interests in mind."

Marguerite sighed deeply as she exclaimed, "I have such regret. This child of mine believes he is alone in this world."

Father Bernard calmly reassured the distraught nun. "No, he knows he is not alone. He came back to you."

Marguerite was not comforted by his reassurances. Her guilt was evident as she mournfully proclaimed, "But he is just a shell of a man, and he wants to retrieve his illegitimate child from the orphanage. I swear God is sending me a message."

Father Bernard could not deny her tortured reasoning as he said, "Possibly. Messages come in all forms."

With those words, Marguerite stepped forward to embrace Father Bernard. This time there was no guilt, just true concern and love communicated in the physicality of their embrace.

Then the priest told her with utter sincerity, "I will completely support whatever decision you make."

He forced a smile as he looked at her, and then quietly slipped out of the chapel. Marguerite was alone again with her thoughts, her regrets, and her God. She instinctively knew what she had to do. With quiet determination, she went to the donation room in the basement. Pouring through the donated clothing, she pulled out a couple of worn dresses, and some sturdy work clothes. Carefully, and with much reverence, she removed her nun's clothing. Donning a sturdy work dress over her lithe body, she looked older than her thirty-eight years, but was strangely attractive. Her dark hair was lightly lined with gray, but her skin was clear and had a porcelain quality to it. She was surprised to find that her shapely body was nicely outlined in the worn dress. The transformation in her appearance made the nun take pause, as she tried to absorb the decision she had just made.

Marguerite thoughtfully carried her nun's habit back to the main sanctuary of the church. Carefully, she smoothed the fabric and arranged the black nun's habit over the stairs leading up to the raised altar. The spectacle of the nun's clothing so artfully arranged was strangely and eerily theatrical. It looked like the clothing's occupant had been drawn away by a heavenly force. The act of placing the religious clothing on the altar steps was symbolic, and it told of a deep reverence and commitment. Marguerite kept her crucifix which hung on a sturdy chain around her neck and slipped it under her coarse work dress. She would continue God's work, but her clothing would bear the markings of a humble woman who worked hard to love and support her son.

CHAPTER 7

The Return to the Farm

1918
Normandy, France

Henri slept soundly, rarely even stirring. It was mid-afternoon when he finally awoke, a bit disoriented, but feeling strangely warm and comfortable in Marguerite's humble bed. He felt at ease in this place, with this woman whom he had known all his life.

Marguerite was soothing as she said, "Good afternoon."

Embarrassed, Henri said, "I'm sorry I slept so long. I guess I must have been exhausted. It was a long walk back to Bayeux."

"Yes, you've been on a long journey. No need to apologize."

"I didn't mean to keep you up all night. I probably talked more than I should have."

Marguerite smiled, as she reassured him, "I'm so glad that you told me about what you've experienced. It was hard to hear parts of your story, but I wanted to know. I really needed to know. Thank you."

Henri looked apologetic as he said, "I know it was tough to hear about the death of your sister, but she did not suffer."

"Yes, I miss Adele...every day. She was always my biggest supporter, my confidante. I could tell her anything...and I did. She knew everything about me."

Henri nodded, knowing that the words she spoke were true. As he looked at Marguerite in her common work dress, he could not help but notice the remarkable similarity to his mother. Her speech, her mannerisms, all so alike, seemed uncanny, and a bit unnerving. He had never seen Marguerite in anything but her nun's habit, and she looked transformed, very much like his mother, disturbingly like his mother. Puzzled, he asked point blank, "Why are you dressed this way?"

Marguerite was equally direct, "I'm leaving my position in the church for a while, to help you on the farm. You're going to need some help, and I want to be there for you."

"No. You can't just leave the church. You're a nun."

"It's my decision. I want to be with you. You are going to need help. The farm has been abandoned for two years now." Marguerite hesitated, afraid to tell him. "And Henri, there's one more thing you need to know. The livestock all disappeared after it became known that your parents had been killed."

Henri bristled, incredulous at what she had said, "What? You mean they were stolen?"

"Yes."

Henri's mind raced, instantly enraged, as he quickly came up with the culprit. "The Dubois."

"Yes, Leo confronted Vincent Dubois, but he was driven off the property at gunpoint. With the war and everything, the police didn't want to get involved."

Henri was explosive, his anger volatile. "I swear...I will kill him!"

Marguerite looked alarmed and unnerved, but she tried to appear calm. "No. You need to keep your wits about you. Vincent is a dangerous, unpredictable drunk."

"I'm a dangerous man, too."

Marguerite visibly gasped, knowing that what he said was true. She looked at him, her eyes pleading. "Henri...I can't lose you, too. I can't. You need to approach this situation with caution."

"I'm always cautious. I was trained to be cautious."

Marguerite tried not to look scared, as she responded, "Henri, the war is over. I can't bear the loss of any more of my loved ones. Do you hear me? I can't!"

Henri was suddenly catapulted back to reality, acutely aware of her fear. "I know you're scared, but I will get my father's livestock back. I will."

Marguerite looked at this young man, her biological son, and knew that the war had changed him.

"Then you better talk with Leo…and you better do it safely. Do you understand me? I've lost enough. No more." Marguerite was struck by how much he had changed, how dangerous he seemed, how unstable.

For years there had been bad blood between the two families, ever since Henri's father had caught Vincent Dubois stealing apples from his orchard. Although Gabriel LeBlanc was known to be easygoing and fair in his dealings, he had a temper, and no tolerance for thievery. The confrontation between the two men was intense, with Gabriel threatening to shoot Vincent if he ever saw him on his property again. Seething with hate, the thieving neighbor skulked back to his dilapidated farm, silently vowing revenge.

Vincent Dubois was a lazy man, with a serious love of liquor. Mean and violent when drunk, people avoided him. Barely sustaining his unruly family, Vincent was regarded with suspicion and blatant dislike by his neighbors. There was a steady disappearance from nearby farms of chickens, eggs, fruit, and locally distilled fruit liquor. Not proud or ethical, Vincent felt more vengeful than embarrassed when he was caught stealing the LeBlanc apples. His lack of integrity carried over to his family life, too.

His wife, Lois, was a timid, ill-looking woman. She had been seen in town with massive bruises on her face. People felt pity for this poor victimized soul, but they were fearful and reluctant to get involved in any way with Vincent. Sister Marguerite had encountered Lois several times, kneeling and praying in the darkest part of the church. In her quiet, observant way, Marguerite would come kneel beside her. Initially, Lois was suspicious of Marguerite, but came to understand that she was a friend. Over time, there was a trust established between the two women, and they would disappear into the nun's nearby apartment to share a cup of coffee and talk. Marguerite did not judge or offer her advice. However, she would sometimes offer clothing from the donation room of the church, which Lois gratefully accepted. The frail, timid woman understood that the townspeople were afraid of her husband, and she appreciated Sister Marguerite's willingness to befriend and help her.

When the two oldest Dubois sons were killed early in the war, Marguerite was the only person to come to their farmhouse with food and comforting words. Lois was profoundly appreciative and touched by Marguerite's care and concern. Vincent drunkenly viewed her with suspicion throughout the visit, but Lois never forgot the kindness.

As Marguerite recounted the story of her friendship with Lois Dubois, Henri was shaking his head. He erupted, "They are disgusting people!"

Marguerite was unnerved by Henri's volatility. She drew a deep breath and responded with all the calmness she could muster, "I understand your anger at Vincent, but his wife is a victim, too. And she is my friend. Lois and her children have suffered mightily because of this man."

Henri responded angrily, "His children are cut from the same cloth! I went to school with them. They're sneaky, violent little thieves!"

Marguerite responded, "Well, the two oldest boys were killed in the war. The youngest boy deserted the army about a year ago. He's been seen in the area, and folks seem to think that he's hiding out at the farm. This family has had their share of grief, too."

Henri took pause for a moment, as he took in what Marguerite had revealed. "I have no doubt that Lois has been through a lot. It's not my aim to increase her grief, but I have no use for Vincent. He stole our farm animals, and I will get them back!"

"Promise me that you will be careful."

Henri responded, "I didn't survive the war by being foolish."

Marguerite looked a bit embarrassed as she said, "I did not mean to belittle you. I don't know all that you've been through, but I do know this…you are a survivor. That tells me quite a bit. I do think it would be wise to talk with Leo first. He's level-headed and he may be able to help."

Henri seemed to soak in the advice as he thoughtfully said, "Yes, Leo is a good man. He was such a good friend to my father. I feel so bad that he lost his only son in the war."

"Yes, Leo and his wife have struggled. The war really has taken quite a toll on them."

Henri reassured Marguerite, "We'll be sure to stop and see them."

Marguerite and Henri planned to walk the three miles to the family farm in the morning. Feeling both excited and apprehensive, Henri helped Marguerite pack some basic food supplies. Several loaves of bread, a ham, cheese, coffee, and some basic cooking supplies all went into a rough burlap bag. It was winter, and the farm had been unoccupied for two years, so there was no telling what they would encounter. Henri was nervous, mentally trying to prepare himself for the return to the farm, a place that was so intricately tied to his dead family. He wanted to go back. Henri felt a powerful pull to return but feared the emptiness that he would encounter. Not surprisingly, they both were preoccupied with their thoughts, and turned in to bed early, exhausted.

They awoke a little before dawn. After a hearty breakfast of eggs, ham, and buttered bread, the two hastily prepared to start their trek to the farm. They were both startled to hear the echo of abrupt knocks on the door. Marguerite hesitantly opened the heavy wooden door to find Father Bernard standing impatiently in the cold. He seemed flustered, and awkwardly expressed that he wanted to talk to Marguerite alone. Henri looked puzzled, as Marguerite silently stepped outside to speak privately with the priest. The muffled sounds of angry exchanges could be heard through the thick wooden door. Finally, Marguerite slipped back into the apartment, visibly upset. She gave no explanation, but quickly busied herself with preparations for their departure. Henri could not help but feel the pull between these two, and he secretly wondered about their relationship. Henri knew they had been long time friends and confidantes, but there seemed to be more. Respectfully, he did not question this woman that he knew as a loving aunt.

As the two exited the apartment with their cache of supplies, Father Bernard watched them from the church entrance, his gaze steady, his face unsmiling. Marguerite stopped and they looked directly at each other for an uncomfortably long time. Henri looked from one to the other, feeling like an intruder in a lover's quarrel. Much seemed to be communicated between the priest and the nun, without a word being spoken. Finally, the priest forced a weak smile and waved. Marguerite looked enormously relieved, taking it as a sign that they would remain friends and confidantes. She returned the wave, and hesitantly smiled. Their friendship had been tested before, and it had always survived.

Marguerite and Henri began their hike to the farm just as the sun was coming up, illuminating the Bayeux Cathedral in eerily beautiful morning light. They were mesmerized by the majesty of the structure that towered over the humble French village. Henri remembered, and he felt grounded in the place, the cathedral a physical anchor to his past, a symbol of hope and permanence that was reassuring to him as a returning soldier.

With a sudden surge of confidence and inspiration, the two began their journey to the farm. When they had barely cleared the buildings of the town, Henri slipped away to a cluster of bushes, and quickly returned, holding a menacing looking rifle. The gun was not pretty, the barrel dull, and the wooden stock marred with scratches, its wooden grain barely visible through the dirt, but Henri handled the weapon with an ease and reverence that spoke volumes. Frankly, there was something unsettling about how he handled the weapon. Marguerite was alarmed by the sight, and she started to protest, but

Henri forcefully asserted that he needed to carry this gun. The weapon had been his constant companion, his friend, his security throughout the war, and it had seen him safely through the horrific ordeal. He obviously drew comfort from it, but Marguerite was unnerved, and her concerns about Henri's mental stability reemerged.

They were mostly quiet on their walk back to the farm. It was unusually cold, and the landscape was lightly dusted with snow. Henri was nostalgic as he walked past the bucolic Normandy farms. Marguerite would periodically update Henri as to news of individual families and their farms. Again, he was made aware of the suffering and loss that Bayeux had endured through the war years. He was certainly not alone in his losses, and that somehow made him even more determined to return to the farm, and to put the war behind him.

As they approached Leo's farm, Henri was flooded with warm memories of his father's best friend. Knowing that it was milking time, Henri walked toward the barn to find the loyal family friend. They had barely started down the path, when Leo emerged from the barn, and stared in disbelief.

The old farmer was tearfully relieved, and his joy was apparent in the long, heartfelt embrace.

Leo smiled as he said, "My, you're a sight for sore eyes. Welcome back, son."

Henri felt the warmth and sincerity in his greeting, and it made him tear up as he said, "Yes, it's been quite a journey. The last few years have been hard on us all."

Leo nodded, "Yes, we've all lost dear loved ones. I miss your father every day. He was truly a special friend to me. He kept me going after my son died in the war."

Henri understood as he said, "Yes, he was a special man. I know that he thought the world of you, too. I'm so sorry about your son."

"Yes, it's been hard. You don't ever expect to outlive your children. Sadly, we're not alone. Almost every family in this area has lost someone in the war."

Marguerite sighed and nodded as she spoke, "Unfortunately, it's true."

Leo was not a maudlin man by nature, and he quickly ended the sad discussion. "Well, come on in and have a fresh cup of hot coffee."

Sitting before the toasty farmhouse stove, Leo's wife warmly welcomed Henri home. She served Marguerite and Henri hot coffee and warm bread with jam. Leo sadly told of the theft of the LeBlanc farm animals. He seemed embarrassed that he was not able to successfully confront Vincent and retrieve all that was stolen.

Henri reassured his father's old friend, "You need not feel bad. I appreciate that you tried. Vincent Dubois is a crazy, violent drunk."

Leo nodded, as he sternly looked Henri in the eyes. "He is a dangerous man, and you need to keep that in mind. You're likely to be killed if you are hell bent on retrieving your father's livestock."

Henri smiled and said, "I've been likely to have been killed many a time over the last few years."

Leo nodded as he responded, "I have no doubt about that. Thankfully, you've made it back from the war alive, so it's best not to tempt fate. Vincent is very dangerous. Don't underestimate him."

Henri's confidence was a bit unnerving to everyone in the little farmhouse kitchen. "I'm not underestimating him, and he would be wise to not underestimate me."

Leo seemed to understand as he said, "Okay, then, let me help you."

Leo's wife was obviously concerned, as she interjected, "Let's not be planning something foolish."

Leo tried to reassure his wife as he said, "I need to help Gabriel's son."

His wife looked visibly upset, but she silently nodded.

Henri clearly appreciated the support as he said, "I suppose it would be safer with your help."

Leo shook his head in agreement as he said, "Yes, but we better think about how to best go about this plan of yours. It's probably smart to head over to his farm early in the morning before he starts drinking. He'll be hungover for sure, but less likely to be stupid drunk."

Leo looked at his wife, reassuring her, "Don't worry. We will be careful."

Leo's wife nodded that she understood. This was a debt he owed to his deceased best friend. Leo had to help Gabriel's son retrieve all that had been stolen from the family farm. The plan had an undeniable element of redemption, and the hope that this would help Henri move forward to rebuild his life.

After their brief visit with Leo and his wife, the two continued on their journey. It was almost noon when they finally reached the family farm. Hesitantly, they approached the faded, arched gate and looked in disbelief at the scene before them. Scattered flakes of snow falling from the gray sky contributed to the aura of bleakness, the feeling of abandonment. The once smoothly beaten path leading to the house was covered with unwelcoming dry, dead vegetation. It was unsettling to see the once vibrant farm in such a state of neglect. Although much had changed, the old two-story stone farmhouse with its faded blue wooden shutters still stood solidly, overlooking the rolling pastures. A mosaic of stone fences charmingly encircled the pastures, and in the distance, a sizable apple orchard could be seen. The massive stone barn was eerily quiet and devoid of any activity. The emptiness was unexpected and felt too harsh for words.

The door to the kitchen easily pushed open to reveal a dusty, disheveled room. The cupboards were haphazardly ajar, their contents mostly gone. Only a few chipped dishes remained, and one very worn pot. It was immediately apparent that more than just the farm animals had been taken. The unattractive, sturdy furnishings remained, but it was clear that the house had been violated, and its most valuable possessions stolen. Henri calculatingly took it all in, and he seemed inordinately, frighteningly calm to Marguerite. There was something subtly dangerous in his reaction to finding his family's home in such a state. Marguerite knew that the war had changed him, and she consciously tried to calm herself as she put her arm around Henri. He gently pushed her away, as he angrily took in the state of the family farm. In the remaining limited daylight of December, Marguerite and Henri steadily worked to clean and tidy the disheveled old farm-house. Although extremely dusty, all four bedrooms were as Adele and Gabriel had left them. The beds appeared as though they were awaiting the return of their long-lost family members. Henri found it disturbing to see the time capsule. He could feel the presence of his family as he walked through the rooms, and he acutely felt their loss. Struggling, he wiped his tears away as he began the work of cleaning out the wood stove. The coldness of the winter had permeated the old stone house, and he was determined to warm it.

With a sense of urgency, Henri left the farmhouse to forage through the barn in search of wood for the stove. He immediately no-ticed that the farm wagon was missing, as were many of the tools. The stolen farm implements had been used by his family for generations, and this saddened Henri even more. He shook his head angrily as he looked at the emptiness of the ancient barn. Fortunately, he found a large stack of split wood next to the door. He scooped up an armload and headed out the door towards the farmhouse.

In the dimming evening light, he clearly saw the silhouette of a slightly built man carrying a gun. Initially Henri was alarmed, but then he noticed something oddly familiar in the visitor's gait. As they walked closer to each other, it became apparent that it was indeed Theo, the young soldier whom he had taken under his wing through the last months of the war.

Theo smiled, his facial features barely visible in the evening light, as he said in his steady drawl, "I'm betting you weren't expecting to see me so soon."

Henri was sincere as he said, "I'm glad to see you, brother."

Theo seemed to truly appreciate the welcome as he sadly said, "I returned to Cherbourg to find my mother and learned that she died a few months ago. My family is all gone. I don't have anyone left."

Henri responded with complete sincerity, "I'm sorry to hear about your mother. I know she meant a lot to you. But I want you to know that I've considered you to be my brother for some time now."

Theo seemed touched, his eyes uncharacteristically tearing as he said, "I think a lot of you, too. I never had a brother before. I kind of like the idea."

Henri smiled as he said, "We've had each other's backs for quite a while now. I trust you completely…and for a while there, I didn't trust anyone or anything."

"Yeah, we do work together well. Although, I think it's time we found a new line of work. Warring doesn't have much of a future to it."

"Honestly, I could use your help. God knows there's plenty to do here if you're up to the task."

"I don't know anything about farming, but I can learn. If you're willing to take me on, I'll prove myself."

Henri responded, "I'm not worried one bit about you. In my mind, you've already proven yourself."

Theo seemed to soak up the acceptance and vote of confidence as he said, "I'm not that fond of cows, but I suppose I'll learn."

Henri chuckled. "Well, the cows were all stolen."

Theo looked puzzled as he said, "Stolen?"

"Yeah, thieving neighbor helped himself to all the livestock, and anything else of value that he could haul off."

Theo shook his head in disbelief. "Doesn't seem wise…messing with the likes of you."

"No. It was not wise."

"Seems like I may have arrived at just the right time, although I do believe that you and I need to move toward a more peaceful existence."

"We have not known much peace, have we?"

"That's true, but the war's over, so I think we've got a pretty good chance of finding some peace, as long as we have a mind to put our warring ways behind us."

Henri had always marveled at Theo's folksy wisdom, so rare in someone his age, and he found himself listening, absorbing his words. "I'm perfectly willing to put my warring ways behind me, once I get my family's livestock and belongings back where they belong."

"I can help you with that…brother."

Henri was obviously pleased, as he responded, "I guess we're meant to be brothers of a sort. Although, I have to say that you're not much to look at."

Theo smirked as he said, "How do you know? You have never seen me cleaned up."

Henri chuckled as he said, "Come on in the house and meet my aunt. She'll make sure that you get cleaned up. I guarantee it. You'll be lucky to have any hide left when she's done with you."

Theo looked uncomfortable as he followed Henri into the ancient stone farmhouse. Initially, Marguerite was startled by the unexpected appearance of one of Henri's war buddies, another young man, clutching a rifle. But she quickly came to understand that the two young men had a very close bond, and she sensed that their sniper rifles had been the link that securely carried them through the war. Their weapons, along with the connection between them, had provided what little security and comfort they could find in the trenches of northern France.

Marguerite instinctively knew that this scrawny, mild-mannered young fellow, needed a good meal and the companionship of friends. She welcomed Theo warmly, like a mother caring for a returning son. Marguerite handed out plates with thick slices of ham and cheese, and delicious buttered bread. Huddled around the warmth of the stove, the two young men ate ravenously.

As the evening wore on and the trio became more comfortable with one another, Marguerite did indeed insist that Theo bathe and change his clothing. Henri was silently amused as he helped haul hot water to the bathing tub. Theo's objections were futile in the face of Marguerite's determination. In the end, Theo emerged clean. Marguerite completed the transformation by insisting that she cut his hair. His thin, lackluster brown hair was a stark contrast to Henri's thick, wavy locks. Slightly built, but wiry, Theo looked unimpressive, but strangely sturdy. The smallness of his physical frame was even more pronounced as he donned Gabriel's old work clothes, which were several sizes too large. Marguerite summarily, almost ritually, burned Theo's lice-infested uniform, and the transition to farm life began.

CHAPTER 8

The Confrontation

1918
The Dubois Farm in Normandy, France

Marguerite was up before dawn, praying quietly as she stoked the wood-burning stove. She was tense, thinking about the dangerous task ahead. It was a comfort to know that Henri would have help in retrieving the family's farm animals and equipment, but still she worried. Theo was an interesting character from Henri's war experience, but in her mind, he was an unknown, and this was unsettling. Although he was younger than Henri, he seemed like an old soul. Quietly reassured, Theo had a way of taking in his surroundings, and there seemed to be an odd aura of wisdom about him for someone so young. He obviously had a strong bond with Henri, and there appeared to be a mutual trust and respect between the two young men. Marguerite tried to calm her worried mind, but she was unnerved by Theo's unwillingness to be far from his sniper rifle. Frankly, Marguerite was worried whether these two young men could handle the predictably volatile confrontation with Vincent Dubois.

Henri and Theo came down the stairs into the kitchen just as Marguerite was pouring her first cup of coffee. The aroma was heavenly.

Henri playfully slapped Theo on the shoulder and remarked, "This is not the same coffee they served us in the trenches. For one thing, it's hot."

Theo grinned and gratefully accepted the steaming cup of wonderfully aromatic coffee. Marguerite was comforted to witness the almost brother-like bond between the two young men. Both had come into the kitchen carrying their sniper rifles, which they carefully leaned against the coat rack near the door. The commonality between the two war comrades was quite remarkable. War had driven them together, and their survival through the terrible ordeal had crafted a bond that was deep and visceral.

Leo predictably arrived shortly after dawn. He had a paternalistic air about him as he sat at the kitchen table and drank coffee with Henri, Theo, and Marguerite. Leo was surprised to meet Henri's wartime comrade but was reassured by the young man's calm and matter-of-fact demeanor. The older man sensed that the two war comrades were indeed close friends, and he was glad that Henri had such a relationship in his life. Leo had leaned heavily on Gabriel when his son died in the war, and he knew the value of such a bond.

Leo sighed, and emphatically stated, "Well, boys, you need to keep in mind that Vincent Dubois is a dangerous drunk. He's quite capable of causing you harm. So, you'll need to keep your wits about you, and let me do the talking. The goal is to retrieve the farm animals and anything else he stole, without anyone getting hurt."

Henri listened respectfully and nodded his head as he said, "I'm not looking to start a fight. I just want my family's animals and possessions back where they belong."

Leo was reassured by Henri's approach and said, "That's exactly how you need to think about this mission. Vincent Dubois is not worth your hatred. Don't waste your energy on that drunken fool."

Theo had been taking it all in as he asked, "Is this fellow likely to have a gun?"

Leo responded, "Oh yes, he'll come out of that ramshackle house of his ready to do battle. He's foul-mouthed, and he'll be hung over. He holds a big grudge against the LeBlanc family, so don't be surprised if he immediately tries to drive us off his property at gunpoint."

Theo smirked as he responded, "He sounds delightful. It's been a whole month since I've been shot at, but I haven't forgotten the experience."

Leo went on to further instruct the two young men, "Keep your rifles inconspicuous, if possible. We don't need to immediately confront him with guns drawn."

Henri turned to Theo and said, "Probably best if you hang back and do over-watch."

Theo nodded. "Yes, I'll find a nice perch to keep an eye on the situation."

Leo was impressed that the two young men seemed to communicate through minimal words. They obviously had instinctively worked together during the war, and this was reassuring.

Leo looked at both men sternly, as he reiterated, "Being hotheaded will only make the situation worse and probably get someone killed."

Henri and Theo both nodded that they understood. They would follow Leo's lead in dealing with Vincent.

Together, the somber group walked out to Leo's farm wagon. The veteran farmer had thought to bring several wire cages for transporting any stolen chickens that they found. Marguerite followed them. All three men were surprised and puzzled as they looked at her settling into the back of the wagon.

Henri immediately spoke up, "Aunt Marguerite, you should stay here. It won't be safe for you at the Dubois farm."

Marguerite squared her shoulders, and said with a certain determination in her voice, "I'm going. It's not safe for any of you at the Dubois farm, and I might be able to help. Lois Dubois and I are friends. It might help with the situation."

The three men gave each other a questioning look, and finally Leo took the lead by saying, "Okay, but you are to stay with the wagon."

There was quiet heaviness in the air, as the four began the short journey to the Dubois farm. As the horse-drawn wagon pulled up to the dilapidated farm, a ferocious, mangy looking dog emerged from the bushes. Barking loudly, then snarling and growling, the animal slowly edged toward the wagon. The commotion awoke the occupants of the farmhouse, and within seconds, a red-eyed, disheveled looking man emerged from the house carrying a gun. He immediately recognized the intruders and knew their intent.

Raising his gun menacingly, Vincent shouted, "Get off my property!" Unnoticed in the excitement, Theo had slipped off the back of the wagon and stood at a distance, observing the situation. His gun was raised as he took in the escalating confrontation.

Leo stood steadily in the wagon as he announced, "Put your gun down, Vincent. We're not here to start trouble. Henri's back from the war and we're here to retrieve his family's livestock and belongings."

Vincent cagily edged toward the wagon. His rifle was aimed directly at Leo. The deranged man screamed, "Get the hell off my property, or I'll shoot you!"

Henri's anger was rapidly escalating, and he jumped down from the wagon. Just as he landed on the ground, the rabid looking dog lunged at his thigh. The crack of a rifle shot pierced the air, and the dog fell at Henri's feet. Stunned, Vincent looked over to the side yard to see Theo standing tall, steadfastly aiming his rifle directly at Vincent.

Theo calmly but loudly said, "Put the gun down, or the next shot goes right between your eyes."

Vincent instinctively knew that this young rifleman meant business. Fumbling with anger and the effects of a night of drinking, he laid his rifle down. The hatred in his eyes was piercing as he looked at the unexpected intruder holding him at gunpoint.

Henri proclaimed, "We're going to be gathering up all the animals and equipment that you stole from my family's farm. I'm not big on forgiveness, so don't test me."

Vincent profanely exclaimed, "You son of a bitch!"

A shot rang out as the bullet whistled past his head. Vincent stiffened, his eyes wide with disbelief, clearly terrified by the very real threat before him.

There was no more resistance as Theo announced, "That was a warning, and a gift. I don't have any more charity for you today, so if you're a smart man, you won't give these folks any more trouble."

Vincent seethed with rage but stood quietly as Leo and Henri went into the barn and began loading the stolen farm tools onto the wagon. Next, they loaded most of the chickens into the wire cages. Then they harnessed the two remaining LeBlanc horses to the stolen farm wagon. The prized Normandy cows were next. The once impressive animals were hardly recognizable. The original LeBlanc herd of thirty cattle had dwindled down to a mere twelve cows, and the remaining cows looked to be starving, their ribs clearly protruding, their hides dull and encrusted with manure. The cattle stood among heaps of rotting manure in the decrepit barn. Henri and Leo gave each other a knowing look as they visibly gasped, appalled at the condition of the animals. Vincent had sold most of the herd to starving families in the area during the last year of the war, and these few animals were all that remained of the previously prized LeBlanc cattle. Disgusted, their anger rising, Henri and Leo began herding the remaining cattle out of the barn and down the lane.

As they were leaving, Lois emerged from the old farmhouse. She had several dishes piled in her arms. With much embarrassment, she quietly loaded them in the wagon. Marguerite attempted to talk with her, but Lois tearfully waved her off, before going back into the house and returning with several pots and pans, silently placing them in the wagon. Marguerite whispered so that Vincent would not hear, "Thank you."

Lois whispered back, "I'm so ashamed." Then she walked back into the house without looking back.

As the odd assemblage of people, animals, and farm wagons started down the lane to the road, Henri turned and pointed menacingly at Vincent.

With his anger barely under control, he shouted, "I do not ever want to see you on my property again! If I do, I will kill you. And furthermore, if I hear that you have mistreated or beaten your wife, I will come after you. If you cause harm to Leo or his farm, there will be serious consequences."

Theo continued to aim his rifle squarely at Vincent's head until the wagons and cattle were out of sight. Then he quietly slipped away, rejoining the group as they began the trek back to the LeBlanc farm. As Theo caught up with the little caravan, he gave a nod of acknowledgment to Henri, a silent communication of a job well done. With deep and heartfelt gratitude, Henri proclaimed, "Nice over-watch, Theo."

The young, slightly built man smiled and said, "I was taught by the best."

Leo was a little unnerved by the nonappearance of the youngest Dubois son during the altercation. He had a feeling of dread that the Dubois version of retribution was coming.

Cautiously he warned, "We had best be on the lookout for Vincent's youngest boy. He's rumored to be hiding at the family farm, and he's every bit as despicable as his old man."

Theo seemed to understand the threat. Quietly, he disappeared into the brush to watch over and protect the caravan. Leo was visibly relieved as the stolen animals and equipment finally made it safely back to his best friend's farm. It was a healing moment, a debt paid to his long-time neighbor and friend. As he said goodbye and shook hands with Henri and Theo, he was proud and appreciative of their strength, and he totally embraced the moment. Leo could not look at these two young men without feeling immense pride in their character, and a steadfast hope for the future.

CHAPTER 9

Settling into Farm Life

1919
LeBlanc Farm in Normandy, France

There was a flurry of activity on the farm over the next few months. Marguerite was an industrious woman, and she thoroughly scrubbed the old farmhouse from top to bottom. She found it healing. Everywhere, there was evidence of her sister. The sturdy furniture, the linens, and even the dishes and cooking pots all reminded her of Adele, and her sister's love of the farm. Marguerite missed her sister terribly. Their relationship had been one of honesty, and sometimes that had been painful. Yet, despite their differences, Marguerite always knew they had an unbreakable bond.

Adele had enjoyed a strong and loving marriage. She just seemed to fit so easily into her life as a mother, and her role as the wife of a farmer. Marguerite marveled at how differently their lives had played out. At times, she had resented Adele for raising her son. But in her most honest moments, she recognized the painful truth. Henri had experienced a very loving, secure childhood, one that she likely would not have been able to provide. It hurt.

Although Henri was not Gabriel's biological son, he was his son, in every way that mattered. He was a farmer at heart. At an early age, Gabriel had insisted that his two boys work hard, and learn the craft of farming. Louis had protested, but Henri eagerly absorbed the lessons. He had loved working the land and managing livestock beside his father and brother. Henri proudly drew his identity from his family, and from their farming legacy.

The first few weeks back on the farm, Henri felt overwhelmed by all the work that needed to be done. Theo was more than willing to help, but he knew nothing about farming. Patiently, very much like his father, Henri began sharing his knowledge with his former war comrade, as they made steady progress toward the repair of the farm operation. It was a long slog, the days filled with hard work, and the results were barely visible in the first weeks, which left Henri dispirited.

There were several pressing needs that worried Henri and kept him awake at night. The cattle were in terrible condition. They had arrived back from the Dubois farm emaciated, encrusted in dried manure, and they had scattered open sores on their hides, along with the fact that they were producing almost no milk. Henri worked diligently with Theo to clean the animals and try and heal their wounds. With no extra grain, and just an abundance of dried pasture grasses, food for the livestock was limited. Henri was worried that the cattle might not survive.

Leo stopped by a few days after the cows were returned and stated how he shared Henri's concern. He offered, "These cattle are in sorry shape. I'll bring some of my extra hay over in the morning."

Henri proudly shook his head as he said, "I can't be accepting charity."

"Your father and I helped each other all the time. I was kind of hoping that we would have a similar relationship. Besides, I'm going to need some apples in the fall. My wife loves to make apple pies, and I like to mix up a few batches of Calvados. Maybe we could do a little bartering?"

Henri smiled and he responded, "I think we can come to some sort of an agreement. You might have to throw in a bottle of your famous apple liquor."

"I'll throw in two bottles of apple liquor. I'm going to need quite a few apples."

Henri looked serious as he said, "Leo, this works both ways. Don't hesitate to ask if you need help with something."

"Oh, I will. I'm farming all by myself now, so I'll need help from time to time."

Henri looked relieved as he said, "I appreciate your help more than you know. It's overwhelming to get this farm up and running again."

Leo reassured him, "Your father always said you were a natural farmer. He wasn't so sure about Louis."

"Yeah, Louis didn't particularly like farming."

Leo nodded, "That's what your father used to say. It didn't make him love Louis any less, though."

"Yes, he was a pretty amazing father."

"Yeah, I have a lot of fond memories of him," Leo sighed. "Well…I better get going. I'll bring that load of hay over tomorrow morning. Take care, boys."

Theo and Henri waved as the old farmer urged his horse-drawn wagon toward the road.

After dinner, Henri, Theo, and Marguerite sat around the wood stove and talked. As they had become increasing more comfortable with one another, they all looked forward to these evening chats. It was an opportunity to reconnect and discuss all the issues they were facing. Marguerite was both entertained and reassured by the easy humor between Henri and Theo, which had the effect of making their worries seem much more manageable.

This didn't keep Henri from becoming serious at times. One evening he proclaimed, "We've got a money problem and a food problem. Until this farm can produce milk and sufficient eggs, we have no income. It's going to be six months before we have any crops to sell."

Theo chuckled, "I'm just saying, I've never eaten so well. You farmers always think you're on the verge of starving."

Henri smiled at his friend as he said, "Well, I think we just might need to cut your rations."

Marguerite chimed in, "You're right. We are running out of supplies. I have a little money to help, but not enough to get us through the next couple months until the garden is producing. We need to let these chickens sit on some eggs, so we can expand the flock."

Theo commented, "I don't have any money, but I've been known to be a pretty good hunter. I noticed that there are a fair number of deer that like to graze in your orchard."

Henri brightened as he said, "That would help a lot. Maybe we could even barter some venison for supplies."

Marguerite agreed, "I can ask around when I go to town. Food has been scarce for over a year. I would not be surprised if we can barter for some of the things we need."

The frenetic work effort to rebuild the farm operation seemed to completely occupy Henri's mind. He did not talk about the loss of his family, or Sophie, or the fact that he had a child. Sequestered on the farm, he consciously avoided contact with the outside world. The isolation and relentless physical work seemed to be therapeutic, allowing him the freedom to readjust to life outside of the military. There were glimmers emerging of the old Henri, less angry, easygoing, smiling, but intensely focused on the farm. Life was hard, but simple. The demons were still there, but they were buried in work.

After the trio had been working on the farm for three weeks, there came an unexpected knock on the door. Alone in the kitchen, Marguerite was suddenly overcome by an uneasy feeling. She opened the door to discover Father Bernard. There was an awkward silence for a moment, and then they both smiled. Marguerite motioned him into the kitchen.

Father Bernard asked, "Well, how are you, Marguerite?"

She responded with complete sincerity, "I am well, really well."

"No regrets?"

Marguerite chuckled as she said, "Oh, I have lots of regrets, just not about my decision to help Henri."

Father Bernard looked at her quizzically as he said, "So, Henri is doing well? He looked pretty unsettled the last time I saw him."

She seemed eager to reveal his progress as she explained, "He's doing remarkably well, working incredibly hard putting this old farm back together. I'm so proud of him."

"And how are you and Henri getting along?"

Marguerite looked genuinely happy as she said, "Honestly, it's been wonderful. I finally feel like a parent."

The priest gingerly asked, "So you told him?"

"No, not yet. It isn't the right time. We're just getting to know each other, really."

Father Bernard nodded as he said, "Does he talk about the death of his family?"

"No, he's been completely occupied with getting this farm up and running."

Father Bernard wisely commented, "He's been through a lot. Probably best to take it one step at a time. The healing will come."

Marguerite was relieved as she said, "I feel that way, too. He's stronger than I ever realized. Obviously, he has a lot to work through, but I have a good feeling that he's on his way."

The priest was pleasantly surprised, and commented, "I'm glad that things are working out for you and Henri. Good news is always welcome. The parish ministry seems empty without you, but I'm glad you're happy."

Marguerite went on to say, "I do miss you and Louise. And I miss working with the children's choir...but I know that I need to be here with Henri."

"You need to follow your heart. I will say, though, that Sister Louise is having quite a struggle with the children's choir." Father Bernard chuckled and added, "She thinks God is testing her patience."

"Yes, she would be the first one to admit that she has no patience for rambunctious children. Please give her my love. She's been such a dear friend to me."

The priest nodded and remarked, "She would love to see you. Stop by when you come to town on market day."

Marguerite felt a little embarrassed as she responded, "Well, I haven't been coming to town on market day. To tell the truth, we don't have anything to sell, and we're short on money. The cows are in rough shape and aren't producing much milk. Henri is trying to nurse them back to health, but he's not sure they're going to survive."

Father Bernard solemnly responded, "That sounds serious."

"It is very serious. It's probably going to be a couple of months before we have farm produce to bring to market. To be honest, we've been living on wild venison and rabbits that the boys have hunted. I was wondering if we might be able to barter in Bayeux for supplies, with some of our wild game?"

"Meat has been in short supply for quite a while now. I have no doubt that you can barter your wild game for supplies. I'll spread the word for you. I do hope you'll stop in to visit. At some point, Henri is going to need to venture out into Bayeux, too."

After a thoughtful pause, Marguerite said, "Henri is not ready for the outside world, yet."

Father Bernard studied Marguerite and then he responded, "Both of you will need to confront the past. You'll know when you're ready. But, until then, I'm going to send some food your way. My parishioners are constantly sharing their food with me. It's one of the benefits of being a priest."

Marguerite looked relieved as she said, "Thank you. Before you go, you must meet Henri's friend from the war. Theo has been such a help." Father Bernard was curious as he followed Marguerite out to the barn.

CHAPTER 10

The Past Returns

1919
LeBlanc Farm in Normandy, France

As signs of spring were emerging over the Normandy landscape, the already busy pace of farm life picked up even more. There was much to be done as Henri and Theo prepared to plant crops. Henri had spent the dark winter evenings painstakingly planning the crops that he would need to sustain the farm for the next year. With literally no money, he had to rely on Leo to buy and share seeds for the extensive planting. Once again, his father's trusted friend had stepped in to make sure that Henri had what he needed to survive. Leo saw this young man as more than just his best friend's son. Without even fully recognizing it, the old friend saw Henri as much needed hope for the future, during a time when France was emerging from the darkness of war.

Most of the cows had survived the winter. Only two had died due to the neglect inflicted on them at the Dubois farm. The remaining ten cows were slowly recovering from their ordeal, and their milk production was steadily improving. Henri was relieved and excited beyond words when a healthy calf was born in mid-April. He stood in quiet appreciation of all the progress that was so visible over the previous months. Their hard work was beginning to pay off, and Henri finally had the sense that the LeBlanc farm was going to make it.

Theo had made good on his word to provide an abundance of wild game. He was regularly making the trip to Bayeux to sell venison and rabbits to one of the local restaurants. Marguerite had secretly winced when she learned that Theo had agreed to supply the Laurent restaurant with wild game. The connection of this family to her past made her shudder with uneasiness. But she could not reveal her misgivings about the arrangement, not without disclosing a deep secret.

As spring continued to unfold, Marguerite felt the need to venture out from the farm. Initially, the seclusion was a welcome relief, as it allowed her to focus her attention on Henri, away from the prying eyes of curious parishioners. But Marguerite was growing restless, and she missed Father Bernard and Sister Louise. She missed their frank talks and candid advice over coffee. The unique relationship among the three, their complete acceptance and steadfast support of one another, had been such a stabilizing force in her life.

Marguerite pulled open the heavy door just as Louise was coming out of the church. The surprised nun squealed with delight, and spontaneously hugged Marguerite.

Sister Louise exclaimed, "I'm so glad to see you. I've been worried about you. So, you must tell me everything."

Marguerite happily returned the hug and said, "I've missed you so much, and I've missed our talks."

Sister Louise looked mischievous as she responded, "Yes, we certainly have been known to talk about everything. I need to hear everything about you and Henri."

The two women quickly walked back to Father Bernard's office. He had heard the excitement and was eagerly waiting as the two women confidently strode into his office.

The priest stood and welcomed Marguerite with a hug. He warmly expressed, "The prodigal daughter has returned. It's good to see you."

Huddled around the priest's cluttered desk, the trio easily settled into talk over coffee. The intimate gathering felt natural, and they immediately spoke in the manner of old friends.

Louise looked at Marguerite as she spontaneously asked, "Are you as well as you look?"

Marguerite chuckled as she answered, "You always did have a way of getting right to the point. I feel that I made the right decision. To tell the truth, I've never been happier."

Louise looked relieved as she asked, "So, Henri is doing well?"

"Yes, he's been incredibly busy with the farm, and I think the work is healing him. He seems more settled, more like his old self."

Father Bernard shook his head as he thoughtfully interjected, "So many of the soldiers who have returned from the war are struggling."

Marguerite acknowledged, "Yes, I have to say that at first, I was worried. He was so angry when he first got back from the war. But, as the months have gone by, I feel that he is finding himself again. It's been good for me, too."

Louise impatiently asked, "Have you told him?"

Suddenly somber, Marguerite shook her head and said, "No. I have been waiting for the right time. To be honest, I'm afraid. For the first time, I feel like we truly have a connection that isn't overshadowed by my sister or her family. I know that sounds selfish."

Louise communicated complete acceptance as she reassured Marguerite, "You are entitled to your feelings. It's good to be honest with yourself."

"Well, I obviously haven't been honest with Henri, and I do intend to tell him. But he's not ready to hear what I have to say. He's getting to seem more like his old self, but he is different. He's more serious, and he angers more easily, although that part is getting much better. I'm not going to lie, I miss that carefree, happy boy who went off to war."

Father Bernard was insightful as he quietly said, "He's not a boy anymore. Henri is a young man who has seen and experienced the horrors of war. Going through something like that, it changes a man."

"I can see that so plainly, but it scares me. I just want Henri to be happy again, and I think he wants it, too. I see it in his hard work, like he's trying to fix everything, and heal himself in the process. Honestly,

I think the endless work on the farm has been necessary for him. It has allowed him to block out the world, especially the pieces that he just can't deal with yet."

Louise probed, "Does he talk about Sophie?"

"No, but he does talk about wanting to meet his child."

Father Bernard suddenly looked alarmed as he said, "What does he know about this child? Who told him?"

"Louis told him as he was dying. Henri knows that he has a little girl somewhere in a convent orphanage. I think he wants to do more than just meet her."

The priest seemed uncomfortable as he said, "I have no doubt that Mr. Bissett will do everything in his power to keep Henri away from this child. He has gone to great lengths to hide the fact that his Sophie, had an illegitimate child with a young man, that he sees as below his daughters' station in life."

Marguerite stated, "I don't think it would be overstating it to say that Henri hates Mr. Bissett. He hates that this man stepped between him and Sophie, and that he decided the fate of their child. To be quite honest, I'm afraid of where this is leading."

Father Bernard's concern was evident in the sudden seriousness of his voice, a warning to Marguerite. "Henri is going to need level-headed support to navigate these troubled waters. You need to start by telling him the truth. He needs to know that you are his mother, and that you will support him if he decides to include this child in his life. This is not going to be easy. He's going to have a lot of hard questions for you. Questions that you need to be prepared to honestly answer."

Marguerite had tears in her eyes as she said, "I know. I know that I need to tell him the whole truth. It's been such a wonderful couple of months, helping my son and getting to know him. I'm afraid that this revelation will destroy our relationship forever."

Louise wisely interjected, "He knows you love him, and that you have always had his best interests in mind. Giving him up to your sister was incredibly hard on you. He may find it shocking initially, but as it sinks in, I think he'll understand."

Father Bernard nodded as he said, "I agree. He's been through a lot with the war, and that has a way of clarifying life's priorities. I believe he will come to appreciate your honesty. And there is no one better qualified to support him as he tries to establish a relationship with his child. You know that I am always here if you need to talk."

"I appreciate that your door is always open. I think he's going to ask you for help finding his child."

The priest was unflappable as he responded, "I will be glad to help Henri in any way that I can. I have absolutely no allegiance to Mr. Bissett, and you can tell him that for me."

Marguerite suddenly brightened as she said, "I will tell him."

It was late afternoon when Marguerite finally left for the farm. She felt loved by these friends who knew her completely. It was acceptance in its purest form. The thought of telling Henri the truth somehow seemed more manageable, and she felt a sudden surge of confidence as she said good-bye to her friends.

The next day Marguerite felt edgy and nervous as she prepared breakfast for Henri and Theo. Deep in thought, she was determined, to make it the day that she revealed the truth to Henri. Marguerite had been waiting for a lull in the farm work, so that he might have more time, and more energy, to absorb the revelation. The two young men had just finished the arduous task of plowing and planting the crops. It was a monumental milestone, and Henri and Theo appeared visibly relieved by their progress. There was still pruning to be done in the apple orchard, but the pace of work had lessened.

After breakfast, Marguerite decided to walk out to the orchard, in hopes of finding Henri alone. Theo was still finishing the milking in the barn as she walked across the rolling pastures toward the orchard. Henri saw her coming and he had the odd sensation that something was amiss. Her gait was somehow hesitant, and she appeared deep in thought. He jumped down from the tree he was pruning as she drew near.

Henri looked worried as he asked, "Are you alright, Aunt Marguerite?"

Marguerite nodded awkwardly as she answered, "Yes, I'm fine. I just wanted to talk with you alone."

Puzzled, Henri said, "It sounds serious."

Marguerite's voice started to quiver with emotion as she went on to say, "I don't hardly know where to begin."

Henri reached over to put his arm around Marguerite. Reassuringly, he said, "We've been through quite a bit together, so I doubt there's much you could say that would shock me."

"Well, this will certainly be the test of that. But before I tell you what I have to say, please know that I did this because I love you. I wanted you to have what I couldn't provide for you."

Henri looked stricken, and the color suddenly drained from his face. He mumbled, "Louis said something very similar before he died. Go on."

Marguerite took a deep breath and looked Henri directly in the eyes as she quietly said, "I am your biological mother."

Henri appeared to not be breathing as he studied Marguerite's face. Finally, he said, "I don't understand."

"I was pregnant with you when I was sixteen years old. My boyfriend did not want anything to do with me once he found out I was pregnant."

Henri seemed to be trying to comprehend what he was hearing. Quietly he commented, his voice puzzled and barely audible, "So, you gave me to your sister to raise?"

Marguerite looked distressed as she responded, "It's more complicated than that. I wanted to keep you and raise you as my own. Honestly, I did."

Gulping for air, his eyes searching, trying to find meaning in her words, Henri struggled to steady the tone of his voice. "Did Louis know that I was not his real brother?"

Marguerite quickly said, "You were his real brother."

Henri responded angrily, his voice suddenly loud, "Did Louis know that I was not his brother?"

"No."

His anger mounting, Henri exclaimed, "I don't believe you. How could you hide your pregnancy and then just have me magically appear in your sister's family?"

Marguerite's voice started to break with emotion as she recounted, "My parents were mortified when they learned I was pregnant. They wanted me to go away to a convent to secretly have you, and then return to Bayeux like nothing had happened. I couldn't leave you in an orphanage. I couldn't. So, Adele and I came up with a plan. I pretended to leave for the convent to become a nun, but I was hiding out at the farm. Shortly after I delivered you, I left for the convent to become a nun."

"So many family secrets. It doesn't seem real."

Marguerite assured him, "It's true. Adele faked her pregnancy, so people in the community were not surprised by your arrival. My sister and her husband welcomed you into their family with open arms. They loved you from the first moment, just as I did."

"I was always so proud of my family. It's hard to believe that I was not one of them."

Marguerite nodded and said, "As difficult as it is to say, you were, without a doubt, the beloved son of Adele and Gabriel. They loved you completely. Gabriel defiantly protected your identity as his son. There's no doubt that Louis had a true brother in you. But I gave up too much...too much. It was hard to watch you grow up so close, but so far away. I desperately wanted to be more than just a doting aunt."

Facing Marguerite with a sense of defiance, he blurted out, "I must know. Who is my real father?"

Marguerite appeared disturbed by the question, as she slowly answered, "Jacob Laurent."

Henri visibly gasped as he responded, "Unbelievable. We've lived so close all these years. How could he not know that I am his son?"

"Honestly, he doesn't know."

Angrily, Henri spouted, "That's what you want to believe! My whole existence in this family has been a hoax."

Marguerite tried to steady herself. With determination, she went on to calmly explain, "Jacob wanted me to secretly have you in a convent, and then give you up to the orphanage. I let him believe that is what happened. Trust me, he was quite disturbed to see me return to Bayeux four years later. But I convinced him that I had left you in an orphanage, and that the secret was safe. I'm sorry to have to tell you all this, but you need to understand something. Giving you up to my sister was the hardest thing I have ever done. I loved you from the moment I could feel you inside of me. I wanted so much more for you than I could give you."

Henri seemed to have reached his saturation point, as he stormily turned away from his mother. "I can't hear another word!"

Suddenly, he turned and stomped toward the barn. If he had looked back, Henri would have seen Marguerite collapsed on the ground, quietly sobbing.

Theo was startled, and puzzled, as Henri entered the barn, obviously upset. He turned to Henri and asked, "What's happened?"

Henri quickly tried to hide his tears as he angrily answered, "Ahh…my beloved aunt has finally decided to reveal a family secret. Apparently, she feels that now is the time."

Theo could easily see the hurt on Henri's face. He gently said, "Family secrets can be pretty damning."

"Yes, and this one calls into question my very identity. It appears I am not who I thought I was."

Theo asked, "So what did you learn from your aunt that has you so upset?"

Henri blurted out angrily, "I am her son!"

Theo looked puzzled, and a little amused, as he said in his folksy way, "I could certainly think of a worse family secret. I'd be proud to have her as my mother."

"I'm her bastard child!"

Theo chuckled as he said, "Welcome to the club. I'm a bastard too."

Henri seemed taken aback by Theo's candor. He said, "You never told me that."

Theo shrugged and said, "It was not something I was particularly proud of."

"Sorry, I didn't know. It must have been a hard childhood."

Theo suddenly seemed sad, as he recounted his youth. He quietly said, "The man that I believe was my father, he drifted in and out of our lives for years. My mother cleaned house for some rich folks. She raised me by herself. It was a rough life."

Henri said, "I suppose I shouldn't complain too much, at least not to you."

Theo smiled at his friend and said, "No, I think you were lucky. You've had a nice life here. I never met the folks that raised you, but I'd say they obviously cared about you. Not everyone finds that in this life. I suspect that Marguerite did what she thought was best for you. I wouldn't judge her too harshly."

Henri shook his head in amazement. Theo never ceased to amaze him. He was clearly an old soul, in a young body. It was this quality that had drawn Henri to the young man.

Henri decided to reveal one more aspect of the story. He blurted out, "Jacob Laurent is my biological father."

Theo was obviously shocked by this revelation. Over the last few months, he had been selling venison to Jacob for his restaurant. He thought for a moment before he mischievously said, "Well, that explains your good looks."

Henri shook his head at his friend and said, "I've gone to the same church with this man for years."

"Well, everybody goes to the same church here."

Henri chuckled, "That's true. We're all good Catholics."

"Jacob doesn't act like he knows your family all that well."

"Marguerite, my mother, swears he does not know that I am his son. I do know that my father did not like doing business with him. Now, it all kind of makes sense."

Theo reassured him, "You had a real father, and it sounds like he was a special man. Honestly, I think you've been fortunate. There's probably nothing to be gained by confronting Jacob. He's never been a part of your life."

"Yes, I think you're right. I don't feel any need to know this man. But I do feel bad for Marguerite. It had to be hard on her. She's been living in the same town with this man for years. That could not have been easy."

Theo agreed as he said, "Marguerite is an amazing woman. It is apparent to me that she would do just about anything for you. I think you owe her an apology. Don't make her suffer more than she already has."

Henri shook his head in wonderment at the slightly built, unimpressive looking young man before him. "I have to say, you're smarter and wiser than you look."

Theo smirked as he said, "Well, we both know I'm not much to look at."

Henri knew that he had to make things right with Marguerite. He turned and walked out of the barn in search of her. He found the woman, his mother, in the kitchen with her back to him. Slowly, he approached her. She could sense his presence, but she did not turn to face him.

Henri was sincere as he said, "I'm sorry. You obviously have suffered a lot. I don't hold any hard feelings against you."

Marguerite turned to face him. Her red, swollen eyes spoke of her grief. She quietly said, "Honestly, I don't think I could blame you. I've had such regret about my decision, all those years ago. I feel like I've missed so much of your life."

"I have known only love and support in this family, and I attribute that to you. I have always felt your love for me. Always."

He moved forward to embrace her. They held onto each other for the longest time. It was so much more healing than words alone. Henri finally pulled away and studied Marguerite. He saw her in a totally different light. He was proud of this woman who had sacrificed so much for him. He vowed to himself to protect his own child with the same fierce level of devotion.

CHAPTER 11

Father Bernard

1875-1897
Eastern Europe and France

Father Bernard came from an unlikely place. His Roma mother died in childbirth. The gypsy women who cared for the fated woman naturally assumed care of the orphaned boy. The child was fierce looking, with wild black hair, and teeth. They named him Danior, which meant, "born with teeth." Superstitious, the Roma women consulted their tarot cards, and were alarmed by their findings. The child was destined to be a fierce warrior, who would abandon his people. Even as an infant, the Roma could sense that he was different.

The gypsy women collectively made sure that the little boy was fed and minimally clothed, but no Roma family came forth to claim him as their own. He was a wild child, fiercely, stubbornly, surviving at the fringe of the nomadic community. Instinctively, he seemed to have a sixth sense for danger, and he trusted no one. His intuition helped him survive the very real dangers of being an unprotected orphan in a band of lawless gypsies.

At an early age, Danior became an adept pickpocket. He had mastered a very useful sleight of hand maneuver. This skill allowed him to lift valuables from unsuspecting people. On the rare occasion when he was discovered, he ran like the wind to escape. He had never been

physically caught. Some of the stolen prizes would be dutifully shared with the larger Roma community, but he always kept a portion for himself. The older, larger Roma boys would attempt to take his spoils, but he was a fierce fighter, and they eventually learned to leave him alone.

Danior's childhood was spent migrating the rivers of Europe in a Roma flotilla. The sizable group of gypsies had spent years in Eastern Europe. As the pattern of their thievery became all too familiar, the flotilla set their sights on new territory. With an air of excitement and the anticipation of pilfered riches, they made their way to Paris. Their migratory progress was followed with alarm, as the towns and cities along the rivers spread the word ahead of their arrival.

The people of Paris warily watched from the riverbanks, as the ramshackle flotilla, crowded with dirty gypsies, floated past. The citizens of Paris had a heavy feeling. Trouble was coming. Hostile looks were exchanged between the Parisians watching from the bridges and riverbanks, and the people on the rafts. At the edge of the great city, the flotilla pulled their rafts to shore and set up camp.

Danior could sense the danger, but he found the beauty and wealth of the city to be captivating. He made his first foray into Paris with a small group of Roma boys. The Parisians were beautifully clothed and wore watches and jewelry in abundance. The boys hastily set to work, to relieve them of their valuables. The thieving boys were surprised to find that the townspeople were alert to their ways, and they were quickly discovered. The local police gave chase, but they caught no one. Over the next few days, the thieving Roma were consistently identified and met with a hostile and effective police presence. The police were ready, as soon as these roving bands of thieves showed up on the streets of Paris.

Danior was the only child who managed to successfully lift a money clip from a pocket. But even he was discovered. Wildly, he ran through the streets and alleys as he attempted to escape the police. Finally, he ducked into the back doorway to the Moulin Rouge. The music and scantily dressed women totally mesmerized him. No one seemed bothered by his presence, and no one asked him to leave.

Finally, as the evening light was fading, he stealthily walked back to the Roma encampment. But as he approached the site, it was apparent that the entire Roma community had hurriedly departed. There were scattered pieces of clothing still drying on bushes, and the fires still smoldered. Hours earlier, the police had descended in mass upon the Roma encampment and had forced them to leave at gunpoint. As Danior eerily walked through the abandoned camp, he was somber, but not distraught. He was used to being alone and had no strong ties to anyone.

Hidden by the cover of night, he walked back to the Moulin Rouge, but the night crowd was different. The sounds of dancing and music were intermixed with the noise of men and women together. The obviously drunken men, who stumbled through the back halls of the Moulin Rouge, radiated true danger. Danior shrunk back as one particularly menacing beast approached him. Cornered, Danior tried to slip past him, but the man roughly grabbed him, trying to pin him against the wall. No stranger to fighting, the wild looking Roma boy struck back with lightning speed. He furiously kicked the man in the groin and bit the top of his ear clear off. The stunned drunk fell back in agony, as Danior scrambled away from him and scurried outside. He ran frantically through the dimly lit alleys until he finally slipped into a dark covered doorway, leading to a basement. Hiding in the tomb-like space, he sunk down onto the stone steps. Fitfully, he listened and tried to rest as the night dissipated, until finally, he saw the peaceful light of dawn.

The streets were nearly empty. An old priest was slowly hobbling down the cobblestone avenue with a baguette-filled basket tucked under his arm. His black robes swung with each rocking, arthritic step. He seemed self-absorbed and hardly noticed the slight nudge of his basket, as Danior lightly lifted a baguette from the basket, and raced away. When the old priest looked up, he saw the young street urchin deftly running toward a side street. The boy briefly looked back and the two caught each other's stare for a brief second. The desperation and hunger evident in the young boy's eyes made the priest shudder.

Three days later, the old priest saw the boy again. The child was maybe twelve years old, with almost black hair, olive-colored skin, and dark eyes. He was remarkably dirty and wore thin, ragged clothing. Despite his rugged, almost feral appearance, he was a beautiful boy.

Father Bernard called out to him in a non-threatening way. "Boy, you look hungry. Here, come get some bread."

Danior stopped, and hesitantly turned toward the priest. He was like a frightened animal, as he studied the old man intensely. Finally, he grabbed the loaf of bread and ran away into a nearby alley.

The following day, the old priest once again encountered the boy as he was returning from his daily trip to the bakery. This time, the priest gently extended a fresh baked pastry and a baguette. Danior warily took the food and said in barely understandable French, "Thank you." The accent was Slovakian, and the priest concluded that the child had been left behind when the Roma flotilla was driven from Paris. The child's face was swollen and bruised, and the old priest feared that he was in grave danger on the streets of Paris.

Father Bernard did not approach him, but quietly asked, "What is your name, son?"

He responded in a thick accent, "Danior."

"That's a good, strong name. Roma, right?"

The boy seemed hesitant to admit it, but he nodded and said, "Yes."

"Well, Danior, I suspect that you already know that the streets of Paris are not a safe place for a young boy. Do you have any family?"

Again, he responded in broken French, "I don't have any family."

"Well, you're going need a safe place to stay at night. I will leave the side door open to my church, the Notre Dame Cathedral. You will find a blanket and food under the last pew after dark. I promise that you will be safe there."

The boy studied the old priest intensely, and then he nodded.

True to his word, Father Bernard left a thick blanket and food under the pew as evening approached. When the old priest checked in the morning, the food was gone, and the blanket neatly folded under the pew. Father Bernard gave a sigh of relief and started off to the bakery shop. Along the way, he again encountered Danior. The boy did not walk beside him, but he did walk closer than he had previously. The priest was relieved to see that he looked more rested, and his bruises were fading.

Father Bernard said, "Good morning, Danior. I hope you slept well?"

The boy awkwardly responded in broken French, "Yes…thank you."

"Well, I'm glad to hear it. I'm on my way to the bakery, and I could certainly use some company. Shall we have a cup of coffee, and a pastry to start the day?"

The boy smiled slightly as he nodded and said, "Yes." He moved a bit closer to the old priest, and they were practically walking side by side. The young boy slowed his pace to match the old man's arthritic movements.

The old priest was true to his word. He did keep Danior safe. The relationship between the priest and the orphan boy grew, and it literally changed the trajectory of Danior's life. During their evenings together, Father Bernard taught the boy to read and write. The adolescent child was extremely bright, and he quickly mastered the French language. It pleased the old priest that the boy loved to read. Although he retained a slight Slovakian accent, Danior's language skills were those of a refined, well-educated young man.

As the old priest's health deteriorated, he worried about Danior's future. Although he didn't know exactly how old the boy was, he guessed his age as currently about fourteen years old. He was a good looking, strong young man with a quick, perceptive mind. With a sense of urgency, Father Bernard approached the boy with serious discussions about his future.

The old priest gently reminded the boy, "Danior, you know I'm not going to be on this earth much longer. My time here is almost done. My heart pains remind me of this almost daily."

The boy looked uncomfortable and sad as he said, "I will help you."

"You have made me very proud. I've never known such a capable student, and such a caring young man, but we need to discuss your future. I need to know that you will be safe when I'm gone."

Danior shook his head, indicating that he did not want to talk about such a serious subject.

The old priest was undeterred. He said, "You have a promising future ahead of you, but we must plan, so that all your potential is not lost. Have you thought about what you want to do?"

"A little. I think I want to be like you, a priest."

"Well, it's not a life that you want 'a little.' There is a fair amount of sacrifice. You would never know the joy of having a wife and children. Quite frankly, that has been the most difficult part for me. You should think about that. But, if you decide that you want to pursue the priesthood, I will help you."

"You have helped me so much. I don't know how I could ever repay you for your compassion."

The old priest smiled and patted the young man's hand. He responded, "You have given me such joy. I think it is I who should thank you. But…we have one more thing to address. You need a last name."

Danior responded quickly, "I would like my last name to be Bernard."

The old man was pleased as he said, "I would be honored. Danior Bernard…it has the sound of greatness, doesn't it?"

Over the next few months, Father Bernard put plans in place for Danior to enter the seminary. It was a sad parting, for they both knew they would not see each other again. Danior easily made the adjustment to seminary life. The quiet solitude, and endless study and prayer, were a good fit for the thoughtful young man. He had a powerful presence for such a young priest and was strangely comfortable leading a church service. It was a remarkable transformation from his humble Roma beginnings.

His first church assignment was to Bayeux, France. He immediately felt at home in the quaint little working-class village. The handsome young priest was a compelling speaker, and his sermons were practical in their direction as to how to live a religious life. The struggling parishioners were drawn to his message, and to him. Father Bernard met Marguerite shortly after his arrival in Bayeux, and it was an extraordinary first encounter. Unknown to him, Marguerite had secretly sought him out. She was desperate and needed to confess a secret that threatened to destroy her from within. The young woman was drawn to him in an almost instinctive way. He was not like any priest she had ever encountered. Father Bernard was strikingly handsome, with a chiseled face, and dark, expressive eyes. His beauty was a bit disarming in a man of the cloth, but it was his sincere interest in people that truly drew her to his confessional. She needed to confess a sin, but more than that, she needed compassion.

Newly appointed to the Bayeux Cathedral, Father Bernard was hearing confessions on a cold, dark evening. The confessional door opened with a certain hesitancy, and he heard a deep sigh before Marguerite began her confession. Father Bernard could only see her outline through the ancient wicker screen, but he could tell that she was a very young woman, stooped in obvious distress.

There was an awkward silence, and then Marguerite began. Through muffled sobs she said, "Forgive me Father, for I have sinned."

The pain in her voice immediately struck Father Bernard and he reassuringly said, "You can feel safe to tell me anything. I am not here to judge you."

Slowly, through tearful sobs, Marguerite started to unfold her sin, "I'm pregnant." She stopped and waited for his condemnation.

Father Bernard gently probed, his slight Slovakian accent strangely comforting. "I'm assuming that you're not married?"

The distressed young girl sighed, and responded, "No, I'm not married, and my boyfriend wants nothing to do with me, or the baby."

The confession was quickly becoming more of a dialogue between the young priest and the pregnant young girl. He gently asked, "Do you love this young man?"

Marguerite was blunt and her pain evident in her response. "I thought I did. But how do you love someone who is so quick to abandon you in your hour of need?"

Father Bernard was insightful in his response, "I think your question answers itself. No doubt it's painful to realize that you have given yourself to someone who does not treasure you and the baby that you carry."

She sobbed and shuddered with such emotion that the young priest regretted his blunt comment.

With a quivering voice she said, "I don't think I can live with this shame."

Father Bernard calmly reassured her, "You are hardly the first person to have a child out of wedlock. Do your parents know of this pregnancy?"

Through muffled sobs, Marguerite explained, "Yes, they are mortified with shame. They want me to go quietly away to a convent, to have this baby."

The young priest silently shook his head in disgust as he tried to sound nonjudgmental. "Do you have any other family that could support you through this pregnancy?"

Marguerite finally sounded a bit hopeful as she answered, "Yes, my older sister has offered to take me in. She totally supports me. Honestly, she's the only person who seems to truly care about me."

The young priest suddenly put a face with the saga he was hearing through the screen of the confessional. He had observed Marguerite hanging around in the back of the church for the last couple of evenings. It was as though she was trying to find the courage to enter the confessional. It all made sense now.

Father Bernard confided impulsively to Marguerite, "I care about you, too." He quickly wondered why he had shared that thought with this vulnerable young woman, and he hoped she did not think him inappropriate.

Marguerite accepted the statement and seemed reassured by it. She brightened a bit as she said, "Thank you for being here for me. I was so afraid that you might condemn me. Honestly, I don't think I can take any more rejection." Suddenly, she grew mindful that she was not having an intimate conversation with a friend, and she grew quiet.

Father Bernard proceeded with some hesitation. He gently said, "Please know that you can talk with me any time. I'm here for confessions most evenings, and as you can see, they are sparsely attended. I am comforted to know that you have the support of your sister. She is a good woman."

Marguerite suddenly sounded embarrassed as she said, "You know who I am?"

The priest answered honestly, "Yes."

Marguerite had hoped that the dark confessional, on a dark night, in a vacant church, would hide her identity. It unnerved her to know that the young priest knew who she was, and that he knew her secret. She suddenly lost her nerve and she fumbled with the confessional door, as she stepped outside the dark cubicle. Father Bernard met her. He stepped forward to put his arm around her shoulder and she accepted the embrace. It was the beginning of an oddly intimate and caring relationship. Marguerite did not know it at the time, but their friendship would guide her through many a storm over the course of her life.

Over the next few weeks, Marguerite did seek out Father Bernard during his scheduled evening confessions. The sessions were less confession-like, and more like intimate problem-solving exchanges between friends. There was no physical contact between them, but they were developing a connection. Less distraught than previously, Marguerite was clearly struggling with Jacob's rejection. Her young boyfriend had been mortified by the news of the pregnancy, and had shown no compassion for Marguerite, or the welfare of the child. Jacob's biggest concern seemed to be that his parents might learn of the pregnancy. It was a brutal realization for the vulnerable young girl. However, over the course of a couple of weeks, Marguerite slowly progressed from anger to fear, and then acceptance of her situation. Initially she hated Jacob, but she quickly realized that this was a waste of her energy. As she accepted the truth, Marguerite started to take steps to make what she hoped was the best decision for herself, and for her unborn child. Surprisingly, she already felt a bond with the child, and she was developing a protectiveness that was growing by the day. Father Bernard was silently impressed with her growing maturity and selflessness.

Marguerite's relationship with her parents was becoming increasingly more strained as the family grappled with the crisis. Angry, and critical of their daughter's lack of Christian character, they demanded that Marguerite go quietly away to a Catholic home for unwed mothers. Their sinful daughter could leave the child in an orphanage and then return to Bayeux, with her reputation, and the family's reputation, unscathed. Marguerite was appalled. The tension within the family inevitably boiled over, and one evening the wayward daughter stormed from her childhood home in a fit of anger, vowing never to return. Silently, her parents were relieved when Marguerite left to go stay with her sister. Adele and Gabriel welcomed her with open arms, offering their unwavering love and support, which was healing for her battered soul.

Father Bernard kept his promise to Marguerite. He visited her weekly on the LeBlanc farm and treated her with respect as she grappled with decisions. Marguerite was clearly tormented. Father Bernard seemed to care for the young woman in a genuine way, and this connection was vital as she confronted devastating life decisions. Marguerite desperately needed someone to believe in her, and she found this in Father Bernard.

The quietness and seclusion of the LeBlanc farm brought tranquility and much needed clarity of thought to the troubled young woman. Already in her second trimester, Marguerite was thankful for the isolation that the farm provided. It helped her to heal emotionally, and to sort through the decisions that she knew had to be made in short order. Adele and Gabriel suggested that Marguerite live with them and raise her child in their family. Initially, Marguerite gave serious consideration to the proposal, but she did not want her child to experience the rejection and condemnation that would surely follow. As the pregnancy progressed, so did her clarity of thought. Marguerite wanted her child to know love and acceptance in their family, and in their community. With a growing sense of urgency, she struggled with how to provide this for her unborn child. Marguerite desperately wanted to be a part of her child's life, but more importantly, she wanted what was best for the child.

It was out of this turmoil that Marguerite and Adele hatched a plan. It was uncharacteristically devious and deceptive, but it had the utmost interests of the unborn child in mind. The plan was complicated, and it took considerable effort to convince Gabriel that it was a realistic solution. Marguerite would announce through her parents that she had decided to join the convent to pursue religious training. Her parents would be predictably proud and spread the word throughout the Bayeux community. In addition, there would be more good news to deliver. Adele was again pregnant. The older sister would feign pregnancy initially with loose fitting clothing. As the pregnancy progressed, she would retreat to the sanctuary of rural life. Quietly hidden away at the secluded LeBlanc farm, Marguerite would deliver the baby to Adele and Gabriel's loving arms. When Marguerite had recovered from the delivery, she would indeed seek admittance to the convent. It was an incredibly tough decision, but Marguerite reluctantly came to conclusion, that this path offered the best future for her child.

Marguerite reluctantly revealed her plan to Father Bernard during one of his weekly visits to the farm. He was shocked, but he quickly came to understand the motivation. Although young, the priest had observed the judgmental cruelty of some of his pious parishioners. It was a contradiction, but a reality.

Father Bernard was concerned, however, about Marguerite's motivation for joining the convent. He quickly and angrily confronted her about her decision. He stared at her in disbelief as he emphatically stated, "You can't run away from your troubles by joining a convent."

Marguerite was defensive as she defiantly replied, "I've decided. This is what is best for my child."

"It's not what's best for you. Being a nun is a hard life. Have you even thought about what your life will be like?"

Marguerite was not prepared for the harsh rebuke. She tried to explain, "I know that I can do it."

Father Bernard stated emphatically, "The nuns will not accept someone into their religious order who is merely trying to hide from the world. It takes great courage and commitment to be a nun. They live hard lives of poverty, serving those in greatest need. You would be giving up the joy of parenthood, and you could never marry. This is not the right answer!"

Marguerite stood up to him and said, "Yes, it is the right answer. It's right for my child, and I will make it right for me."

"You're being impulsive."

Tearfully, she responded, "No, I have thought long and hard about what is best for this child. I want my baby to grow up in a loving, well-respected family. Adele and Gabriel will be amazing parents to my child, and Louis will gain a sibling. I am not being impulsive."

The young priest was distraught as he saw Marguerite's conviction to pursue the twisted plan. He threw out questions with a desperate rapidity, "How are you going to hide this from Jacob? Do you think he will be fooled? His child will be growing up in clear sight of him!"

Marguerite was calm as she answered. "Jacob will think that I left to have the child in a convent orphanage. He will conveniently believe that I, and my problem child, are gone from his life. He's a simple, selfish boy!"

"He's not that simple."

"Oh, you are wrong. He'll see it as a simple solution to an embarrassing problem." Father Bernard did not stop his attack on her plan. He pointedly asked, "Do you honestly think that you can make this kind of commitment to become a nun?"

"Do I appear to be a nonbeliever?"

"No, but this lifestyle requires much more than being a Christian believer. I fear that you will look back with great regret if you give up your child to your sister."

Marguerite tried to sound convincing as she responded, "My sister and I have talked, and she wants me to be part of this child's life. Adele and Gabriel do want to include me, as a loving aunt. It will not be the same as raising my own child, but it will be enough."

"No, I don't think it will be enough. Living as a nun, it's unlikely that you will have much opportunity to even see this child."

"Adele and Gabriel want what is best for this child, too. They will bring the child to visit me."

The priest shook his head in frustration as he said, "I don't think you are being honest with yourself."

Her voice quivering, Marguerite said, "Oh, I'm being very honest with myself. I know this is going to be painful, but it is the best decision for my child. I need you to write me a recommendation. I am going to become a nun." With a sense of hesitation and sadness, Father Bernard finally wrote a glowing recommendation for Marguerite, as she sought admittance to a convent outside of Paris. It was close enough that her family could visit from time to time. Although she would be mostly sequestered during her religious training, she would have the opportunity to have some contact with those she loved. There would clearly be significant sacrifice on the part of Marguerite, and the young priest worried whether she could emotionally survive the separation from her baby.

Unknown to Father Bernard, he would observe and participate in the dilemma surrounding these decisions for the rest of his life. Through the lens of this complicated deception, he would witness this unborn child grow through milestones, from infancy to adulthood, and go on to experience love and loss on a scale that was almost unfathomable.

CHAPTER 12

A Difficult Birth

1897
The LeBlanc Farm in Normandy, France

The cold winter air was refreshing as Marguerite walked through the barren apple orchard. Carefully stepping through the tall, dried grass, her massive pregnant belly was pendulous and felt heavy. Suddenly she gasped, as a sharp pain clenched her protuberant mid-section. She took a long, steadying breath and felt the trickle of warm liquid running down her legs. The moment was sobering, and a bit scary, as Marguerite realized that the time had come. With much deliberation, she haltingly made her way back to the farmhouse. Intermittently, she stopped and braced herself as she felt the intensity of a contraction rise like a wave.

Marguerite slowly pushed the kitchen door open, just as a contraction was starting to grip her. She grimaced and looked up to see her sister staring at her. Adele immediately knew. The older sister rushed forward, and quickly noticed the wetness on Marguerite's dress and socks. Adele could see the pain and fear on her sister's face.

With a forced calmness, Adele said, "Ahh…I think it is time."

Marguerite forced a smile and said, "It certainly feels like it's time."

"You will be fine. I will be right here with you. Let's get you out of this dress." Adele gently steered her sister toward the bedroom near the kitchen, but Marguerite shook her head.

Wincing with pain, she said, "No, I want the privacy of my own bedroom upstairs. Just in case I get a bit noisy."

Adele reassured her, "You can be as noisy as you want."

With the pains gripping and briefly paralyzing her, one after another, it was a slow, deliberate process to get Marguerite up the stairs and into her bedroom. As Adele helped Marguerite out of her wet dress, she was alarmed to see a slow, steady stream of bright red blood flowing down her leg. Marguerite's labor appeared to be starting in a manner completely different from her own experience with Louis' birth a year earlier, and it was worrisome. The older sister immediately had the sense that something was terribly wrong.

Once she had Marguerite lying uncomfortably in her bed, Adele slipped away and raced to the barn to get Gabriel. She found him stacking firewood against the wall of the barn. He looked up with concern as she frantically ran into the barn, calling his name. Gabriel could see the fear in Adele's eyes.

She made no attempt to appear calm as she cried out, "Marguerite is in labor, and something is not right! She's bleeding…a lot!"

Gabriel quickly stepped forward and embraced his agitated wife. He reassured her, "I will get Mrs. Durand. You're going to need to stay calm for Marguerite's sake. I'll be back as soon as I can." He raced to ready the horses and wagon. Gabriel's mind was clouded with worry as he hurriedly urged the horses toward the Durand farm.

Adele consciously took several deep breaths to calm her racing heart. Slowly, she centered herself, forcing herself to stay focused, to not fall apart with fear, as she reentered the house. The sounds of muffled screams assaulted her ears, as she hesitantly climbed the stairs to the bedroom.

Mrs. Durand recognized the panicked look on Gabriel's face. Although she was not medically trained, she had an almost legendary reputation for skillfully guiding laboring mothers through difficult deliveries. In her sixties, the old woman had delivered hundreds of babies over her lifetime. She was credited with saving several local women and their babies from almost certain death. Calm and pragmatic, her mere presence with a laboring mother had the effect of inspiring confidence that the situation could be handled.

Marguerite's skin was ghostly white, and her brow was speckled with beads of perspiration. Restlessly, she tossed with the almost continuous contractions. Adele tried to coach her through the jarring pains, but Marguerite seemed barely conscious as she continued to lose blood. Terrified, Adele anxiously awaited the arrival of Mrs. Durand.

Finally, Gabriel burst into the room, followed by the older woman. Mrs. Durand quickly assessed the situation. Throwing off her lumpy, practical coat, she rolled up her sleeves, and then pulled back the blankets covering Marguerite. The small lake of bright red blood confirmed her suspicions. Deftly running her hands over Marguerite's convulsing, pregnant abdomen, she tried to ascertain the intrauterine position of the infant.

Calmly, but with an air of authority, the old woman said, "Marguerite, I need you to listen to me. Can you hear me?"

Marguerite nodded weakly and focused intently on Mrs. Durand through half-opened eyes.

"I'm going to check inside of you. This is going to hurt, so I need you to take a deep breath." As the old woman expertly inserted two fingers into the birth canal to assess the degree of cervical dilation, Marguerite screamed. Ignoring the laboring woman's obvious pain, she focused on her internal examination. Thankfully, the cervix was almost completely dilated, but she felt a tiny foot. Quickly assessing the gravity of the situation, she announced with calm determination, "Marguerite, I am going to manually dilate your cervix so that we can get this baby out. On the count of three, I need you to take a deep breath. One, two, three…"

Marguerite took a deep breath and then screamed in agony as the old woman stretched the cervical opening.

As the scream exhausted itself, Mrs. Durand instructed, "Now, listen to me. Look at me, Marguerite."

Spent, and barely conscious, Marguerite again opened her eyes and put her trust in the woman before her.

Mrs. Durand spoke loudly, but with confidence, "With the next contraction, I need you to push with everything in you. Everything! I will tell you when. OK, push, push…PUSH!"

Marguerite rallied her physical reserves, and she pushed mightily. As her abdomen convulsed with the muscular contraction, the old woman grabbed onto the tiny foot and gently, steadily, pulled the baby out. The little boy was blue and not moving. Mrs. Durand quickly turned the newborn face down and wiped the secretions from his nose and mouth. She smacked the tiny being on the back, and he weakly began to cry. Within seconds, the cry strengthened to a full-fledged wail. His skin color rapidly changed from a dusky blue to a ruddy pink, and he started to move his arms and legs.

Mrs. Durand gently handed the now wailing infant to a shaking Adele. Tears were streaming down her face, as she clumsily held the slippery baby. Without speaking a word, the old woman turned her full attention to Marguerite. She was relieved to see that the placenta had slipped out, but the bleeding that followed was horrendous. She expertly packed the loose sheets tightly into the blood-filled opening. Then she set about vigorously kneading the soft abdomen. As the uterus contracted in response to the kneading, the blood flow slowed. Marguerite had lost a lot of blood, but she was conscious, and she eagerly followed the wailing baby with her eyes. Weakly, she lifted her arms and Adele gently placed the baby on her chest. Tears of relief and joy were pouring down her face, as Marguerite gently, lovingly, stroked the beautiful little boy.

There was an overwhelming sense of relief in the room, but the old woman knew there was still danger. The loss of blood had left Marguerite weak and vulnerable. If the bleeding were to resume, it seemed likely that she would not survive. Carefully, Mrs. Durand began to educate Adele and Marguerite about the dangers. Both listened attentively, as they absorbed the vital instructions.

The bond between mother and child was immediately apparent, for Marguerite was totally mesmerized and in love with her baby. She named him Henri. There was no consultation with Adele and Gabriel. Her child would bear the unique identity of a name chosen specifically for him. Marguerite quietly claimed this privilege as her own.

Father Bernard was a regular visitor to the farm as Marguerite recovered. He was concerned as he witnessed the bond between the mother and child. Finally, one day when they were alone, he asked, "Marguerite, do you honestly think you can go forward with your plan to leave this child with your sister to raise?"

Marguerite was downcast, as she nodded and said, "Yes."

"I believe you are not being honest with yourself."

Suddenly, her eyes filled with tears as she said, "You're wrong. I know what I need to do for Henri. I will not have him grow up as an illegitimate child."

"You love him more than life itself. You can give him what he needs."

She shook her head sorrowfully, and responded, "I want him to grow up in a respected, loving family. My sister and brother-in-law will be amazing parents. It is what's best for Henri."

The priest was frustrated as he bluntly said, "Well, it's not what is best for you. I think you need to take some time and reconsider your decision."

"I've made up my mind."

"Henri is almost six weeks old. How long do you think you can hide out here on the farm? Admit it. You can't leave him. Be honest with yourself!"

Marguerite knew that the priest was correct. If her plan was to work, she must leave soon. Stubbornly, defiantly, she responded, "You are right. I am struggling. But I am going to leave for the convent… soon. However, I don't think I can do it by myself. Will you, please, go with me?"

"You're asking me to help you do something that I think is not right for you?"

"Please."

Father Bernard gave her an exasperated look as he stubbornly replied, "No, I will not help you abandon your child. I know what it feels like to grow up without a mother. You are not thinking clearly!"

Suddenly, Marguerite seemed to cave under the weight of his criticism, and she slumped forward, crying. She said between sobs, "Why are you questioning my decisions?"

"Frankly, I'm worried. You have stubbornly stuck to this plan to leave your child with your sister, despite the obvious reality that you love Henri, endlessly. And Marguerite...I see your anger and bitterness toward Jacob and your parents. It's not healthy to hold such resentment inside you. Have you even spoken with your parents since you left their house?"

"No. I cannot forgive them. Last week, they came to meet Adele's beautiful new baby boy. I hid upstairs and listened as they gushed on and on about how excited they were to have another grandchild. They did not even ask Adele about me. It was like I never existed. Yes, I am angry!"

Father Bernard seemed relieved that Marguerite was finally being candid. He probed, "And what about Jacob? Do you hate him, too?"

"Maybe. But honestly, I don't even miss him. At first, I was crushed by his rejection, but he's more of a disappointment than anything. I don't want him in my life, or Henri's life."

The emotional conversation had grown painfully honest as he asked, "Do you seriously believe that Henri's true identity can remain a secret as he grows up in plain sight of Jacob?"

"Yes, I do. Already, Henri has been accepted as the newest addition to Adele and Gabriel's family. No one suspects, and I know that you would never tell anyone the truth."

The priest smirked as he said, "Given my profession, I'm pretty sure that's not a compliment."

Marguerite smiled slightly in return as she said, "I know I have put you in a difficult spot. But...I do trust you."

"Well, promise me that you will think long and hard about what your life will be like without Henri. Be honest with yourself. It would be hard as an unmarried woman to raise Henri, but I would support you. Don't be hasty, think about it."

"I have thought about it every day since he was born. I'm not being impulsive. I'm trying to give him the life he deserves. I can see that Adele and Gabriel already love Henri, and Louis is excited to have a little brother. Henri will grow up as a respected, loved child, in my sister's family. He deserves a secure future, one that I cannot give him."

The priest was speechless as he absorbed Marguerite's determination. Finally, he said, "I don't agree, but I do respect your right to make your own decisions. I will contact the Mother Superior and set up an appointment for your interview. I must forewarn you. She is a strong-willed woman, and she will make her own determinations as to your suitability. I think you need to realize, she's not likely to accept someone who is merely running away from a difficult life. Being a nun is a religious calling and requires tremendous commitment and sacrifice."

Marguerite looked embarrassed, but she nodded her understanding.

Father Bernard silently grieved her decision. The truth was more complicated than he even wanted to admit. He had fallen in love with Marguerite. Although he found her frighteningly stubborn, he admired and respected her love for her child. She was a flawed, vulnerable person, but his draw to her was undeniable.

As the time drew near for Marguerite to leave for the convent, Adele and Gabriel became increasingly concerned. Marguerite was clearly struggling. Adele did everything in her power to make the last days of mother-son time meaningful. Marguerite rocked, fed, and sang to her young son without the constraints of household chores. It was her time with her son, and Marguerite did not waste it.

Father Bernard arrived on a cold day in December with a horse and cart, to begin the journey to the convent outside of Paris. There was a profound sadness that saturated the parting. Marguerite looked as though she might be physically ill, and indeed she did feel ill. She was barely able to climb up onto the seat of the wagon. Clearly distraught, she held Henri one last time from her perched seat. Marguerite was crying and kissing him, as she handed Henri to her sister. It was a supremely sad parting, of mother and child.

The long trip to the convent was heavy with silence as Father Bernard and Marguerite allowed their feelings to occupy the time and space. As they closed in on the convent gates, Father Bernard could feel the tenseness in his jaw, as he repeatedly, furtively, glanced at the young woman seated beside him. Her stoic, determined face quivered with the emotion dammed within, threatening to break loose into a tsunami of sadness. The priest instinctively knew that the Mother Superior would not accept a despondent candidate for religious training. The life of a nun was demanding and selfless, and not suited for someone floundering in regret and despair.

CHAPTER 13

The Convent

1897-1901
Orphanage Outside Paris, France

The enormous gray building looked cold and austere as the horse drawn cart pulled through the wrought iron gates. With great hesitancy, Marguerite and Father Bernard walked haltingly toward the heavy doors guarding the entrance to the forbidding looking building. The formidable doors were made of ancient wood, and reinforced with bands of wrought iron, which gave the appearance of a rather severe looking religious fortress. Marguerite shuddered as she stood waiting at the doorway to her future.

The Mother Superior met with Marguerite and Father Bernard upon their arrival. The old nun's lively eyes took in the scene before her. Her astute assessment quickly recognized that Marguerite was distraught, and that she appeared to be leaking breastmilk. The old nun did not confront Marguerite, but merely stated, in a matter-of-fact way, that those entering the convent must do so willingly, with an open heart. It was no place for a reluctant participant. She went on to say that Marguerite was welcome to stay for a brief period of observation, to expose and immerse herself in the actual daily life of a nun. The period would not only be an exploration for Marguerite, but also one for the Mother Superior. Marguerite was free to leave at any time, for any reason, during this period.

In the words of the Mother Superior, "There are no prisoners here. You enter and stay of your own free will. But only I can recommend that you continue to further religious training as a nun. Only those whom I truly believe are a good fit for this life, will stay." She looked directly into Marguerite's eyes as she spoke these words. The visibly upset young woman numbly nodded her understanding.

The elderly nun went on to say in a sterner tone, "Although it may seem odd as you see me today, I too was once a young, impetuous girl. I am fully aware that young girls seek this life for all manner of reasons. Some truly are looking to serve God, others are running away from something, or somebody. I am not here to judge you. However, know that the rigors of life in a convent are not a good match for someone retreating from a devastating life experience. I am here for you if you wish to talk, but I will not make any effort to convince you to stay. At the end of this month, you and I will have a candid discussion about your future. Do you have any questions?"

Marguerite quietly, almost imperceptibly, said, "No." There was sadness to her demeanor, but also a subtle determination to stay, to see her journey through.

Sensing that the meeting was over, Father Bernard interjected, "May I speak with Marguerite alone?"

"Most certainly," the aged nun said as she quietly got up from her chair and left the office, closing the door behind her.

Marguerite let out a gasping sob as the door closed. Father Bernard rushed to her side and opened his arms, fully embracing her, desperately wanting to erase her pain. Marguerite did not resist. Both had tears running down their faces as they held each other.

Marguerite was the first to speak as she pushed herself away from Father Bernard. She spoke through muffled sobs, "I have to do this."

He looked directly into her eyes and gently shook her shoulders as he spoke, "No, you don't. This is clearly not the life you were meant to live. I will take you back to the farm. You belong with your son."

She shook her head and replied, "I can't have my son growing up in Bayeux, the child of an unmarried mother. People will speculate about the identity of his father and nothing good will come of it. I will not do this to my innocent Henri."

Father Bernard felt defeat as he uttered, "You are innocent, too."

"No, I am not innocent, and I know my community. Henri and I would suffer tremendously. Even my own parents would not stand with me. Jacob would deny being the father, and it would be an ugly environment in which to raise a child. I cannot do that to my son!"

The priest knew what she said was true. He sighed and said, "Please don't do this. You deserve to be with your son. You are accountable only to God."

She defiantly looked into his eyes as she said, "It is not that simple. The controversy surrounding my illegitimate child would follow Henri all through his childhood. He deserves better."

Father Bernard looked exasperated as he proclaimed, "I care too much for you to let you do this."

Marguerite sighed and looked lovingly at him, and with a soft, almost whisper-like voice, she said, "I care for you too, and that's part of the problem. You are the most amazing man I have ever encountered, but there is no future for the two of us. It scares me to be with you. My love for you only complicates an already messy situation. It's not fair to either of us to be so close, but so far. Please let me go."

Father Bernard looked stunned and strangely pleased by Marguerite's honest proclamation. He nodded in acknowledgment of this previously unspoken truth and stammered his response, his mostly hidden Slovakian accent suddenly more evident. "I…love you, too. It's painful for me to even say these words. The temptation to violate my vows has become a daily struggle, of which I am not proud."

Marguerite felt relief that his words, as well as hers, had finally been spoken. She smiled weakly at the young priest as she said, "I know that we cannot be together, but it does warm my heart to know that you love me. I will carry that with me."

The priest looked as though his resolve was weakening as he again moved toward her. She held up her hands as if to push him away and stepped back. A sudden burst of firmness was evident in her voice as she exclaimed, "You and I have responsibilities. We have made commitments that we both need to honor."

"That is true. I do not take my vows lightly. However, it does not stop me from thinking about you and worrying about how these decisions will impact your life, and mine. I admit that I selfishly want to keep you close. I'm not proud to tell you this, but it is true."

Marguerite was somber as she said, "Please watch over and protect my son. I am going to become a nun. I do hope that you will visit me, from time to time. It would be a comfort, but I do understand if you decide that it wouldn't be appropriate. I seem to have a way of complicating things. I am so sorry."

She stepped forward to embrace him and lightly kissed him on the lips. He instantly encircled her with his strong arms and returned her expression of affection, with a deeply passionate, lingering kiss. They both shuddered, stunned by the electricity between them. Shaken, Marguerite pulled back and abruptly opened the door, quickly stepping out of the Mother Superior's office, leaving the young priest standing there, trembling and wildly conflicted. He desperately fought the urge to run after her, trying to make sense of his feelings, and the trajectory of his life. It was several minutes before Father Bernard could compose himself enough to emerge from the seclusion of the office. He was still reeling from the interaction, as he searched the deserted hallway. Conflicted by the feelings racing through his mind, he was sick with confusion. He tried to calm himself as he considered searching for Marguerite and begging that she return with him. But he instinctively knew that she was stronger than he was, and that she would not change her mind. Sadly, he understood, but it didn't diminish his feelings for her in any way.

Father Bernard half stumbled back to his horse and cart, and with much reluctance he climbed into the seat. The long journey back to Bayeux was filled with rumination and doubt. At times there were tears, too. When he finally arrived back in Bayeux, Father Bernard had pulled himself together enough to at least feign normalcy. The demands of the busy parish quickly garnered his attention, and he felt a sense of relief as he threw himself into his duties as a parish priest.

Marguerite's first evening at the convent was a lonely, harsh affair. Tormented by her feelings for the priest and her son, she gave serious thought to running out of the convent into the night. Finally, she calmed herself. Just as reason was starting to settle in, the Mother Superior appeared with a middle-aged nun at her side. The nun was to be her mentor during her trial period, and Marguerite could not have imagined a less welcoming looking nun. Sister Mary Monica was a slightly built, severe looking woman with deeply etched frown lines around her mouth. Marguerite guessed her to be in her late forties, but she looked remarkably worn, and drawn, for her years. Dressed in the full regalia of her black nun's habit, she gave off an intimidating air. The austere nun made it perfectly clear that Marguerite would be expected to participate fully in all the obligations and duties of a nun. Her purpose was to show Marguerite the deprivation and hardship that would occupy her days in the convent. Sister Mary Monica was not by Marguerite's side to comfort or encourage the young girl. She was assigned to mentor Marguerite, and to test her resolve to become a nun. The Mother Superior had correctly interpreted Marguerite's emotional reluctance, and she had tasked Sister Mary Monica with this rather harsh assignment. In the Mother Superior's mind, she was doing Marguerite a favor. She knew that Marguerite would need to be fully committed to this path and she intended to test her mental toughness and ability to contribute to the mission of the religious order. It was a brutal, yet necessary, introduction to life in the convent.

After a somewhat abrupt introduction, Sister Mary Monica ushered Marguerite away to an enormous dining room filled with children of all ages and sizes. Long harvest style tables with benches were crowded with youngsters, busily eating, laughing, and speaking loudly over the din in the massive room. Marguerite guessed that there were over two hundred children crowded into the huge dining hall. The activity and noise in the room had a distinct energy that buzzed like a beehive. Although there was chaos in the room, there was a certain level of order and efficiency too. Older children were helping to feed toddlers, and there were several nuns who were shepherding the distribution of food and seemed to instinctively know which child needed encouragement to eat. It was an impressive operation. It was not warm and friendly, but it seemed to be accomplishing the task of feeding an enormous number of orphaned children in a surprisingly organized manner.

Marguerite was relieved to hear joy in the overcrowded room. It boasted a feeling of humanity. There was laughter and playful teasing as these children, who knew each other well, ate in a communal setting. The busy nuns were constantly redirecting children to eat and quit their playing. The admonishments were brisk and delivered with efficiency, but there was still a level of mischievous playfulness in the room. It was reassuring to Marguerite to see the resilience of these orphaned children. On some level, they appeared at first glance to be surviving both physically and emotionally. No doubt there was severe mental anguish buried within them, but there was vibrant life, too. Although plainly dressed in a mismatched assortment of worn clothing, they all appeared to be relatively clean and well-nourished. It was a testament to the hard work and efficiency of the nuns who were doing a huge humanitarian service.

The children who lived in the orphanage came from all backgrounds and circumstances. It was a literal collection of all the societal remnants of human depravity. There were infants abandoned on the steps of the orphanage by the daughters of wealth and privilege, and an even larger number of infants and children who came from the poorest segments of society. Rampant epidemics had left large numbers of orphans, and these too became part of the population. The Catholic mission took them all in.

The Mother Superior was a tough and efficient manager of this enormous French orphanage. She was at first blush a no-nonsense person, but she had retained a quietly hidden sense of tenderness when dealing with those under her care. Absolutely insistent upon order and cleanliness, she demanded that those nuns working under her perform their duties with discipline and consistency. The Mother Superior was revered in the Catholic Church in an almost legendary manner for the skills she possessed.

In addition to managing the daily care of over two hundred orphans, the Mother Superior was known to be a very effective fundraiser. Wealthy benefactors, some with family members who had entrusted their illegitimate children or grandchildren to the care of the convent, provided generous endowments to the orphanage. An accomplished writer, the Mother Superior used her letter writing skills to garner funds and ongoing support for the orphanage, always maintaining relationships with the orphanage's wealthy Christian benefactors. Over the years, she had built a continuous stream of income to support the never-ending stream of children entering her doors. She efficiently used these funds to provide healthy food and sensible clothing for the children. It was impressive, and it did not go unnoticed by the benefactors, or the hierarchy of the Catholic Church.

Like most of those who entered convent life, the Mother Superior had a secret. She had spent time in a French orphanage as a young child, and it had been a brutal experience. Orphaned at the age of ten, she and her younger brother had endured physical and emotional abuse in a remote orphanage, before escaping to the French countryside. Luckily, a farm family had discovered the children hiding in their barn. The frightened children were fed and given warm beds for the night. As the children unfolded their story, the rescuing family took them into their care. The older farm couple provided them with food, warm clothing, and gave the battered children love and a sense of belonging. The Mother Superior never forgot the humanity that she and her brother encountered.

At the age of seventeen, she willingly entered the convent, with the personal mission of someday providing sanctuary and safe care to orphaned children. It was a cause that had endless need, and she quickly found herself immersed in their care and protection. Quickly, she had risen to leadership positions in the religious organization. She was a highly perceptive and intuitive administrator, who used her skills to effectively assess the potential of those seeking entrance to the convent. Her strategy was to saturate the young aspirant to the rigors of the physical care of orphaned children, and diligently observe and evaluate their response to the trial. The mission was to recruit and retain only those who could willingly provide compassionate, efficient care. She was also widely known to have no tolerance for those nuns who were physically or emotionally abusive to orphaned children, having summarily dismissed four nuns during her first year as Mother Superior when she observed them being abusive to the children. Her reputation for the competent and compassionate care of orphaned children was widely known and revered. At the age of sixty-four, the Mother Superior was an energetic and esteemed figure.

Although tired and mentally spent, Marguerite dutifully followed Sister Mary Monica into the huge dining hall buzzing with the noise of children. Immediately, her no-nonsense mentor tasked her with helping to feed a fussy toddler. Marguerite easily fell into soothing the toddler and urging her to eat the food before her. The child seemed to welcome the attention and did begin to eat. It was a mutually comforting interaction. Marguerite's life in the convent had gotten off to a tumultuous start, but she could clearly see the overwhelming need in this sea of young children.

As the meal ended, Sister Mary Monica shepherded the children to an enormous room filled with rows and rows of beds. Marguerite followed and was quickly assigned the duty of undressing toddlers and getting them into their sleeping gowns. Prayers followed, and then the children were tucked into warm, clean beds. The scope of the operation continued to astound her. There was some fussiness and brief crying by some of the youngest orphans, but several of the older children took the initiative to comfort and tuck these youngest orphans in for the night. There seemed to be a culture of caring in the rather chaotic room. It gave Marguerite hope that maybe she truly could survive, and even contribute to life in this convent orphanage.

Marguerite felt exhausted as Sister Mary Monica next led her to a more remote room that housed six infants in separate wooden bassinets. Again, the linens were clean, and the babies looked well cared for, and healthy. Marguerite estimated that the six infants ranged in age from less than a week old, to possibly three months of age. The nun who had been tending to the needs of the infants thankfully acknowledged her relief from duty, and she quickly left the room. One of the youngest infants was crying in her corner bassinet. Marguerite instinctively and confidently went to the bassinet and picked up the fussy baby. Rocking the baby as she walked, she picked up one of the prepared bottles. Knowingly, she lowered herself and the baby into a sturdy rocking chair. Lulled by the physical comfort, and the rhythmic rocking, the infant was soon sucking voraciously and consuming the contents of the bottle. Sister Mary Monica was silently impressed, but she said nothing to Marguerite. Throughout the night, Marguerite repeatedly rose from her bedside cot to tend to the babies' needs. It was calming to both the infants and to Marguerite, as she thought endlessly of Henri. She pragmatically told herself over and over that her son was safe and well cared for in her sister's family.

As the early morning light started to peek through the eastern windows, an efficient, almost friendly nun arrived to relieve Marguerite and Sister Mary Monica from their duties. Sister Theresa was pleased to find the nursery in good order, and the infants sleeping calmly in their bassinets.

Marguerite had survived her first night. She was tired, but strangely fulfilled. Her mentor was surprisingly impressed with the convent's newest aspirant. As the Mother Superior made her morning rounds, there was a brief, quiet sharing between the mentor and the administrator. Marguerite had made quite a favorable impression on one of the most critical and stringent of the established nuns. It was a noteworthy beginning for Marguerite.

To the surprise and the quiet delight of the Mother Superior, Marguerite sailed through her trial period of exposure to convent life. There were no reservations as she was recommended to continue her training as a nun. The hard, physical demands of convent life were not overly challenging to Marguerite. She was used to hard physical labor and took comfort in it. Being physically strong and fit was a huge advantage, as she navigated the demands of training. The work suited her soul and she approached it with maturity and energy. Quite frankly, she was a natural asset to the Mother Superior's mission.

Over the course of several years, Marguerite completed her training and prepared to take her final vows as a nun. It had been a long journey, but she was very proud of her accomplishment. Over the period of her training, Marguerite had received regular letters from her sister, generously sharing information about Henri and his developmental accomplishments. The steady flow of news about Henri and the LeBlanc family was welcome, reassuring Marguerite that she had made the right decision after all. Although Adele and Gabriel had offered many times to bring Henri to visit her at the convent, Marguerite had refused. Still deeply conflicted, Marguerite worried that seeing her child would threaten her resolve to follow through on her plan to provide the best future for Henri.

When the news arrived that her parents had died during an influenza outbreak, Marguerite was plagued with guilt. She had not seen or communicated with her parents since she had abruptly left their home as a pregnant teenager. The emotional wound was abruptly reopened, and she desperately longed to see her family. In a short letter, Marguerite simply asked Adele to come visit her at the convent. Adele was relieved, and promptly planned to make the journey with Gabriel, Louis, and Henri.

Marguerite was nervous and excited as she rushed to meet her family in the lobby of the orphanage. From a distance, she could see the little group huddled in the enormous entry, and she instinctively ran toward them. Adele looked up, smiling, and she too rushed to meet her sister. They fell together in a warm, encompassing hug, as Gabriel and the two little boys watched. Marguerite's eyes grew wide as she stared at the little fair-haired boy, she knew was her own. Still entangled in her sister's arms, she could hardly breathe as she studied him over her sister's shoulder. Henri was bright-eyed and alert as he looked quizzically at the interaction between his mother and the strange woman before him.

The two little boys stood side by side, but they could not have looked more different. The older boy was stocky, with dark eyes, olive skin, and dark, wavy hair. But it was the younger boy who made Marguerite gasp when she first saw him. He looked so much like Jacob that she could hardly breathe. Henri had the same thick, blondish brown hair, and the same clear green eyes with brown highlights. The fair complexion and finely chiseled facial features were alarmingly, and distinctively Jacob's. He was truly a beautiful little boy.

Slowly, Marguerite disentangled herself from Adele and dropped to her knees in front of Henri. He looked puzzled and backed away toward Gabriel.

Gently, Adele nudged the little boy forward as she said, "Henri, this is your Aunt Marguerite. She has been looking forward to spending time with you. She is my sister."

Henri smiled shyly, and then reached up to grab Gabriel's hand.

Marguerite was still taking in the wonder of him when she smiled and said, "Hello, Henri." She resisted the urge to just scoop him up in her arms. Suddenly aware that the whole family was watching her intently, she quickly stood to greet Gabriel and Louis. Unknown to Marguerite, the Mother Superior was taking in the reunification scene from the shadows of her doorway, and in her intuitive way, she knew that Henri was Marguerite's son.

The family of visitors spent the entire day picnicking and playing together in a nearby meadow. The two sisters spoke like they had never been apart, and it was healing. But the focus of the day was clearly on Henri. Marguerite played silly games with the boys and read them stories. As Marguerite spent time with Henri, she quickly came to know the essence of the young boy who was her child. He was bright and inquisitive, with a playful nature, and this made her smile inwardly.

Henri seemed to be thriving in his loving, energetic family. Although she was thrilled to see her son, there was sadness, too. She had given up so much. Marguerite hid her sadness and regret as Henri, Adele, Gabriel, and Louis hugged her and said their goodbyes. But, in a final moment before they climbed into the wagon, Marguerite lifted Henri into her arms and hugged him for the longest time, before handing him back to Adele. Tears streaming down her face, she turned and waved as she opened the heavy door and disappeared inside of the orphanage.

CHAPTER 14

Sister Marguerite Has a Change in Plans

1901
Orphanage Outside Paris, France

Marguerite couldn't sleep. Her mind kept drifting back to thoughts of Henri. Finally, with a sense of resignation, she climbed out of bed and got dressed for the day. Feeling tired and edgy, Marguerite slipped from the quiet orphanage and restlessly walked around the grassy yard. She loved the early morning. Normally, Marguerite felt like she was at her best when the sun was just coming up, but not today. The tranquility of the early morning light seemed to evade her, as tormented thoughts tumbled through her mind. With a deep sigh, she quietly opened the front door and stepped back into the building. The Mother Superior was waiting for her.

The wise old nun looked at her quizzically, and said, "I'm worried about you. I think we need to talk."

With a sense of dread, Marguerite dutifully followed her down the hall to her office. The desk was cluttered in a busy, yet organized way that spoke of her many responsibilities. Silently, Marguerite slunk down into a chair.

The Mother Superior did not look angry, but she did look stern. Frankly, she said, "Marguerite, you have not been yourself since your family visited."

The young nun said nothing in response. She looked embarrassed, as she weakly nodded.

Gently, the Mother Superior said, "You do not need to carry this burden by yourself. Marguerite, I know that you have a child."

Stunned, Marguerite felt like someone had knocked the wind right out of her. Unable to respond for an uncomfortable amount of time, she finally looked up and acknowledged, "Yes, I do have a little boy. How did you know?"

There was no condemnation, just concern, as the Mother Superior said, "I've known since the first day you arrived here."

Marguerite was incredulous as she asked, "How?"

"Well, you were distraught, and I could see that you were leaking breastmilk. It wasn't hard to figure out."

"So why did you not confront me?"

"You were not ready to share that part of your life."

"Yet you let me stay?"

"To be honest, I did not intend to let you stay."

"So, what made you change your mind?"

With a sense of pride, the old woman responded, "You did. Despite your obvious pain, you immediately engaged in giving comfort to the orphan children."

"Well, I think it would be more truthful to say, that they gave comfort to me."

"I suspect that's true. But you demonstrated great personal strength and determination. I was impressed."

Marguerite seemed to soak up the compliment as she responded, "I am thankful that you gave me a chance."

"It was an easy decision, but what are we to do with you now?"

Marguerite looked alarmed as she let the question soak in. Quietly, she admitted, "I have been tormented by my decision to give up Henri to my sister."

"Yes, I can see that. But your child is thriving in your sister's family, is he not?"

"Henri does appear to be thriving. He's a happy, energetic little boy, who clearly loves his family, and I am relieved to see him doing so well. But I am so, so sad that I can't be part of his life. I feel such guilt."

"That's not productive. You obviously tried to make the best decision for your child. That took amazing strength to put his well-being ahead of your own."

Marguerite sighed and said, "I'm not sure it was the right decision, but it's too late now."

Wisely, the Mother Superior continued, "Well, your son is firmly embedded in your sister's family. It would be very unfair to him to disrupt the stability of his life."

"I could not do that to Henri, or to my sister's family."

"But you want to be a part of his life?"

"Yes, I do."

The Mother Superior got right to the heart of the matter by asking, "Is your sister willing to share Henri?"

"Yes, she has been quite generous. Adele writes to me regularly and tells me all about Henri. And I know she worries about me, too."

"Possibly, they could visit more often?"

"The distance is too great to visit frequently. They are dairy farmers, so they have animals that require attention daily. Gabriel's friend can help from time to time, but it's really a lot to ask of a neighbor on a regular basis."

Thoughtfully, the old nun probed further as she directly asked, "So what do you want your role to be in Henri's life?"

"Well, I know that I can't be his mother."

"Go on."

Marguerite responded, "I suppose, I would like to be a doting, fun loving aunt."

The Mother Superior nodded her approval as she said, "Now that sounds like a realistic plan."

"But, not from this distance."

"You want to go back to Bayeux, don't you?"

"Yes."

With a deep sigh, the old nun said, "Now that makes me sad. But I have made a few connections in the church over the years, so maybe I can help you."

Marguerite brightened as she responded, "I would be so grateful."

"Well, let me write to Father Bernard and see if I can get you an assignment with the Bayeux parish. You would have more flexibility there than in the Bayeux convent."

Marguerite looked suddenly uncomfortable at the mention of Father Bernard. She tried to appear unruffled as she responded, "That would be wonderful."

Smiling slyly, the Mother Superior said, "You know, Marguerite, I have grown quite fond of you. Please don't tell anyone, though. I need to preserve my reputation."

"I won't. I won't tell a soul."

The letter arrived on Father Bernard's desk a week later. It was a warmly worded missive, written to a trusted colleague, that addressed the desired reassignment of their mutual friend, Marguerite. The letter outlined her prior work and accomplishments in the convent orphanage and made it clear that her leaving would be a great loss to the operation of the orphanage. As he read the letter, Father Bernard was stunned. He paused and tried to calm his sudden inner turmoil. After so many years, just the thought of Marguerite still stirred feelings that he had fought hard to suppress. Over the next few days, Father Bernard tormented over how he should respond to the request. There was overwhelming need in the Bayeux parish, and Marguerite's services could easily be put to good use. Try as he might, he could not come up with any rational reason to turn down such a qualified applicant. Still, he was reluctant to accept Marguerite into his parish. The letter had evoked long suppressed feelings for the young nun, and he thought it not wise to have her close. He had fought his inner battle for years and had finally felt like it was behind him. Painful as it had been, they both had committed their lives to a purpose bigger than their personal relationship, or so they told themselves.

Deep down, Father Bernard was hurt by such an officially written request from Marguerite's Mother Superior. Although there had been no contact between the two since he left Marguerite at the convent over four years ago, he felt slighted that she had not written him directly. But he sensed that Marguerite also had reservations about her return to Bayeux. He knew her to be a thoughtful, caring person, and decided, after much rumination, that she intended no offense. Father Bernard finally concluded that Marguerite's primary motivation for wanting to return to Bayeux was indeed to be close to her son. The awkwardness and pain that emanated from their feelings for each other was secondary. They were both committed to their chosen religious lives, and would hopefully forge an effective, mature, working relationship. With that thought in mind, he decided to accept Marguerite into his parish mission.

It was three weeks before the response letter arrived at the convent. Marguerite had become increasingly worried that her request would be denied. In her heart, Marguerite had decided that she could understand any reluctance that the priest might have about her returning to Bayeux. The secrets of their past created a heaviness between them that was undeniable. But as she waited to hear, Marguerite felt a growing confidence that Father Bernard would not keep her from her son.

As the Mother Superior called Marguerite to her office, the young nun felt almost physically ill. The moment of truth was at hand, and Marguerite could barely hold onto her composure. Nervously, she sat. Slowly, and with deliberate purpose, the Mother Superior opened the letter to read it. Her facial expression did not give away the contents of the letter. Marguerite visibly gulped air as she tried to steady herself. Looking concerned, the Mother Superior quietly handed the letter to Marguerite. With shaking hands, Marguerite tried to focus and read the missive. Finally, the old nun said, "Your request for assignment to Bayeux has been granted."

Marguerite let out a soft sob of relief as she responded, "I am so grateful for all you have done for me."

The Mother Superior studied Marguerite for the longest time before she said, "I pray that you find solace in this assignment. You do know that you are always welcome to return here. If you find that this assignment does not suit you, please come back to us. You are a very special young woman. I can't even begin to tell you how much I will miss you."

Marguerite smiled weakly through her tears and said, "I will miss you, too."

The Mother Superior personally made the arrangements for Marguerite to be delivered to her sister's farm outside of Bayeux. In her masterfully intuitive way, she also granted the young nun a two-week leave to spend time with her family before reporting to Father Bernard in Bayeux. It was an unexpected gift that overwhelmed Marguerite with gratitude, as she eagerly anticipated the opportunity to be with her son.

The news of Marguerite's leaving spread like a wildfire through the crowded orphanage. The children were clearly saddened by the news. There were tears and hugs, as Sister Marguerite spent her last days immersed in the care of these young orphans that she had come to love. She could not help but feel that she had made a difference in their young lives. The orphaned children did have the ability to care about someone, and this bolstered her belief in their resilience.

As she was helping the sea of orphans with their last supper together, Marguerite playfully climbed onto one of the sturdy tables in the center of the enormous dining hall. There were titters and laughing as she clapped her hands to get their attention. The children immediately quieted to hear what she had to say. Marguerite was not maudlin as she spoke. With a loud, clear voice, she said, "I want you to know that I will miss you all. You are very, very dear to me and I have enjoyed being a part of your life. I've even enjoyed the antics and pranks of our little Charles." The room burst into laughter at the mention of one of the orphanage's most mischievous children. She went on to say, "Please take care of one another and give each other the love that you have given me. I will carry your beautiful faces with me forever. Now, please join me in singing one last song together."

Marguerite led the crowded room filled with children of all ages in a popular children's song. Loud and boisterous, the children sang along. At the conclusion of the rousing song, there was clapping and shouts of good wishes. As the children filed out of the dining hall, Marguerite quietly left to go pack her few possessions. She would leave the next morning at daybreak.

CHAPTER 15

Sister Marguerite Returns

1901
The LeBlanc Farm in Normandy, France

Marguerite had her bag heavily slung over her shoulder as she pushed open the massive door, ready to leave and start her new life. She immediately recognized the voice as she stepped outside, but there was a lightness to it, a teasing chuckle that was almost unrecognizable. The Mother Superior stood closely by an elderly man, and there was an obvious ease between them. Marguerite was puzzled, and more than a little curious. She had seen the old farmer many times, always coming and going from the Mother Superior's office.

Hearing the door open, the old nun was suddenly more serious, her voice authoritative, as she turned to greet Marguerite. "Good morning, Marguerite! I see you're prompt as usual."

Marguerite smiled awkwardly, feeling like she was intruding on an intimate conversation. "Good morning! I certainly try to be prompt."

"I'd like you to meet my brother, Elliot."

Suddenly, Marguerite could see the similarity in the two siblings, as she smiled warmly, and extended her hand to the farmer. "So nice to meet you."

"Ahh…the pleasure's all mine. My sister has told me all about you." There was a twinkle in his eyes, as he added, "I think you might be her favorite."

"Well, I don't know about that. I think I've certainly tested her patience."

He chuckled and said, "As the younger brother, I've given her a few challenges myself. But…I have to say, she still claims me as family."

His sister looked amused, and more playful than Marguerite was accustomed to seeing her. She responded, "Alright you two, I don't think that we need to hear tales of all your misbehavior. We'll be here all day."

Elliot responded to the cue and efficiently took Marguerite's bag from her to place in the back of the wagon. Suddenly, Marguerite felt tears welling in her eyes as she turned to say goodbye. The old nun, also teary, stepped closer and gave Marguerite a big, long hug.

The Mother Superior whispered, "Go make the life that you want with your son."

Barely audible, Marguerite responded, "I will."

Marguerite turned and climbed into the seat beside Elliot. The tears were flowing freely now, as she waved goodbye, unable to express her immense gratitude for all that the Mother Superior had done to help her. As the horse and buggy pulled away, the old nun called out to Marguerite, "Travel safely. Give my regards to your family!"

They traveled for quite a distance, Elliot respecting her mood, her sorrow at the parting. Finally, he said, "She's a special one, an angel really."

"Yes, she saved me. I was so lost when I came to the convent."

He nodded, and said with complete sincerity, "She saved me, too. After our parents died, we were sent to an orphanage. It was a scary place, and even at the age of ten, she understood that I was in danger. She watched over me, protected me."

Marguerite sensed his reluctance to tell the tale, but she wanted to understand this woman, and her story, so she gently asked, "Why were you in danger?"

"Ahh…it's an ugly tale." He sighed, and then said, "There was a priest there who liked little boys, and I had caught his fancy. My sister had heard stories from some of the other children, and she watched over me, and warned me to stay away from him. When she saw him, trying to corral me into his office, she fiercely confronted him, screamed at him. Told him, to 'Leave my brother alone!' He was furious, and beat her with a wooden paddle, pretending all the while that he was disciplining an unruly child. I tried to fend him off her, but he beat me, too. That night, my sister came to my bedside, and we escaped into the French countryside. We ran for most of the night, desperately trying to get as far away from the orphanage as possible. As the sun was coming up, we slipped into a barn and fell asleep in the hay. Of course, the farmer found us when he came to tend his horses. He could see that we had been beaten. Our faces were bruised and swollen. He was so caring. I will never forget his compassion…not if I live to be a hundred. He and his wife listened to our story, believed us, and reassured us that we were safe with them. And we were safe with them. They cared for us, fed us, and took us into their family, into their home. Pierre and Marie were older and had never had any children. They saw us as a gift, and they raised us as their own. It was really a miracle."

"That's quite a story."

"Yes, it is, and every word is true. I'm proud of my sister. Even as a child, she had incredible courage, incredible insight. I shudder to think what would have happened, if she had not pulled me out of that orphanage in the dark of night."

"Yes, there is evil in this world. Thankfully, she was your guardian angel. She has watched over me, too."

"Yes…it's her way. She comes across as a tough old bird, but you'll never find a more caring, compassionate woman."

Marguerite chuckled as she said, "Well said. So, tell me something about the esteemed Mother Superior that would surprise me."

"She loves horses," he said, without hesitation.

"Now, that really does surprise me."

Elliot seemed pleased to share a different side of his sister. "She has a beautiful horse…loves to ride him."

Marguerite looked dumbfounded, and this seemed to please Elliot. He grinned as he explained, "She is quite an accomplished rider. Loves to ride like the wind. Every Sunday, she visits my farm, has a bit of dinner with my wife and I, and then takes Ronan for a ride. He's really a beautiful horse. I tease her that I'm going to hook him up to a plow, but she knows I wouldn't dare."

Marguerite laughed at this unexpected intimate peek into the Mother Superior's relationship with her brother. She quickly decided that she liked this man, his humility, his honesty, his love for his sister.

The long day of travel seemed to go by quickly, as Marguerite and Elliot shared pieces of their lives. It was a surprisingly comfortable relationship, and the young nun marveled that she trusted this man that she had just met, not only with her safety, but with her life story. He listened, accepting her, and respecting her choices…like he had heard it before. Somehow it was healing for Marguerite to tell the tale, from the perspective of time and maturity.

As evening light was starting to fade, the wagon pulled into the lane of the LeBlanc farm. The family had heard the approaching horses, and the door swung open as Adele and Gabriel poured out, followed by the boys. As Marguerite jumped to the ground, the sisters embraced, and the little boys giggled, waving with excitement. It was a joyful reunion, and Elliot took it all in, happy to see the love that encircled the young woman whom he had quickly come to know. He had a sense that she would find her way in her new life.

The days ahead were filled with playful times, as Marguerite got to know Henri and Louis. The little boys had fond memories of their first meeting with Marguerite, and they eagerly played games and read books with her. Although they were a year apart in age, the two boys were remarkably similar in size, but that is where their physical similarities ended. They were rough and tumble for sure, but they were also respectful, well-raised young boys. Marguerite was impressed and she couldn't help but feel pleased. Adele and Gabriel had proven to be capable, loving parents, but it was also apparent that they expected the boys to participate in the daily chores. Henri and Louis would feed the chickens and retrieve eggs every morning before breakfast. Initially, she felt like voicing her objection that the boys were too young for such chores, but then she was abruptly jarred by the realization that she had no right to voice her opinion.

As the week wore on, thoughts and worry started to invade the blissful little cocoon of farm life, as Marguerite thought ahead to the transition that she must make to successfully be a part of her son's life. It was daunting, and the gravity could not have weighed heavier on her, as she suddenly faced the reality of confronting Jacob, and being near Father Bernard again. She repeatedly told herself that she could make this transition, for her son, for herself.

Marguerite's past involvements with both Jacob and Father Bernard hung heavily over her, but it was the young priest who dominated her thoughts. Her mind kept going back to their emotional parting over four years ago, and the raw, honest acknowledgment that they both loved each other. She had not seen or communicated with Father Bernard since their parting, and somehow it had felt safer that way. Her feelings for him had been safely buried in the endless work of caring for orphaned children. But upon her return, Marguerite guiltily had to admit to herself how she still thought of his beautiful body, and his sharp mind, and his compassion, and she knew without a doubt that she still had feelings for him. It was going to be a monumental test of her commitment to her vows to work closely with Father Bernard. She knew his character, his integrity, almost more than she knew herself. Sadly, she had to acknowledge that he would not allow her close again. Their relationship would have to be different, or they could not co-exist in the same church, the same village.

Marguerite's concern about her inevitable confrontation with Jacob was an entirely different matter. In her most honest moments, she had to admit that she despised him. Marguerite marveled over how she could have ever been attracted to him, but they had been young lovers overtaken by a powerful physical draw, one that had cataclysmically brought them together, clouding their perceptions of each other. The pregnancy, and the dejection that followed, had brought the intoxicating love affair to a quick, painful end. Marguerite still shuddered with the memory, but she smiled inwardly at the thought of Henri, safe and happy, hidden away in her sister's loving family.

Surprisingly, Marguerite was not overtaken by concern regarding her inevitable meeting with her past teenage lover. She had learned from Adele that Jacob was now married to a pretty, young woman and had an infant son. He had predictably married well and was working towards taking over the family restaurant. Adele was bitter as she described his blissfully successful young life. She could not, and would not, forgive Jacob for his treatment of Marguerite. Stubbornly, she refused to acknowledge him when she inadvertently encountered him in church, or on the street. Jacob, in return, pretended to not see Adele. It perfectly exemplified the secrets of Bayeux.

Marguerite had long ago decided that Jacob was a person of low character and not worthy of her hate. She shocked even herself at how little she thought of him. It was as if he had never been a part of her life, which of course was not true. Whether they openly acknowledged it or not, Jacob and Marguerite had been together as adolescent lovers, and they had a child. It was the uncomfortable reality. She knew that Jacob would not be pleased to see her reappear. But she also knew that Jacob would never acknowledge their prior love affair and their illegitimate child. This fact was strangely empowering and had an unexpected calming effect on Marguerite. She felt relatively certain that their past would remain a secret. With a sense of confidence and maybe a dose of defiance, she thought that any discomfort that Jacob felt by her reemergence into Bayeux was his problem. He was no longer a part of Marguerite's life, and she would not alter the course of her life, especially not for the likes of him.

After Marguerite had been on the farm for a couple of days, Adele left for her weekly trip to Bayeux to sell cheese, eggs, and poultry to the local restaurants. Marguerite was excited to have time alone with Henri and Louis. Secretly, she was determined to make the most of this time as she planned to play hide and seek, and other games. The little boys loved her willingness to endlessly play the games they enjoyed. Henri proudly proclaimed that she was his "favorite aunt." Marguerite smiled, and silently thought how this was the highest compliment she could ever hope to hear. Adele was pleased that the reunion between Henri and Marguerite was going well, and that her sister finally seemed to be healing.

As Adele made her weekly rounds selling farm produce to local restaurants, she ran into Father Bernard. They had been close since the priest had befriended and discreetly helped her sister, as she struggled with decisions surrounding her unplanned pregnancy. Adele had been forever grateful to the priest for his support of Marguerite during her time of crisis. She was convinced that her sister could not have survived emotionally without him.

As Adele approached Father Bernard, she said, "I was hoping that I would bump into my favorite priest today."

He smiled in an amused way as he responded, "I think my status has been elevated since we last met."

Adele shook her head as she reassured him, "I think you well know that your status could not be higher in my eyes."

He teasingly responded, "I'm not sure what that says about your judgment, but I am glad to see you, Adele."

She looked at him sincerely and said, "I want to thank you for approving Marguerite's request for reassignment to Bayeux. It means the world to me, and to Marguerite. I can only imagine the amount of thought and worry that went into granting that request. You do know that she would never do anything to disrupt Henri's life, or yours, for that matter."

Father Bernard thoughtfully looked at Adele before speaking. "I would not have agreed to her reassignment here if I thought otherwise."

Adele spoke bluntly, "She is not the same devastated young girl who left here four years ago. She has matured into a formidable young woman, one who wants to be near her son."

Father Bernard looked uncomfortable as he said, "I fear that she will struggle with guilt, as she watches her child grow up so close, but so far from her. And her reappearance in Bayeux has the potential to stir up questions and angst with Jacob Laurent. I hope that I have made the right decision in allowing her to be assigned to the Bayeux parish."

Adele looked Father Bernard straight in the eyes and said, "You have made the right decision. Marguerite wants to be close to her son and be involved in his life as a loving aunt. She would never do anything to hurt Henri. Trust me. Jacob means nothing to her. He wounded her terribly by abandoning her, and not even acknowledging her pregnancy to his parents. Jacob may be uncomfortable initially when Marguerite reappears in Bayeux, but he most certainly will not want to acknowledge their past. It will remain an awkward secret."

He nodded as he said, "I hope you are right. The level of deception that I willingly participated in has bothered me all these years."

Adele spoke from the heart, "You saved her, and I will be forever grateful for all that you have done. I assure you, that you have not made a mistake in allowing Marguerite to return."

"Marguerite and I have not spoken, or even written to each other, in over four years," he said quietly.

Adele nodded her understanding as she said, "Well, part of the reason that I was hoping to see you today was to invite you to the farm for dinner. It would be a chance for you and Marguerite to talk in private, away from the prying eyes of your parishioners. I think it might do you both good."

Father Bernard was silent for a moment and then thoughtfully said, "There certainly has been a lot of history between Marguerite and I, and that scares me, too. I will think about your invitation. Please do not think me rude if I cannot give you an answer now."

Adele understood completely as she said, "You are welcome anytime. I do hope that you have the chance to talk with Marguerite before she reports for duty. It would be good to clear the air and get reacquainted. You will see that she has grown to be a capable, thoughtful young woman. She will be an amazing addition to your church mission."

Father Bernard was somewhat reticent as he said, "Marguerite was always a thoughtful person."

As Adele started to walk back to her cart, she handed Father Bernard a wedge of her famous cheese. He nodded and smiled as he accepted the gift.

Over the next day, Father Bernard thought about going to the LeBlanc farm to visit Marguerite. He knew in his heart that Adele was right. It would be wise to speak with Marguerite before they were expected to work together. As he thought about their prior relationship, the overwhelming memory was one of honesty. They had always been blatantly honest with each other. Honesty could be a good beginning as they forged ahead to a working relationship. With that thought in mind, Father Bernard made plans to visit the LeBlanc farm the next morning.

It was midmorning when Father Bernard arrived at the LeBlanc farm. The little boys raced out to meet him, followed by Adele, Gabriel, and finally Marguerite. After a brief exchange of pleasantries, Marguerite and Father Bernard strolled over to the pasture. Separated from the group, they awkwardly, and with much hesitancy, began to talk. Father Bernard could not help but notice how much Marguerite had changed. No longer an uncertain teenage girl, she was poised and confident, and she spoke with an ease that communicated her maturity. She was darkly beautiful in a very natural way, and Father Bernard could easily see that Marguerite was not the girl whom he had left at the convent over four years prior.

Father Bernard began by saying, "You look well, Marguerite."

She smiled weakly and acknowledged, "I'm much better than when you last saw me."

Father Bernard nodded and said, "I think we're both in better shape. We have been through a lot together, haven't we?"

Marguerite looked into his eyes and said, "I can never repay you for all that you have done for me. Honestly, I don't know what I would have done if I had not encountered you in that confessional. You listened to me without judging and you gave me sound advice."

He chuckled and said, "Advice you did not follow, as I remember it."

Marguerite smiled demurely and nodded as she responded, "You respected me, and ultimately supported me as I made my own decisions. I am so thankful. Honestly, you stood by me when I needed someone to believe in me."

Father Bernard spoke with some reluctance as he said, "To tell the truth, I have not felt good about my part in this deception."

Marguerite listened respectfully, and then responded, "There is no need for you to feel guilt. I feel that I made the right decision. Henri is thriving in my sister's loving family. He is part of a well-respected family, and no one in the community suspects that he is anything but the child of Adele and Gabriel. Yes, I have forfeited for his welfare, but I am gratified to see him happy and healthy. I have returned here to be part of his life, as a loving aunt."

The priest nodded, studying her intensely, as he asked, "Did you ever resolve the issues with your parents? The relationship was so broken."

"I feel tremendous guilt over how I treated my parents. I was so angry with them for essentially abandoning me, that I never spoke, or even wrote to them again. I heard through Adele, that they were pleased that I had left for the convent orphanage to have my illegitimate child, and that they were proud that I had decided to become a nun. Just hearing Adele speak of my parents' relief, regarding the solution to their embarrassing wayward daughter, made me, so very, very angry. Honestly, even after they died unexpectedly in the influenza outbreak, I still could not forgive them. I'm not proud of that. Surprisingly, they never seemed to put the pieces together, that Henri was really my child."

Father Bernard sensed the pain, the sincerity in her words. He responded, "You're only human, Marguerite. Forgiveness takes time and perspective, and it needs to come from the heart. I believe that you will get there…someday. For your own healing, I hope that you do forgive your parents."

Marguerite sighed, appreciating his words, as she said, "I believe my path to healing is through my relationship with my son. I need to be a part of Henri's life, to truly know him, and have him know me."

"I think it's going to be hard for you to live so close to Henri, and not have a larger role in his life. Being an aunt is not the same as being a parent."

Marguerite sighed, obviously uncomfortable, not expecting him to be so blunt. "I can make this work. You know I'm a strong person."

The priest smiled faintly, as the smallest inkling of their previous friendship, their previous honesty, resurfaced. "Yes, I have noticed that you're a strong person, and more than a little pig-headed."

"My pigheadedness may very well be my saving grace. I am determined to make this work, for my son's sake, and for my own. I want to be part of his life."

Father Bernard was suddenly taken by her beauty and her poise, but he pretended not to notice. Quietly, he looked at her, taking in the mature woman before him, as he responded in an equally direct manner, the authority of his position evident in his voice. "You are going to have to prove to me that you can make this work. As you well know, your presence here is complicated, and has the potential to stir up the past, a past that some would rather forget. Your return to Bayeux is going to put you face to face with Jacob Laurent. His restaurant is close to the church, and he regularly attends mass at the Bayeux Cathedral. Have you thought about how you are going to deal with seeing him almost daily?"

Marguerite was steadfast in her response. She said, "I have thought about Jacob…a lot. To tell the truth, I don't really care what he thinks of me. As soon as I told him that I was pregnant, he wanted nothing to do with me. I know for a fact that he did not tell his parents about the pregnancy. I'm quite certain that he believes that I left to have my child in a home for unwed mothers. As to his discomfort in being around me, I really don't care. I'm not trying to stir up trouble, and I'm not trying to seek vengeance. I only want to be near my son and be a part of his life. So, I will do whatever it takes to convince Jacob that I'm not here to stir up the past or cause him embarrassment. I feel confident that I can reassure him that I have returned to do the work of the church. I will make this work. Trust me."

Father Bernard was quiet for a long bit, looking at her, regrettably still feeling drawn to her, trying to take in what she had said. Inwardly he smiled, and marveled at how much she had changed, how confident she had become, how fearless. He admired this more mature version of the young woman who had previously driven him so perilously close to violating his vows, and he responded with his own brand of compassion and honesty, a touch of authority now evident in his voice. "I do trust you, and quite frankly, I always have. I think that's what drew me to you. In a different circumstance, I believe you and I could have had a future together. But we have both chosen a religious life, and we need to follow through on those commitments. I can't live with the torment of having you near, if we do not both agree here and now, that we can only be friends and coworkers. I will not allow you to stay if it is uncomfortable between us. Do you understand?"

Marguerite was a little taken aback by his bluntness. She responded with equal clarity, "I do understand. I promise, this will work."

There was a somberness in the air, a residual of the frank conversation, as Father Bernard and Marguerite walked back to his wagon.

Together they decided that Marguerite would start her work with the Bayeux parish the following week. Marguerite knew that she would have to redefine herself and prove beyond a doubt that she could be a valuable addition to the Bayeux parish, through her work in the community. She would make this work, for the sake of being close to her son.

CHAPTER 16

A Daunting Return to the Bayeux Cathedral

1901
Bayeux, France

Marguerite had risen early to make Henri's favorite breakfast. In anticipation of their aunt's last morning with them, Henri and Louis had been excused from their morning chores. They were jubilant. The little boys knew they would see Marguerite often, so there was no dread or sadness. They pulled on the skirt of her black nun's habit, as she playfully attempted to make pancakes in the shape of cows. Peals of laughter echoed through the kitchen as Henri and Louis examined the misshapen results.

Henri screeched with laughter as he proclaimed, "They look like cow poop!"

Marguerite pretended to be offended as she said, "I don't hardly think so. These are extremely hairy cows."

Louis chimed in, "No, they look like cow splats!"

Marguerite smiled and teasingly said, "Well, then I guess you won't want any of my pancakes? I'll probably just have to eat them all myself."

Henri immediately shouted his objection, "You can't eat all the pancakes! They're for all of us!"

Marguerite suddenly became tearful, as she leaned over and scooped Henri into her arms. She said, "I am going to miss you so much!"

Fresh strawberries and warm syrup had already been placed on the primitive harvest table, and it had the look and feel of a special goodbye breakfast. As Marguerite sat down with Adele, Gabriel, and the boys, she felt overwhelming gratitude. The opportunity to spend two weeks with Henri had been such a gift to her spirit. Yes, there was some sadness, but she had used every second of her time to build a relationship with Henri. The love and inclusiveness that she felt sitting at the table truly bolstered her resolve to make the transition back to her home community.

After breakfast, Gabriel insisted upon driving Marguerite to the church. The little boys shouted exuberant goodbyes as Marguerite and Gabriel started on their short journey. Once they were out of sight, Marguerite became visibly subdued, her shoulders slumping as she seemed to suddenly feel the weight of the task ahead of her, the controversies of her past still present. Gabriel sensed that she did not want to talk, and he respected her somber mood. For most of the journey, the clopping of horse hooves was the only sound that echoed through the tranquil morning. As the horse-drawn wagon pulled up in front of the Bayeux Cathedral, Gabriel broke the silence.

He smiled in a reassuring way as he said, "Marguerite, it's nice to have you back. Just remember, Adele and I are with you as you make this journey. You are not alone."

Marguerite smiled weakly and nodded before saying, "I appreciate your support, more than you know. Seeing and spending time with Henri has given me the strength to see this through. I really am determined to make this work."

Gabriel acknowledged, "Yes, for what it's worth, I think you've made the right decision."

With that, Marguerite nodded her appreciation of the words spoken, and jumped down from the wagon with her small bag of belongings and entered the church. She did not look back. Once inside the cathedral, she stopped to take in the beautiful morning light coming through the stained-glass windows. The colorful, muted light filtering into the majestic church had a way of calming her, centering her, as she stepped back into her life in Bayeux. She was a believer, a religious person, who had dedicated her life to God, but surprisingly she was not overly religious. She did not embrace the ritual, nor was she mesmerized by religious idols, but rather, she believed in the goodness of deeds, as the expression of her commitment to God. Briefly, she knelt in the dark recesses of the church to have a quiet conversation with God before approaching the door to Father Bernard's office. She could see light coming from under the door, and Marguerite could sense his presence. Hesitant, she stopped and took a deep breath before knocking on the door. The familiar voice called out, "Please come in."

As she entered the ancient, cluttered office, Father Bernard rose from his chair.

There was a moment of quiet contemplation as he extended a somewhat formal welcome, "Good morning, Marguerite. I hope that your time with your family has been restful and restorative."

Marguerite was humble, but confident, as she said, "It was wonderful to spend time with my family. Honestly, I could not have asked for a greater gift."

Father Bernard nodded soberly as he got right down to the business of explaining her new position. There was not a hint of their past relationship, just a straightforward discussion of the business of the parish. Marguerite was strangely comforted by the formality, and it seemed to smooth out the awkwardness that existed between them.

Father Bernard seamlessly began describing Marguerite's new assignment. "You will find your new role in the Bayeux parish a little unconventional. Although it is not obvious, there is a lot of suffering here. Our mission is to help those in need, and to ease their burden. I think you're going to find the work quite demanding."

Marguerite nodded her acknowledgment as she said, "I am not afraid of challenges, and I think you will quickly see that I am no stranger to work."

The priest smiled and said, "I am not worried about your work ethic. Any concerns I have relate to your past involvements in this community. But I would not have accepted you into this position if I thought you could not make peace with your past. I believe in you now, as I always have."

Marguerite breathed a sigh of relief, knowing that on some level she had his support. She responded, "I appreciate your confidence in me. I will make this work, and you will see that my past will not be a distraction."

"You will be directly accountable to me. Although the church does have a relationship with the Bayeux convent, they have taken a hands-off stance regarding my parish nuns. It may very well be a result of my insistence that I personally direct the efforts of my nuns. Anyway, I do believe I have frustrated the Mother Superior at the Bayeux convent. I think it would be safe to say that she is not accustomed to having her authority challenged. I suppose what I'm trying to say is that I will be the one who decides if you can stay in Bayeux. You will have to show me that you can navigate the issues related to your relationship with Jacob, and with me. I can't allow you to stay if you are not accepted as a competent, respected nun in this community. We'll be working closely together, so this must be a comfortable relationship."

Marguerite felt a queasiness sweep through her, as she nodded and quietly said, "I understand."

The priest looked concerned at the obvious fear on Marguerite's face. With a less stern voice, he went on to say, "I do want you to be successful in this quest, but I need you to understand that I will be honest in my assessment of you."

"I expect you to be honest. You will not regret my returning to Bayeux."

Abruptly, Father Bernard stood and began walking toward the door of the office, all the while talking.

He said, "Well, I think it is time to meet Sister Louise. She's a unique character, but she has been an amazing addition to our parish mission. I was somehow able to pry her from the clutches of the convent. She's friendly and compassionate, and totally committed to the needs of the people in this community. It has been invaluable to have a woman who will listen and support grieving widows, address the needs of the poor, and support unwed mothers." Father Bernard stopped, as he suddenly seemed a little uncomfortable.

Marguerite nodded as she said, "She sounds wonderful."

The priest chuckled as he responded, "She's a bit of character, and I mean that she's a good character. Like you, she's experienced some rough aspects of life. But I'm not here to tell her story. I will say, though, that she has earned the love and respect of this rather tough community."

Marguerite was intrigued as she commented, "She sounds interesting."

Father Bernard nodded as he went on to say, "She is certainly not boring. Louise is quite a joyful presence, not the typical dour, reserved nun. The same characteristics that draw the townspeople to her, made her a bit of an outcast in the convent. I like to think that I may have rescued her from that life."

Marguerite knowingly responded, "You do have a knack for rescuing young women in distress." As soon as the words left her mouth, Marguerite regretted them.

For a moment, there was awkward silence. Father Bernard looked briefly like he was going to respond to Marguerite's comment, but then he resumed his explanation of her role as a parish nun.

"The people in this community trust her and hold her in very high regard. The demands of the parish are hard for me to explain, but I believe that Sister Louise will capably train you in the needs of this ministry. Although you will be free from the regimen of convent life, I think you will find this role uniquely demanding. You will have a small, but adequate, apartment, so you will have more privacy than you have experienced in the convent. Sister Louise has enjoyed having private space, and I think you will, too. In addition, you'll have some free time on Sunday afternoons and evenings to spend as you please. I suspect you'll use this time to be with Henri."

Again, there was a brief, awkward silence, as the past between them exerted its undeniable presence. She responded with complete sincerity, "I cannot thank you enough."

Father Bernard nodded and said, "Like I said, Sister Louise has found the living arrangements and work schedule to her liking. It has been my experience that even nuns have to attend to their personal needs. Now, if you don't have any questions, I will introduce you to Sister Louise."

He quickly left the office, leading Marguerite down the steps to the basement of the church. Light was emanating from a room near the stairs, and faint humming could be heard. Sister Louise turned to greet the two, as they entered a room filled with piles of used clothing that the nun was folding and sorting according to size. She was a strikingly beautiful blonde woman with a deep, ragged scar that traversed her left cheek. It was hard not to stare at the disfigurement. The beautiful, scarred nun was a little older than Marguerite and had a noticeable positive energy about her. She immediately extended her hand in friendship and gave Sister Marguerite a genuine, welcoming smile. Father Bernard seemed relieved as he quickly excused himself and left the two nuns to get to know each other. Marguerite was immediately impressed with her mentor's warmth and exuberance. Louise made it clear that she was eager to have help with her extensive duties, but also there was the sense that she welcomed the camaraderie of a fellow nun.

Sister Louise's energy was infectious as she spoke. "I think you'll find this assignment quite different from life in the convent. For me, I have found it far more demanding, but also liberating. Father Bernard has given me a lot of freedom in my schedule to do my work in the parish. To tell the truth, I feel blessed to have been chosen for this role. I can honestly say, I love my work here." Sister Louise explained that they were currently in the church donation room. The room was filled with clothing of all sizes for men, women, and children. Although there were a few pieces of relatively new clothing, most of the garments were quite worn. The two young nuns sorted and folded clothing as they talked. Louise explained that the donation center was open to the parishioners every Thursday morning. It was a valuable, practical resource for the community. She sighed as she further explained that some of the most impoverished people were reluctant to take charity. But then she admitted that she had ways of slipping needed clothing to families, and especially children, in a manner that did not offend. Marguerite was quickly coming to the realization that she liked this young nun.

Sister Louise went on to explain that the nuns were also expected to work with the children's choir. She smirked as she said, "It's a lot like herding cats. I admit that I'm not very musical, and I struggle with corralling the little demons. Honestly, I don't think Father Bernard could have found a less qualified children's choir director."

Marguerite chuckled. She was not used to such candor in a fellow nun, and it felt refreshing. She quickly offered, "I have a fair amount of experience with children, and I have assisted with a children's choir in the past. I love music, and I love most children."

They laughed in mutual understanding. Sister Louise seemed pleased that her counterpart was confident in her ability to help. It was a pleasant discovery and a huge relief.

Sister Louise sighed and said, "The thing that I find most gratifying is working with women in need. It has been my experience that women are more comfortable approaching a nun when they are confronted with a crisis. In my time here, I have given comfort to and helped individuals with abusive husbands, unexpected pregnancies, and devastating illness and death. I don't want you to think that I only work with women, but I have to say I believe it is my gift. For whatever reason, I think people trust me with their problems, and I have developed a reputation for maintaining that trust. In my mind, there is no room for judgment, or cruel discrimination, of these poor, tormented souls."

Marguerite felt like this young nun was speaking to her soul as she responded, "Well spoken."

Sister Louise was candidly honest as she went on to exclaim, "In looking at me, it must be apparent that I have had my own colorful past. I don't deny it. I have been shunned and judged in the cruelest manner, and I will not inflict pain, nor judgment, on another living soul. My entry into the convent is an unconventional story, and I may share it with you someday, but not today."

Marguerite quietly marveled at Louise's blatant honesty. Although they had just met, she already felt a bond forming between them.

Marguerite responded, "I am very much looking forward to working with you, and you are not the only one with an interesting life story." Although Marguerite was favorably impressed with Sister Louise, she was not yet ready to share her own life story.

Next, Sister Louise led Marguerite to her new apartment. It was located right next to the church and was a small, but adequate, one room affair. A wood-burning stove was putting forth wonderful heat. The room was simply furnished with a small, primitive, wooden table and two chairs, along with a simple bed nestled in the corner of the room. Spotlessly clean, the cozy little apartment was adorned with a vase of dried flowers. However, the most beautiful thing about the room was the large window. With the brightly colored blue curtains pulled back, the morning light streamed into the room, and it gave a warmth and brightness to the tiny apartment. Marguerite was impressed and touched by the care and thoughtfulness that was evident in the room's preparation.

Almost at a loss for words, Marguerite tearfully said, "It is a beautiful apartment. Thank you."

Louise smiled and said, "I'm glad that you like it. I have found the privacy of my own personal apartment to be so restorative to my spirit. I love to read, and it is heavenly to have a quiet, beautiful space in which to do so. But you need to know that occasionally, those in need, sometimes women in danger, will seek you out in the dark of night, hidden away from prying eyes. They will knock on your apartment door, as though it is the only refuge in the darkness. It does not happen often, but I do make my best effort to help those in distress, no matter what the hour."

Marguerite suddenly knew why Father Bernard had chosen Sister Louise. She said, "I hope to live up to your standards."

Sister Louise nodded, as she said, "I have heard only good things about you from Father Bernard and through the convent. I understand that you are originally from the Bayeux community, which will be a challenge. People will have impressions of you as a child or possibly a teenager that they may hang on to, somehow overlooking that you are now a grown woman. You will have to prove yourself in this role."

Marguerite nodded her understanding. Silently, she thought that her presence in Bayeux was far more complicated than this young nun could ever imagine.

Sister Louise went on, "Father Bernard allows almost complete freedom to address parish needs without the constraints of a strict schedule. Your prayer time is your own. Every Sunday after morning mass is your personal time to spend as you see fit. One more thing… Father Bernard is quite an effective administrator, and you will find him to be very supportive. You can tell him anything. I have found him to be a trusted friend and confidante."

Marguerite nodded knowingly, as she realized that she had nothing that she wanted to add to this assessment. As the two nuns left Marguerite's apartment and stepped into the street, Louise indicated that her apartment was next to Marguerite's. They had just started down the street when a well-dressed young man briskly walked past them, in an obvious hurry.

Sister Louise cheerfully called out, "Good morning, Mr. Laurent!"

He turned to respond to the greeting, and suddenly stopped in his tracks, momentarily dumbstruck. Both Jacob and Marguerite stared awkwardly at each other.

Jacob seemed stricken as he looked directly at Marguerite and accusingly blurted out, "What are you doing here?"

Marguerite bristled, her anger suddenly present, as she was equally direct in her response. "I live and work here in Bayeux," she said. In her mind, she had thought that she no longer had any feelings for this man who had fathered her child and summarily abandoned her as a frightened teenager. It was not true. She hated this man, with a ferocity that frightened her.

Jacob looked flustered and obviously wanted to say more, but he felt embarrassed to have such an interaction in front of Sister Louise. He nodded and mumbled, "Oh…have a good day, Sister Louise." Abruptly, he turned and hurriedly walked away, escaping down the street.

Marguerite appeared wounded by the interaction and was clearly taken aback.

Louise was concerned as she quizzically looked at her fellow nun and said, "Are you okay?"

Marguerite nodded and numbly said, "I'm fine."

Sister Louise was puzzled by the depth of emotion, and blatant uneasiness between Jacob and Marguerite. She quietly commented, "I thought I was the only interesting nun with a past."

Marguerite looked embarrassed, and smiled weakly as she said, "Trust me. You are not the only one."

Louise returned the smile and said, "That's good to know. Well, I'm a very good listener, if you need to talk. And you can rest assured that I don't tell secrets. You can trust me."

Marguerite felt a small sense of relief. She nodded and felt that maybe she had found a friend. There was a true sense of appreciation as she said, "Thank you. I'll keep that it in mind."

As Jacob scurried down the street, he abruptly turned and slipped into the Bayeux Cathedral. He was not thinking clearly as he marched into Father Bernard's office with an entitled sense of purpose. The priest was inwardly startled by Jacob's sudden appearance, but he managed to portray an aura of detached calmness to his uninvited guest.

Father Bernard greeted Jacob with a certain pastoral formality when he said, "Good morning, Jacob. What can I do for you?"

Jacob was direct in his answer. "I would like to talk with you about your newest nun."

The priest responded, "Yes, Marguerite has recently joined our parish mission. We are very fortunate to have her. She has come to us with the highest recommendations."

Jacob blurted out, "She cannot stay here."

Father Bernard feigned surprise. He knew the character of this young man, and Jacob's behavior was not unexpected. The priest respectfully probed, "I'm curious as to why you think Marguerite should not stay here?"

Jacob responded with an indignant sense of entitlement. "Marguerite is a poor fit to work in the Bayeux community. There are many qualified nuns in the convent that would better serve your purposes. As you are aware, my family gives generously to your church."

Father Bernard was repulsed, as inwardly his anger and disgust threatened to erupt, but he maintained his composure. He responded with a sense of authority, "We are, of course, appreciative of your family's generosity. However, I disagree with your assessment that Marguerite is a poor choice for this assignment. I chose her. She came here with the highest recommendation from a trusted colleague."

Jacob renewed his assertion with even more force, "She cannot stay here. My family will not allow it."

Father Bernard responded, "Jacob, I know why you personally object to Marguerite's presence in Bayeux. She has told me about your youthful love affair, and that she left Bayeux years ago, to have your child."

Jacob was suddenly ashen and could not bring himself to speak.

Father Bernard went on, "Marguerite is not here to stir up the past. She is here at my request to work in the Bayeux parish. I can reassure you that she has no intention to reveal any embarrassing aspects of your adolescent relationship. It would not be good for either of you. Your secret is safe with me, and with Marguerite."

Jacob was angrily indignant, his emotions, his fears, on full display, as he confronted Father Bernard. "I will not allow you to ruin my life! Marguerite cannot stay here. I will not allow it!"

His anger, no longer concealed, Father Bernard responded forcefully with an air of authority. "It is not your decision to make."

Jacob quickly blurted out, "I will go to the Bayeux convent and speak with the Mother Superior about this matter."

Father Bernard looked menacingly at Jacob as he said, "If you decide to speak with the Mother Superior, I will have no choice but to divulge the circumstances of your past relationship with Marguerite. As you well know, there are very few secrets in the Bayeux convent. Your parents, and your wife, would be very disappointed."

Jacob looked at Father Bernard like he had been outwitted. He shook his head in obvious confusion and defeat as he said, "How do I know that you and Marguerite will keep this secret?"

With total sincerity, Father Bernard said, "I give you...my word. Marguerite and I have spoken of this, and her return to Bayeux was contingent upon her discretion regarding this matter. She does not want to disrupt your life. I swear on my Bible that I am telling you the truth."

Jacob looked deflated as he came to the realization that he had no say in the matter. Reluctantly, he made anguished eye contact with the priest, and gave a subtle nod as he stormed out of the office.

Father Bernard took a deep breath and reflected on the encounter with Jacob. It had come more quickly than he had anticipated, but he felt satisfied in his steady defense of Marguerite and certain that he had not allowed this young man who had caused Marguerite incalculable pain, to inflict even more. It was not justice, but it was a small step in that direction.

The two nuns entered the church shortly after the explosive interaction between the priest and Jacob. Father Bernard greeted them and asked to speak with Marguerite alone. Again, Sister Louise had the sense that this newest nun came with a certain amount of intrigue. She smiled at the thought that, for once, she may not be the most scandalous nun in the religious order. Sister Louise quietly left the priest and the young nun alone to talk privately.

Father Bernard spoke first, "Jacob just left here."

Marguerite nodded and said, "It didn't take long for him to object to my presence."

"No, he wasted no time in registering his objection to your assignment with the parish."

Marguerite looked stricken as she weakly said, "I just encountered him on the street. He was furious and demanded to know what I was doing here. I'm sure he would have said much more, had I not been with Sister Louise."

Father Bernard acknowledged that Jacob was indeed angry. He went on to say, "He was insistent that you not, be allowed to stay in Bayeux. He reminded me how his family gives generously to the church. He is such a pompous ass. I have watched Jacob over the last few years, as he has gone blithely about his privileged life, while you have struggled greatly with all the repercussions of your involvement with him."

Marguerite was taken aback by his honesty and said, "I do not expect you to protect me. I am accountable for my life, as I have lived it."

Father Bernard quickly responded, "I too, am accountable for my decisions, and I have chosen to not let Jacob wreak any more havoc on your life. He suggested that he might talk with the Mother Superior to have you replaced by another nun from the Bayeux convent. I informed him that if he followed through on this threat, I would have no choice but to share information about his past relationship with you, and that there were very few secrets in Bayeux. He stormed out of my office."

Marguerite looked dismayed as she apologetically said, "I am so sorry that you have been thrown into this."

Father Bernard waved off her apology and said, "Jacob desperately wants to keep the secret of your pregnancy hidden from his wife, parents, and the town of Bayeux. He won't risk his reputation."

Marguerite agreed. She said, "I believe you are right. But it's going to be uncomfortable for both of us. He desperately wants me to disappear."

The priest reassured her, "You are not going anywhere. Jacob will need to come to terms with the demons of his past. I will not allow him to bully you, or me. He is a despicable person. Of course, you and I will have to learn to coexist peacefully with him, or this controversy will damage us both."

Marguerite nodded and said, "I will quietly meet with him and reassure him that I mean him no harm, and that the past will remain in the past. I can make this work. He sees me as insignificant. With time, I will become just a part of the Bayeux scenery."

The priest reluctantly agreed. "I think you are correct, but I fear that both of us will struggle as we live in such close proximity to this poor excuse of a man."

Marguerite reassured him as she spoke, "I will not let him separate me from my son. I have no interest in purposely dredging up the past."

"Yes, retribution will not serve any purpose, but I will not sit quietly by while Jacob continues to cause you pain. You deserve the freedom to pursue your religious mission here, and to reestablish your connection with Henri."

Marguerite was somehow soothed by his confidence in her, and deeply appreciative of the support. They both had been tested, and were still standing, in the wake of a considerable storm. The path was being strategically and painfully laid for Marguerite's reentry into Bayeux.

Early the next morning, as Marguerite was leaving her apartment, she turned to close her heavy apartment door. Suddenly, she could feel a menacing presence lingering in the shadows of the dawn light. Abruptly, she spun around to face the threat, and was confronted with Jacob standing steadfastly before her, his arms crossed, his facial expression angry and accusing. The streets of Bayeux were eerily deserted, and Marguerite felt unexpectantly vulnerable. She was startled by his presence, but she breathed deeply and tried to convey an aura of calmness.

He did not greet her, but rather launched into an impassioned plea, "You cannot stay here in Bayeux. I'm sure that the Mother Superior would welcome you into the convent community."

Marguerite was instantly angry and fought to control her reaction to Jacob. Summoning a sense of self-control, she did not feel, she calmly responded, "Jacob, I know that you find my presence here uncomfortable. I have no intention to bring up our past. It would serve no purpose to either you, or me. Trust me."

Jacob appeared undeterred as he implored, "I have a wife and a child now. My family and restaurant business cannot fall prey to the stories of our past."

Marguerite shook with rage at his arrogance. "I have lived those stories of our past! You abandoned me and our child, so do not speak to me of inconvenience!"

Jacob was visibly angered and grabbed her roughly by both shoulders and violently shook her as he shouted, "How dare you threaten me!"

Marguerite felt an overwhelming desire to strike him, as she barely managed to shake free of his grip, and forcefully state, "I fully intend to stay and work in Bayeux. I have no intention to threaten your reputation in this community. I promise you, the past will remain the past, if you treat me with the respect I deserve. So, let's move forward, and act like responsible adults."

Jacob calmed a little as he asked, "What happened to the child?"

Marguerite's heart raced as she fought to be convincing, "The child is lost to me. I have spent the last four and a half years working in a convent. My life is dedicated to God, and I will spend the rest of my days devoted to this religious mission. You should not fear my presence in Bayeux. I will cause no harm to your reputation."

Jacob seemed to reluctantly acknowledge that she might possibly be speaking the truth. He quietly commented, "I think it will be uncomfortable to have you in Bayeux"

Marguerite feigned a weak smile as she said, "Initially maybe, but we will learn to share this place. It will be fine. Our lives intercepted briefly when we were children, but we are adults now. I have every intention to respect your life and your family, and I expect you to do the same for me."

Jacob reluctantly nodded and said, "Maybe you're right. We were children when our lives crossed paths, and now we are adults. The past does not need to resurface. It serves no purpose to either of us."

Marguerite took a deep breath and told Jacob, "I assure you...I have no rational reason to revisit the past between us. It would only cause pain and destruction to us both. Believe me when I say, I wish you no harm. Trust me."

Jacob finally appeared to absorb that her words might be truthful. He nodded and said, "Okay, Marguerite, I must agree that neither of us would benefit from revealing our past relationship. It is not my purpose to hurt you, but you can certainly understand my position."

Marguerite silently fumed, her eyes intense, as she tried to sound convincing. "I do understand your position. We can respectfully live in this community together. Agreed?"

Silently, Jacob was impressed by Marguerite's confidence and maturity. She clearly was not the same girl he had known years before. Jacob thought for a second, and then reluctantly said, "I agree." Hesitantly, he turned, and slowly began walking toward his restaurant, mentally trying to process the interaction. Marguerite sighed and had the first semblance of a feeling, that she could reconcile the past and move forward to the future that she wanted to live. It was a small victory, a beginning.

CHAPTER 17

Sisterhood

1901
Bayeux, France

L ouise was walking past her apartment window, suddenly jolted from her sleepiness by the drama unfolding in the street outside. She was transfixed, as she watched Jacob angrily shaking Marguerite in an obviously tense confrontation. Momentarily frozen, she watched, then scrambled toward the door, flinging it open. Racing forward, Louise suddenly stopped, bewildered, as Jacob and Marguerite appeared engrossed in a heated discussion. The flash of conflict between the two seemed to dissipate as quickly as it erupted. After a momentary pause in the exchange between the two former lovers, Jacob hesitantly turned from Marguerite, the anger so visible only moments before, seemingly resolved, or, at the very least, dampened, as he slowly walked away, his eyes cast downward as though he were deep in some troubling thought. Marguerite was pale and shaking when Louise reached her. Although the two women did not know each other well, they instinctively fell together in an embrace of comfort and support.

Louise frantically asked, "Are you alright?"

Marguerite was too choked with emotion to respond. Gulping air, and trying to compose herself, she nodded.

"I'm worried that you are in danger here. What is going on between you and Jacob?"

"I'm not in danger."

"I know what I saw. Jacob was shaking you, clearly threatening you. He looks like he is quite capable of hurting you."

Marguerite responded with as much calm as she could muster. "I know it looks bad. But honestly, Jacob and I have come to an agreement."

Louise looked at her fellow nun intensely, studying her, trying to absorb her words and make sense of the situation. Silently, with the aid of her sixth sense, she was putting the pieces together. In a reassuring voice, she said, "Believe me when I say…you can tell me anything. You can trust me. I will not judge you or run to the Mother Superior with stories. I never betray a confidence. There is nothing that you can tell me, that I will find shocking."

Marguerite was touched, and truly appreciative of the colorful honesty in this unusual nun. She responded, forcing herself to sound calmer, and more controlled than she felt, "I really do value your support and understanding, more than you know. Maybe someday I will tell you the story between Jacob and I, but I cannot tell you now."

Sister Louise looked worried as she said, "You should not carry this burden alone."

"I'm not carrying it alone. I know it looks otherwise, but Jacob and I have come to an agreement that we can coexist peacefully in the same village."

Sister Louise gave Marguerite a questioning look, as she asked, "Does Father Bernard know your history with Jacob?"

Marguerite nodded as she said, "He knows everything."

Sister Louise wasn't completely surprised, as she had sensed that there was something mysterious about the relationship between this newest nun and the priest. "I'm glad that you have Father Bernard's wise counsel in this matter. Please know, I am here too. You can talk with me anytime, about anything."

Sister Louise sensed that they had both said what they needed to say, and that Marguerite did not want to talk any more about the situation. There was a brief, awkward silence between them as she began ushering Marguerite toward the church, so that they could prepare for the children's choir practice.

Sister Louise chuckled and said, "Okay, now, you're about to meet the true demons of the parish." The tension seemed to lift as they both laughed with relief.

As the two nuns entered the church, a chaotic group of noisy children was gathering near the organ. The organist seemed genuinely annoyed and shouted out for the children to be quiet. Marguerite smiled as she approached the group. The children were scattered in age from approximately eight to fourteen years, and their clothing and manner of dress was as varied as their ages. There were a few children dressed in clean, well-pressed, stylish attire, but the majority wore a conglomeration of mismatched and rugged, patched clothing. It was a blunt visual reminder to Marguerite that there were distinctly different social classes in Bayeux, and she instantly saw the need for the clothing bank. Although she had grown up in the Bayeux community, she felt like she was seeing it for the first time, and it was sobering to see the disparity.

Sister Louise wasted no time in introducing Marguerite to the youngsters, and to the organist. Children and music had always brought Marguerite peace and happiness, and the children seemed to sense her pleasure, instinctively liking her, and miraculously quieting down to listen to her instructions. Marguerite began by leading the group, singing a silly children's song, trying all the while to get a sense of the voices in the choir. Then she called out individuals to sing a line, or two, of the well-known song. Most of the children seemed embarrassed to sing solo, and there was some awkward tittering when a couple of the less talented children sang. Marguerite was positive and encouraging. She reassured them that their voices melded together beautifully, and they had all the makings of fabulous choir. Marguerite went on to explain that choirs were the blending of a wide range of voices, and that their group had a beautiful range.

Marguerite's brief exploration of the talent in her choir had brought to her attention two clear, beautiful voices. One of these talented children was a young teenage girl named Marie. Approximately fourteen years old, she was thin, with beautiful porcelain skin and curly blonde hair. Marie was painfully shy, and obviously poor, wearing clothing that was patched, and several sizes too big, making her look waif-like. The strength and clarity of Marie's voice was a stark contrast to her physical appearance. Marguerite was intrigued and excited to have the opportunity to work with this young girl. Ethan was the other child whom Marguerite had identified as having an exceptionally beautiful voice. Well-dressed, with shiny new shoes, the eight-year-old boy looked to have come from a wealthy family. He was confident to the point of cockiness. Clearly, he enjoyed singing in the choir, and he eagerly quieted down to hear Marguerite's instructions. Her initial encounter with the children's choir left Marguerite excited and hopeful, as she eagerly anticipated putting together musical programs to showcase their talent.

Father Bernard watched the choir practice from the back of the church. He was impressed with Marguerite's ability to corral the children's energy. She clearly enjoyed the role, and it was having quite an effect on the choir, even though she had just begun. Father Bernard smiled to himself, a reassuring feeling suddenly washing over him, as he thought that maybe the pieces of Marguerite's transition to Bayeux were coming together.

As the children finished their choir practice, Marguerite again ended by having them all sing a playful children's song. They sang lustily and seemed to enjoy the chance to be silly. It was a clear signal that there had been a significant change in the nature of the children's choir. The sudden infusion of energy and fun with the arrival of Sister Marguerite was like a breath of fresh air to the children, and to the organist. As the children filed out of the church, Marguerite reminded them of their next practice. Quietly, she was already making plans for adding a few solos to the music program. Music had always been a refuge for her. It stilled her worries and lifted her spirits, taking her to places that calmed her heart. She hoped to instill her love of music into the children.

Sister Louise was thrilled that her new counterpart seemed to have a natural affinity for working with children, as it had been her own biggest weakness. She hugged Marguerite, effusively complimenting her, exclaiming her wonder at Marguerite's patience and skill as a choir director. Marguerite was pleased to receive the positive feedback. Frankly, she was unaccustomed to the warmth and generosity of spirit she was finding in Sister Louise, as she had not usually found it in her fellow nuns.

CHAPTER 18

Night Terror

1901
Bayeux, France

Through the fogginess of deep sleep, Louise heard desperate knocking, and it sent her heart racing, her consciousness erupting into a suddenly fearful state of instinctive survival. At first, she thought it was just another nightmare that had returned to haunt her. Her heart pounded, and a clamminess swept over her body, making her feel suddenly cold, as she fought to suppress the images that were racing through her mind. But then she heard the muffled sobs, and she knew that it was real. Mentally, she tried to calm herself, and control the sense of foreboding that was quickly enveloping her. Slowly, purposefully, she climbed out of bed. Her loose nightgown hung limply on her fearful body, as she guardedly walked to the door. Taking a deep breath, she opened the heavy wooden door, just a crack.

In the light of the full moon, she immediately recognized the swollen, bloody face of the woman standing before her. In obvious pain, Emma reached out to Louise. Instinctively, defiantly, the young nun stepped into the street to steady the injured woman. Louise was suddenly alert, in survival mode, as she visually scanned the streets of Bayeux for a pursuer before pulling Emma into her apartment. She carefully supported and half carried the seriously injured woman to her bed. With a gentleness that spoke much of her compassion, Louise lowered Emma onto the bed. Then she rushed to the door, and abruptly bolted the lock with a loud metallic snap. Falling backwards against the thick wooden door, Louise gasped as she tried to take in the scene before her.

Through hysterical, pain-racked sobs, Emma cried, "He's going to kill me! Please! Help me!"

Moving forward to calm Emma, Louise firmly held her hand as she said, "I will not let him hurt you again. You're safe here." But, in her mind, the nun knew it was not true.

Emma recognized the lie, and she responded with slow, pain-filled, halting words. "You're...wrong. He'll...come looking...for me here. He...warned me....to stay far away...from you."

Louise nodded, before responding with as much reassurance as she could muster. "You're right. We need to find a safe place for you. But first I need to tend to your wounds."

After closing the curtains, Louise lit a candle, and slowly cast the light around the woman to assess her injuries. She took in a worried breath, as she steadied the lighted candle in front of Emma's face. There was a deep gash above her left eye. Steadily, bright red blood was streaming down into her swollen eye, and then spilling down onto her already blood-soaked gown. It was a grotesque scene, and, for a moment, Louise felt faint. Then, taking a deep breath, she mustered her resolve, and reached for a clean towel as she applied steady pressure to the wound. It obviously caused Emma pain, but she did not complain. After about ten minutes of steady pressure, Louise lifted the bloody towel and examined the wound. The bleeding had slowed to a trickle. Carefully, the nun pulled the gash apart to assess it depth, and she discovered bone.

Alarmed, but trying to project a sense of confidence, Louise said, "Well, it looks like we'll need to get the doctor to sew you up."

"No!"

"Your wound is right down to the bone. It needs to be sewn back together."

Gasping in panic, Emma implored Louise to not take her elsewhere. Her words were halting, as she spoke guardedly through the pain, "He'll find me…if you go to…the doctor. There are no secrets… here. You have…to sew me up."

"I've never done anything like this. Honestly, it would be safer with the doctor."

"No…I will be safer with you."

Louise studied Emma's fearful face, and then reluctantly went to get her sewing kit. She approached the task tentatively. There was a part of her that wanted to feign confidence, but she could not fully convince herself. With her needle threaded, her hand hesitantly hovered above the deep, jagged wound.

Finally, Emma said, "Just do it."

Squeamish, Louise poked the needle into the battered skin. She felt the resistance as she dug deep, and then pulled the thread up. Surprisingly, there was very little bleeding. Emma was totally quiet, and she lay perfectly still, which encouraged Louise to proceed. With each successive stitch, she became more confident. Quickly, she developed a rhythm, and the stitches became more uniform. When the cavernous wound was completed closed, she stood back and examined her handiwork, feeling a strange sense of pride.

Louise quietly proclaimed, "Well, I've done it. I think…it looks pretty good."

"Thank you."

There was palpable relief in the air as the two women quietly took a moment to ponder the situation. Finally, Louise said, "It's not safe for you here. I know you don't want to involve anyone else, but I can't protect you by myself. Your husband will be here soon, and neither one of us will be safe. I need to go get help."

Once again panicked, Emma moaned, "No!"

"Trust me. I will keep you safe, but I need to get help from Sister Marguerite and Father Bernard. They will not betray you…I promise."

Looking helpless, and feeling as though she had no other options, Emma reluctantly nodded. Louise wasted no time. She slipped out of the apartment and hurried to Marguerite's apartment next door.

Marguerite was abruptly jolted awake by the urgent knocking. Momentarily disoriented, she immediately sensed that something was terribly wrong. Trying to shake her sleepiness, she hurried out of bed. Stopping for a moment, she purposely took a deep breath, before cautiously opening the door. The full moon clearly illuminated her friend standing in a blood-soaked nightgown, looking fearful and distraught. Marguerite gasped as she took in the vision before her. Frantically, Louise held her finger to her lips, indicating that they needed to be quiet. Marguerite instinctively heeded her silent instruction, as she visually scanned the cobblestone street for imminent danger.

Marguerite followed Louise into the candle-lit apartment and was horrified by the scene before her. There was a trail of blood leading to a badly bruised and bloodied woman who was lying in Louise's bed. The woman looked vaguely familiar, despite her grotesquely bloody appearance. Then she realized that it was Emma, the butcher's wife. It had been rumored for years that the local butcher regularly drank to excess and beat his poor, docile wife.

Quickly putting together in her mind, the situation before her, Marguerite spoke to the injured woman. "Did your husband do this to you?"

Looking at Marguerite through the one eye that was not swollen shut, Emma responded through soft sobs, "Yes…he's going to kill me."

Marguerite responded, "No, he's not going to kill you. We are going to protect you."

Emma was despondent, as she answered, "You can't protect me… from him."

Marguerite was determined, as she defiantly reassured Emma, "I promise you…we can, and we will, protect you."

Marguerite turned to confer with Louise, and was startled to see her previously confident friend, staring blankly at the floor, pale and visibly shaking. Marguerite stepped forward, not sure how to comfort her trembling friend. Awkwardly she hugged Louise, trying to infuse some strength, some calm into the obviously unnerved fellow nun. Attempting to sound steady, Marguerite softly said in a comforting voice, "I'm going to get Father Bernard. I will be right back."

Without further explanation, she slipped out the door and ran to the priest's nearby apartment, her panic rising as her mind wildly tried to process the scene she had just witnessed. The urgency of her knocks on the ancient wooden door had an agitated quality, rhythmic but chaotic. After what seemed like an eternity, the door opened to reveal a mostly undressed Father Bernard. Stepping into the moonlit doorway, the priest wore only hastily donned trousers, still unbuttoned at the waist. Marguerite was taken aback by his state of undress, and she couldn't take her eyes away from his nakedness. His broad shoulders only served to emphasize his muscled chest and flat abdomen. He was beautiful in a truly masculine way, and she was instinctively drawn to him.

Father Bernard could see that Marguerite was frightened and upset, and he instinctively, protectively, rushed forward to comfort her. All aspects of their previous agreement to keep their personal interactions dispassionate and professional, were suddenly forgotten. Briefly, they embraced. The priest and the nun, both felt the electricity between them, and they quickly, and purposefully, pushed away from each other. Father Bernard turned away from her, his face hidden, as he fumbled to pull on a loose cotton shirt, buttoning it as they headed to the door. Marguerite spilled out the events of night, the panic in her voice, escalating the sense of crisis, as she tried to prepare the priest for what he was about to encounter.

As the priest rushed through the doorway, he was aghast at the bloody scene before him. He instantly knew what had happened to Emma, and rage began to overtake him. Father Bernard knew the people in his village well. He knew their strengths, their weaknesses, their kindness, and their capacity for evil. He silently vowed that he would not let this injustice go unpunished. He was not a perfect priest, but he was a man who believed in justice.

With a quiet resolve, he purposefully walked to Emma's side and said, "You don't need to be afraid. We will take care of you. But first we must find a safe place for you to heal and recover."

Emma was comforted by the priest's take-charge manner, but she still had her doubts. Shakily, she told him, "He'll find me."

"No, I believe we can find a safe place outside of town for you to recover."

Louise suddenly seemed to have pulled herself back together, as she suggested, "Mrs. Durand would help Emma. She's such an amazing healer."

The priest was thoughtful as he responded, "Normally, I would agree with you, but her husband just died a month ago."

Marguerite listened with heightened interest, as they spoke about the woman who had most certainly saved her life, and the life of her son, when she was in labor with Henri. The past was everywhere in Bayeux, and she shuddered.

Almost without thinking, Marguerite said, "I know that her husband just died, but Mrs. Durand would want to help. I do believe that Emma would get the best care and be safe there."

Louise, looking and acting more like her previous confident self, chimed in, "I visited with her last week, and she is lonely, and grieving, but she is still the same strong woman."

"Well, if you are both pretty sure that she's up to the challenge, then I agree she would do an excellent job of caring for Emma. Her farm is out of the way, too. But we had better get going while it's still dark. I don't want anyone to see us leaving Bayeux with Emma."

Louise agreed, "Yes, we need to get going. I fear that Emma's husband will be sobering up soon, and he'll come looking for her here, for sure."

The injured woman said nothing as the three rescuers nodded in agreement, and then quickly dispersed to get dressed and assemble the horse and wagon for the trip. When they returned, the trio furiously worked together to gather some supplies, and make a bed in the back of the wagon. Father Bernard gently scooped Emma into his arms and placed her on the blankets. Emma winced in pain, as she fearfully searched the street for signs of her tormentor. The sound of the horse hooves echoing off the cobblestones seemed deafening to the anxious travelers, as they made their way through the streets of Bayeux. Pensively, they held their breath, hoping and praying that their escape would go unnoticed. Once they cleared the town, the wary group visibly relaxed. There was a palpable sense of urgency as Father Bernard pushed the team of horses swiftly onward toward the Durand farm.

The normally friendly collie barked loudly, as they pulled down the farm lane. A full moon brightly illuminated the bucolic scene before them. Emerging from the ancient farmhouse, they saw the silhouette of an older woman in a nightgown. As they drew nearer, Mrs. Durand stepped confidently forward and greeted her nighttime visitors. Over the years, the woman had been awakened countless times, to assist with a difficult childbirth or other medical issue. She had always given her assistance willingly, no matter what the hour. It was her nature, her gift.

The old woman looked sturdy, and alert, even in the moonlight. She stepped even closer and instantly recognized the occupants of the wagon. With a sense of calm, she said, "Well, what brings this group of my favorite people to me in the middle of the night?"

Louise jumped down from the wagon and hugged the old woman. They were obviously more than just friends. Mrs. Durand returned the embrace, and said, "Oh my, you're shaking."

Father Bernard seemed to understand the scene before him as he said, "I apologize for our midnight visit. I know you're suffering from the recent loss of your husband, and I am hesitant to ask this favor of you."

The old woman responded, "I do miss my husband, but I was fortunate enough to have been married to a good man for forty-five years. So, I suppose, I was one of the lucky ones. But that's not why you're here at this hour of the night, is it?"

"No, we need your healing hands. Our friend, Emma, has been badly beaten by her husband, and she needs your help, if you're able."

Mrs. Durand smiled slightly as she said, "I am old, but I'm still fairly able."

The priest chuckled slightly. "I wasn't implying that you weren't able. You obviously don't suffer from ineptitude. But...I have to say that there is a certain amount of danger in taking care of Emma in your home. Although it seems unlikely, her husband could find her here, and he is a dangerous man."

Mrs. Durand was characteristically her old self as she said, "I'm too old to die young, and I don't have any tolerance for violence against women. It would be an honor to help Emma. She is more than welcome to stay here."

"You are a special one," Father Bernard said.

"Well, why don't you carry Emma in, and I'll have you put her in the bedroom downstairs."

Carefully, he lifted Emma from the wagon and followed the old woman into the house. Once Emma was settled into the bed, Mrs. Durand began to assess her wounds. Then she turned and said, "I think I can handle it from here. I suppose you had better get back to Bayeux before the sun comes up, or this won't be a secret for long."

Father Bernard nodded reluctantly to the wise old woman as he said, "Yes, we do need to get back under the cover of night. Are you sure you're fine with taking care of Emma by yourself?"

"Yes, I think we'll manage just fine."

"Thank you again. We will check on you tomorrow."

Mrs. Durand was confident as she responded, "I'll take good care of her."

As they started to walk toward the door, Marguerite meekly said, "Thank you for all that you do."

The old woman looked knowingly at the young nun and said, "You're welcome. And Marguerite, I'm glad that you are looking well."

As Marguerite purposely fell behind the group, she whispered, "I never got a chance to thank you for saving my life, and for saving my baby. You were an angel. I can never thank you enough."

The old woman whispered back, "Just seeing you vital and healthy is payment enough. And I have enjoyed watching your son grow. He's a beautiful boy."

Marguerite was shaken by the revelation that Mrs. Durand knew of Henri's identity. She was an astute woman, so of course she knew.

The old woman squeezed Marguerite's hand as she whispered, "I'm not in the business of telling secrets. I want only the best for you and your son."

Marguerite nodded as she said, "I'll be out to check on you."

There was very little conversation, as the priest hurriedly pushed the horses to return to Bayeux. Even in the dark of night, the priest was acutely aware of Louise's fragility, of the wound that had been reopened. He could not talk of it, or risk betraying a confidence in Marguerite's presence, but it was undeniably there as they traveled back to town.

Finally, he said as they reentered Bayeux, "You girls need to be careful. Lock your doors. Emma's husband will be sobering up, and I expect that he'll come looking for her. So…get some rest, and don't open your door for anyone."

Marguerite looked concerned, as she turned toward the priest. "You need to rest, too."

"I'll try and catch a few winks, but I'll keep my door open, so I can hear any commotion that may arise."

Louise suddenly interjected, "Be careful. We're not the only ones in danger."

There was something innately confident in his response. "I can take care of myself. If it's a fight he's looking for, he may very well find it."

The two nuns looked uneasily at each other, puzzled by a side of Father Bernard that they had never seen.

CHAPTER 19

A Wound Reopened

1901
Bayeux, France

He looked nothing like a priest, as he huddled on the floor of his apartment, the door slightly ajar. In many ways, he was once again the boy, Danior. Although now a grown man, the survival instincts of his youth were fully engaged. At an early age, he had learned to meet threat with threat, and it had assured his survival in the Roma clan. Tired, and spent from the night's happenings, he intermittently dozed, and then would startle as he heard a cat jump down from a windowsill, or a bird chortle. Just as the sun was coming up, Danior heard heavy, fumbling steps on the cobblestones. He pulled himself fully awake, as he listened attentively, and tried to assess the threat.

His movements were stealthy as he quietly opened the door. Peering down the street toward Sister Louise's apartment, he saw him, clumsily, drunkenly walking toward the nun's apartment. Instinctively, the priest readied himself, bracing for battle, as he slipped out the door and began running toward the threat with a swiftness that was uncharacteristic of a middle-aged man. But Emma's husband made it to the door before him, and Louise was ready to confront him. With the first angry pound on the door, the nun threw it open, defiantly facing him.

Staggering toward Louise, red-eyed and smelling foul, he bel-lowed, "Get out of my way, you bitch! I know she's here!"

His violent rage was sadly familiar to her. The drunken man violent-ly threw Louise aside, sending her tumbling against the doorway, as he stormed inside. He could easily see that his wife was not hidden away in the sparsely furnished apartment. Angry and hellbent on revenge, he turned and stumbled toward Louise, his hand raised to strike. But Louise had a wellspring of rage too, and she stepped forward to meet the threat. The two collided with a ferocity that was feral in nature. The foul-smelling drunk landed a blow into Louise's shoulder, which violently propelled her against the stone wall. It was as though she didn't feel the injury, for she leaped up and dove forcefully into the stumbling, drunken man, kneeing him in the groin with a strength she did not know she possessed. He toppled backward, writhing in pain and curs-ing, his words thick and foul. Louise landed on top of him, pummeling him with her fists, seeming to have a need to vent her fury. The release of her assault was cathartic, and wildly beyond her control.

Father Bernard stormed into the chaotic scene, quickly followed by Marguerite. The priest immediately pulled Louise from the entan-glement and pushed her into Marguerite's open arms. Emma's hus-band was unsteady, trying to pull himself to his feet, still reeling from Louise's assault. Now even more enraged, he turned toward the priest, his fists raised, foul curses spewing from his mouth.

Father Bernard looked like a man possessed, his dark eyes flashing with the fierceness of a wild animal. Without a single word, he pulled back his muscled arm and struck the fumbling drunk with his tightly clenched fist. The man fell back haphazardly, and collapsed against the stone wall, his face covered in blood. Before he could recover, Father Bernard jumped upon him, and began to mercilessly pummel his face. Stunned and disoriented, there was no resistance on the part of the drunken man, as the priest's clenched fist slammed repeatedly into the bloody and broken face. The sound of breaking bones and teeth shockingly filled the room, adding a terrifying element to the scene.

Marguerite was frightened and appalled, as she screamed, "Stop!" before rushing over to the priest whom she barely recognized, desperately pulling back on his arm, as he was about to deliver a final, fatal blow. She had tears in her eyes as she searched the priest's face for some semblance of the reasoned, compassionate man she knew and loved. Looking dazed, Father Bernard abruptly stopped the assault and turned toward her, their eyes connecting, her intensely puzzled gaze bridging the gap between them, as a flush of embarrassment swept over him. Suddenly, Marguerite's hands were firmly around his clenched fist. Feeling her strength, her reasoning, he stood, trying to calm himself.

As the calamity was finally settling down, the village policeman rushed into the apartment. He immediately recognized the bloodied drunk, lying barely conscious on the floor. The badly bleeding man with broken teeth, and a deep gash above his left eye, told the story to the seasoned policeman. He was accustomed to breaking up the occasional drunken brawl, but the man's injuries had the look of vengeful, uncontrolled violence. The policeman studied Father Bernard quizzically before he spoke.

Looking squarely at the drunken man, the officer said, "You're at it again. Tell me that your poor, ill-fated wife has not suffered from your drunken rage."

Stunned from the violent blows to his head, the bloodied man was dazed and sullen. He did not respond to the policeman's inquiry.

Father Bernard stepped forward, trying to sound calm and reasonable, as he said, "I'm afraid he has beaten his wife badly, and he physically assaulted one of my nuns."

The policeman shook his head in disgust as he said, "I don't want you stinking up my jail, but I think I'd better protect you from the good priest here."

Father Bernard roughly nudged the drunk with his foot to get his attention. He glared at the man's bloody face and threatened him in a clear voice, his slight Slovakian accent suddenly more pronounced, "Your wife is not your property to abuse as you please. If you ever harm Emma, or my nuns again, I will visit you, and we will settle it between us." There was shocked silence in the room, as the sincerity of what he said sunk in.

The evil man glared back hatefully as he haltingly said through his pain, "Father, you've got a bit of the devil in you. I do believe…that you're…going to burn in hell."

Father Bernard was steadfast as he said, "I meant what I said. Don't doubt me, for I am a man of my word. It may very well be that we'll meet in hell."

The policeman looked stunned by the priest's blatant threat, but he said nothing. Pulling the bloodied drunk to his feet, the officer half dragged, half carried, the man out of the apartment.

An immediate sense of relief filled the room, as Marguerite, Louise, and Father Bernard were suddenly alone. Marguerite was still clutching the priest's bloodied hand, and she was fighting the need to hold him, to comfort him. He felt it too, as a vacuous silence and awkwardness filled the space between them. But over four years had gone by, and they were no longer intimate friends who shared pieces of their lives. Marguerite was looking deep into his eyes, questioning, as she gently let go of his hand, reluctantly letting go of his touch.

A suppressed sob from Louise seemed to break the spell between Marguerite and Father Bernard. The priest turned toward Louise, a semblance of his previous self, reappearing, genuine concern in his voice, as he asked, "Are you hurt?"

Louise was shaking, her voice oddly different, as she answered, "I'm fine."

But it was apparent that she was not fine. She was fighting to regain some sense of composure, but failing miserably, as deep, gulping sobs overtook her.

Marguerite rushed forward, pulling Louise into her arms, trying to comfort her, calm her. Louise's response was primal, as her past pain and fear came out in louder sobs. Father Bernard looked on helplessly, as Marguerite silently waved for him to leave them alone. Worried as he witnessed the raw scene before him, he nodded to Marguerite and reluctantly turned and slipped out of the apartment.

Once Father Bernard left the room, Louise no longer made any effort, and she collapsed on the floor like a deflated balloon. Marguerite gently lowered herself beside her friend, feeling her sadness, feeling her pain. Feeling helpless as she held on tightly to the distraught woman, Marguerite had a sense of being overwhelmed by the grief that was oozing from her friend. It was disturbing to witness the pain and wounding that had been reopened by Emma's abuse.

Marguerite stroked Sister Louise's head lovingly as she softly said, "I am so sorry that you have had to live with this pain."

Sister Louise mumbled through her sobs, "I have tried to forget, but it keeps coming back. I don't believe I'll ever escape it."

Sister Marguerite nodded knowingly as she reassured her, "No, I don't think we can ever completely escape our past. I suppose the best we can do is to make some sort of peace with it."

"Just when I think I've made peace with all that has happened to me, it comes roaring back with a vengeance."

Marguerite gently probed, "You've been abused by a man?"

"I was raped as a young girl!"

Marguerite could see the raw pain as she responded, "I'm so sorry that you've had to live with this memory…this pain. Emma's abuse must have brought all this to the surface again."

"Oh yes, I saw myself in her…all bloody, and beaten. It brought it all back…just when I thought I had put it behind me."

"How can I help you?"

The sobs had quieted somewhat, as Louise thoughtfully answered, "By being a friend…by listening, and not judging."

Marguerite marveled at this thoughtful, caring young woman, and she reassured her, "I am here to listen. At some point, I think you need to tell this story, this part of your life, that causes you so much pain."

"I do need to unburden myself. I have never told anyone the complete truth about what happened to me."

"You can trust me."

"I had a good feeling, the first time I met you."

Marguerite smiled as she said, "I had the same feeling about you."

"You know…I think we were destined to be friends. Maybe it's God's way of offering healing."

"You could be right. I have my own wounds, my own ugly story. You are not the only one who suffers."

Louise seemed relieved by Marguerite's honesty. She went on to say, "I could sense that in you, too. I do think it would help us both, to tell our ugly stories."

"Yes, I think we both could benefit from some healing."

There was a commonality in their grief despite their very different stories. It was amazing how they had ended up together in such an intimate church assignment. It seemed like fate, or possibly divine intervention. The two were destined to be close confidantes and would ultimately help each other heal their very real wounds.

CHAPTER 20

An Ugly Story

1901
Bayeux, France

The afternoon sky cast an ominous light as the clouds gathered over Bayeux. The wind was picking up, and the air was heavy with humidity, as dark clouds gathered over the suddenly deserted streets. Clearly, there was a storm coming.

Father Bernard was apprehensive as he watched Louise and Marguerite load the wagon to head out to the Durand farm. His dark eyes were alert and searching, as he visually scanned the town's streets. He knew that Emma's husband had been released from jail, after a brief incarceration to allow him to sober up. The local police had made only a cursory effort to punish him, and it left Father Bernard angry and frustrated. In his heart, he hoped and prayed that he had instilled a sufficient sense of fear into the evil, abusive husband. It was a strangely odd prayer for a man of the cloth.

Father Bernard had implored the nuns to wait until the next day to visit the Durand farm, so that he might accompany them. He had a funeral service to officiate for a local family that required his attention that afternoon. The two nuns were equally emphatic that they needed to check in on Emma and Mrs. Durand. Father Bernard knew in his heart that he would not be able to guard the nuns continually as they went about their parish duties, but it was an uneasy realization.

Marguerite and Louise wasted no time spiriting out of town, with their supplies of clothing and food for Emma and Mrs. Durand. They too, were apprehensive and edgy as they warily watched the streets of Bayeux. When they had finally cleared the town and were on their way to the Durand farm, they both breathed a huge sigh of relief.

Sister Louise looked ravaged from the night's horrific events. Tired and pale, her large, jagged facial scar was even more pronounced than usual. Outwardly, she fought to present her usual confidence and sense of purpose, but it was just not there. Sitting beside Marguerite, as the horses steadily pulled them toward the Durand farm, Louise felt empty and numb.

Marguerite could sense her friend's fragility. Although she tried not to show it, she was alarmed by the startling change in Louise's appearance and demeanor. She emanated sincere concern as she gently asked, "Are you sure that you feel up to this?"

Louise answered in a voice that sounded strange and hollow, "Yes, of course."

Marguerite reached over and put her arm around Louise. She could feel the silent sobs, but there was no sound. Quietly, Marguerite whispered, "You are not okay."

Looking straight ahead, in a voice completely devoid of any emotion, Louise numbly responded, "I've never told anyone what happened to me."

"You need to let this out. It's eating you alive."

The sky had suddenly darkened, and large, cool raindrops began to fall. The women did not try to shield themselves from the rain as it washed over them, cooling them in a wetness that heightened their senses. The horses slowed, and the rhythm of their gait seemed to fit perfectly with the rain. For the longest time, the two just absorbed the rain, and the almost surreal tranquility.

Finally, Louise began, her voice hollow and flat, "I killed him…I killed him…and I'm not sorry."

There was no judgment in her eyes, as Marguerite just nodded, saying nothing.

"I planned it. I was ready for him."

"He hurt you."

Louise appeared to be almost in a trance as she said, "Yes, he was an evil, evil man."

Gently, Marguerite urged, "Tell me what happened to you."

Sister Louise looked up at the rain-filled sky, her jagged cheek scar prominent on her beautiful face. She looked sad as she said, "I don't know where to begin."

Marguerite understood that she felt overwhelmed, and said, "Tell me about your family."

"It was just my mother and me. Her name was Brigette, and I was her only child. My father left her shortly after I was born, so I did not know him. My parents were never married, and my mother bore the stigma of bearing an illegitimate child. When I would ask about my father, my mother would bitterly answer that he was not worth knowing. She would tell me to forget about him."

"Did you have other family, maybe grandparents?"

Louise nodded and said, "Yes, my mother's parents lived north of Paris, in Lille. They were farmers and quite comfortable. My mother caused quite a stir within the family when she ran away to Paris with one of the local farm boys. She was only sixteen years old when she got pregnant with me. They lived together for a while, but when my father disappeared after I was born, he left my mother destitute and full of shame. Somehow, she did muster the courage to make the journey back to her family, but her parents were bitter and wanted nothing to do with their daughter, or with me. That was the last time that my mother ever saw or heard from her parents. She felt so dejected, so bitter. She never got over it."

Marguerite was intrigued by the sad story and gently asked, "So how did your mother support herself as a single parent in Paris?"

Louise responded, "Well, she could not leave me, so she took in laundry for wealthy families. She would take me with her, in a little handcart, to pick up and drop off laundry. It is my first real memory of her. She would wash and iron clothing well into the night. We were desperately poor. Sometimes her wealthy clients would give us old clothing that they no longer wanted. She would take the fabric from these unwanted clothes and make them into quite nice dresses, for the two of us."

"Obviously, she was very committed to you."

Louise looked deep in thought as she responded, "Yes, she worked very hard to provide for me. It was surely not a joyful childhood, but I felt cared for."

Marguerite hesitantly asked, "Did she love you?"

Louise nodded and said, "Yes, she did. My mother was very suspicious and fearful that harm would come to me, and it clouded my entire childhood. She would not let me play in the streets of Paris by myself. Although I did go to school, she walked me to and from, every day. I was the poor, illegitimate child of the local laundry woman. It was a very lonely childhood. I don't remember ever feeling carefree, or ever having any friends. My favorite time of the week was when we went to church. I loved the sense of peace and security I felt in that building. My mother seemed to relax, to be at peace in the church, and she would linger after the service to pray, and marvel at the beauty of the stained-glass windows. It was her refuge, and it became mine."

Marguerite was reluctant to ask the next question, but she gingerly proceeded. "So where is your mother now?"

Louise's face darkened, as she answered, "She's dead."

Marguerite could tell that Louise was emotionally shutting down. Gently, she asked, "I'm sorry. May I ask how she died?"

Louise looked lost as she answered, "She died of consumption. Slowly, over the course of a year, she became weaker, and weaker, and finally her lungs just gave out. I tried endlessly to nurse her back to health, but she just kept getting weaker. Those last months were awful. I had taken over her laundry duties, so that we could have food, and pay the rent. I was so young, so physically and emotionally overwhelmed. My mother knew she was dying, and she would try to warn me against all the danger that she saw looming. She would repeatedly tell me that beauty was a curse, and that I should be wary of men. It was a terrifying message to tell a fourteen-year-old girl. The closer she came to death, the more paranoid she became."

"Was there no one to help?"

Sister Louise shook her head as she answered, "No, my mother had successfully alienated herself, and me, from all those who even tried to help. She was so fearful of everyone, so we were literally alone. There was one man in our tenement who would approach me and ask questions about my mother's health. In my despair, I would sometimes share the news of her declining health. My mother repeatedly warned me to stay away from him, but honestly, she warned me about everybody."

Marguerite had a sense of where Louise's story was going as she asked, "Were her suspicions justified?"

Louise nodded and began to cry as she said, "Oh, yes. Shortly after my mother died, he showed up at my apartment in the middle of the night…and raped me. I can still smell his foul breath. I cannot describe to you how dirty, and how violated, I felt. But…it was almost more frightening to feel the rage. I felt like I was possessed…a crazy person, filled with hate. When he returned the next night, I was ready. I lay quietly in my bed, clutching a butcher knife that I had carefully sharpened, and when he climbed on top of me, I pushed the knife deep into his chest. I can still see the disbelief, the shock on his face as he hovered over me. He fought back and wrestled the knife from my hands. In his frantic attempts to save himself, he pulled the knife out of his chest, and, in doing so, sliced my face wide open. Bleeding rivers all over me, he fell on top of me, dead. In my nightmares, I can still feel and taste the warmth of his blood raining down into my mouth. He was a big, heavy man and I struggled to push his dead body off mine. My screams brought the neighbors from nearby apartments, and they seemed to instantly recognize what had happened. An old couple quickly pulled me from the apartment and tried to stop my face from bleeding. They were so kind, as they whisked me away to the local convent hospital before the police arrived. There was no surprise among my neighbors that this man had committed such an atrocity."

With great sadness, Marguerite asked, "Did you ever see the old couple again?"

Louise smiled slightly as she responded, "Oh, yes. They came every day for the next two weeks. Honestly, I think they did more to restore my faith in humanity than I can even describe. The old woman was so kind and comforting, and she just let me talk. She encouraged me to let out all my feelings, and she told me over and over that I was a beautiful person. This woman who saved my life, she was Mrs. Durand's twin sister. They are so much alike in every way. At the end of my stay in the hospital, I decided to join the convent. Although it has not always been a pleasant experience, I have found peace and purpose in the Catholic order. It has given me so much opportunity to help others, and I have never known such friendships as those I have formed in Bayeux."

Sister Marguerite nodded as she said, "Yes, you are much loved and admired in this community. Do you mind if I ask one more question?"

Sister Louise hesitantly responded, "Of course."

Marguerite asked, "So did the police ever question you about the man they found in your apartment?"

Louise shook her head as she answered, "No, the old couple told me that he was well-known to the police, and they basically thought he got what he deserved. Thankfully, the old couple had gone to the police station and told them what happened. The police quickly closed the investigation, and they didn't even question me. It was a blessing because I did not want to retell the story to anyone."

The rain had stopped, and there was a rainbow emerging on the horizon. Louise suddenly had a feeling of lightness, of being unburdened, and it felt liberating. As the horse pulled into the lane at the Durand farm, the old woman stepped outside of the ancient farmhouse to greet them.

She smiled and shook her head as she said, "You look like a couple of drowned rats."

Sister Louise quickly responded, "Ahh…the rain felt refreshing. It's good to cleanse the soul. How is our patient?"

Mrs. Durand had a satisfied look as she responded, "She's doing remarkably well. Come on in and see for yourself."

The two nuns jumped down from the wagon and followed the old woman into the house. Emma was sitting at the sturdy farm table, gingerly sipping coffee. Her face was massively bruised, and one eye was completely swollen shut. But the wound appeared to be well approximated and was surprisingly clear of signs of infection. Although tired looking, Emma appeared relatively relaxed as she greeted them. She had the look of a survivor, one who had gone through a terrible storm, yet was still standing. As the four women huddled together in the simple country kitchen, there was hope, and for the moment, that was enough.

The trip back to Bayeux was particularly peaceful. It was late afternoon, and Marguerite and Louise were tired, with the kind of exhaustion that is satisfying. They continued to talk, and Marguerite could not help but marvel at the story.

Sister Marguerite asked Louise, "How did you end up in Bayeux?"

Louise confessed, "I was assigned to the Bayeux convent after taking my final vows. Through my involvement in the church, I gradually got to know Father Bernard. Quite frankly, I was shocked to learn that he had requested that I be assigned to work directly with the

Bayeux community, under his direction. It wasn't well-received by the Mother Superior, but ultimately Father Bernard was able to wrestle me away from the Bayeux convent. Honestly, it was the best thing that ever happened to me. I have never known such purpose, or happiness. When I was first assigned to the Bayeux parish, I immediately noticed Mrs. Durand in church. She is the spitting image of her Parisian sister. I finally approached her after church one Sunday and introduced myself. Mrs. Durand knew all about me through her sister's letters, and she treated me like long-lost family. This remarkable woman warmly welcomed me to Bayeux and provided me with such a sense of support and belonging. We have been friends and confidantes ever since that day. When her husband died, it was my turn to return the kindness. The widow Durand is the closest thing I have to family."

Sister Marguerite was beginning to understand the bond that she felt existed between these two women. It was an extraordinary coincidence, and it suggested, divine intervention.

Louise chuckled as she went on to explain her placement in the Bayeux parish. "Apparently, my predecessor was witnessed using her ruler to hit some of the poorly behaved choir children. It didn't meet with Father Bernard's approval, and he demanded that the Mother Superior replace this nun. He insisted that he be allowed to pick the candidate. The Mother Superior was not happy, and they have not been on good terms since that protracted battle. But to tell the truth, I don't know why he chose me. I certainly don't have much patience for unruly choir children."

Marguerite chimed in, "I know why he chose you. It is your compassion and ability to sense the needs of others. You have a gift."

Louise seemed embarrassed, as she was not accustomed to praise. She felt hugely proud to hear these words from her fellow nun and new friend. She hugged Marguerite and reminded her, "Please know, that I am here for you…when you're ready to tell your ugly story."

Marguerite smiled wistfully and said, "Mine is a long story. Probably better save it for our next ride out to the farm."

CHAPTER 21

The Present Meets the Past

1901
Bayeux Cathedral

The squeal of delight echoed through the massive, arched church entryway, filling the somber space with spontaneous joy. All eyes were drawn to Henri, as he tugged relentlessly on Adele's hand, finally breaking free, running haphazardly through the crowd of churchgoers. Marguerite was equally uninhibited, as she scooped the little boy up in her arms, and gave him a long, loving bear hug, and a kiss on the forehead. The exuberance and sheer happiness permeated the austere stone entry, and people could not help but smile, and they wondered, and whispered. Adele and Gabriel seemed embarrassed by Henri's outburst, as they pried the little boy from Marguerite's arms. They quickly carried Henri to a pew in the back of the church, as they tried unsuccessfully to calm his excitement.

Jacob was entering the church with his beautifully dressed young wife and infant son, just as Adele was prying Henri from Marguerite. He seemed stricken, as he took in the interaction between the pretty young nun and the little boy. He quickly scurried past, shielding his family from the scene, his eyes downcast. There was no acknowledgment between the two former lovers, just a palpable sense of unease. Jacob and his young family proceeded to the front of the church to join his parents. The Laurent family routinely occupied a prominent pew in the Bayeux Cathedral for the weekly Sunday morning mass. The negotiated peace between Marguerite and Jacob seemed tenuous and untested, as the two occupied this sacred space, for their very first Sunday mass together in several years. The bustling, crowded church was lost to Jacob, as he struggled to remain calm and detached from the entanglements of his past.

Sister Louise was mesmerized by the interaction between Marguerite and Henri, as she watched the reunification scene from a short distance. Always intuitive, always wise in the ways of the world, she could not help but feel the love and connection between the nun and the young child. Louise instinctively knew, without a doubt, that this little boy was more than just a nephew to Marguerite.

Sister Marguerite moved confidently, her long black dress swaying gently with each graceful step, as she moved toward the choir. The children were a mass of barely contained, bubbling energy. Fidgeting, giggling, they attempted to settle themselves as Marguerite stepped in front of the eager group. Her back to the congregation, the pretty young nun secretly winked to the youngsters, and they smiled back, ready to begin. Not prideful by nature, Marguerite was uncharacteristically proud to showcase the talent and diligent work of the young choir. She knew the group of rather ordinary looking children had unusual choral talent. The children felt it too, and they were confidently eager to perform for the normally sleepy congregation.

Marguerite stood tall, focused, expectant, as she directed the children. The beautifully blended pubescent voices started out low, and then rose to a bone-chilling height, completely harmonized, as they sang "Ave Maria." Rising to the high-arched ceilings, the beautiful sounds filled the space, and transfixed the congregation. There was no shuffling, or whispering, or other human sounds, only the glorious music.

Midway through the powerful hymn, one of the youngest members of the choir broke into a brief solo. Only eight years old, Alex was blond and beautiful, and confident in the manner of a child born to privilege, one who had never known criticism, or defeat. Although he was one of the shortest children, he stood tall, as he sang powerfully, with the self-assurance of one who knows his gift. The church congregation fell completely and utterly silent, as they took in the purity of the child's voice. The morning light streaming through the mosaic of colorful stained glass magnified and provided a surreal aura of beauty to the musical experience.

As the hymn came to an end, there was a prolonged, eerie silence, and then something happened that had never happened before. It started with a few sparse claps, but it quickly rose to an explosion of applause, as hands came together in celebration of the magnificent music. Marguerite turned shyly, surprised. She nodded in recognition, and then swung her arm up, pointing in the direction of the children. The youngsters beamed, as they stood tall, proudly taking in the applause.

It was a moment of definition for this rather common looking church choir, and it was the reintroduction of Sister Marguerite to the Bayeux parish. Of course, she had grown up in the community, but her absence during the last few years made her unfamiliar to most of the local churchgoers. She looked and acted like a totally different person. Even in her plain nun's habit, Marguerite was beautiful, and she carried herself with confidence and grace. As Jacob sat with his family in the front of the church, he could not stop looking at her.

His wife elbowed him and quietly asked, "Do you know this nun?"

Jacob shook his head as he whispered to his wife, "She looks a little familiar. It's possible that we went to the same school as children."

Jacob's wife commented, "She does look to be about your age. She's done absolute wonders with the children's choir."

Jacob was nervous and tried desperately to look disinterested, as he nodded his agreement. Internally, he felt great emotional upheaval, and maybe even a deeply buried twinge of regret. As Marguerite turned to face the congregation, the former lovers briefly made eye contact. Marguerite, however, remained unflappable, as she pretended not to see the young man from her past. She was vastly different from the fragile, young adolescent girl whom Jacob had rejected only five years prior.

Ever observant, Father Bernard took in Jacob's apprehension, noticing his unease, as he delivered his sermon on integrity. The message seemed strangely lost on the irreverent young man, as Jacob obsessively focused his dumbstruck gaze on Marguerite. The priest was unnerved by what he saw in Jacob, who sat beside his beautiful young wife and child. He feared that Marguerite would be undone by Jacob's proximity, but he need not have worried. Marguerite appeared confident and seemed completely oblivious to the awkward stares that he focused on her. Inwardly, silently, she noticed, and maybe even felt a bit vengeful, as she rightfully occupied space in this church, in this town, that Jacob had so arrogantly claimed. Seeing him ashen and shaken made her even more confident that she was going to be a vital part of this church, and more importantly, of Henri's life. In her mind, Jacob could be damned. He was no longer going to hurt her or exert any pull over her life.

As the final hymn filled the beautiful cathedral with heavenly sounds, Father Bernard slowly walked down the main aisle toward the back of the church, smiling and nodding to his people. The parishioners returned the silent acknowledgment, as they looked approvingly at the man, the priest, who seemed to understand them so well. It was the perfect ending to Sunday mass. Positioning himself near the impressive arched doors, Father Bernard spoke warmly with the individuals of his parish, as they walked out of the church and into the cobbled streets of Bayeux. As the Laurent family filed out of the church, Father Bernard and Jacob acknowledged each other with a knowing nod. The history between Marguerite, Jacob, and Father Bernard was a subtle but powerful presence in the cathedral on this Sunday morning.

Adele and Gabriel waited patiently outside of the church with the boys, for Marguerite to emerge after the service. As the young nun approached them, Henri and Louis jumped up and down, and ran excitedly toward Marguerite. She swept the two little boys up in her arms and swung them around, as they laughed in delight. Trying not to alert his wife, Jacob discreetly shielded the scene from her view, all the while watching as Marguerite climbed into the wagon with the joyful family. Sounds of laughter could be heard as the wagon left the town of Bayeux, heading for the LeBlanc farm.

Jacob's angst had not lessened. He could not take his eyes off Marguerite, and he could not help but notice that one of the little boys looked like a Laurent. Feeling faint, and physically stricken, Jacob walked with his wife and young child back to the family restaurant.

CHAPTER 22

The Unhidden Truth

1901
Bayeux, France

There was a trust between them. Although the two young nuns had known each other only a short time, they felt at ease with each other. The events of the previous week had revealed aspects and mysteries about themselves, all of which had peeled back the layers of who they were. Neither had been shocked or repulsed, but rather instinctively liked, and had grown to respect, each other even more. Both had come from convent life, regimented, austere, and more prone to gracious, measured human contact, largely devoid of passion. Religious life had provided a haven for them, but there had been something missing. Although Louise and Marguerite were not fully aware of the missing piece, they were vaguely aware of a common spirit between them, and this fostered a connection, and the beginning of a deep friendship. There was an honesty between them that felt natural. When the two were together, they unwittingly revealed their deeply suppressed passion for life with a candor that would surely raise the eyebrows of their peers in the convent. They felt at home together, a sisterhood that was treasured.

Marguerite and Louise were like two bees busily building a hive, as they prepared for a trip to the Durand farm. Gathering food and more clothing items from the donation room, they worked seamlessly together. At the last minute, they pulled the horse drawn wagon in front of their apartments. Father Bernard nervously helped them load supplies, all the while watching the busy street for any sign of Emma's husband. The priest's wariness had lessened somewhat, but he would never be completely free, as he was hardwired to constantly assess threat. It was a residual from his tough, hardscrabble childhood with the gypsies.

Father Bernard said, "I would not dally getting out of town. There are a lot of eyes here on the streets of Bayeux."

Marguerite tried to reassure him, "We'll be careful."

The two nuns wasted no time climbing into the wagon, quickly urging the horses out of town, towards the Durand farm. As they cleared the perimeter of the town, they were visibly relieved, and seemed to relax.

With an ease that spoke volumes about their relationship, Louise confidently said, "I believe you promised me an ugly story." There was no malice or condemnation in her voice, just acceptance and true friendship.

Marguerite was surprisingly open, as she chuckled and said, "You certainly don't beat around the bush."

Louise smirked lightheartedly. "I don't want to be the only nun with an ugly story."

"Trust me, you're not."

"So, tell me."

Marguerite hesitated for a moment, and then said, "I have a child."

"I know."

Marguerite turned to her, incredulous, doubting. She fired back, "How could you know?"

"I've seen you with your sister's boys. The youngest one is yours."

Aghast, Marguerite felt shocked. "Why would you say that?"

"I can see the love between the two of you. He is your child. You cannot take your eyes off him."

Marguerite sounded suddenly agitated and distressed as she lamented, "No one must know! I don't want Henri to grow up being the illegitimate child of a wayward nun."

Louise was suddenly very serious as she warned, "If you truly want to keep this secret, then you need to stop drawing attention to Henri. People talk. It wasn't hard for me to figure out, and it's just a matter of time before others do, too."

There were tears in Marguerite's eyes as she said, "I came back here to be with him."

"Then be wise. You cannot be making a big scene in the back of the church when you see Henri. People are already talking and wondering. Your secret will not stay safe for long, not if you continue to have these public displays of affection with your son. Your whole face lights up when you are in his presence. It's wonderful, but it does threaten to reveal Henri's real identity."

"I can't do that to him. And Gabriel and Adele would never forgive me. They love my son as much as I do."

"Yes, and it would be very confusing to Henri."

Marguerite was talking softly, almost to herself as she said, "Gabriel is fiercely protective of Henri. There is such a bond between them. He could not love this little boy more, than if he was his own."

"I'm assuming you made this decision of your own free will?"

Marguerite nodded reluctantly, "Yes, it was my decision. But...I have had doubts."

Louise looked at her friend with understanding as she said, "How old were you when you had Henri?"

"Seventeen. Just a naïve girl."

"I think that describes most seventeen-year-old girls."

Marguerite seemed mired in the past as she said, "It seems like a lifetime ago. I can hardly remember how I first felt when I was with this boy who got me pregnant."

"It was Jacob, right?"

Marguerite again stared at her in disbelief. "How could you know that?"

"You forget, I witnessed your little altercation in the street with Jacob. And…I'm very good at reading people. It finally made sense to me, especially when I saw you with Henri in the back of the church. Your son looks very much like his father."

Groaning in despair, Marguerite asked, "Do you really think so?"

"Yes, Jacob would be a fool not to suspect."

"Jacob is a fool! He only cares about his reputation! He never cared one bit about me, or the child I was carrying. It was all my problem!"

"Yes, I can see that in him. He may be a fool, but he's a vindictive one. So, don't you be foolish in underestimating him. An illegitimate child would be embarrassing to him and his family, so you need to be careful. The Laurent family gives generously to the church, and they would not hesitate to use their influence to have you removed from Bayeux."

"Jacob has already tried to do so. Father Bernard will protect me from them. I know he will."

"He can't protect you if they go to the higher-ups in the church. Father Bernard is not all-powerful. Money can buy a lot in the Catholic Church. I don't understand, how could Jacob not know, that Henri is his child?" Louise asked, puzzled.

"Honestly, it was a twisted plan, all based on deception and lies. I did not want my child to grow up in an orphanage, or to feel the shame of being an illegitimate child. Adele was reluctant at first, but she loves me, and finally agreed to the charade."

Louise nodded, taking in the story, "She was worried about you."

"Very much so. She tried to talk me out of the plan, tried to convince me that I would have grave regrets. But I would not listen. I was so obsessed with providing my child with a secure, loving family, that I really didn't consider my own needs."

"And now you have regrets."

"Yes."

Louise could easily see the regret in her friend's face, feel her pain, as she softly said, "I'm so sorry."

"It was my decision completely. Father Bernard and Adele both tried to convince me to stay in Bayeux and raise my child as a single mother, but I wanted more for Henri, more than I could give him."

"I still don't understand how Jacob could not know that Henri is his son."

Marguerite sighed, the anguish still there as she responded, "Jacob wanted nothing to do with me after I told him I was pregnant. He completely avoided me, and his only concern was that his parents might find out. I was devastated. Honestly, I was at my wits' end, when I first encountered Father Bernard in a confessional on a dark, rainy night. He made me feel like I had a friend, an ally, that I wasn't alone."

"Ahh…that sounds like Father Bernard."

"He listened, and didn't judge, and he gave me hope."

Louise smiled as she said, "But, it sounds like he didn't approve of your plan."

"No, he didn't. At first, he refused to go along with it."

"But you convinced him."

Marguerite looked a little guilty as she said, "Yes, I pushed him to do something that he wasn't comfortable with, a lie that faces him daily."

"And now you feel guilty about that, too."

"Yes, I do."

Louise nodded, understanding, as she said, "I'm confused. In a town so caught up in gossip and stories, how did your pregnancy go unnoticed? How did Adele and Gabriel suddenly have a second child, a little boy?"

"It was easier that you might think. My parents essentially dis-owned me after I told them my disgraceful news, so I moved to Adele's farm. Shortly thereafter, I let it be known that I had left to join the convent. My parents, and probably Jacob, were greatly relieved to avoid the embarrassment and disgrace. In their minds, it was a prob-lem solved. I hid out on Adele's farm until after the birth. My sister pretended to be pregnant, by wearing loose clothing, and disappearing into her remote farm life. It was a completely believable narrative, especially if that's what you wanted to believe."

Louise nodded, understanding, and then she said, "You must hate Jacob for how he treated you."

Marguerite shook her head, trying to convince herself and Louise. "No. I don't feel anything for him."

"I've seen the two of you together. That is not the look of feeling nothing."

Marguerite was taken aback by the bluntness. She fumbled with her words, as she tried to convince Louise that she felt nothing for the man who had wounded her. "He's...he's nothing...just a poor excuse...of a man."

"Well, I have to agree with you on that point."

"I returned to Bayeux to be near Henri, so that I can be a part of his life. I will not allow Jacob to interfere with my relationship with my son."

The tone of her voice was suddenly stern as she warned, "Then you need to be more discreet. After your reunification scene with Henri in the back of the church, the town is already whispering, already wondering, and I'm sure Jacob is, too."

Marguerite gasped, horrified by the thought. "Do you really think that he's suspicious?"

"Yes, I do. He may be an evil person, but he's not stupid, and he'll do anything to protect his reputation. I would not underestimate him."

Suddenly tears were flowing down Marguerite's cheeks, the reality sinking in, that this man still had the ability to hurt her. But she was no longer passive, no longer weak, and she responded defiantly, "I will not allow him to separate me from my son. I won't!"

"Then you need to proceed carefully if you want your plan to succeed. You need to convince him beyond a doubt that Henri is not his son, that you are here to do the work of the church, and that revealing your past will only serve to harm you both. He needs to trust you, to know that you will not harm his reputation."

"I can, and I will…do it."

Louise tried to be reassuring as she pragmatically gave her assessment. "Well, I don't think all is lost…yet. Jacob may suspect, but he will not want to draw attention to the possibility that he has an illegitimate son, and he will conveniently ignore this remnant from his past, provided it is not thrown in his face. If you are sincere that you want this plan to work, you need to get the word out that you love spending time with both of your nephews, but do not display that love so openly. And it may be a good idea for Adele and Gabriel to not come to Sunday mass for a while, until the town has a new focus for their gossip."

Marguerite brightened a bit as she said, "I think you're right. I'm sure Adele and Gabriel would agree. They are so protective of Henri, and they would do anything to keep him safe from controversy."

"You can still have your time with Henri, on the farm, away from curious eyes." Suddenly there seemed to be a sense of resolution.

As they pulled into the lane of the Durand farm, the mixed breed dog barked and wagged its tail. Emma opened the door and watched the visitors approach, her face a mass of mostly faded, greenish-purple bruises surrounding her worried eyes. Louise immediately knew that something was wrong. She jumped down from the wagon even before it came to a complete stop.

Emma's shoulders were slumped in burden, as she stepped forward to meet Louise. Trying not to cry, she said, "I think she's had a stroke."

Louise gasped, as the news hit her like a brick. "No! Is she conscious?"

Emma nodded sadly as she said, "Yes, but she's paralyzed on her left side, and her speech is very garbled, but I do think she understands. I can't get her to swallow water. She chokes."

Louise began to cry, her shoulders shaking. "I am not ready to lose her. She has helped me so much."

There was somberness as the three women entered the bedroom. Slumped deep in the bed, Mrs. Durand looked gray, her breathing had a noisy, snoring quality, and she looked barely conscious. Her eyes fluttered open as she recognized her visitors. A startling right-sided facial droop was evident as she smiled weakly, giving her face a distorted, lopsided appearance. Louise rushed to her bedside and started to cry, as she leaned forward to hug the old woman. Clear drool was running unabated from her distorted, droopy mouth, her speech garbled and barely understandable. Mrs. Durand struggled to say, "On't…cwry." Laboriously, the dying woman lifted her non-paralyzed arm, and clumsily began stroking Louise's head. So much was communicated between the two, with this awkward, fumbling human touch. Marguerite suddenly felt like an intruder, as she watched the intimate scene. Slowly, she and Emma backed out of the room to give them privacy. From the kitchen, Marguerite could hear garbled sounds, and Louise responding earnestly, lovingly, to the old woman who meant the world to her. It was the language of love, the language of final messages, and despite the garbled words, the two women understood each other perfectly.

Marguerite turned toward Emma, as they listened to the sounds in the adjoining room. Quietly, so as not to disturb Mrs. Durand and Louise, she near whispered, "How are you doing, Emma?"

"I'm healing inside and out. My time out here on the farm has given me the solitude to think and put my life in perspective. Honestly, I feel better than I've felt in a very long time."

Marguerite nodded as she studied Emma's face. The prominent scar was healing well, but it promised to be a permanent visual reminder of her abuse. "I'm glad. Your face looks much, much better, a lot less swollen, and the bruising is starting to fade."

Emma reassured her, "I'm going to be fine. I'll have a pretty good scar above my eye, but overall, I'm lucky."

"Have you thought about what's next for you?"

Emma was emphatic as she said, "I'm not going back to him. I don't ever want to see him again."

"You deserve so much better than that man. I would be disappointed in you if you even thought about going back to him."

Emma nodded as she said, "Mrs. Durand said the very same thing. Before she had her stroke, she helped me put together a plan. She even wrote her sister in Paris, asking her to find me work. We just received a letter two days ago. I have been offered a position, as a live-in maid, to a wealthy couple in Paris. Mrs. Durand's sister knows this couple personally, and she assures me that they are good people, and will pay me a decent wage."

"That's wonderful, Emma!"

"Yes, some good news to offset the sadness."

"Mrs. Durand would be so happy for you."

"Oh, she read the letter to me, the evening before she had her stroke. We celebrated with a glass of wine. She has been such a dear, such an angel."

"Yes, it seems to be her legacy…and not such a bad one."

Louise emerged from the bedroom, looking sad, but no longer crying. She said, "I'm staying with her until she leaves this world. I don't think she'll live through the night."

Marguerite understood, and said, "Yes, I think that would be good for you both. Mrs. Durand deserves to be with someone who loves her, as she gets ready to depart this world. Is there anything that I can do to help?"

"No, I don't think so. I think Emma and I can keep her comfortable."

Marguerite looked concerned about her friend as she said, "Are you sure?"

"I want to be with her. I need to be with her."

"Of course. Then you should stay. I will be back first thing in the morning to check on you all." Louise and Marguerite embraced, holding each other for the longest time. There was a peace in the old farmhouse, as Marguerite started down the lane, on her solitary journey back to Bayeux.

The round the clock care that Louise and Emma gave to the widow, as she lay dying, was so much more than contrition. Suddenly, the roles were reversed, as the scarred women were determined to return the kindnesses that had been extended to them by the old woman. The care and love given to Mrs. Durand by the two women was empowering, and it did as much for the scarred women as it did for the dying, old healer. It was the power of love, pure and raw.

CHAPTER 23

Suspicions

1901
Bayeux, France

The arrival of Marguerite back in Bayeux had initially gone largely unnoticed. There were respectful nods, and mumbled greetings as the townsfolk encountered the newest nun on the streets. Some thought she looked vaguely familiar, but she had changed so much since she had lived in Bayeux as a child, and then an adolescent, that she was barely recognizable to the community. But her stellar performance as the newly appointed choir director, and the spectacle of her reunion with Henri in the normally sedate church entry, suddenly jogged the memories of parishioners. People were remembering her, but the contrast between the timid adolescent girl who had left five years before, and the confident, mature woman who had returned as the newest addition to the parish staff, was quite remarkable.

Most Sunday mornings, as churchgoers slowly filed out of the cathedral, they would spill into the street, gathering into small groups to exchange greetings, and share the happenings of their lives. Intermixed with the overt cordial greetings, there were often whispered bits of gossip, and stilted opinions about the sermon, and who might benefit from such priestly instruction. Father Bernard moved easily among his parishioners, smiling, quietly, astutely, absorbing the conversations around him. He slowed his amble through the crowd, edging near a young woman who had been a classmate of Marguerite's before her departure to the convent. Celeste coyly huddled closer to the group of women who gathered eagerly around her, expectant, awaiting a tidbit of gossip that would entertain them, and distract them from their hard, mundane lives.

Well-known as a malicious gossip, Celeste captivated those around her, as she said, "Marguerite and I went to school together. She used to be painfully timid. I always thought it was quite odd that she left for the convent so suddenly. She was sweet on Jacob Laurent. I used to see them together, holding hands."

The women leaned even closer, mesmerized by Celeste's revelations. There were hushed whispers exchanged, within the tittering group of local gossipers, leaving those nearby to wonder what had them all aflutter. Father Bernard sighed, as he winced with the realization that Marguerite's secret was fragile, at best. He quickly made plans to speak with Marguerite, to help divert the attention that she had drawn and stop the speculation, and hopefully prevent the likely revelation to Jacob, and the painful consequences that would most surely follow.

The following morning, Father Bernard abruptly stopped Marguerite as she entered the sanctuary of the church, and said he needed to talk with her. Marguerite sighed deeply and looked at him with a great sense of dread. She knew what he was going to say, and it was painful to have the topic resurface so quickly after her arrival in Bayeux.

The priest looked somber as he said, "I'm concerned about some of the gossip that I overheard as I made the rounds after church yesterday. You seem to have drawn the attention of a few of our most notorious story-spreaders. I'm worried that your very public display of affection for Henri may have led to some unwelcome speculation. Jacob is a restaurant owner in this town, and he will undoubtably hear the gossip, if this is not stopped…now."

Marguerite looked crestfallen as she responded, "I know, I know. Louise has warned me, but I fear it is too late to stop the gossip."

Father Bernard seemed undaunted, chuckling as he said, "Gossip is a mainstay of this town. The stories fade away as quickly as they come, especially when they originate from our most prolific, and least credible gossip mongers. In a week it will be old news, provided you do not continue to draw attention to yourself, or Henri."

Marguerite looked worried as she asked, "Do you think Jacob noticed?"

Father Bernard responded in a serious tone, "Yes, I think he noticed. As you know, he is not a man of integrity, so I would not flaunt any potential controversy in front of him. He is quite willing to go to my superiors and ask for your removal from Bayeux. Although I have a good relationship with them, I do not have unlimited influence. So, please be careful."

Marguerite felt ill. Her hopes and dreams of spending time with Henri suddenly seemed threatened. She began to cry softly, and she turned away from the young priest. He instinctively stepped forward to comfort her, but she held up her hand as though to keep him away. Quietly, she then turned and slipped out of the church.

Marguerite was sad, and starting to feel overwhelmed and a little frightened, as she thought about the gossip swirling around her and Henri. She knew that she had to speak with Adele and Gabriel, and it was a conversation that she truly dreaded. Although her sister and brother-in-law were sensible people, she also knew they were fiercely protective of their family, and they would be angry that their peaceful existence was being threatened. Marguerite knew without a doubt that they loved Henri, just as much as they loved their own biological son, Louis. Although Adele and Gabriel had tried to include her in Henri's life, at times she felt like an outsider, an observer, to their loving family unit. Henri had the childhood that she had envisioned for him, but in her most honest moments, Marguerite had to admit that it was painful to watch, as she dreamily considered the possibilities of what could have been.

Just as Marguerite was getting ready to leave her apartment, hoping to find Gabriel at the weekly farmer's market, there was a knock on her door. The strong rhythmic knocking echoed through her small apartment and jarred her from her heavy thoughts. Hesitantly, Marguerite opened the door to find Gabriel standing pensively in the street. He was dressed in his well-worn farm clothes, and he shuffled nervously as he greeted Marguerite.

With an overly loud, forced friendliness, Gabriel said, "Good morning, Marguerite! I…I need to talk with you."

Marguerite could sense the heaviness as she motioned him into her apartment. She responded, "Of course, come on in."

Normally even-keeled, Gabriel struggled as he said somewhat angrily, "You promised that you would make this work, that you wanted to be a part of Henri's life, as a loving aunt…but already stories are going around. This is not fair to my family!"

"Yes, I know."

Gabriel had always struggled with his temper, and it was quickly rising out of control as he said, "Henri is my son! He is not going to be the subject of gossip and speculation!" As soon as the words left his mouth, Gabriel felt incredible guilt, as he absorbed the stricken response on his sister-in-law's face.

Marguerite was wounded by his words, and it was written all over her stunned expression. Tears flowing, and trembling with anger, she shouted, "He's my son, too! Don't you ever forget that!"

The outburst jolted Gabriel, and he struggled to calm himself. He knew his sister-in-law well, mostly through his wife, but there was an undeniable bond between them. Gabriel respected, and was protective of Marguerite, who had selflessly gifted her only child to his family. It was a complicated relationship, one that waxed and waned between love and jealousy. Gabriel knew he had touched on the nerve that went to the very core of Marguerite, and he felt guilty.

"I'm sorry. I'm sorry. I know this has been hard on you, and I'm not trying to hurt you. Honestly, I'm not."

"You have no idea how painful this has been, to see my child so close, but so far away. He is my child! My son!"

"I have not forgotten that he is your child, I haven't. I love this little boy so much, that I cannot imagine living life without him. It troubles me greatly to hear people question, and gossip, about his relationship with you."

Marguerite was remorseful as she said, "Yes, it was not supposed to go like this. I fear I have been very naïve, and careless, and I'm so sorry."

Gabriel nodded, and then he said, "I think Adele and I have been careless, too. I don't think I've ever told you this, but I'm so thankful that you trusted Adele and me with your son. I could not love him more. Honestly, he has been such a gift to our family. But I do feel bad for you. He is rightfully your child, and you have had to live your life at a distance from him."

Marguerite very much appreciated Gabriel's acknowledgment that she was indeed Henri's mother. She needed to hear it from him to ease some of the pain and soothe the rift between them. Marguerite said in a manner-of-fact way, "It was my decision that Henri would grow up in your family, as your son. You have been an amazing father to him, and for that I am thankful. Obviously, I have sacrificed a lot to give him the life I imagined for him. And...I swear on a stack of Bibles, I am going to do everything in my power to make sure that his life is not disrupted."

Gabriel appeared almost fearful of the answer, as he asked, "What about Jacob? Is he asking questions?"

"Well, he's not happy that I'm back in Bayeux. I'm an inconvenient reminder of his past."

"But...does he suspect that Henri is his son?"

"I don't think he knows, but I'm not completely certain. Honestly, his biggest concern is his reputation."

Gabriel responded forcefully, "I hate him for how he treated you, and I will not let him harm my son."

Marguerite gave him a worried look as she said, "Gabriel, you need to let me deal with this. Getting hot-headed will add nothing good to this situation."

He smiled slightly, as he listened to this woman who looked and sounded so much like his wife. With a forced calmness, he asked, "Okay, so how do we end all this speculation and gossip?"

Marguerite looked a bit devilish as she smirked and said, "We lie."

There was complete silence for a moment, and then the somberness suddenly lifted, as Gabriel shook his head and laughed, deep and spontaneous, his belly heaving. Although he found this woman deeply conflicted, he also loved her in a sisterly way. When the air had cleared, and the laughter subsided, he said, "Well, nothing new there. We've been lying all along, right?"

"Yes, it's been a rather elaborate lie, but I think we need to be a lot more convincing. We need to speak and act as though Henri and Louis are my adorable, much beloved little nephews."

"Yes! And...I think it would be wise if we didn't bring the boys to church for a while. I'm not sure we could control the boys' excitement around you, and it makes no sense to spark any more curiosity and gossip."

Marguerite nodded as she said, "Yes, I think that would be wise. I was going to speak with you about that. If it's okay with you, I'll drive myself out to the farm to visit on Sunday afternoons. That way, I will get to see Henri, and not have to be concerned about the curiosity of the townspeople."

"You are always welcome at the farm, and I think you know that you're a very important part of our family."

Marguerite appreciated the words, the inclusiveness. She seemed to relax a bit as she said, "I've already been talking about Henri and Louis to my children's choir, describing them as my mischievous, fun-loving nephews. The children love these stories, and I'm sure they'll help spread the word in town, that Henri and Louis are my nephews."

Gabriel looked visibly relieved and appeared to be more convinced, as Marguerite tried to reassure him that Henri's identity and security in his family was safe.

Finally, he said, "I'm sorry if I hurt you. That was certainly not my intent. As a matter of fact, Adele did not want me to come talk with you. She thought I was too hot-headed, and I would say things that I might regret."

"Ahh...that does sound like Adele. Well, I'm glad that you did stop by, even if you did have a few moments of hotheadedness. I think Henri is a very lucky little boy, to have you as his father."

Gabriel seemed truly touched by Marguerite's admission. He awkwardly smiled as he stepped out of the apartment and returned to the busy weekly farmer's market, to sell his produce.

Marguerite felt inordinately tired. She was deep in thought, hunched over, methodically staring at the cobblestones, as she ambled trance-like toward Louise's apartment. In her state of preoccupation, she barely heard her name being called. She turned around to look and saw Jacob in the distance. Her heart suddenly began beating fast, and she quickly ducked into Louise's nearby apartment. She slammed the door with a ferocity that made the metal hinges echo the jarring sound. Marguerite spun around and collapsed against the door, silently gasping as she waited for him to knock. Louise stared dumbfounded at her friend, as she instinctively knew to remain quiet, waiting for the threat to pass. Blessedly, the knock did not come.

After what seemed like an eternity, finally Marguerite spoke, "Jacob followed me here."

Louise was always her most determined self when she was dealing with other people's problems. She was fierce and decisive, and she put her hands on her hips and declared, "Don't you dare let that poor excuse of a man ruin your life!"

Marguerite was feeling uncharacteristically defeated, and uncertain, as she responded, "It's become such a tangle of lies. I'm not sure that I can do this anymore."

"What about Jacob's lies? His lies are so much bigger and more damning! Jacob lies every time he pretends not to know you. He lies every time he pretends that he does not have a child. Don't tell me how sad you are that you have had to lie. This is about doing the right thing for your child. You're stronger than this man. Don't even think about letting him bully you into a corner!"

Marguerite was soaking up Louise's tirade, trying to muster the gumption to truly confront this man whom she hated. Finally, she admitted, "I don't really know what to say to Jacob to make him leave me alone."

Louise instantly responded, "You need to convince him that, without a doubt, Henri is your nephew."

Marguerite sounded deflated and hopeless as she answered, "I don't think I can do that…he'll see through my lies."

"You can and must do this! I'll help you. We'll practice the conversation that you need to have with Jacob. We'll do so until the story, the lie, is totally convincing coming out of your mouth. There can be no uncertainty, no doubt in your voice. You are only going to get one chance to convince Jacob. Only one chance."

Marguerite appreciated her friend with a depth that went beyond words. She nodded her agreement, and they set to work repeatedly role-playing the anticipated interaction. It really did help Marguerite relax and practice her lie. The play-acting had humorous moments too, as Marguerite let loose with her most candid, profane thoughts about Jacob. Louise laughed, as they prepared for the inevitable show-down between the two former lovers. Louise was forceful as the rehearsal progressed, and she emphasized in a determined voice, "You need to convince Jacob without any doubt that Adele, Gabriel, and their boys are all the family that you have in this world. For this reason alone, of course you hope to be close to your nephews."

Marguerite was shaking as she asked, "What do I say if he asks me if Henri is his child?"

Louise answered without hesitation, "You…tell him that he is not Henri's father. This man abandoned you, and your child. He is not Henri's father in all the ways that truly matter. He has not earned the right to make any decisions that affect Henri's life. I would not let him have any more opportunity to separate you from your son. Yes, it's a lie, but it's the lesser of two evils. This man does not have Henri's best interests in mind."

Marguerite was thankful to hear Louise's perspective, and it gave her the confidence that she needed to convincingly enact her lie. She knew Jacob would be persistent, probably menacingly confrontational, as he fought to suppress his inconvenient, unsavory past. But she also understood the man better than she wanted to admit.

In her most honest moments, Marguerite marveled that she could have ever loved, or even liked, Jacob. Yes, it had been a youthful love affair, driven by physical attraction, but she had not been just another young victim. Marguerite had sought him out, the pretty son of privilege, who flattered her, and made her feel like more than just a poor farm girl. For a brief, blissful time in her adolescence, she had felt attractive, witty, and desired. It had been an intoxicating feeling, and it had led Marguerite deep into a dreamy, unrealistic relationship with Jacob. As Marguerite nervously revealed her pregnancy to the young man whom she idolized, she was totally unprepared for his response, his immediate rejection of her, and of their baby. In disbelief, she fell completely into a numbing despair, as she tried to understand the rejection. Marguerite wondered out loud how she could have been so wrong about him. But, in her more insightful moments, she ultimately came to understand that he had offered an escape, and had allowed her to be a very different, more exciting version of herself. Initially, the anger consumed her and clouded her judgment. But that useless emotion quickly gave way to defiantly plotting a very practical plan for her child's future. She was determined that Henri would never have to bear the stigma of her youthful indiscretions. As Marguerite thought about how Jacob threatened her life, she knew that he was a simple man, and that he wanted to believe simple truths. Understanding him was powerful, for it revealed the answer to her dilemma. She knew that Jacob wanted to believe that Henri was not his son. It was more convenient, and certainly less complicated, and that fit with the way he lived his life. So, Marguerite was determined to deliver this convenient version of the truth to him. She would be absolutely, unblinkingly convincing. Marguerite's future with her son depended on her performance. Soon Marguerite sounded convincing, even to herself.

It was the next morning while Marguerite was just about to enter the church, that she heard Jacob calling to her. She turned, purposely took a deep breath to steady her nerves, then stopped to face Jacob.

Awkwardly, he demanded to speak with her. "You and I need to talk," he said.

Marguerite was calm and poised as she responded, "What can I help you with, Jacob?"

He seemed unnerved and a bit puzzled by her direct and confident interaction with him. He stuttered as he tried to sound like he was in command of the situation. "I...I need to know the...the truth. Is that youngest boy...mine?"

Marguerite was inwardly pleased that he was so obviously flustered, and she drew confidence from it. For once, she did not feel inferior to Jacob. He was just an imperfect man, nothing more. She looked and sounded indignant, as she answered, "Absolutely not! Those two boys are my nephews. They are very precious to me, so of course I make every effort to spoil them."

Jacob accusingly blurted out, "The youngest one looks a little like...like me."

Marguerite shook her head vehemently, as she quickly responded, "I understand your guilt, but that child's father is Gabriel LeBlanc. Making crazy accusations is hardly productive, and I'm quite certain that Gabriel would not be amused."

Jacob seemed taken aback by her forcefulness, but he also looked visibly relieved, as he muttered, "You can understand my concern."

Marguerite shook her head again, and said, "Not really. I thought we had agreed to put our past behind us and move on. Jacob, we can't keep having the same conversation, over and over. It's destructive to us both. Our lives came together when we were young for a brief time, but we're grown up now, and we need to move on, and live and act like adults."

Jacob seemed embarrassed, as he said, "I'm sorry. It's been bothering me ever since I saw you with that little boy in the back of the church."

Marguerite confidently told him what he ultimately wanted to hear, "For your own peace of mind, you need to understand…that little boy is one of my nephews. I am very close to my sister and her family, and they mean everything to me. They're all the family I have left in this world, and I have every intention of spending as much time as I can with them. And yes, I do plan to be the doting aunt, and spoil those little boys."

Jacob seemed to relax a bit, and to be predictably reassured, as he said in a superficial way, "Well, maybe now that we've cleared that up…maybe we can be friends?"

Marguerite was inwardly, silently appalled, but she disguised her disgust with the expertise of an experienced actress. She graciously responded in a calculating manner, "Jacob, I do think we can be friendly, but not friends. Too much has happened between us. I want to go forward with my life. So, no, we cannot be friends."

He seemed hurt, and a little startled by her self-assurance. He asked, "Do you hate me?"

"No. I don't hate you."

He was uncharacteristically meek as he proclaimed, "I…I am sorry. But how could we have ever ended up together? We're from such different backgrounds."

Marguerite's eyes flashed, and she knew in that instant that she did hate him. But she kept her composure, and responded in a detached, disinterested manner. "Yes, we're very different people, not meant to be together. We're in agreement on that point." There was pause, as though there was more to be said, and then a thoughtful, determined silence, as Marguerite turned and opened the heavy church door, and disappeared into the depths of the building. Once inside, she breathed a huge sigh of relief, and physically collapsed against the wooden door. She smiled to herself, and thought how the lie had been convincing, and that she must surely be on the path to hell.

CHAPTER 24

Henri's Childhood

1901-1909
Bayeux, France

Marguerite never regretted moving back to Bayeux to be near Henri, but there were moments of anguish as she watched her child grow up. With an almost equal measure of joy and pain, she obsessively watched Henri, as he achieved the ordinary developmental milestones of childhood. However, they were not ordinary to Marguerite. She marveled as Henri demonstrated his ability to skip, and she gushed to an extreme when he read his first words. She prided herself, probably more than she should have, that he was a thriving, happy, bright little boy. She loved watching him mature into a unique, strong-willed person, but all the while, she quietly lamented her small role in his life.

Adele and Gabriel were capable, loving parents, but Marguerite found herself quietly at odds with some of their child rearing practices. She admired Gabriel's relationship with his boys, but he was a strict, demanding father. He expected that the boys be up at the crack of dawn, helping with the feeding of the livestock and the milking of the cows. Gabriel worked side by side with his sons, teaching them the intricacies of farm life. He had no tolerance for shoddy work, and he was not afraid to admonish his boys if he thought their efforts were lacking. There was never any pushback from his sons, for they loved and respected their father. They were the descendants of Normandy farmers, and the craft was being melded into the newest generation.

On one of her rare overnight stays with the family, Marguerite finally decided to say something to Gabriel about his expectation that the boys learn to work the farm at such a young age. It had bothered her to see the little boys wake while it was still dark, and go out and feed the chickens, long before breakfast. One morning, after the family had eaten together, and the boys had left to go outside, Marguerite hesitantly broached the subject with Gabriel and Adele.

Marguerite fussed nervously with her coffee cup as she said, "Gabriel, I have wanted to talk with you for quite a while."

Gabriel and Adele exchanged knowing glances, as a heaviness settled over the trio. Never one to shy away from controversy, Gabriel asked, "What's your concern, Marguerite?"

"Well, I'm worried about the boys…that they're being worked too hard. They're too young to be doing all this heavy farm work."

Gabriel visibly stiffened, as he tried to respond in a civil manner. With a little too much force, and a little too much volume, he quickly reacted. "Nonsense! My sons need to learn how to work. It's good for them."

Marguerite was a bit shaken, as she tried to respond calmly, "I want Henri to have a childhood."

Gabriel looked at Adele, and she shook her head, signaling to him that he needed to remain calm, but he did not heed the silent signal, and he sounded threatened as he proclaimed in a booming voice, "My sons do have a childhood! What, are you saying, Marguerite? That you think we are not good parents?"

"No, I'm not saying that you are bad parents. I just want my son to be able to play, to be a little boy."

Adele, always the peacemaker, could see the fury building in Gabriel, and she turned to Marguerite and quickly interjected, "You trusted us with your son. You trusted that we would raise him with strong values, and that's what we're trying to accomplish. We are not trying to rob him of his childhood."

Gabriel quickly added, "My sons are going to know how to work. We're farmers. Our family has worked this land for five generations, and they didn't learn to run a successful farm by playing all day!"

Marguerite's heart was pounding, her face red, as she forcefully said, "I think I've earned the right to have a say in how you raise my son."

The silence was awkward, and deafening. Finally, Adele spoke, "I know this is hard for you, but Henri is our son, too. He is a joyful, headstrong little boy, and yes, he does know how to work."

Gabriel was noticeably relieved that Adele had spoken, and this time he did heed her looks. Marguerite felt like an outsider as she looked at the two adults before her whom she had entrusted with her son's care. Frustrated, and feeling defeated, she stormed from the kitchen and began packing her bag, so that she could leave.

Adele followed Marguerite into her bedroom, watching her stormily pack. Finally, she said, "I'm sorry if we hurt you. Honesty, we do appreciate your input. But you need to understand that farming is not only the livelihood, but also the identity, of this family."

Marguerite was abrupt in her answer, still throwing clothing items in her bag as she exclaimed, "I can see that farming is everything to Gabriel!"

"That's not true. He cares deeply for his family, and you of all people, should know that by now."

With jealousy and regret bubbling out, Marguerite said with a hint of sarcasm, "Yes, you have the perfect family, with the perfect husband, and the perfect children."

Adele was taken aback, wounded by her words. She was silent for an uncomfortable amount of time, as the sisters stared defiantly at each other. Finally, she said in a quiet, sad voice, "I know this has been hard on you. I am reminded of that constantly, as I see you with Henri. We have tried to include you in our family, in Henri's life, but I get the sense that it is never enough."

"It never feels like enough," Marguerite sadly admitted, tears streaming down her face.

Adele moved forward to embrace her sister. Both were crying, trying to find their way through the complicated family relationship that they had created.

Although there were tensions from time to time, the relationship between the sisters and Gabriel was strong, and they seemed to weather the ups and downs of their convoluted family dynamics. Marguerite was a definite part of the family, and the boys grew up knowing her well.

Marguerite had long dreamed of having Henri in her church choir. She fantasized, and smiled inwardly, when she thought about Henri attending choir practice, and spending valuable time with her. Sadly, it was not to be. Henri had no interest in singing, and forcefully pushed back when she tried to encourage him to join the choir.

One Sunday, Marguerite brightly said to Henri with more than just a subtle hint of suggestion, "You have a beautiful voice! I can't wait to hear you sing your first solo in front of the entire congregation."

Henri was appalled, and his youthful face displayed it. He looked to Gabriel, and his father gave him a warning look. But Henri was a spontaneous child, and he said what he thought, with unfiltered honesty. He declared, "I'm not joining the choir! I hate to sing!"

Marguerite was taken aback, but time and previous trials had helped her remember the boundaries of this complicated relationship. She responded, with remarkable ease, "No one would make you join the choir. Music is a calling. Only those who truly enjoy singing should join the choir."

Henri was instantly relieved, and he smiled at Marguerite.

Louis chuckled, a mischievous look in his eyes, as he remarked, "He sounds like a braying donkey when he sings."

The family laughed, and Henri playfully punched his brother in the arm, as they comfortably enjoyed their Sunday picnic. Gabriel looked at Marguerite and nodded approvingly. It was complicated, but their unusual family seemed to be thriving, and navigating life together.

In the winter of 1909, when Henri was twelve years old, a particularly lethal influenza descended upon Bayeux and the surrounding area. Outbreaks of influenza always triggered fear, for most families had experienced its ravages, and had stories to tell of their losses from prior outbreaks. Marguerite had lost both of her parents to the disease. This seasonal threat sparked true fear in the Bayeux community. Families kept their children home from school, and the attendance at Sunday mass plummeted. Likewise, Sister Marguerite canceled choir practice for the month of January. Still, the number of individuals affected by the disease grew to a startling number.

Father Bernard sat at his desk, sipping coffee, soaking up the companionship of Marguerite and Louise. Over the years, they had developed the morning ritual of gathering in the priest's office to enjoy coffee, and intimate, candid conversations. There were very few topics that were off the table, as they all shared their feelings and innermost thoughts with an almost startling candor.

Father Bernard looked troubled as he shared the news, "Jacob Laurent's son died last night."

Louise looked concerned and sad, as she said, "That was his only son. I'm not particularly fond of Jacob, but I do feel bad for him, and his family."

Marguerite seemed deep in thought, as she responded, "Yes, he's suffered a lot in the last year, with the loss of his parents. I even find myself feeling sorry for him."

The priest nodded, "I'm not his biggest supporter, but I'm worried about him. He is not cut of a very substantial cloth, if you know what I mean."

Marguerite sadly chuckled and nodded her head in agreement as she said, "Trust me, I know what you mean."

The priest went on to say, "His wife and newborn baby are sick, too."

Louise gave Marguerite a discreet glance as she quickly volunteered, "I can check in on them, and make sure that they have what they need."

Father Bernard looked sternly at both nuns, as he said, "Seven people have died in Bayeux in the last week. This influenza outbreak is racing through the community, and I'm afraid that it's going to kill a lot more people. I've seen this before when I was child…whole families wiped out."

Marguerite somberly added, "I saw several children die from influenza during the first winter I spent in the convent orphanage. It was terrifying. I got quite sick myself. But I have to say, I haven't been sick since."

"Well, I know this will sound a bit uncaring, but I do not want either of you having any direct contact with any of the sick people in the parish. If people need food, we can leave it on their doorsteps. It will accomplish nothing if we all come down with the illness."

Marguerite started to argue, "Honestly, I seem to have immunity from all the time I spent in the orphanage, so I don't think I would get sick."

Father Bernard was stern as he responded, hands on his hips, "Marguerite, I'm serious. I do not want you, or Louise, to have any direct contact with the sick, or their families. This outbreak of influenza will only stop if people refrain from having person to person contact. I'm canceling mass for the next month, and I will not be conducting any funeral services during this time. We need to be sensible and responsible, even if it is not popular. I've already been in contact with the church hierarchy, and they agree that it is not safe to have large gatherings of people. It will just result in more people dying."

There was a somber silence, as the threesome seemed to absorb the situation, and then Father Bernard said, "Marguerite, I do not want you to visit Henri for at least a month, until this outbreak calms down."

Marguerite bristled, and was starting to object, when Louise forcefully interjected, "He's right. It would be very unwise and unsafe for Henri, and the rest of the family. They should be fine on the farm. They're already isolated."

The priest gave Louise an appreciative look, as Marguerite sullenly accepted the decision. The friends could palpably feel the pall of illness and death that was invading their French community. Over the next weeks, the influenza outbreak did seep through the town and outlying area. Sadly, the infectious disease had spread widely in the schools before they were closed, and this had a particularly cruel impact on young families.

In the second week of the outbreak, news came that Henri and Adele were very ill. Leo, Gabriel's trusted neighbor and best friend, knocked hesitantly on Marguerite's apartment door. The burly farmer looked sad and anxious, as he waited for the door to open. He had been sent to deliver a message. Marguerite opened the door, fully expecting more bad news, as had been the pattern over the previous weeks. She gasped when she saw Gabriel's friend standing in her doorway. She could see by his demeanor, and his sad, sorry eyes, that he was about to deliver disturbing news of her family.

Leo's eyes communicated his regret, before he even said a word. He had a warm, deep voice and he looked sincere as he said, "I'm so sorry to bring you this news."

Marguerite choked back the tears, as she listened expectantly. Impatiently, she interjected, "They're sick, aren't they?"

"Yes, your sister and Henri are very ill. Gabriel sent me to come get you. He's afraid that they're not going to make it."

Her heart pounded in her chest, and for a moment, Marguerite felt faint. She steadied herself against the doorframe, then nodded, unable to speak.

Leo reached out to steady her, as he went on to explain, "Gabriel is beside himself. Frankly, I'm worried about him. He hasn't slept more than an hour or two, in days. For whatever reason, Gabriel and Louis are not sick, which has been a blessing."

"Well, I'm glad for that bit of news."

Leo wanted to be clear, to forewarn Marguerite, as he went on, "Adele and Henri are in rough shape. They both have pneumonia, and they've been drifting in and out of consciousness. It isn't very hopeful, I'm afraid. I think you should know that…to prepare yourself."

Nodding, as her sad eyes met Leo's, Marguerite responded, "I appreciate you coming to get me, and I appreciate your honesty." She sincerely meant every word.

Just as she turned and began quickly packing a burlap bag with clothing and extra food, Father Bernard joined Leo in the doorway. Always perceptive, he saw the stricken look on Marguerite's face, and he instinctively concluded that Henri was sick. The priest knew that he could not dissuade her from leaving to care for Henri, and he didn't even try. He watched helplessly as she frantically gathered supplies, readying herself to leave for the farm. Trying to sound calm, he finally said, "I can see that Leo has brought some bad news from the farm. What can I do to help?"

"Pray…pray for my Henri, and for Adele."

Momentarily, oblivious to Leo's presence, the priest placed a hand on Marguerite's shoulder and looked in her worried eyes, as he said, "I will most certainly pray for you, and your family, but you need to promise me that you will take care of yourself. Promise."

Marguerite tried to smile, as she acknowledged his sincere concern for her. "I promise."

Suddenly aware that Leo was awkwardly watching, wondering about the intimate scene, Father Bernard straightened and said with a forced pastoral formality, "I'll stop out in a few days to check on you."

Marguerite nodded, and briskly marched out the door, her supplies slung over her shoulder. Father Bernard felt deflated as he watched her leave, and he worried that Marguerite would not survive if Henri died. It was a terrifying thought. Sister Louise was anxiously standing next to the priest, as Leo and Marguerite hurriedly urged the horse-drawn wagon out of town, on their way to the farm. Together, Louise and Father Bernard walked quietly, somberly into the church. They went to the first pew that they encountered in the back of the church, and knelt side by side, as they fervently prayed to an already overburdened God.

As Leo pulled the wagon up to the farmhouse, Marguerite jumped down, and hurriedly gathered her burlap bag filled with food and personal clothing. The old door creaked as Gabriel pushed it open and stepped outside. He waved weakly to Leo and gave a nod of appreciation and thanks to his best friend. No words were spoken between them, as Leo urged the horses back to his neighboring farm. Exhaustion and defeat were written all over his face, as he turned to greet Marguerite. Tears were welling up in his eyes, his voice breaking, as he tried to speak. In that moment, the true gravity of the situation hit her like a massive rock. Marguerite trembled and had the terrifying thought that she was too late. Gabriel motioned her inside without speaking.

Marguerite could smell the sickness. The dank odor of fever seemed to permeate the farmhouse. She walked almost trance-like to the bedroom near the kitchen, and was aghast as she saw her sister, gray and sunken, in the simple bed. Instinctively, she rushed to Adele's bedside and knelt by her, tenderly kissing her forehead.

Adele spoke first, her voice hoarse and weak, and barely audible, "I'm sorry. I've done my best for Henri."

Marguerite's heart lurched, as she tried to comprehend what her sister was attempting to tell her. Through muffled sobs, Marguerite asked, "You're sorry for what?"

Adele looked lovingly at her sister as she whispered, "I have tried to keep Henri safe for you."

Marguerite could hold it in no longer, as she let out a feral yowl, her sobs suddenly loud and uninhibited. She struggled to speak through her convulsive sobs, "My Henri's…dead?"

Her sister weakly shook her head and reached out to comfort her sister. "No, but he's very ill and I do not think he's going to make it. I'm sorry."

Marguerite abruptly demanded, "Where is he?"

At this point, Gabriel entered the room, and gently led Marguerite up the stairs to a small, dimly lit bedroom. The sight that confronted Marguerite took her breath away. Her normally vibrant child lay ashen and diaphoretic in the sweat-soaked bed. His breathing was shallow, and she could hear a distinct rattle in his chest, as he labored for oxygen. Marguerite gasped and felt like she was sinking under a wave of grief. Purposely, she steadied herself, and took several deep breaths before moving to his bedside. Henri was listless, and barely responded to her kisses and strokes. Finally, his eyes fluttered open, as Marguerite spoke with him gently, lovingly. There was a flicker of recognition, and maybe even the faintest evidence of a smile. The spark of recognition had an amazing, transformative effect on Marguerite. In that moment, she consciously emerged from her overwhelming grief, and made the decision to fight with everything in her, for her son's survival. Her thoughts immediately went to her experiences in the orphanage, and specifically to Sister Monica, a scary, disciplined, demanding old nun. The terrifying old woman had taught her how to care for children with deadly influenza. The survival rates of afflicted children in the orphanage were remarkably good under her guidance, and Marguerite never forgot her lessons of care. She would use this knowledge to care for Henri, and for her sister.

Marguerite leaned into Henri's ear and said, "I'm here, Henri, to help you. I love you very, very much and I need you to fight to get well."

Henri stirred, then opened his eyes weakly. There was a look of recognition, and he seemed comforted by her presence. Marguerite quickly ordered Gabriel to bring tepid water so that she could bathe Henri and bring his temperature down. There was no embarrassment on Henri's part. In his weakened state, he felt only love in his aunt's touch. Next, Marguerite set about changing the soiled bed linens, and propped Henri up to a semi-sitting position. Although he initially resisted, Marguerite spooned water, and then thin broth, into his parched mouth. Gabriel gazed at the scene from the bedroom doorway, a bit of hope easing into his tired body. He did not know if Henri would survive, but he did know that Marguerite would do everything in her power to nurse Henri back to health. Gabriel moved quietly from the doorway, and hugged Louis, who had been peering anxiously into the bedroom. The father and son cried tears of gratitude, for the care and hope that Marguerite so willingly delivered.

Over the next three days and nights, Marguerite worked tirelessly to nurture both Henri and Adele back to health. The principles of care that Marguerite had learned, under the rather severe direction of Sister Monica, were diligently enacted. She directed Gabriel and Louis to help, making sure that Adele and Henri were hydrated, their linens clean, tepid baths given when fevers spiked, and that both patients were sitting at their bedsides, and even in their chairs, daily. The progress was slow, but steady, as both Henri and Adele showed signs of recovery.

On the third day after her arrival on the farm, Marguerite was feeling satisfied that both Henri and Adele were doing much better. Although both were weak as kittens, they were alert, coughing less, and breathing easier. Their fevers had subsided, and they were both drinking water and eating simple soups. Henri seemed to be regaining his strength much more quickly than Adele. He even tried to walk around the room, but became suddenly dizzy, and fell into Gabriel's arms. Initially, Marguerite was alarmed, but then she realized that Henri was showing promising signs of his former vibrant self, and that made her smile. Marguerite had observed from her time in the orphanage, how the young had a remarkable ability to recover from serious illness. Adele's recovery was destined to be longer and more complicated. Although she was making steady progress, Adele's energy was severely compromised. She became weak, and even a little short of breath when doing even light activity. But Gabriel was so relieved, so happy, he did not mind giving his wife the extra attention and care necessary for her recovery. The truth was, the family was grateful and almost giddy with relief, that they had escaped the travails of such a deadly influenza outbreak.

On Marguerite's fourth day, there was a knock on the door. Father Bernard stood expectantly outside, and he looked relieved beyond words when a tired, but smiling, Marguerite opened the door. He stepped forward and gave her a heartfelt hug. She did not resist but seemed to soak up the comfort and love that she felt in his touch.

Marguerite gently pulled from the embrace and mischievously said, "I thought that those in quarantined homes were to have no physical contact from the parish staff."

The priest chuckled, and said, "It's my rule, so I suppose I can break it."

"So that's how it goes."

A bit of teasing was evident in his voice as he said, "I would hardly count you as a rule follower."

"No, I'm much more likely to follow my heart, and for this, I have no regrets. Henri and Adele were in rough shape when I got here. Honestly, I was terrified that they might die."

The priest asked, "So they are doing better?"

Marguerite sighed, and gave a weary smile, as she said, "Oh yes. They both are doing much better. Henri seems to be quickly regaining his strength, but Adele is extremely weak. I think she'll do fine, but it's going to take quite a while before she's fully recovered."

Father Bernard could sense Marguerite's fatigue, and he knew that she had put her heart and soul into caring for Henri and Adele. He loved this about her. The relationship between the priest and the nun had many contradictory aspects, but the mutual respect, trust, and admiration for each other, made it an oddly intimate, but distantly professional affair.

Gabriel came out of the barn just as the priest was leaving. The two men were friends, and it was apparent in the ease and openness of their conversation. In many ways, the priest had become an unofficial part of their family. Father Bernard had weathered many a storm with Marguerite, and Gabriel was thankful that his beloved sister-in-law had such a meaningful relationship in her life.

Marguerite stayed at the farm another two weeks, as she helped nurse both Henri and Adele back to health. It was valuable time with Henri. She read to him daily, and eventually took him for walks around the farm as he regained his strength. She was fascinated with his interests, and his zest for life. The unexpected circumstance of her spending time with Henri on the farm had presented an opportunity to get to know her son even better. It was a gift of time that Marguerite accepted gratefully. Secretly she wished that her role in his life was different, but Marguerite knew that Henri loved her, and that was enough – most of the time.

CHAPTER 25

Love and War

1914
Bayeux, France

In Henri's seventeenth year, the inevitable happened. He fell in love. The joyful, charismatic young man with the distinct, fine facial features of his biological father, and the well-built, muscled body of a Normandy farmer, had drawn the attention of Sophie Bissett. It was an unlikely match, and in many ways an old story, oft repeated throughout time, as the two young lovers were from distinctly different backgrounds.

Sophie was a tall girl, lithe, but shapely in a voluptuous way, and she moved with the grace of a trained dancer. Her thick, almost black, hair glistened, and framed her finely boned facial features, but it was her gorgeous alabaster skin, and dark, arresting eyes, that drew young boys to her like a magnet. Sophie was the only daughter of a wealthy, ruthless banker, and she had an innate confidence and wore all the vestiges of a life of privilege, like a finely adorned prize. Despite repeated warnings from her father, Sophie was drawn to Henri. Initially, it was an act of defiance. He was the forbidden fruit, the beautiful, common farm boy, from a social class that was unacceptable to her father.

Although he was not born of privilege, Henri was equally good-looking and mesmerizing. The beautiful child had grown to be a beautiful young man, but he looked to be an anomaly in his family, for he did not have the short, stocky build, or the thick, dark hair of his father and brother. He was taller than Louis by a good six inches, and he had a thin, muscular build that suggested an innate athleticism. The finely chiseled facial features were crowned by thick, wavy brown hair that contained gold and red highlights. But, like Sophie, his eyes were his most noticeable feature. They were intelligent and alert, light green in color with flecks of brown, and were framed by thick, feathery, long brown lashes. His eyes radiated warmth, friendliness, and a confidence that was contrary to his common station in life.

Henri's personality was radiant and big. He was, by his youthful nature, mischievously cocky and impulsive, which made him a favorite among his peers, and drew the admiring attention of a rebellious Sophie. His carefree, naïve confidence knew no bounds, for he had led a sheltered life, and in practical terms, had never known anything but love and acceptance.

The attraction between Sophie and Henri started as playful flirtation, and quickly became a collision, as the two naively responded to the physical draw between them. Initially, Sophie was just tugging at his heart, flirting, teasing, and exerting her newfound power over the male sex, but she found herself to be the one who was helplessly smitten. Henri's draw over her proved to be a tsunami of love and playfulness, and it pulled her into a relationship that intriguingly encompassed respect and friendship. It was all new, and it was much more than the ecstasy of their physical relationship. She had not grown up in a stable, loving home, and she absolutely marveled at Henri's close-knit family. Sophie's mother had died when she was only one year old, and she had been raised by an assortment of hired nannies, each of whom inevitably left after experiencing demeaning encounters with her domineering father. Mr. Bissett was known to be verbally abusive, and condescending toward his staff, summarily firing anyone who questioned, or challenged him. It was a tumultuous childhood, and one that had left Sophie uncertain and mistrusting of family, and suspicious of life in general. Meeting Henri was like finding the missing piece to a complicated puzzle.

Sophie's father, Mr. Bissett, could feel his anger rising, his temples suddenly pounding, as he watched his daughter passionately kiss Henri goodbye, in the shadows at the edge of town. The young man turned, and playfully blew a kiss to Sophie as he walked away. Mr. Bissett was furious as he stormed from the entrance of his bank, marching purposely toward his daughter.

Sophie was so distracted by Henri that she did not see her father, not until he grabbed her arm roughly, and demanded, "What are you doing with him?"

Angrily, Sophie shook her arm free from her father's grip, and defiantly said, "He is not what you think!"

"I know what he is…he's a common farm boy, nothing more. I told you to stay away from him!"

Sophie was shaking with anger, as she stepped forward to face her father more squarely. Loudly, with a clear, determined voice, she said, "Henri is wonderful. You should give him a chance."

His patience wearing even more thin, he hurtfully declared, "No! I am not going to give him a chance, and you are going to stop seeing him at once."

"No, I'm not! I love Henri, and he loves me."

"You don't know the first thing about love. How would this poor farm boy ever provide for you? Have you thought about that?"

Sophie seemed to suddenly lose confidence in the face of her father's fury, as she responded, "He cares about what I think, and what I want out of life."

"He doesn't have a clue about what you need. He's just a simple farm boy that has captured your fancy. Nothing more!"

Her anger and rebelliousness came spewing out, her restraint falling to the wayside, as Sophie shouted, "Oh, he's much more than you'll ever be! He's kind and thoughtful, and hard-working!"

Smugly, Mr. Bissett said, "Of course he is…and if you end up with him, you'll be hard-working too. You'll be a common farm wife! I did not raise you to become a common farm wife! You are better than that! I forbid you to see this boy ever again!"

Defiantly, Sophie responded, "I will see him. You cannot stop me!" Trembling with anger, at this man who had given so little of himself during her childhood, she stormed away.

The relationship between the father and daughter had always been cold and strained, but it steadily grew worse. Sophie spent more and more time with Henri, and she purposely avoided dinner, which was the one time of the day she and her father typically spent together. Mr. Bissett was not used to being openly defied, and he fumed, plotting as to how he could break his daughter away from Henri. In his most irrational moments, he thought about confronting Henri directly, but he decided this would only serve to alienate him further from Sophie. In the end, he decided to have a talk with Henri's father.

Mr. Bissett approached Gabriel cautiously at the farmer's market, for there was something powerful and unpredictable about the sturdy farmer. Gabriel saw him approaching out of the corner of his eye, and he was ready. He bristled and did not move when Mr. Bissett indicated with his thumb that they should move away from Gabriel's cart, so they could talk privately. The interaction between the two men began had a thinly veiled aura of threat hanging between them.

Mr. Bissett seemed flustered, nervously gesturing with his hands as he declared in a purposely quiet, controlled voice, "I need to talk with you."

Gabriel had heard the rumors of Mr. Bissett's disdain for his son, and it did not sit well with him. He squinted, and took measure of the well-dressed banker, eyeing him in a threatening way. Bluntly, he said, "So talk."

"Your son needs to stay away from my daughter."

Now, Gabriel stepped closer, squaring himself up next to this man he did not like, and did not respect. With a measured calmness, he spoke, "My son is a good person, and I trust him to make his own judgments as to who he spends his time with."

Mr. Bissett cowered ever so slightly, as he tried to project authority over the rough looking farmer. With an air of disdain, he said, "Let me be perfectly clear. Your son needs to spend his time with someone else…preferably some common farm girl, not my daughter."

For one fleeting moment, it looked like Gabriel was going to physically strike Mr. Bissett, but then he thought better of it, instead saying, "My son is more than good enough to be with your daughter. Henri and Sophie are young adults, capable of making their own decisions about who they spend their precious time with. I will not be exerting any influence over them, and neither should you."

Mr. Bissett stiffened, his eyes flashing with anger, as he pronounced, "They are not adult enough, to know the difference between an infatuation, and a true, lasting relationship."

His voice rising in anger, Gabriel indignantly proclaimed, "Well, my son may not be viewed as adult enough to be involved with your daughter, but apparently he is adult enough to go fight the Germans."

The significance of the comment was sinking in as Mr. Bissett suddenly changed his tenor and asked, "Henri has joined the military?"

Gabrielle bristled with anger, his temper giving way, as he forcefully said, "In case you haven't noticed, there's a war with Germany brewing, and both of my sons will be leaving soon to fight."

Mr. Bissett's mind, ever deviant and plotting, instantly recognized the solution to his problem, and his demeanor changed. In an obviously obsequious voice, he said, "That's very gallant of your sons."

Gabriel could easily see through the shallow, calculating man before him, and stared defiantly at him.

Sophie's father nodded to Gabriel in a feigned attempt at parental camaraderie, as he went on to say, "Yes, these are troubling times.

Thankfully, we have brave young men, like your sons, to defend us against Germany."

Gabriel inwardly fumed, as he correctly assumed that this hated man was pleased that Henri would soon be gone from Bayeux, and from his daughter's life.

Mr. Bissett abruptly ended the uncomfortable interaction, with a forced, overly friendly, "Well, you have a good day." Quickly, he walked to his bank, not looking back.

Henri's family had been concerned almost from the beginning. Adele and Gabriel could not help but smile when they saw Sophie and Henri playfully running through the orchard, but they worried that this love affair between children of vastly different means was destined for disaster. Marguerite tried to get involved in the private family discussions regarding Henri's relationship with Sophie, but Gabriel became increasingly frustrated with her worried laments, and so she was pushed to the outside, helplessly watching, and worrying. Marguerite heard rumors, and watched the inevitable calamity, from a tormented distance. In many ways, it was like reliving her own youthful love affair, and the painful rejection, all over again.

The relationship between Henri and Louis was complicated, with all the elements of love, competitiveness, and sibling rivalry. Before the arrival of Sophie into Henri's life, the two brothers had been inseparable, but that all quickly changed, and Louis began to feel rejected, and more than a little jealous. The beautiful young girl, from a wealthy family, had chosen his younger brother. Louis was suspicious of her sophisticated airs, and her beautiful clothes, and he quickly deemed her shallow and frivolous. In his world, all people of substance had to lead purposeful, hard-working lives, and this girl clearly did not meet that mark. And there was another rather remarkable coincidence, one that divided them even further. Louis had a girlfriend, who worked as a maid in the Bissett household. Bernadette was attractive in the way that all young people are, with youthful firm skin, and an energy for life, but she was not pretty. Her speech, and her manner of dress, were common, and they clearly communicated her low social class. The disparity between the brothers, and their girlfriends, was stark, and it served to escalate the inevitable sibling rivalry.

Louis would hear through his girlfriend, of the gossip that raced through the Bissett household, and it alarmed him to learn of Mr. Bissett's hatred toward his brother. It sparked an odd struggle in the older sibling. On one hand, he was jealous, and on the other hand, he was protective and fearful that harm would come to Henri, whom he loved dearly.

The last weeks before the brothers left for war were a whirlwind of emotion, a fog of family dinners and desperate moments, as the family clung to their time together. Sophie and Henri were inseparable through this time, always holding hands. They would slip away from these intimate family gatherings for private walks and precious time together, and no one dared object to Sophie's presence. The unlikely young woman had woven herself into Henri's life, and it was indisputable, even to Louis. The family could easily see and feel the draw between the two, and they worried and wondered how their love story would end. Desperately, they clung to the last moments of prewar normalcy.

The final farewell was a calamitous affair. Patriotic music filled the densely packed town square, crowded with families, all saying goodbye to their young men. There were pockets of all manner of farewells, some tearful, some full of patriotic bravado, some remarkably casual, as though these men were merely going off to boarding school. It was humanity, with all the differences in human connection on display. Henri pulled Sophie away from the family members who had gathered in the town square to say goodbye to the brothers. He led her into the deep recesses of the arched entryway to the church. Half hidden in the shadows, the two young lovers fell together, their bodies melding, fitting perfectly.

Sophie sobbed, her body shaking, as she said, "I don't want you to go."

Henri, sensing her love, and her fragility, tried to sound reassuring. He said, "We'll be together soon. I promise. I don't think this war is going to last very long."

"You'll write to me?"

"Everyday. I'll bore you with all the humdrum aspects of soldiering."

Sophie smiled through her tears. "I want to hear it all...everything that you're going through. Promise me you'll be safe. Promise."

"I am coming back to you. I promise."

"You better."

"Ahhh...now that sounds like a threat."

Sophie loved his playfulness, and it made her chuckle as she said, "Well, I am my father's daughter."

"You are nothing like your father. You are the most loving and giving person I have ever met. Oh...and you're gorgeous."

Sophie looked in his eyes, seeing his tears, sensing his sincerity, and suddenly feeling more at ease. "I'll write you every day. I'll bore you to tears, with all the happenings of my life here in Bayeux."

"I want to hear it all...everything you're thinking, even the torment of being with your father."

"I'm not sure I can bear living here without you."

Henri nodded, knowing the truth of what she said. "We'll get through this...and then we'll be together." He smiled devilishly, as he added, "It will drive your father wild."

"I don't care what my father thinks about you. I love you and I want to be with you...forever."

Henri sighed, so happy to hear her words, as his voice broke with emotion, and he said, "I love you, too. I promise...I will come back to you, and we will be together...forever. So, stay strong for me, and write." Smirking, he added, "I'll cherish every boring letter."

They came together again, kissing passionately, clinging, not wanting to part from each other. Finally, they pulled apart, vaguely aware that Henri's family was waiting nearby. Holding hands, they walked back toward the anxious group, who were waiting to see the brothers off to war. From across the town square, Mr. Bissett smugly observed the sad scene, as he thought to himself that time and distance would certainly extinguish the unfortunate infatuation.

There was exhilaration and pride in the air, as the military truck packed with young recruits heading for war, waved wildly, and called out their goodbyes to loved ones, and friends. The band playing patriotic songs seemed to elevate the celebratory mood of the crowd to an even higher pitch, allowing those who had tearfully said their goodbyes only minutes before, to momentarily forget their fears and sorrows. In this brief time, with flags waving, and the adoration of the town, these young men and their families were bursting with pride, and there was a strange and ominous joy in the town square, as the truck drove out of sight.

Sophie was caught up in the frenzy. For one brief second, their eyes met, and it settled them both. Henri thought in that moment, frozen in time, "My God, she's beautiful. I can't believe that she's mine." In the weeks and years ahead, he would vividly remember that moment, and revisit it, time and time again. It would become burned into his memory.

In the days following Henri's departure, Sophie felt physically ill. A tiredness had descended upon her, and she attributed it to her sadness. True to her word, she wrote to Henri every day, and the act did seem to lift her spirits, if only briefly. Impatiently, she waited for that first letter, that lifeline from Henri, but it did not come. Initially, she was puzzled, but still confident that he would write.

Sophie's father was suddenly friendly, as though they had never had harsh words between them. The house seemed bleak, and her life empty without Henri, and so she started to have dinner with her father again. These dinners were strained, awkward affairs, which left Sophie feeling more alone than ever. Her father pretended not to notice the tension between them, as he plied her favor with gifts, and promises of shopping trips to Paris. Mr. Bissett was in his most sinister, plotting mode. Unbeknownst to Sophie, he had arranged to have all the mail coming and going from the house carefully screened, so that Sophie would never receive any letters from Henri, and her letters to him never made it to the post office. It was a simple solution to a complicated problem.

One evening, as Mr. Bissett waited impatiently for his daughter to show up at the dinner table, he heard the distinct sounds of someone getting sick, retching violently. A disturbing thought crossed his mind, as he stood up and deliberately walked towards the sounds. He found Sophie leaning far out of an open window, pale and convulsively vomiting. As her stomach calmed, she pulled herself back from the window, and steadied herself. Ashamed and embarrassed, she looked up and met her father's furious eyes. In that moment, he knew the truth.

His voice shaking with anger, he yelled, "You're pregnant!"

Her head hanging, she nodded.

"Is this how you repay me, for all that I've done for you? You get yourself pregnant by a common farm boy!"

Still feeling waves of nausea, Sophie struggled to speak. Haltingly, she said with a visceral hate, "Don't talk about him...like that. We love...each other."

"Oh, really. Is that why he hasn't written you?"

"I'm sure he'll write when he can."

Mr. Bissett knew his daughter's vulnerability, and he used it to full advantage as he said, "He's been gone for three weeks. You don't think he could have found time to write you a letter in three weeks? He's forgotten all about you."

"You're wrong. He hasn't forgotten about me."

Sneering, Mr. Bissett said, "Oh, I think you're probably a distant memory. He's on to the next girl who is willing to open her legs for him."

Sophie gasped at her father's cruel words and started to cry.

"Well, I assume he doesn't know that he's about to become a father."

Sniffling, and feeling faint, Sophie quietly admitted, "No, he doesn't know."

Mr. Bissett suddenly brightened, as if he had an idea. "Have you told anyone?"

"No."

"Well, there might be a way to rescue your reputation and mine… but you need to do exactly as I say."

Sophie felt imprisoned by her father as she listened, scared, and confused. She hated her submissiveness to him.

"You can't tell anyone…not anyone! You're not the first young girl to get pregnant out of wedlock. There are solutions. I can make some arrangements to have you placed in a convent until you have this child. We'll have to come up with a cover story, so that people don't suspect, but I think it's doable."

Sophie was in shock at the speed with which her father conveniently planned to deal with her embarrassing pregnancy. She suddenly felt utterly defeated and helpless, as another wave of nausea overwhelmed her. The inner strength and confidence that she had felt when she was with Henri was fading, soon to be a distant memory.

Pale and shaking, the smell of vomit assaulting her nostrils, Sophie rushed to escape the room, and the reality of her life. With a swiftness that she did not feel, she clumsily, frantically ran out of the oppressive room, practically knocking over the young maid who had been listening outside of the door. In a very short amount of time, Louis would hear from his girlfriend, Bernadette, who worked in the Bissett household, that Sophie was pregnant. Conflicted and tormented, Louis made the decision to keep the information from his brother. He told himself he was protecting his younger brother from a relationship that had no future and would almost certainly guarantee Henri a life of grief. It was a decision he would live to regret.

In the coming days, Mr. Bissett reassured Sophie that he would protect her reputation, and that no one would ever know about her pregnancy. He would arrange to have her sent to a convent under a different name. Quietly, she could have the baby, and then he would put her up in a luxury apartment in Paris, and she could start her young life anew. Dazed and traumatized, Sophie listened passively, completely immobilized by fear, as her father planned the solution to her pregnancy, and her life. Through it all, she looked for a letter from Henri every day, but found none.

Father Bernard was surprised to see Mr. Bissett at his office door. The look of concern on his face instinctively told the priest that he came to discuss a private matter. He welcomed Mr. Bissett into the office, and quietly closed the door behind him. The wealthy parishioner wasted no time in explaining the reason for his visit.

Mr. Bissett abruptly blurted out, "I need your help with a matter that requires the utmost confidentiality."

Father Bernard was immediately suspicious, but he calmly asked, "What can I help you with, Mr. Bissett?"

The arrogant banker quickly responded, "My daughter has gotten herself into a bit of unfortunate trouble."

The priest had a sense of where the conversation was leading and he discreetly asked, "What kind of unfortunate trouble are we talking about?"

Mr. Bissett hesitated a moment before proceeding. "She has gotten pregnant by a common farm boy."

Father Bernard felt his anger rising as he tried to remain calm. "In my experience, there's nothing common about a common farmer."

The aristocratic banker was dismissive as he disagreed with the priest. "This one is as common as they come."

Father Bernard looked Mr. Bissett in the eyes and sternly asked, "Does Henri know about Sophie's pregnancy?"

The wealthy, entitled man looked stunned that the priest seemed to know about his daughter's involvement with Henri. He asked, "So you know this young man?"

Father Bernard responded very directly. "I know him very well. He's a fine young man and he comes from a strong, hard-working family."

Mr. Bissett sounded annoyed as he responded, "I will not have my daughter tied to a life of poverty and manual labor. She cannot marry this poor farmer. I will not allow it!"

The priest was equally forceful as he said, "I think it is only fair that Henri be involved in this decision. It is his child."

Sophie's father was suddenly enraged as he insisted, "Absolutely not! This common farm boy has bewitched my daughter, and I will not have him making any decisions regarding her future!"

Father Bernard struggled to maintain his composure as he took a deep breath and said, "Sophie and Henri are young adults. It seems only fair that any decisions regarding this pregnancy, and their future, be made by them."

Mr. Bissett was indignant that this local priest would dare counsel him regarding his daughter. His voice was quivering with anger as he exclaimed, "I did not come here to seek your advice! I give a lot of money to this church, and I expect you to discreetly help with this unfortunate situation. If I need to, I will go over your head to the church leaders. I'm certain that I can make your life here miserable. Now, can we talk about admitting my daughter to a convent orphanage under a different name?"

Father Bernard was furious. For an uncomfortably long period of time, he said nothing, and then he quietly surrendered the discussion to the evil man before him. He felt shame as he slowly said, "Mr. Bissett, I do believe you have me in a vulnerable position."

Sophie's father smiled as he proclaimed, "You are in no position to challenge my decisions. My daughter's situation will not become known to Henri, or to anyone else. Sophie's reputation will be preserved. Do we understand each other?"

The priest nodded, with obvious regret.

Mr. Bissett demanded, "Now, I need you to make a private referral to a convent orphanage, so that my daughter can be hidden away until this problem can be resolved."

Father Bernard felt disgust with himself as he assured Sophie's father that he would address the issue promptly. He said, "I do have a contact who can help with this situation, and I will write to her today."

The discussion abruptly ended as Mr. Bissett declared, "Good... I'll make sure there is a sizable contribution in the offering plate next Sunday."

The wealthy banker displayed a confidence and entitlement that the priest found repulsive. It was an uncomfortable interaction, but in the end, Father Bernard agreed to help Mr. Bissett find a convent near Paris, where his daughter could be hidden away, until she delivered the child.

Inwardly, Father Bernard was tragically torn between his loyalty to Marguerite, and the confidence he had pledged to Mr. Bissett. In his heart, the priest knew that telling Marguerite would cause pain, and re-open a wound that had long been festering. History had repeated itself. In the end, he decided to conceal the secret, at least for the time being.

The priest did not want this unborn child to suffer the loss of its biological family and grow up in an orphanage. It seemed a particularly cruel injustice, so that a prominent family could avoid embarrassment. The unborn child was in part descending from a strong, loving, Normandy family, and it seemed sacrilege that Henri and Marguerite did not know of the child's existence. He fervently prayed for the child, for the family, and vowed that he would not let Henri and Sophie's child grow up in obscurity.

CHAPTER 26

The Battle Within

1914
French Military Encampment in
the Early Days of WWI

The first days of basic training were physically grueling, but they somehow lacked the urgency of war. Many of the young recruits knew each other, and the training challenges took on the aura of a competitive boys' camp, as the lethal threat of war was not yet real.

Henri was true to his promise, and he wrote to Sophie every night. Although he was physically and mentally exhausted, writing to Sophie seemed to calm him, and offered an outlet for the humorous mishaps of basic training. The first week went by without a single letter arriving from anyone, and Henri accepted it as the inefficiency of mail delivery during a war. His confidence in himself, and in his relationship with Sophie, was high, and he threw himself into the rigors of training. By the end of the second week, letters had arrived from his parents, and his Aunt Marguerite, but not a single letter from Sophie. A sadness started to settle over Henri. He continued to write every day, but the tone of the letters was more questioning than confident. In the third week, more letters arrived from his parents and aunt, but Henri could hardly read them.

Louis could see the change in his brother, and he was worried. Although he did not care for Sophie, it concerned him to see Henri sad and dejected. At night, after a long day of training, the brothers would talk, and it was inevitably about Sophie, and why she had not written. Strangely, Louis found himself reassuring his brother that Sophie loved him, that her letters were somehow lost, but he too, was puzzled. Finally, in the fourth week of basic training, Louis received a letter from his girlfriend, Bernadette, who worked in the Bissett household. It was crudely written, and full of misspelled words and grammatical errors, but it shed light on the mystery. The letter relayed in a gossipy, small-town manner, that Sophie was pregnant, and that her father had sent her off to a convent to hide away, and secretly have the baby. Louis felt ill, the gravity of the news hitting him hard.

The letter was a gut punch, as he listened to Henri tearfully lament his angst and sorrow that Sophie had not written. Louis had never seen his normally cocky younger brother so emotionally fragile and dejected, and it was scary to watch. Physically, Henri looked drained and exhausted, and for the first time, he was struggling to keep up with the challenges of basic training. The deterioration in his mental and physical condition was quite remarkable.

All the jealousy and sibling rivalry between the two brothers fell to the wayside, as Louis grappled with the decision to tell Henri the truth. In his most honest moments, he had to admit that he did not like Sophie, and he despised her father. He knew that if he told Henri the truth, his younger brother would insist upon marrying Sophie, and this would tie him to an awful family, and a lifetime of misery. It was hugely presumptive of Louis to even consider making this decision, but he told himself that he was responsible for protecting his baby brother, and once the lie was enacted, it was hard to undo. Louis slowly started to back away from his repeated reassurances to his brother that Sophie loved him and started to say out loud that maybe she wasn't really in love with Henri after all. Surprisingly, Henri listened, and did not argue, or try to defend Sophie.

His letters to Sophie became less frequent, and less about his day, and more about the questions between them. Finally, Henri wrote to his parents and asked if they had any news of Sophie. A puzzled response came in the next letter. They had learned from her father that Sophie had left Bayeux for Paris. There was no other news that they could procure. It was all very mysterious, and Henri felt devastated, as letter after letter to Sophie went unanswered.

As inner turmoil boiled within Henri, there were rumors and news of German troop movements in northern France. In many ways, the winds of war were a welcome distraction to the pain and rejection. While the young troops around him became suddenly somber, Henri felt numb, and methodically prepared for the long march to northern France.

Heavily laden with all their combat gear, the rookie troops began the march before dawn. It felt very real, right from the start. The playfulness between the young men suddenly ceased, and they struggled to help each other, as they hiked for miles and miles through the beautiful French countryside. Over the next week, the troops marched approximately twenty miles a day in full combat gear. It was grueling, and many of the weaker soldiers fell out of the march. There were wagons that picked up the stragglers and those who had collapsed from the exertion. It was a humiliation that both Henri and Louis were determined not to experience.

The brothers had a distinct advantage over many, in that they were well accustomed to physical work on the farm, and they had a great reserve of endurance. Side by side, mostly silent, the two brothers steadfastly marched to meet the enemy in northern France. Henri seemed to welcome the physical pain, the extreme exertion, as if he needed to bury his sadness. Louis felt guilty as he marched next to his grief-stricken brother. Each was immersed in his own inner turmoil, a disquieting prelude to the days ahead. Steadily, they were marching toward a storm, one of unimaginable fury.

On the seventh day of the march, news started filtering back of a rapidly approaching German force. The commanders urged the soldiers to close ranks and to keep their weapons at the ready. The orders brought a sudden awareness of danger, making the rookie troops apprehensive and edgy. Scouts were continually going out, and coming back, to report to the commanders. As the sun was going down, the troops were ordered to halt at the edge of a high, flat field.

From the slightly elevated rise, Henri looked across the field at the German army that was amassing in the field opposite them. Peering from the distance of a little over a mile, it looked like an ant hill, buzzing with coordinated frenetic activity. The German soldiers were digging trenches, and there was a disquieting rumble of tanks and trucks as the army got ready. The puffs of dust, and the acrid smell, cast an ominous spell over the eerie scene. For the first time in over a week, Henri's senses felt alive, almost tingling.

There was a surreal quiet among the young troops as the order came down to start digging protective trenches. The men were exhausted from the grueling seven-day march, but their fear served as a powerful motivator. Looking a little stunned, as the grizzled old commander shouted his orders, the rookie soldiers dropped their backpacks and weapons, and fumbled to find their trenching shovels. The task seemed overwhelming, and not realistic, but they started to dig along the high ridge. By midnight, the troops had managed to dig a mile-long trench to the depth of approximately four feet. It would give the troops some cover from advancing forces, and hopefully provide a strong defensive position. The protective trench would be deepened and reinforced in the days ahead, but it would do for the time being.

The commander posted sentries and ordered the men to get some rest. He let his young, inexperienced force know that he fully expected an attack at dawn. The news had a disturbing effect on the exhausted men. The rumbling, and sounds of the German army at work, had quieted, and the silence was disturbing. Most of the men slept very little, if at all, that night.

Louis had been unusually quiet as he and Henri worked side by side, digging their portion of the trench. For the first time in several weeks, it was Henri reaching out and offering encouragement to his older brother. Finally, with the order to settle in and get some sleep, the two huddled together in the freshly dug trench, the smell of the earth strangely comforting to them. Henri could feel his brother trembling, and he was worried.

Finally, he said, "Hey, we're going to be fine."

Louis sounded hollow and uncertain as he said, "I don't think I'm cut out to be a soldier."

Henri tried to sound reassuring as he whispered, "I'm scared, too. Pretty hard to imagine what it's going to be like."

"I'm not sure I can kill someone."

Henri was rattled to hear these honest words come out of his brother's mouth. Again, he tried to reassure Louis. "I am going to be right by your side. We're going to fight side by side."

"You're more cut out for war than I am."

"Don't talk like that. Everyone is scared. It's normal."

Louis did not respond, but instead snuggled his head into Henri's shoulder, as if he was physically trying to soak up the comfort of his brother. For the first time in weeks, their roles had reversed. It was Henri who was trying to comfort Louis, and the conversation had nothing to do with Sophie.

The brothers huddled together, their blankets wrapped tightly around them, as they tried to stave off the cold. They nodded off from time to time, but the impending battle had them both anxious, and full of dread. They worried that they would not perform well under fire, or that they might not survive. It was a fitful night as they restlessly waited through the pitch black, dreading what the dawn would bring.

CHAPTER 27

The Grim Reality of War

1914
Battlefield in Northern France

The light of dawn was just beginning to peek over the horizon, when an unnerving rumble could be heard in the distance. Sentries sounded the alarm, and the unit commanders immediately shouted to the troops collapsed in their trenches that an attack was underway.

Sergeant Pelletier walked forcefully through the narrow, sodden trench, his body stooped to stay hidden from German snipers, calling out as he went, "All right boys, time to shake the sleep off. The Germans are heading this way!" He was weather worn, with leathery skin, and his eyes had a flinty alertness that missed nothing. There was no spit and polish to him, but he radiated an ingrained experience, and he wore it with steadiness and pride. He wasn't afraid, and this drew the attention and respect of his young troops. They were alert to his commands, and although most were terrified, they made every attempt to comply.

Just as the ant-like group of soldiers began to move toward the French trenches, the German artillery barrage began. The loud, concussive sounds seemed surreal, but not too menacing, as shells splattered mud, and cratered the field, far in front of the trenches. But the

German artillery was finding its range, and the shells started to fall closer. The old sergeant seemed oblivious, like it was exactly what he expected to happen.

His tenor raising slightly, he shouted out above the explosions, "Check your weapons! Make sure your ammo is within arms' reach!"

There was a cadence to his orders, a timing that allowed the troops to listen attentively, and comply. In an even tone, he shouted, "Load your weapons! Safety off…be ready! Do not fire until you hear my order! Do you hear me?" There was silence, and the old sergeant roared, "DO YOU HEAR ME?"

In almost complete unison, the troops shouted, "Yes, Sergeant!" The collective response seemed to steady them, to remind them that they were in the fight together.

The grizzled old soldier continued, shouting in a measured, calm manner. "Okay…boys! They're moving this way! I want you to focus your sights on a soldier directly in front of you! Don't fire…yet!"

The German soldiers advanced shoulder to shoulder, across the open, grassy field. Henri thought it was absurd that they would march so openly toward an enemy position. He could almost see their individual faces when the order came.

Explosively, the shout pierced the chaotic scene, "FIRE!"

The synchronized explosion of gunfire was deafening and followed by a surprising number of German soldiers falling, in all manner of contortions. The advancing line of men now had gaps in it, and there was a hesitancy and panic evident in their move forward.

Sergeant Pelletier took in the scene of the faltering line of advancing troops, as he walked back and forth behind the men. Seeing the result of the first discharge, he quickly and calmly shouted, "Well done! Now reload!"

Henri and Louis fumbled as they tried to comply with the command. Their fingers were leaden, uncoordinated, and they labored to perform the simple, familiar task. Henri could see that his brother was dazed, barely moving, as he shouted over the explosions, "Come on Louis…

reload!" Finally, the two brothers and a good number of the young men in the trenches were once again reloaded and perched at the ready, awaiting the sergeant's command. The artillery rounds were creeping closer, showering the troops with mud, and heightening the panic.

Now covered in mud, Sergeant Pelletier yelled fiercely above the fray with the same calm, perfectly timed cadence, "Okay boys... steady aim...FIRE!" Again, the line of German soldiers thinned, and there were now ragged openings in the line of advancing infantry. The French troops watched with an immense sense of relief as a few of the soldiers hesitated, and then abruptly turned and retreated, panicked, running like frightened rabbits, back to the German lines. The trickle of fleeing soldiers suddenly became a tsunami, as the entire assault force turned and ran haphazardly, leaping over the dead and wounded, as they raced back to their trenches.

His eyes were encircled with mud, and this made them even more piercing, as they took in the scene of the retreating German troops. There was a sense of relief in his voice, as the sergeant shouted over the artillery, "Nicely done, boys!"

The words had barely left his mouth, when an artillery round landed in the trench, not twenty feet from the old warrior. An instant eruption of concussive horror filled the sodden trench. The sound was deafening, as mud and body parts rained down on the stunned troops. When the air had cleared somewhat, Henri saw the old sergeant laying against the earthen wall, dazed, but trying to stand. Next to him lay the shattered remains of Joseph, a boy from Bayeux. Louis gasped, and fell over vomiting, as he recognized the mutilated remains of his friend. Henri, stricken with shock and disbelief, took deep, gulping breaths, as he reached over to comfort his brother.

Sergeant Pelletier knew that his rookie troops needed to hear his voice. Standing now, somewhat stooped to protect himself from German snipers, he shouted, "Okay...boys. Check yourself for injuries, and let's get the wounded back to the aid station. Keep your heads down! Let's not give the snipers any easy targets."

The stunned troops seemed to be steadying themselves, under the sergeant's guidance. There were moans and cries of pain infiltrating the bloody trench, as the young men worked together to move the wounded.

The grizzled, mud-covered old soldier was again calling out instructions, "Claus, I need you to keep a sharp eye out for any German movement coming this way. The rest of you…take out your entrenching tools. We need to make this position a lot more defensible."

There was a collective look of disbelief, as the battle-shocked troops said nothing. The grizzled old sergeant was not feeling patient as he roared, "MOVE! Get your shovels out and start digging! I need this trench three feet wider, and three feet deeper." The task seemed overwhelming, but no one dared challenge the old man. They trusted him to lead them through the horrific ordeal, and the seemingly monumental task had the effect of distracting the inexperienced troops from their thoughts.

As the sun set, Henri and Louis were slumped against the earthen wall, physically and mentally exhausted. The defensive trench was now wider and deeper, which allowed for safer movement of troops and more protection from enemy snipers. The young troops naively felt safer, and they were strangely proud that they had survived until dusk.

The gruff old sergeant approached them directly, walking with a slight limp. He brusquely pointed at them and ordered, "You two… follow me." The brothers looked at each other, dazed and puzzled. Dutifully, without speaking, they got to their feet and followed the old man, struggling to keep up. He led them to a tent, about one hundred yards behind the trenches.

Sergeant Pelletier approached the tent directly, and called out in a gravelly voice, "Permission to enter."

A refined, steady voice answered, "Come in, Sergeant."

The old soldier pushed the tent flaps aside and motioned for Henri and Louis to follow him inside. Louis hesitated and gave his younger brother a worried look as he reluctantly stepped into the shadowy tent. A kerosene lantern hanging from the tent's center pole cast an eerie light over the simple furnishings. A clothing locker was neatly placed at the foot of a single army cot in the farthest corner. Directly in front of the entrance was a wooden desk, covered with topographical maps and crudely drawn diagrams.

Captain Dupont was deep in thought as he sat at a desk, trying to analyze the bevy of information before him. He looked up and studied the trio who had just entered his space, as though he were taking their measure. He had the look of a man who had come from privilege, his posture regal, and his movements poised. His uniform was remarkably clean and well-pressed, and it showed no evidence of the day's grisly battle. The stark contrast between the old sergeant and the captain was quite breathtaking.

Captain Dupont addressed the sergeant, getting right to the point. "Are these my new recruits for sniper training?"

His military training was on full display, as the sergeant answered with respectful deference, "Yes, sir. These two are brothers. They seem to have an aptitude for guns."

The captain nodded approvingly, as he turned to Henri and Louis. "What are your names?"

Henri quickly responded, "I'm Henri, and this is my older brother, Louis. Sir."

"You don't look like brothers. Where are you from?"

Louis looked stunned, so Henri once again jumped in to respond. "We're from Bayeux. Sir."

Intrigued, the captain inquired, "Where did you learn to handle guns?"

Henri again answered, "On the farm. My father taught us to hunt rabbits and pheasants. Sir."

"Yes, you look like farmers. Some of my best marksmen come from farms. Well, I want you both to report to Sergeant Moreau for sniper training in the morning. I warn you...he's very demanding and he expects a lot out of his trainees, so be prepared to fully apply yourselves. One more thing. As a trained sniper, you are a valuable resource, and we make every effort to protect our snipers. You are never to participate in an assault on an enemy position. Do you understand me?"

Both Henri and Louis gave each other a quick, disbelieving glance, trying desperately to take in his words, and then they responded in unison, "Yes, sir!"

The captain nodded, and quickly resumed his study of the maps before him. "Dismissed!"

The sergeant held the tent flaps open, as Henri and Louis stepped through the opening into the night. Once the brothers were out of earshot, Henri clutched his brother's arm and whispered, a sense of urgency in his voice, "Did you hear him? Did you hear him? They make every effort to protect their snipers."

Louis angrily shook free from his brother's grip, and he sounded accusing, as he whispered, "Henri, they want us to be snipers. Snipers!"

"Louis, people kill people in wars! That's what war is all about." Although he could not see Louis' face in the dark, Henri knew that his brother was crying.

Softly, trying to speak through his tears, Louis said, "I killed to-day...two boys...no older than I am. I shot them in the head. Henri, I hardly recognize myself...I didn't know I could kill so easily."

Henri could sense the fragility in his brother, and it scared him as he tried to sound convincing, "Louis...you're a soldier. I know that you're shook up about today...about killing your first Germans, and about seeing your friend Joseph killed. I am, too. But listen to me... we need to survive this war...you and me...we need to survive."

The events of the day had stripped away all their bravado and false confidence. Louis sounded defeated, hopeless, as he said, "I'm not cut out for this. How can you be excited about being sent to sniper school?"

Now it was Henri who was angry, as he responded, "I'll tell you why I'm excited...it's a chance to survive...to not have to charge across an open field into enemy machine gun fire! Louis...they just gave us a gift…an opportunity to survive! Don't you dare play the part of the sorry soldier who just discovered that he was expected to kill people. This is war! People are going to die!"

Louis was trying to pull himself together, as he said in a less than convincing voice, "Henri…I know that. I know. I'm sorry."

"Promise me…that you'll do this with me…go through sniper training. This is our chance to make it through this war."

"Hey…we're brothers, right? Yes…we'll do this together…to survive." Louis sounded meek, and reluctantly agreeable.

When the brothers made it back to the trench, their whispered conversation ceased, as the uneasy agreement between them settled in. Silently, they unwrapped their blankets and tried to make themselves comfortable for another night of fitful sleep in the earthen trench. As the brothers huddled together, Henri thought briefly of Sophie, but his vision of her was like an apparition, barely visible in the fog. For the second night in a row, there was no talk of Sophie. All the brothers' mental resources had shifted toward survival.

Henri and Louis were up at the crack of dawn, and they promptly reported to Sergeant Moreau. He was a short, stocky, well-built man, and there was a no-nonsense, intimidating presence about him. His speech was abrupt, with a machine gun burst cadence to it.

Sergeant Moreau turned to face the young men approaching him, and said, "You must be my new recruits. You're late. I was expecting you an hour ago."

Henri stepped forward, as if to shield his brother from the verbal assault. "Sorry, sir…we weren't told to report at any particular time."

The sergeant sounded irritated, as he responded, "I don't want to hear any excuses. Snipers are up at four in the morning. I will not tolerate sloppiness."

Henri looked straight ahead, as he responded in a dispassionate, military manner, "Yes, sir."

The sergeant stepped closer to the two brothers, looking them over with unobscured curiosity. He demanded, "What are your names?"

Henri answered, "This is my brother Louis, and I am Henri LeBlanc."

Sergeant Moreau was antagonistic and probing, as he bluntly asked, "What makes you think you want to be a sniper?"

Again, Henri answered, "We were referred here by Sergeant Pelletier. Sir."

Impatient and irritated, the sergeant barked, "The question is, do you want to become a sniper?"

Henri quickly answered, "Yes, sir. We want to become snipers."

The stocky sergeant pushed past Henri, and stood solidly before Louis, as he demanded, "I want to hear you speak for yourself. Do you want to become a sniper?"

Louis was less than convincing, his voice quivering as he answered, "Yes, sir. I want to become a sniper."

Sergeant Moreau squinted and looked at Louis with a bit of doubt in his eyes. Finally, he said, "Well, we'll figure that out in short order. Let's find out what you boys are made of. Not everybody makes it through my training program."

Over the next few weeks, the sergeant put his new recruits through the paces, and he came to respect their rifle skills. The brothers worked together well, but they seemed to need each other to function in the heat of an assault. Henri and Louis' dependence on each other was concerning, but they were highly effective snipers, and the sergeant decided not to address it. The brothers both made it through Sergeant Moreau's demanding training program, and they steadily gained a reputation for their lethal rifle skills.

The proximity of the two entrenched armies made a sniper's job never ending, and it was killing on an insanely personal level. Henri marveled that the two enemies could exist so close, constantly poking at one another, gnawing at their vital parts, but never completely consuming or defeating their rival.

The back-and-forth assaults across the barren land between the trenches, added a bizarre, hopeless aspect to the loss of life, and it had a profound effect on the brothers. At night, they would huddle together in their blankets for warmth, talking quietly, trying to find some semblance of normalcy, as they remembered their lives before the war. Although talk of Sophie was less frequent, even that pain was a welcome relief from the events of the day. Louis quietly listened, struggling with guilt, and troubled that his brother could not forget this woman. Although physically together, the brothers seemed to be struggling with their own inner battles, as they both fought to survive.

CHAPTER 28

Dark Times

1916
Bayeux, France

As the Battle of the Somme raged in northern France, Marguerite nervously awaited news. It had been two weeks since Adele and Gabriel had learned that Louis had been gravely wounded. Their hurried departure to the field hospital in northern France to be with their son had left Marguerite completely unnerved. The war news that came trickling back to Bayeux was all bad. Several families had been notified that their sons had been killed in the battle, and a pall had fallen over the town. Puzzled, and worried beyond measure, Marguerite tried to rationalize that the chaos of battle had slowed the mail and made the news sporadic and unreliable. But in her heart, she had a gnawing, sinking feeling, that something was terribly wrong. Adele and Gabriel should have been back with Louis, unless he was so seriously wounded that he couldn't be moved, or he had died. The thought made Marguerite shudder.

The letter arrived in the daily mail delivery. Marguerite's heart skipped a beat, as she quickly noticed that it was in Henri's handwriting. He had written so few letters to her, that she was momentarily excited, and then a sobering, frightening feeling settled in. Her hands shook as she awkwardly opened the thin letter. It was simply written in the throes of grief, and it plainly stated what had happened to Louis, Adele, and Gabriel. The words had barely sunk in, when Marguerite dropped the letter, and let it flutter to the cobblestone street. A faintness overcame her, and there was a brief blinding light, as she collapsed in her doorway. Momentarily, she was unconscious, her mind trying to escape the reality that the letter had delivered.

When she awoke, Louise and Father Bernard were by her side. They had found the letter beside her, and read its brief, poignant message. They had been expecting news that Louis had not survived, but this news was overwhelming, and almost beyond comprehension.

Father Bernard gently lifted Marguerite from the street and carried her into her apartment. He softly, reverently, laid her on the bed. Dazed, and grief stricken, Marguerite began to sob, uninhibited, and loudly. Louise and the priest both fell to their knees beside her, holding onto her hands, crying with her. No one spoke for some time. The three friends just seemed to cry themselves out, the sadness was so visceral.

The woman who had offered comfort and hope to so many families that had lost soldiers in the war, fell completely and utterly into the abyss of despair. In the days following the letter's arrival, Marguerite was almost unrecognizable to Father Bernard, her skin sallow, her hair wildly unkempt, and the light completely gone from her beautiful eyes. Louise stayed with her for three days and three nights, listening, comforting, and encouraging her to eat and sleep. On the fourth day, another thin letter arrived. The writing was neat and precise, and the envelope appeared to have a smear of dried blood on it. Both Louise and Marguerite stared at it, frozen with fear, afraid to open it.

Shaking, with tears running down her cheeks, Marguerite sobbed, "I can't lose Henri…I can't!"

Louise, ever the steadfast one with other people's grief and problems, clasped her hand firmly and said, "Whatever is in this letter, we're going to face it together."

At that moment, Father Bernard entered the apartment, but he stopped short when he saw the stricken looks on their faces. Trying to project a calmness that he did not feel, he said, "Did this just arrive?"

Louise nodded, and Marguerite stared blankly at the unopened letter, her eyes focusing on the smear of blood.

The priest carefully picked up the letter like it might burn him, and he hesitantly tore it open. The single sheet of plain paper fell from his hands and fluttered to the table, landing with the written side up. The three leaned over the letter, transfixed, and slowly, purposely, read it, as it lay sideways on the table. Father Bernard was the first to look up, and he had tears in his eyes. He knew compassion and human kindness when he saw it, and this letter, written by the combat surgeon who had cared for Louis, exemplified humanity at its best. It was a message that Marguerite very much needed to hear.

11/11/1916

Dear Marguerite,

As a combat surgeon, I rarely write letters to the families of soldiers whom I have cared for, but I was so touched by Louis and Henri that I felt inclined to share a bit of their final days together. Henri arrived with Louis in the ambulance, and he did not leave his brother's side until their parents arrived. Over the course of five days, I watched them talk, laugh, and cry together. They seemed incredibly bonded in their love for each other. Both Louis and Henri displayed a loving selflessness that I have rarely seen in this war. As he lay dying, Louis was most concerned that Henri live, and live a full, happy life.

I extend my sincere condolences to you, as you grieve the loss of your nephew, and your sister and brother-in-law. Undoubtedly, you are numb with grief, and reeling from the loss of your family, but I caution you, do not let it define you. This war has brought forth the very worst, and the very best, in mankind. Your family is, in my mind, an example of the very best. Henri will need your help, and your love and support, when this war ends. So please take time to grieve, but do not let your grief turn love into hate.

I wish you the very best in the years to come, and I sincerely hope that I have the pleasure to meet you, after this terrible war is over.

Dr. Lamont

Marguerite picked up the letter, the relief that Henri was not dead seemingly allowing her to breathe deeper. She slowly walked in a circle, holding the letter, rereading it, letting the words, the sentiment, soak into her grief-fogged mind. There was a visible strength returning to her, and it was evident as she turned to speak with her friends. "This is such a kind and thoughtful letter," she professed.

The priest quickly agreed, "Yes, I would love to meet this man, although it seems unlikely that I ever will. While caring for the many wounded, he made the effort to write this letter. He was obviously impressed with Louis and Henri's relationship."

Louise added, "He's right, Henri is going to need your help when he returns from this war. Yes, you need to grieve, but you also need to move forward with life."

Father Bernard's emotions were evident, his slight Slovakian accent suddenly more pronounced as his voice trembled, "Marguerite, you have always been an incredibly strong person." He hesitated and then said, "I need you to survive this grief." The priest shifted uncomfortably as he looked at Louise. But the scarred nurse nodded in agreement, her expression understanding, as she encouraged him to go on. "We both need you, and Henri will need you when this war is over."

Marguerite looked touch by the priest's candid admission, but she sounded uncertain as she said, "I don't feel very strong."

Louise quickly countered, "You are the strongest person I know. We will help you get through this. Every step of the way."

Marguerite nodded, the sadness still there, but there was a determination to move forward out of the darkness.

Over the next week, Marguerite did return to her regular duties in the parish. Louise pushed her, challenged her in a loving way, to do the overwhelming work of providing comfort to the families who had lost loved ones in the recent battles. It served to help Marguerite heal her own wounds, and people knew on a visceral level, that she understood their loss. It was the second year of the war, and Bayeux was on its knees in grief. Almost a quarter of the town's young men had been killed in the war. It was truly a dark time.

The winter of 1916 was long and dark, but out of all the tragic war news, people came together, supporting one another, and collectively caring for the neediest among them. It was truly remarkable that from these most desperate times, the community pulled together to help each other, in the most practical, caring manner. Farmers shared their food with those in the community who were struggling to feed their families. There was no talk of payment, just an understanding that they were all in it together. News spread from house to house about the needs that were most urgent, and people shared what little they had. There was a pluckiness, and a sense of defiant survival, that would not let the community be defeated.

Father Bernard, Louise, and Marguerite were pivotal to the community's wartime response. They were tireless beacons of light in a terrible storm. Their quiet, sturdy leadership gave hope to the people of Bayeux, and it had the effect of magnifying the compassion that neighbor offered neighbor. In many ways, it was the best and worst of times. For decades after, people would reflect with pride upon the community's response during the last years of the war.

CHAPTER 29

Hidden Truth

1917
Bayeux, France

Marguerite and Louise would gather every morning in the priest's office to talk. The trio came to cherish this time together, as they got to really know one another in ways they never could have imagined. Although they had always been close, the relationship between the three grew even more candid, and more intimate. Their talks covered an amazing variety of subjects, as the friends shared the most private parts of their lives.

The nuns listened, spellbound, as the priest described his childhood, growing up with the gypsies. They could barely believe that this educated, articulate, compassionate priest had started his life in a migratory colony of Roma thieves. Marguerite chuckled that she had seen glimpses of the fiery Roma child, when Father Bernard's ire was up. There was no judgment among the trio, just acceptance, and more than a bit of fascination with their individual life stories. The two nuns even came to call the priest by his Roma name, Danior, when they were alone.

One morning, the topic of conversation turned to Henri and Sophie. The priest became uncharacteristically quiet, as Marguerite mused aloud, "I do wonder what Henri will be like, when this war is finally over. I will never forget the last time I saw him. He was waving wildly from the back of a truck, filled with local boys leaving for the war. Sophie was waving and blowing him kisses. It was such a touching moment. They seemed to be crazy about each other. I was shocked to learn that Sophie never wrote to Henri."

Louise looked puzzled as she asked, "How do you know that she never wrote to him?"

Marguerite sighed as she remembered, "Adele told me that she received a letter from Henri, asking if she knew anything about Sophie. He was heartbroken...said that he had written her every day for a month, and that none of his letters had been answered. Adele was worried about him, but she was also a little relieved."

Louise, in her matter-of-fact way, asked, "Why would she be relieved?"

Marguerite sighed, and seemed deep in thought as she said, "Adele knew that Sophie's father did not like Henri. He thought Henri was too common for his daughter. It made Gabriel furious, that someone would think his son was not good enough."

Father Bernard shifted in his chair uncomfortably, as he looked worriedly at Marguerite, and then fidgeted with the papers on his desk. Louise, with her sixth sense, her ability to read people, to sense their true intent, had the sinking feeling that the priest was about to reveal something uncomfortable. She looked at him, and Danior did not look away, but rather had a sorry, regretful expression.

Marguerite caught the look between the two, and she was immediately suspicious. Pointedly she accused him, "You know something about why Sophie didn't write, don't you?"

The priest looked ashamed as he nodded, unable to make eye contact with her.

Marguerite seemed incredulous, as she proclaimed, "I thought we had no secrets between us. Seriously, you're going to tell me something about Sophie and Henri...now?"

"It's complicated, and to tell the truth, I'm not sure it's my story to tell."

Marguerite was growing angrier by the second, as she demanded, "If you have information about Henri, I need to know! I deserve to know. I'm his mother!"

Louise looked aghast, as she witnessed this raw exchange between her two friends. In her own way, she knew what Danior was going to reveal. Quietly, with deliberate calmness, she asked, "Do you want me to leave, so you two can discuss this in private?"

Both Marguerite and Danior looked at her, and were briefly silent, and then they shook their heads, and said in unison, "No." The three had grown incredibly close, and they had learned to lean on one another through all the ups and downs of an uncertain life. Intently, the focus turned to Father Bernard.

He sighed, and hesitantly looked at Marguerite, as he said, "Sophie was pregnant with Henri's child when he left for the war."

Marguerite's mouth dropped open, and she looked bewildered as she numbly asked, "Did Henri know?"

"No."

"Why would Sophie not tell him?"

Danior hesitated, and then he said, "She was scared."

Marguerite grew quiet as the memory of her own adolescent pregnancy suddenly overtook her, and she started to cry softly. "She was scared. Just like me."

Father Bernard hesitated before revealing, "Well, there was a bit more to the story than that. Her father found out about the pregnancy, and he arranged for her to go secretly away to a convent to have the baby."

Marguerite turned, directly facing him eye to eye, her anger suddenly explosive as she realized that he had been a part of the deception. Her voice quivering with emotion, she demanded, "How could you not tell me?"

Finding it hard to utter the words, the priest struggled to say, "He...he made me...promise...that I...I would tell no one."

Marguerite gasped as she took in his tortured words. Lashing out, she confronted him, "Your loyalty lies with HIM? Does all we've gone through together over the years mean nothing? I thought you cared about me!"

Louise looked truly uncomfortable, and she felt like an intruder in an intimate tug of war. She started to leave, when Danior turned toward her and forcefully said, "Stay!" Quietly, she sunk down in her chair, spellbound, missing nothing in the exchange.

Then the priest turned his full attention to Marguerite, his confidence returned, as he attempted to explain, "I do care about you… and you must certainly know that by now. I have no loyalty or respect for Mr. Bissett. None."

Trying to control her anger, she exclaimed in an exasperated voice, "I'm confused. I deserved to know."

"Sophie made the decision to not tell Henri about her pregnancy. As much as we like to think of them as children, they are not. Frankly, I did not want to cause you pain. I did express my opinion quite forcefully to Mr. Bissett, that Henri needed to know about the pregnancy, but he was furious, and threatened to make my life in this parish a living hell. I'm not proud that I caved to his extortion, and that I helped find placement for Sophie in a convent until she delivered. I'm not proud of what I did." He hung his head and looked as though he might cry.

Marguerite was suddenly awakened from her anger and stepped toward him, placing her hand gently on his shoulder. He looked up and smiled slightly, appreciating the comfort of her touch.

Louise watched awkwardly, a witness to the scene. Finally, she gently probed, "Where is Sophie now?"

The priest answered honestly, "I'm not certain, but I think she lives in Paris. To my knowledge, she never returned to Bayeux after she left for the convent."

Marguerite quickly asked, "What about the child?"

"I did make a discreet inquiry to the Mother Superior, and I learned that Sophie had a healthy little girl. She would be about three years old now. I don't know anything else. Honest."

Louise was thinking out loud, as she said, "I'm quite friendly with the girl who works as the maid in the Bissett household. I bet I could find out about Sophie, and what happened to the baby."

Marguerite and Danior looked at each other, the sobering truth about their friend evident, as they both chuckled. Louise had a way with people. They trusted her with their deepest, darkest secrets, and she knew the townspeople in ways that were both intimate and damning. She did not betray confidences, so their secrets were safe, but she forgot nothing. Her wisdom, her innate sense of people, was built on her connections, which knew no bounds in the little French village. Marguerite and the priest had no doubt that Louise had the ability to find out about Sophie and her child.

Marguerite gave Louise an imploring look, as she admitted, "I do want to know." Then she paused, a slight smile evident, as she said, "Somewhere out there, I have a granddaughter, and Henri has a child. He'll want to know that...when this war is over."

Louise was quick to agree, "Yes, I suspect that Henri will want to know, and he's going to need your support to get back on his feet and rebuild his life."

The next day, Louise waited nearby as Bernadette left the Bissett estate after a day of work. Although only in her early twenties, Bernadette looked much older, and more worn than her years. Her skin was sallow, and her eyes did not dance with the excitement of youth. There was a tiredness to her walk, a slight stoop in her shoulders that spoke of her resignation to a life of toil, of hardship. Although spent from her day's work, Bernadette brightened as she saw Louise approaching her.

Looking concerned, but still smiling, Louise asked, "How is my friend, Bernadette?"

"I'm doing alright. I do believe that Mr. Bissett got a full day's work out of me."

"You work too hard, Bernadette."

The maid was quick to answer, "I do work hard, but I'm lucky to have a job that pays, so I won't be complaining." There was a toughness to the young woman, a defiance to survive through her own physical labor, no matter how it extinguished her youth.

Louise looked concerned as she said, "I do hope you take care of yourself."

Bernadette nodded, appreciating her concern, as the two women walked side by side back to town. Louise gently asked, "I know you're still reeling from Louis' death, but can I ask you a question?"

There was a brief hesitation in her voice as she answered, "Of course. Anything."

Louise was acutely aware that the young woman's life was hard and made even harder by the death of her boyfriend in the war. Gently, she asked, "Did Louis know that Sophie was pregnant with Henri's child?"

Bernadette looked hauntingly surprised that the secret had escaped, but she took a deep breath and responded honestly, "Yes...I told him in a letter, shortly after they left for the war."

"So, did he tell Henri?"

She thought for a second, hesitating before saying, "I don't think so. He certainly did not want Henri to marry Sophie."

Louise was puzzled as she probed further, "You sound uncertain."

Bernadette looked sad and troubled, as she responded, "To be honest, we wrote each other less and less, as the war went on. In his letters, Louis sounded like he was really struggling...mentally. I don't think he was cut out to be a soldier."

Louise reached over and placed a hand on Bernadette's shoulder as she said, "I'm sorry that you lost Louis in this war."

The tiredness seemed to envelop Bernadette, as she said in a weak, hollow voice, "Yes, the war has taken a lot...from all of us."

Louise looked suddenly sad for her friend, for her life, but she pressed on to ask, "I'm so puzzled. Why did Sophie not write to Henri? They seemed to be so in love."

Suddenly Bernadette's steps slowed, and then stopped. Her gaze lowered until she was staring blankly at the gravel path, the memory of her role in the deception suddenly washing over her, causing her eyes to fill with tears. For what seemed like an eternity, she stood saying nothing, her tears falling on her soiled uniform.

Louise went to her tenderly, truly concerned for her friend, as she took her in her arms, trying to comfort Bernadette with her touch, with her words, "I'm here for you."

Embarrassed and ashamed, Bernadette numbly told the truth, "Sophie wrote to Henri every day before she left for the convent. She would spend hours and hours writing to him. Mr. Bissett made it perfectly clear…that if a single letter made it out, or if one of Henri's letters made to Sophie…that I would be fired on the spot. It makes me sick, to think that I did this horrible thing."

Louise nodded numbly and was not judgmental. In a sincerely sympathetic voice, she said, "We all do what we must do to survive. Don't be so hard on yourself."

Her voice was breaking as she struggled to speak, "It was so wrong. I can't forgive myself."

Louise reassured her, "God will forgive you, and so do I. You were threatened. Don't be so hard on yourself."

"No, I've ruined lives. Henri and Sophie had a special relationship. It was the kind of love that most people don't find in this life."

Louise nodded in understanding, as she gently probed, "So what happened to Sophie?"

"Well, after she had the baby, Mr. Bissett set her up in a fancy apartment in Paris. She hasn't been back to Bayeux for even a visit. Sophie and her father were never close…and they have grown even further apart since she left pregnant."

Louise carefully asked, "What happened to the baby?"

Bernadette responded, "I'm not supposed to know…but I did see in a letter from the Mother Superior that Sophie had a healthy little girl. I'm not sure what happened to the child after Sophie left for Paris."

Louise mumbled, "So many secrets."

Bernadette responded, "Yes, I work in the house of secrets."

The two were entering the town square, and they instinctively sensed that their conversation was no longer private, but rather open to the eyes of the townspeople. Awkwardly, Bernadette wiped her tears away and straightened herself as she walked side by side with Louise through the streets of Bayeux.

Finally, Louise took her hand and said, "I know this was hard, but I appreciate your honesty. You need to forgive yourself. You need to lay this burden down. Promise me that you will stop by my apartment for coffee next Thursday when you come to the farmer's market. Promise me."

Bernadette smiled weakly, as she said, "I promise."

"Good. I'll have a fresh cup of coffee waiting for you. We'll talk. Please take care of yourself, my friend."

Marguerite watched pensively from her apartment window, as the two women walked into the town square. Louise and Bernadette walked slowly, halting from time to time, obviously in a serious discussion. Marguerite studied the two women, trying desperately to read the body language, to get a sense of the message that Bernadette had conveyed. Even from the distance of her apartment window, Marguerite could see that Bernadette was slumped in sadness, and appeared like she had been crying. The news could not be good, and she fought the urge to run from her apartment, and demand to hear Bernadette's story, which undoubtedly involved her son. But in the end, Marguerite stayed in her apartment, impatiently waiting for Louise, whom she knew would come.

As Louise left Bernadette, she headed toward Marguerite's apartment, but once outside, she paused, uncharacteristically hesitant, not wanting to share her discoveries. Before she could knock, Marguerite threw the door open and stepped into the doorway, her eyes piercing, questioning, as she stared at her friend. Louise gently brushed past her and then turned to face Marguerite.

The words erupted from Marguerite, "Just tell me!"

For once the roles were reversed, it was Louise who cautiously approached the conversation, her tendency for bluntness no longer evident. She took a deep breath before responding. "Marguerite, before I tell you what I have learned, I want you to understand that Bernadette is a victim, too. She is terribly sad, and regretful, about her part in this deception."

Marguerite's anguish was rising, her voice shaky as she said, "What are you trying to say? What has Bernadette done?"

Louise's honesty, her bluntness, returned, she said, "Mr. Bissett threatened to fire Bernadette on the spot, if she did not intercept and hide all of the letters between Sophie and Henri."

Marguerite looked wounded, the words sinking in. She paced around the apartment, shaking her head in anger and sadness. Finally, she said, "I hate that man."

"Yes, he is evil, beyond words."

Marguerite quietly responded, "I hate her, too."

"That is not fair. She is a poor young woman, who is the sole support of herself and her widowed mother. She fell prey to Mr. Bissett's manipulation. It wasn't a moral decision, for sure, but it does point out that she is a victim, too."

Marguerite was indignant as she said, "My son is the true victim. He has lost the most in this evil plan to save the Bissett reputation."

"True. But please, you need to remember that Bernadette is a victim, too."

"Louise, you know I am not good at forgiveness. Do not preach to me. Not now."

Nodding her understanding, her support, Louise was silent.

Pointedly, Marguerite asked, "So what happened to the child?"

Louise responded honesty, "Bernadette only knew that Sophie had a healthy little girl. She did not know what happened to the child after that. I believe her."

Marguerite shook her head, not so sure.

"Sophie left for Paris after she had the baby. Apparently, Mr. Bissett put her up in a fancy apartment."

"Of course, he did. Is it true, that she doesn't visit her father?"

Louise nodded, as she said, "Bernadette said that Sophie has not been back to Bayeux to visit. The relationship with her father was never good, but it deteriorated even more, after she left Bayeux pregnant."

Marguerite looked deep in thought as she softly said, "I always felt sorry for Sophie. She seemed so wanting…of a real family. Honesty, I think that was part of what drew her to Henri. He came from the kind of family that she wanted."

"You may be right."

Suddenly, there was a knock on the partially opened door. Father Bernard peeked in, and he looked at the serious faces, sensing that the meeting with Bernadette had unearthed troubling new revelations, disturbing truths that hung heavily over the intimate group of friends. He sighed, and stepped inside of the apartment, readying himself to hear the story, to listen and hopefully be the voice of reason, as an emotionally charged tale of deception and secrecy came to light. Father Bernard knew that Henri's return to Bayeux after the war was going to be complicated by the secrets of the past, and would ultimately test his fortitude, and his ability to forgive.

CHAPTER 30

Sophie Leaves Breadcrumbs

1915
Orphanage Outside Paris, France

When Mr. Bissett forcefully demanded Father's Bernard's discreet help in finding a convent to house and care for his daughter, the priest turned to a trusted confidante. It was the very same Mother Superior who had accepted Marguerite into her convent years before. She was in her eighties now, but remarkably, still mentally sharp. Physically, she was stooped and moved more slowly, but there was no doubt that she was completely in charge of the convent orphanage. Yes, she had mentored a planned successor, but she still stubbornly hung on to the daily operations.

Sophie was sent to the remote convent to wait out her pregnancy in secrecy, just as the first battles of the war raged. She arrived on a bleak day, with her cold, aristocratic father.

Mr. Bissett stood before the massive old wooden door that was scarred by weather and time. Impatiently, he repeatedly struck the enormous iron door knocker, announcing his arrival. A diminutive looking nun gingerly opened the door and peeked her head through the opening. The woman looked too small, and too young, to be a nun.

She greeted Mr. Bissett with a nod, and said in a respectful, direct voice, "How may I help you, sir?"

Mr. Bissett responded in a commanding manner, "I'm here to see the Mother Superior. She's expecting me."

"Please come in."

Sophie watched from the family's beautiful, shiny new car, as her father refused. He stood firmly, and said, "No, I'll wait here for her."

The young nun looked confused, but she did not argue. Quietly, she responded, "I will try and locate her." She closed the door in Mr. Bissett's face, and he turned toward his daughter, his irritation and impatience evident. Minutes passed before the door finally opened. A tall, regal old nun stepped confidently through the doorway. The long black dress, crowned with the black cloth headpiece that encircled her wrinkled face, made for an intimidating presentation. She approached Mr. Bissett directly, her gaze steady, and her alert eyes taking in the man before her.

Her voice was gravelly, and no nonsense, as she greeted him. "You must be Mr. Bissett."

Sounding a bit flustered, he responded, "Yes. I'm here to drop off my daughter. I believe Father Bernard wrote you about our situation."

"He did, indeed."

Mr. Bissett sighed with relief, not wanting to explain or further prolong the uncomfortable interaction. "Good. Then I'll get my daughter's suitcase."

Now, it was the Mother Superior's turn to look irritated. She curtly asked, "Does your daughter have a name?"

Mr. Bissett was taken aback, but he seemed to submit to the rather indomitable presence before him. "Of course." He turned toward his daughter, sitting uncomfortably in the car. "This is Sophie."

The nun walked to the car and extended her hand. "Welcome, Sophie. I'm glad to meet you." Sophie looked at the old nun, tears in her eyes. She said nothing but acknowledged the greeting with a meek nod.

Mr. Bissett seemed hurried and dismissive as he rattled off his demands. "As I'm sure you can understand, this is a private matter...a very private matter. You are not to discuss my daughter's confinement here with anyone. When her time here is over, you can contact Father Bernard in a letter. Do we understand each other?"

The old nun bristled, and gave him a flinty-eyed look, as she responded with a practiced calmness, "I do believe I've got the picture of what is going on here."

Mr. Bissett did not like her tone, or the look in her eyes. He reemphasized, "This is a very embarrassing situation, and it threatens the family name, not to mention my business. It is of the utmost importance that we understand each other."

Her voice was unwavering, her gaze serious, as she responded, "I suspect that your reputation is well-established, Mr. Bissett. But, let me be clear. I am not in the business of revealing family secrets. It's hurtful, and contrary to my line of work. We are all God's people. Even you."

He seemed satisfied as he reached in his suit pocket and pulled out a packet of money and extended it to the old nun. "I'm sure you have expenses here, that you could use a little help with."

The old nun's eyes flashed with anger, her pride threatening to overtake her practical need for money, to feed the many orphans in her care. With a determined, steady look on her face, she reached up and accepted the money. She did not express her thanks, just looked at Mr. Bissett with the experienced understanding of someone who has lived a long time. Mr. Bissett turned abruptly and went to help his obviously pregnant daughter from the vehicle. Leaving Sophie standing beside her large, overstuffed suitcase, Mr. Bissett climbed into the shiny car, and escaped quickly down the long drive, leaving a cloud of dust billowing behind him.

Sophie collapsed into sobs, as the dust settled over them. The Mother Superior reached over and put her arm around the distraught young girl, offering her words of comfort. "You poor thing. I promise we'll help you get through this time." The elderly nun picked up the heavy suitcase with surprising ease and led Sophie inside of the imposing building. Once inside, Sophie calmed a bit, and reached over to carry her own suitcase. Smiling slightly, the nun started to walk to her office, Sophie following.

Sophie stepped hesitantly into the ancient office. Illuminated by a small window, dust mites were visible as the morning sun streamed into the cluttered space. At first glance, the desk looked like a trash heap, but with further study, one could discern distinct piles of bills and letters. The Mother Superior pointed to a hard, wooden chair opposite her desk, and Sophie sat herself down gingerly, intrigued by both the office and the old nun.

The Mother Superior relaxed in her chair and studied the girl before she spoke, her deep, gravelly voice projecting surprising compassion. "I know you're feeling overwhelmed right now."

Sophie looked wounded, as she wiped her tears and said, "You probably wonder why someone like me…is here."

With no malice in her voice, the aged nun responded, "I'm pretty sure I know why you're here."

"You're wondering why a girl from a wealthy family has been sent away."

The nun shook her head, as she looked directly at Sophie. "Honestly, you're not the first young woman from a wealthy family who has been sent here to conceal an embarrassing pregnancy."

Sophie's response was angry, and childlike. Accusingly, she spouted, "You think I'm just another spoiled rich girl that got herself into trouble and had to be sent away to save the family reputation."

Calmly, deliberately, the Mother Superior said, "I think no such thing. As you can well imagine, I've seen a lot over my life, and I don't judge, or make assumptions."

"I'm pregnant because I fell in love with a boy, and he loved me, too. I'm not sorry about that."

With complete sincerity, the Mother Superior responded, "You're fortunate to have known that kind of a relationship. Not everyone finds that in this life."

Sophie did not expect this response, and her surprise was apparent on her face. Somewhat guardedly, she said, "My father didn't approve of Henri, thought him too common for someone like me."

"Ahh...so where is Henri now?"

"He's off fighting in northern France."

The interaction between the young girl and the old woman seemed to have fallen into an awkward conversation. Her bright eyes alert, she pointedly asked, "So what does Henri think about your father bringing you here?"

She hung her head, as she answered, "He doesn't know I'm pregnant."

The old nun looked puzzled. Not wanting to wound her further, but needing to know, she reluctantly probed, "You did tell him?"

The memory caused Sophie to cry, and she responded, "I didn't know I was pregnant when he left for the war, but I wrote to him, and told him in a letter."

"He must have been shocked to learn such news."

Crying harder now, Sophie was barely understandable. "I don't know. He never wrote back."

"You haven't heard from him since he left?"

"No. Not a single letter. I wrote to him every day for months. Not a single letter came back to me."

The Mother Superior sighed and nodded in sympathy. She said, "Which of course has left you wondering, and feeling hurt."

"Honestly, this was not just a fling. We love each other. I just don't understand why he would do this to me."

"You're sure your young man is alive and well? The war has taken so many."

Sophie nodded and said, "I have heard through his parents that he's with his brother in northern France, and that they are well. I couldn't uncover any other news of him."

"I'm sorry."

Sophie was again defiant as she said, "I don't want your pity."

"I don't pity you. I only want you to know that I feel empathy for your pain. The loss of a loved one, either through death, or through separation, is a true loss. The heart aches just the same."

Sophie surprisingly defended Henri. "He is a good person with an amazing family. I don't regret our love affair. I have never felt more loved, more complete, than when I was with Henri."

The old nun smiled, her wrinkles more pronounced, as she said, "I'm glad you feel that way. Life is way too short to live with regret. It is best to remember and savor the good we experience along the way. I hope that we can help you through this next chapter."

"I never thought I'd be in this situation. I don't know what to do."

"Well…you're here now, and I suspect that gives you a bit of space away from your father, and his ideas for your future."

"Oh, you underestimate him. My father is not a good person. He cares much more about his business and his reputation, than he ever did about me."

"Sophie, you are an adult."

"I may be an adult, but I have no way of supporting myself, or this child. My father will disown me if I go against his wishes."

The nun looked dismayed as she calmly said, "You appear to be quite a capable young woman."

Sounding defeated, Sophie quietly said, "I've never been able to stand up to my father."

Sensing her fragility, the Mother Superior changed the subject. "Sophie, we will talk more about your situation soon. But right now, let's get you settled in. You will be rooming with another young woman. Marie is about your age, a pleasant girl, and she's about five months pregnant. Everyone works in the convent orphanage. It's not meant to be punitive. It's just the culture here, and how we survive. I've assigned you to work with Marie and Sister Mary Margaret, in the preschool area. Let's drop your suitcase off in your room, and head over to the preschool, and I will introduce you to them."

Sophie nodded, as she tried to imagine what this new chapter in her life would be like. Strangely, she did feel enormous relief to be away from her father, as she followed the Mother Superior out of the office.

The adjustment to life in the convent was surprisingly smooth for Sophie. Although she had never worked a day in her life, she fell easily into the tasks of caring for young children in the orphanage. She enjoyed the routine and felt satisfied with her care of the young boys and girls. It was a window into a part of life she had never seen, and she found it fascinating. The nuns and pregnant young girls worked together like bees in a buzzing hive of activity. There was little time for consternation, as the collective effort of the operation required so much focus and physical exertion, that there was little time or energy for anything else.

Sophie's pregnancy was no longer the center of everyone's attention, and this helped her think about her future devoid of outside influences. In the evening, she would sometimes wander down to the Mother Superior's office, where she would always find her busy at work, writing letters, and making plans for the operation of her orphanage.

The old nun always stopped what she was doing and welcomed Sophie in to talk.

Sophie peeked her head around the open door, and looked at the old face, which was deep in thought, carefully composing a letter. She gently asked, reluctant to interrupt the busy administrator, "Are you up for some company?"

The Mother Superior's face broke into a mass of wrinkles, as she smiled and said, "Come on in, Sophie."

"You look like you're busy."

There was a genuine warmth to her gravelly voice as she responded, "Nonsense. I always look forward to our talks. Please, have a seat."

Sophie moved with an awkwardness, as she sat down on the hard, wooden chair, her rounded belly prominently protruding. She shifted in the chair, trying to find a comfortable position. She sighed as she said, "I'm as big as an elephant."

"I think you're exaggerating a bit, but you are getting close to having this child. How are you feeling?"

"Scared."

In a reassuring voice, the nun said, "That's normal. You'll be fine. We'll help you get through labor."

"I'm more worried about what happens after labor."

"Ahh…have you made any decisions?"

Sophie looked thoughtful, as she said, "Well, I've decided on names. If it's a boy, I'm going to name him Henri, and if it's a girl, I'm going to name her Marguerite."

"You look like you thought long and hard about these names."

"I care about this child, and I want them to have a meaningful name, one that ties them to their father. I don't want them to be some poor, fatherless child."

The Mother Superior looked puzzled, as she said, "I certainly understand why you chose the name Henri, but why did you choose the name Marguerite?"

"Well, Henri adored his Aunt Marguerite. He thought she was a very strong, caring woman. If this child is a girl, I know she's going to need to be strong and caring, like Marguerite. And…I've decided to give this child, their father's last name."

The old nun looked a bit surprised, but then she smiled and said, "That's not customary when the mother is not married."

"I think I'm well beyond customary at this point. If Henri survives this war, I want him to be able to find his child. In my heart, I know that he would be an amazing father."

Gently, the Mother Superior asked, "So have you decided to leave the child here in the orphanage?"

"Yes. I have no way to support myself, or this child. My father will not lift a finger to help either of us, if I go against his wishes. That is the reality. I cannot leave here with a child that I can't provide for. I can't."

"You underestimate yourself."

"No. I'm being realistic. I don't have a clue as to how to be a parent, and I have no way to support myself."

The old nun sighed, her disappointment evident as she said, "Sophie, you're an adult. This decision is yours to make."

"I know you're disappointed in me."

"Well, actually, I'm more worried that you may regret not knowing this child."

Sophie took a deep breath as she hesitantly said, "I know you're going to think this is unusual, but I want to visit my child, and I want them to know me. My father plans to give me a generous allowance if I move to Paris after the baby is born, and I intend to use it to support my child, and maybe other children."

"In all my years, I've not encountered a plan quite like yours. Sophie, you do know that I wish only the best for you, and this child."

"Then let me visit as often as I want."

"I think that it would be good for the child to know their mother, and no doubt it would be good for you. You are welcome here anytime. It works out well for me, too. I don't have to say goodbye to someone of whom I've grown quite fond."

On a warm summer day, Sophie delivered a beautiful, healthy little girl. The bond between mother and child was immediately apparent, but Sophie was not a natural mother. She looked helpless when the little girl cried, and she was hesitant to pick her up and offer comfort. The nuns, ever observant, noticed her innate lack of parenting skills. Sophie instinctively knew that this was due to the complete absence of love and parenting that she had experienced as a child. But she wanted much more for her baby and was completely receptive, as the nuns patiently taught her how to care for and comfort little Marguerite.

The Mother Superior watched from a distance, as Sophie tenderly held her newborn, seemingly in awe of the little creature.

Sophie was oblivious to the old nun, as she spoke lovingly to her little girl, "You are named after a very special person, someone who means the world to your father – his Aunt Marguerite. She is a very strong woman, someone who is kind, and fun, and she loves music. And she's a nun."

The light of recognition went on, as the Mother Superior finally connected the dots. She vividly remembered the young woman who had come to her years before, distraught, and leaking breastmilk, who went on to become a nun. She remembered the visit from the young nun's family, and the obvious draw between Marguerite and one of the supposed nephews. Suddenly, it all made sense. The Mother Superior shook her head, as she thought, wistfully, that she had been slow to make the connection. She smiled to herself, as she thought, "I must be getting old."

True to her word, Sophie did return to visit and spend time with little Marguerite. She drove up to the orphanage in her shiny new car, every Friday morning. As the child grew to be a toddler, she anxiously awaited the weekly arrival of her mother. Although she did bear some of the harbingers of a child being raised in an orphanage, little Marguerite was certainly doing better than most of the orphans. She was a bright little girl, confident, and engaging. It was not the childhood that Henri would have wanted for his child, but little Marguerite was more than just surviving.

The war years had proven to be an unimaginable strain on the Mother Superior, as she struggled to handle the huge influx of orphaned children. Traumatized war orphans poured into the austere old institution, which was the last and only hope for those who ended up on its doorstep. The aged administrator rallied her last life resources to meet this challenge, as she struggled to save the orphaned children of France. Her stamina had lessened with age, but her determination had grown far beyond her physical strength. Old and determined, she fought relentlessly to nurture, and provide food and clothing for those under her care.

It certainly helped, that the Mother Superior was a prolific letter writer, and she was not above reminding those of wealth and privilege of how her convent had been there to help in their time of most urgent need. It was only fitting that they reciprocate and support her mission in its own time of crisis. The survival of France's children was the hope and future of a country that was tittering on the brink of collapse, as the war ground on.

CHAPTER 31

Long Lost Letters

1919
Bayeux, France

The summer of 1919 had been a summer of healing for Henri. As he worked with his war time comrade to repair the farm, he was also repairing himself. Henri still had nightmares and flashbacks of the wounding of Louis, but overall, they were less severe, and had become more of a recurring, frightening dream. He knew he would never completely leave the war behind, and there was a part of him that wanted to remember. It had been a painful, but formative part of his life, and he ultimately came to accept it as part of his journey.

The after-supper talks that Henri, Theo, and Marguerite engaged in had grown more intimate, and were now more open, more inclusive of previously off-limit topics. Henri seemed less fragile, more willing to discuss issues that previously would have been unimaginable. One evening as Henri wondered aloud why Sophie never answered his letters, Marguerite answered him honestly. The revelation left Henri dumbfounded, and then angry. His anger was initially at Marguerite for keeping the secret for so long, and then it shifted to Bernadette, the Bissett maid, and his brother's former girlfriend.

The very next day, Henri was waiting outside of the gate at the Bissett estate when Bernadette left work for the day. He was shocked to see how much Bernadette had changed since he had last seen her five years prior. Her youth was gone, her body bent with the exertion of the day, and her skin and hair looked lifeless and dull. It saddened him to see her looking so defeated, so tired. Preoccupied and physically spent, Bernadette looked up and saw Henri staring at her with a steely glare. She froze, and then her eyes teared up as he approached her.

Without an explanation or greeting, Bernadette looked at Henri and said through tear-filled eyes, "I'm sorry."

Henri tried to control his anger, but it gushed out, as he half-shouted, "You're sorry?! That's all you have to say?!"

Gulping air, she tried to explain while crying, "Mr. Bissett threatened to fire me if I didn't hide the letters. I didn't want to...honest. This job isn't much, but it supports my mother and me."

Henri suddenly felt sorry for the poor, defeated woman, for she too was a victim of Sophie's evil father. Accusingly, he said to Bernadette, "But...you told Louis."

"I did tell him in a letter. I'm sorry, but Louis did not want you to end up with Sophie. He thought she would ruin your life."

Henri sighed and acknowledged, "Yes, I know that now. He told me before he died."

Bernadette looked incredibly sad as she said, "Yes, we both lost Louis. I think about him all the time. It seems like a million years ago that we were together."

Henri's anger was subsiding, and he was almost overcome by pity for Bernadette, as he knew how much it hurt to lose a loved one. He responded, "Yes. I think the war has aged us all. It doesn't seem possible that we were all together, young and innocent, only five years ago."

Bernadette nodded, and quietly said, "I kept the letters."

Henri looked stunned, as he urgently asked, "You kept the letters? You have the letters?"

She smiled slightly, as she said, "Yes, I hid them in a chest in the basement. Stay here. I'll get them for you."

Henri's mind was racing, his thoughts tumbling, as he waited for Bernadette to return. A few minutes later, she returned holding two bundles of envelopes tightly bound together with twine. The letters were unopened, the sanctity of their words preserved for him. Henri gingerly took the two bundles from her. He looked pale and a little unsteady as he studied the familiar writing on the envelopes, mesmerized.

Bernadette smiled, seeming to enjoy this act of defiance, this rebellion against Mr. Bissett. She reassured Henri, "She loved you. She really loved you."

Henri wanted to hear the words, and he let them soak in. Finally, he admitted, "I was so hurt when I didn't get any letters from her."

"She was devastated, too, when she didn't hear from you. It made me sick to be a part of his evil plan. I'm so sorry."

Henri had tears in his eyes as he nodded, and said, "I know you cared about Louis."

She nodded thoughtfully. "I did care about your brother."

Henri held the letters close to his heart, then turned and walked away. When he was barely out of sight, he retreated to the shade of a tree at the edge of town. He lowered himself to the ground, the grass, and wildflowers fragrant around him. Hesitantly, Henri untied the bundle of letters written by Sophie. They had been carefully placed in chronological order, with a reverence that made them seem like something out of a time capsule. Nestled in the long grasses, Henri laid on his stomach, invisible to the casual passerby, as he opened the first letter, and began to read. He could vividly hear her voice, feel her love, while he read. It was almost as if time had stood still, and the awful happenings of the past few years had not happened. There was an innocence to her words, a hope, that seemed foreign now. He could not stop the tears from flowing, and he did not try. Letter after letter he read, and Henri was saddened by the progressive bewilderment, and eventual dejection, sadly expressed by Sophie. The pregnancy was revealed in a letter about three weeks after he had left for the war.

Initially Sophie had expressed a sense of excitement, that their love had created something wonderful, but then there was a sense of fear and regret as her father's influence overcame her. In the final letter, written the day she left for the convent, Sophie sounded so incredibly sad, bewildered, and frightened that Henri could barely stand to read it. The final letter was beautifully written in Sophie's artful script, a rawness so exposed, that it communicated completely the love she still felt for him, and the futility of the future that loomed before her. Henri could hardly breathe as he soaked in the words, feeling incredible sadness and anger that their love for each other had been manipulated so completely by Mr. Bissett, that it had extinguished the very existence of their relationship.

It was dusk, the daylight quickly fading, as he carefully reassembled the letters, and retied the bundles with twine. Henri marched directly to the church and walked inside, and he immediately noticed the light coming from under Father Bernard's office door. The priest looked up as Henri stepped into the office unannounced. His eyes fell on the bundles of letters that Henri cradled so tenderly, and he immediately knew.

Father Bernard looked embarrassed, as he said, "I see you recovered the lost letters from Sophie. I'm so sorry for my part in this deception."

Henri was angry and insistent, as he proclaimed, "I don't want to hear how sorry you are."

The priest offered no more apologies. He just hung his head.

"I need your help."

The priest looked up, with an aura of gratitude that maybe something could be done to help alleviate this young man's pain. He meekly asked, "Anything. What can I do to help you?"

Henri was direct, and decisive. "I need you to find out where my daughter is, and what happened to Sophie. I don't want to hear rumors. I need the truth."

"I think I can get that for you. I have a trusted friend, the Mother Superior at the convent where Sophie went to have the baby."

Henri was cynical, and distrustful as he asked, "Are you sure she hasn't been bought off by Mr. Bissett? He seems to have his fingers deep into every aspect of this."

"She is not someone who can be bought."

"Well, she would be the only one that hasn't been tainted by threats, or money."

Father Bernard again looked embarrassed as he answered honestly, "Trust me. She can't be bought. You need to understand that she will not mince words and may tell you something that you do not want to hear."

"I want the truth...the complete truth."

The priest nodded that he understood. He said, "I will write her this evening, and have a letter in the mail tomorrow morning."

Henri nodded, and their eyes met in understanding. Despite the recent revelation, he still thought highly of this man, this priest, who had stood with Marguerite and his entire family through the ups and downs of their many years together.

Without even knowing it, Theo, was an integral part of Henri's summer of healing. The unassuming young man was a wise and attentive listener, and as a veteran he understood what Henri had been through in the war. This understanding, without need for explanation, really bonded the two, and helped them both move forward, without continually falling into the despair of the past. Almost always working side by side, the two young men had an ease between them, an honesty, as though they were real brothers.

Theo had changed over the course of the summer, too. His slight build had become muscled, and he carried himself with a confidence that had not been there previously. He was not a handsome man, but there was something attractive in his manner.

Theo seemed a little hesitant, as he asked, "Do you know that Picard girl...Audrey?"

Henri looked at his friend and smiled as he responded, "Yes, she's a nice girl. You sweet on her?"

"We've been talking at the farm market, and I think she's pretty. She's nice, but I don't know if she would ever be interested in someone like me."

"You're not as scrawny as you used to be. You just might turn some young girl's head."

Theo chuckled, "I'm hardly a lady's man, but I would like to find a nice girl."

"Well, Audrey's a nice girl. Why don't you ask her out for some coffee and a pastry?"

"I'm afraid she'll say no."

Henri was suddenly adamant, "Don't be a fool. You can't live in fear, so take a chance. I don't want to give you a big head, but you are a good guy, and a lot of girls would love to find someone like you."

"You really think so?"

"I do."

Theo smiled to himself, and then he turned to Henri and asked, "What about you?"

"I don't want to get involved with any women. My life's complicated enough."

Theo looked concerned as he said, "You're still thinking about Sophie and your little girl, aren't you?"

Henri looked sad. He stared at the ground and said, "Yeah, I think about her all the time, especially since I read all those letters that Bernadette hid. I still can't believe that Sophie's father would go to those lengths to keep us apart. Honestly, I think I could kill him. I have that much hatred for him."

"You and I have both done enough killing. No more. It serves no purpose to go around hating someone."

Henri was defensive as he said, "Well, that's easy for you to say. You haven't gone through what I have. I've lost Sophie and our child."

"You've been talking more and more about your little girl. Are you going to try and find her?"

"Yes. Father Bernard is helping me. He wrote to the Mother Superior in charge of the orphanage where Sophie went to have the baby. He seems to think that she'll help us find my little girl. Honestly, I don't know what I'll do if someone has adopted her. It's hard for me to accept that Sophie would have left her in an orphanage. I can't forgive her, either."

"You have a lot to sort through, my friend. Can't say that I'm particularly good at giving advice, but I'm here for you, if you want to talk."

Henri was quietly honest as he admitted, "You know what? I'm almost more afraid that they will find this little girl. I don't know anything about taking care of a child."

"Well, I know you took care of me during the war. I suspect that you'd figure out how to take care of a little girl, and you know that Marguerite would help. So, I wouldn't worry too much about that piece. Take it one step at a time. But you better lay your hatred aside. It will eat you alive. You promised your brother on his deathbed that you would get on with life, and I'm going to keep reminding you of that."

It was the very next morning, as Theo and Henri were leaving the barn after milking, that they saw Father Bernard approaching them smiling, and holding up a letter. Henri stopped for a second, as he readied himself for the news he was about to hear.

The priest called out a friendly, "Good morning!"

Henri responded with a tentative, "You're up a bit early, aren't you, Father?"

Father Bernard nodded as he smiled and said, "I wanted to get this letter to you." The priest hesitated as he looked at Theo standing beside Henri.

Henri understood the hesitation, and he said, "You can say anything in front of Theo. He seems to know more about me, than I know about myself."

The priest nodded to Theo with a look of approval, and then he said, "It's good news. Your little girl has not been adopted. She's still at the orphanage. The Mother Superior describes her as a beautiful, healthy, spirited little girl."

Henri choked up as he breathed a sigh of relief. Theo was relieved and excited for his friend as he said, "That's great news, Henri. I'm happy for you."

Father Bernard could see that Henri was shaken and trying to absorb the news. "The Mother Superior wants you to come and meet your little girl…next Friday."

Wiping a tear from his eye, Henri's voice was filled with emotion as he responded, "I can't believe this is happening."

"There's something else I need to tell you."

Henri looked guarded, like the good news was going to be shattered, as he said, "Just tell me. No more secrets."

Father Bernard sighed in silent recognition of his part in the deception. He revealed, "Sophie named your daughter Marguerite LeBlanc, because she wanted you to find her after you came back from the war."

Henri looked stunned as he asked, "Are you sure about that?"

"I have a long, trusted relationship with the Mother Superior. She is not one to mince words or exaggerate. She wrote that Sophie named this child Marguerite, because you always had such admiration and respect for your Aunt Marguerite. Sophie was also insistent that this little girl should bare the last name of her father, and understand that she descended from a strong, loving family."

Henri looked dumbfounded and a little unsteady, as he looked wide-eyed and puzzled at the priest.

The days before Henri left for the orphanage were a time of excitement, mixed with worry. He struggled to carry through on routine chores, his emotional turmoil evident. The past was colliding with the present, and there were so many unknowns, causing Henri to have truly mixed feelings.

Henri was distracted and deep in thought as he uncrated the weekly produce and cheese for sale at the farmer's market. He looked up and saw a diminutive looking man in an impeccable suit walking briskly toward the bank. For a split second, the two men made eye contact, and then the small, well-dressed man looked down and pretended not to see him. Henri immediately recognized the man, and he could feel his ire rising uncontrollably. He stopped what he was doing, and quickly strode toward Sophie's father, all reason dissipating.

Henri stepped before Mr. Bissett, full and tall, as he demanded, "Do you remember me?"

Sophie's father looked flustered, as he tried to respond in a calm, take-charge manner. "I think you're someone who went to school with my daughter. I'm sorry, I can't remember your name."

Henri didn't hesitate. He drew back his clenched fist and forcefully punched Mr. Bissett in the face, splitting his lip, and spraying blood everywhere. Father Bernard was just emerging from the church, as he quickly took in the scene before him. He slowly let the conflict unfold, wanting the dominant player to deliver the decisive blow, the final statement. With the third blow, the priest intervened, offering words of peace and reconciliation. At that point, Mr. Bissett lay bloodied on the cobblestone pavement, dazed and barely conscious.

Father Bernard got between the two men and feigned neutrality, as he whispered to Henri, "Do you feel better?"

Henri looked at the priest, and whispered back, "I do."

The scene drew the town's market goers and, while they had no idea as to the substance of the conflict, they quickly sided with Henri, for they did not like Mr. Bissett. As the banker lay bleeding, no one offered to help him, but instead lined up to buy the LeBlanc produce. It was telling and said much about whom the town trusted and respected.

CHAPTER 32

Little Marguerite

1919
Convent Orphanage Outside of Paris

Marguerite and Henri started out for the orphanage at the first light of dawn. The sound of birds and the rhythmic clopping of horse hooves permeated the quietness of the morning, as they steadily made progress into the French countryside. Both mother and son were deeply immersed in their own thoughts, sitting side by side, the rough wooden seat of the wagon hard and uncomfortable, as they jostled toward their past, and an unknown future.

It had been over twenty years since Marguerite had made her initial journey to the convent orphanage with Father Bernard, and she was again remembering the angst of that first journey, as though it were yesterday. Marguerite had wanted to make the journey back to the convent to support Henri, but she now felt unexpectedly shaken, as the memories came roaring back. It was as though she was once again the devastated young girl who had left her newborn son behind, to start her life as a nun. Silently, Marguerite tried to calm herself, to hide her turmoil from Henri. She rationalized that it was silly, that she could still be grappling with these memories so many years later.

Marguerite desperately tried to refocus her thoughts. She looked out over the French countryside noting how much had changed since her first journey. She was startled by the physical ramifications of the passage of time. There were cars mixed with raggedy horse drawn wagons, and both shared the narrow, rutted road. The war had left the countryside and farms looking forlorn and neglected, but if one looked carefully, there were signs of a people who were rebuilding, reemerging into life. The battered barns and fences were being repaired, and the fields were planted with crops that had not been seen for the last few years. The war-weary people of France were rising out of the ashes of destruction, and they were steadily putting their lives back together.

Henri was completely self-absorbed, as he thought about Sophie, and meeting his child for the very first time. His feelings were raw and conflicted, and the certainty and confidence that had driven him to this journey had begun to dissipate. In his mind, he rehashed the words that Sophie had written to him, wondering if she still even thought of him. It felt like a lifetime ago. The war had created a chasm that made the past seem even more remote. He was hardly the same person who had fallen hopelessly in love with the beautiful Sophie as an adolescent. That naive, impulsive young man had not survived the war. He was a different person now, old beyond his years, with too many tragic life experiences to ever be considered naive again.

Hours passed as mother and son, seated side by side, traveled in tormented silence. Although, no words were spoken between them, they were both comforted by their physical proximity. Neither one wanted to talk or share the jumbled thoughts racing through their minds. Finally, Henri looked over at his mother. He could sense her turmoil, and he reached over to put his arm around her. The gesture, the comforting touch of her son, awoke Marguerite to the realization of just how far they had come. Life had come full circle, and she was back with Henri again, this time as his mother. She gave Henri a reassuring and appreciative smile. Hope and anticipation seemed to suddenly fill the air as they drew closer to the convent orphanage.

The massive, gray building loomed high on the hill, and it looked unchanged, still forbidding and fortress like. But everything else around the orphanage was different. The previously grassy play area had been converted into numerous large garden plots, filled with the remnants of a bountiful summer crop. There were also chickens, lots of chickens, that industriously rummaged through the gardens looking for insects. A good-sized hen house was positioned a short distance from the gardens, and there was a clatter of cackling, as two older children emerged from the building, their baskets filled with fresh eggs. Marguerite was astounded as she took in the transformation of the once familiar ground. The scene was a reminder of how much the war had changed the operation of the orphanage, demanding more self-sufficiency and adaptability to feed the huge influx of war orphans. Oddly, there was a shiny, black automobile parked in front of the massive old wooden door.

The heavy wrought iron door knocker looked cold and unwelcoming, as Marguerite and Henri readied themselves for whatever was on the other side of the formidable entryway. The mother and son stood and looked at each other pensively, as Marguerite reached up to lift the door knocker. The clang echoed and loudly announced their arrival. Nervously, the two waited. In short order, the door hesitantly opened a crack. A middle aged, very plain looking nun peeked through and politely asked them to state their business. Marguerite stepped forward, and instantly the two women recognized each other. The nun smiled at Marguerite and flung the door open. Sister Elsa and Marguerite had been young nuns together in the convent over twenty years prior. Although the two women were approximately the same age, the years had not been kind to Sister Elsa. She looked remarkably more worn, and much older than Marguerite. The two women hugged and were genuinely happy to be reunited. Marguerite introduced Henri to her old friend.

Elsa smiled at Henri and said, "Any friend of Marguerite's is a friend of mine."

Marguerite swallowed and hesitantly said, "He is my son."

Elsa tried not to look surprised as she said, "He's a very handsome young man."

"Yes, he is. There are obviously things about my past that I did not share during my time here."

Sister Elsa was nonplussed as she responded, "We all have pasts. I doubt that there is anything in your past that would make me think less of you."

Although they had never been confidantes, there had always been an acceptance between the two nuns. The physical hardship of working together in the orphanage had forged a bond between the two women. They both had similar work ethics, and this had led to the development of a mutual respect between them.

Marguerite got directly to the point of the visit. She stated, "We're here to speak to the Mother Superior."

Elsa nodded as she responded, "As you well know, she's quite a force of nature. The church hierarchy has tried to replace her, but she refuses to step down until she has a competent replacement. She just turned eighty-four years old." Elsa chuckled as she went on, "Of course, it would be an act of God himself, if such a replacement could be found. She's still sharp as a tack. There's nothing that gets by her. I should warn you that she's gotten more and more impatient with age. The war years have been hard on her."

Marguerite was relieved that the legendary church icon had remained vital. The aged administrator had always been remarkably direct and perceptive. It had made her an intimidating, yet effective leader. Elsa led Henri and Marguerite to the office of the Mother Superior. Hesitantly, Marguerite knocked on the closed door.

A strong, gravelly voice instructed Henri and Marguerite, "Come in."

Marguerite stepped through the door first, with Henri hesitantly entering behind her. Marguerite smiled weakly and said, "Hello."

The old nun looked curiously at Marguerite. Her eyes were indeed alert and perceptive, and she instantly recognized Marguerite.

She quietly took stock of the situation as she returned the greeting, "Well, hello Marguerite."

Marguerite was flustered, her confidence suddenly wavering, as she said, "I'd like to introduce my son, Henri."

The old woman stood and extended her hand to Henri. He took her bony hand in his, and he could feel the strength that still radiated from the old body.

Henri was intrigued by the mysterious, wise woman. He looked directly into her eyes and said, "It's nice to meet you."

The Mother Superior smiled and said with complete sincerity, "I'm very glad to finally meet you, too. I've heard so much about you. Please, have a seat." She walked behind Marguerite and Henri, and quietly closed the door. Although slightly stooped, she had a remarkable physical presence, and moved with the ease and energy of a much younger person.

As the mother and son moved to seat themselves on the rigid wooden chairs, Marguerite awkwardly said, "I should tell you why we are here."

"I know why you are here."

Marguerite and Henri looked uncomfortable with her bluntness and there was a tortured pause in the conversation.

Finally, Henri blurted out, "We are here to get my daughter."

The Mother Superior suddenly focused on Henri, taking in the essence of him, her gaze piercing and stern. She asked him directly, "Are you sure that you are ready and capable of providing care for a young child?"

Henri felt uncomfortable and threatened as he responded defensively, "Yes, she is my child. I'm the only parent she's ever going to know."

The old nun looked annoyed with his self-righteous behavior, and she quickly corrected the young man. "Well, that's not true. Her mother visits her on a regular basis."

Henri looked shaken, and turned suddenly pale, as he tried to soak in the words. Marguerite audibly gasped and gave a puzzled look to the old nun.

Henri fumbled for words, his speech suddenly almost a whisper of disbelief. "I thought Sophie abandoned our child shortly after her birth."

"Sophie truly struggled with the decision. We talked many times over the course of her pregnancy. You know, she really loved you, even when you didn't write."

Henri was tearing up, and indignant, as he forcefully said, "I did write! I wrote to her every day for months!"

The nun was surprised, and she instinctively knew that he was telling the truth. She breathed deeply to calm her anger and conceal her disgust, as she quickly surmised that Mr. Bissett had orchestrated the missing letters.

She nodded to Henri, a sincere look of compassion on her face, as she said, "I'm guessing that the letters went missing. I wouldn't put something like that past Mr. Bissett."

Henri looked incredibly sad, as he responded, "Yes, Sophie's father went to great lengths to make sure that all the letters between us were intercepted. Sophie and I wrote each other every day for months. Not a single letter made it through."

The Mother Superior sighed, remembering Sophie and all the tearful conversations, along with the girl's angst. "Well, I don't believe that Sophie ever figured it out, or suspected, that her father hid the letters. We had many a conversation about you, and her disbelief that you did not respond to her letters. Sophie was completely brokenhearted. To be quite honest, I was very worried about her, and I was disappointed."

Henri looked up, puzzled, as he asked, "Why were you disappointed?"

"Sophie is a very capable, smart woman, but she had no confidence in her ability to lead her life. Her father threatened to disown her and leave her penniless if she didn't leave her child hidden here in the orphanage. She was angry and felt manipulated, but in the end, she completely surrendered to her father's wishes. Suffice it to say, I was disappointed."

"He is an evil man."

"Yes, he is."

Henri was uncharacteristically open and honest with his feelings, as he admitted, "I just don't know where to go from here."

After getting a sense of Henri's character, the Mother Superior knew he was as Sophie had described. The old nun was reassuring as she said, "Ahh, that's understandable. Well, you should know that Sophie didn't abandon little Marguerite. She comes to visit and spend the day with her child, every Friday. She has never missed a week." She looked directly into Henri's eyes and gave him a nod and a knowing look.

Henri could hardly breathe as he tried to comprehend what she had just told him. Barely audible, he whispered, "Today is Friday. She's here?"

The old nun smiled, her wrinkles suddenly more pronounced as she quietly said, "Yes."

Henri looked hopeful and scared. He stood and looked toward the door. Marguerite felt like a spectator as she silently reached over and touched his hand. He looked at his mother briefly, comforted by her quiet presence. The Mother Superior walked behind them and opened the door widely, motioning them through. Henri stood and walked ahead of them, his steps hesitant, guarded, his mind racing with a tumult of different emotions. The noises of playful children, and the familiar laugh of a young woman, pulled him forward. Henri found himself walking more quickly, his heart racing, expectant and scared, as he moved closer to the sound of her voice.

Henri held his breath as he stepped into the entry of the large room, and then he stopped, frozen, as he saw her. He could not stop the tears as he took in the sight of Sophie, older, but even more beautiful than he remembered. As she was laughing and playing with little Marguerite, Sophie looked up and saw Henri standing in the doorway, and her laughter suddenly stopped; she was transfixed by the sight of him. Her eyes watered, and she looked to Henri, taking in his essence. He was older, more muscular, ruggedly handsome, and his eyes communicated so much. The little girl looked at her mother, puzzled, and then she looked quizzically at Henri. Little Marguerite brightened as she seemed to understand, and began jumping up and down, excited and smiling.

She tugged on her mother's arm, her joy contagious, as she excitably asked, "Is that him? Is that him?"

Sophie tenderly leaned over and scooped up the little girl, as she said, "Yes, that's your father."

Henri heard the exchange between mother and child, and he felt a flush of warmth, as he walked slowly toward them, his tear-filled eyes locked on Sophie and little Marguerite.

As he drew near, Sophie looked into his eyes, smiled through her tears, and said, "I knew that you would come to find us."

Henri instantly could feel her love, and he tenderly embraced Sophie and their child. Little Marguerite reached up in the entanglement, delighted, as she touched his face. He smiled at his daughter, and gently took her from Sophie's arms. He looked at her in wonder, recognizing his hair color and his eyes mirrored in this tiny, beautiful little girl.

"I've been wanting to meet you for the longest time."

Little Marguerite grinned, and said confidently, "I've been waiting for you, too. Mama said that you would come, and that I would know it was you…because you're the handsomest man in all of France."

"Is that so?"

Little Marguerite nodded her head earnestly, grinning. Sophie touched his face tenderly, trying to fully believe that he was truly with her. She moved closer, their faces almost touching, as she whispered so that only he could hear, "I still love you."

Henri melted, his hopes and dreams complete in those four words. He leaned in, and their lips tenderly touched, the electricity still there, only stronger. He smiled, incredulous that this could really be happening, and said, "I love you, too. You need to know that I did not abandon you. I wrote you every day for months, until I thought you wanted nothing to do with me. I was crushed. I thought I was going to die."

Sophie nodded, and tears filled her eyes, as she remembered. "I know. I know. I just got a letter from Bernadette, saying she was so sorry."

They fell together, tears flowing freely, as they grieved the tragic circumstances of the last few years. Little Marguerite looked puzzled and worried as she clung to her mother. Finally, Henri broke away from Sophie and looked earnestly at his little girl. "When I see this one, I can't be sad anymore. I don't want to waste any more time."

Sophie was unbelievably relieved to hear his words, and to feel his love. She was so grateful, so deeply appreciative of Henri, whom she had never stopped loving. His love and regard for family had always made such an impression on her, but never more than in this moment. For the first time in her life, she felt secure and loved, and was looking hopefully forward to their future.

Marguerite and the Mother Superior stood side by side in the doorway, taking in the reunification scene, not able to hear their words, but understanding. The old nun had tears in her eyes as she reached over and grasped Marguerite's hand, the act a statement of closure, of past injustices rectified. Both women were silently bonded in their hope for the young family.

www.ingramcontent.com/pod-product-compliance
Lightning Source LLC
Chambersburg PA
CBHW020302200626
46814CB00006BA/2044